GLENMILL

This book is a mi

It is largely set in Dumfries which is, of course,
very much a real town. However most of the places,
and all of the characters are purely fictional.
The book is not meant to be a documentary.
It is a fictional thriller. I have tried hard to research
each aspect of the book as carefully as possible.

I have tried to paint a fictional picture
of things that are very real indeed.

Obviously I hope that you will enjoy reading the book.
That is what it is intended for: entertainment.
When you have finished, I hope that
I will have given you some food for thought.

Mark Frankland

"Reporters from the Daily Record went 'undercover'
to expose evil heroin dealers at the beginning
of our award winning anti-heroin campaign.
Around 300 were named and shamed in the newspaper
and this was only the tip of the iceberg.

The response from Record readers was huge.
We found that heroin is not solely an urban problem.
The reach of the dealers and the emotional
and social problems they cause impacts
on all walks of life in all of Scotland's communities."

Keith McLeod, Daily Record News Reporter

The Cull

Mark Frankland

A Glenmill Publication

First published in 2001

Glenmill

Dumfries

Scotland

DG2 8PX

tel: 0776 149 3542

http://www.thecull.com

British Library Cataloguing in Publication Data.
A catalogue record of this book is available from the British Library.

ISBN 0 9535944 3 2

Design, Layout & Typesetting by Yasmin
email: nomad@yazzy.net

Acknowledgements

First off, I must thank Sandra, the bravest person I know,
without whom this edition would not have been possible.

Attempting to earn a living from writing is not an easy thing.
In fact, at times it seems well nigh impossible.
I really don't believe that I would have found the energy
to keep bashing my head against a brick wall
were it not for my partner, Carol. She never gives up on me,
even when I give up on myself. She reads everything
as I write it and tells it how it is. For all this, thanks.

I must also thank my Mum and Dad who are
also always four square behind my writing efforts.

Likewise I must thank my two boys, Dyonne and Courtney,
who have to put up with a Dad who locks himself away to
write and spends more time than he should being grumpy.

Thanks also to Keith and Ian at the Daily record for their support.

This was not an easy book to write.
Many of the topics are grim to say the least.
I would like to thank all the people who have guided
me through the shadowy world of hard drugs.

In particular I must thank Gavin, Debs and my two
anonymous mentors. Both have seen their lives blighted
by heroin for many, many years. Thankfully at the time
of writing, one has at last freed himself, and is en-route
to a Rehab centre and a new life. Without their help
and insight I would have never dared to write this story.

Contents

Part One
Infection

"The crew were mainly just kids.
Rock and Rollers with one foot in the grave."

Apocalypse Now

Chapter 1
East Wind

For thousands of miles the batch of heroin had a completely normal and uneventful journey. In cars and jeeps and trucks and a container ship and then more cars, it made sedate progress all the way from Afghanistan through Southern Russia to Turkey to Italy to Cork to Belfast. Business as usual. All deadlines were met as it passed through the hands of various wholesalers. There were no storms at sea, no paid-off officials changing their minds, no sudden outbreaks of violent, barely noticed wars. Nothing whatsoever. A nice smooth delivery.

The consignment was broken down and repackaged on a bleak estate on the outskirts of Belfast where Union Jacks hung from every lamp-post and the two men loaded up the Glasgow package into the hidden compartment under the boot of their car. It was when they landed up at the ferry terminal in Larne that the dreaded influence of Sod's Law decided to play its hand. When they had left the estate the weather had been drizzly and dreary but nothing more. By the time they arrived in Larne, having stopped for two trays of pie and chips with curry sauce, the wind was beginning to blow. An hour later the wind had become a gale and the rain was blowing across the tarmac in horizontal sheets.

Half an hour later a flustered official wrapped from head to toe in bright yellow waterproofs tapped on the window and told the two men that the crossing had been cancelled. He told them that the forecast was shite. He told them that he doubted if the ten o' clock would make it either. He happily agreed with their appraisal that the whole business was a bag of shite, that the weather was a bag of shite and that life in general was a bag of shite.

When they reported their situation back to their boss on the estate in Belfast he too was of the opinion that it was a bag of shite. He didn't fancy the idea of them holing-up in a B&B in Larne with such a hefty package and so he told them to come back and that he would change things about a bit.

When he called his customer in Glasgow to report that the weather had put paid to the delivery he received a response that has hardly cordial. He was informed that he was a 'fucking useless cunt' and that 'every fucker in the South of Scotland' was waiting for the delivery. The man from Belfast held the phone away from his ear and grimaced to his colleagues as he lit up a cigarette. Eventually he managed to promise that he would complete the delivery just as soon as the weather improved and the ferries started running again and that there really was fuck all that he could do about the weather.

When the conversation eventually ended he dropped the phone back on its cradle and stared at it for a moment.

"Scottish Tosser."

Bob Bennet sat at his desk and gazed out of the window rather dolefully. There was little in the vista outside to cheer him up. Beyond the car park there was a small industrial estate of aluminium-cladded units which were mainly vacant. Beyond them a greasy grey sky looked as if it spread all the way to New York.

It was bloody cold. The central heating system was well short of being up to the job. He had not been able to take his jacket off all day and was wishing that he had thought to bring a jumper into work. He took a sip of coffee and tried to summon up the energy to relaunch his attack on the mountain of paperwork that spread all over his desk.

Energy and enthusiasm. Once-upon-a-time he had been filled with an abundance of each. Once-upon-a-time. Now he found it hard to remember the days when he hadn't been miserable all the time. It wasn't surprising really. It was now nearly 30 years. Thirty years since he had graduated from Stirling University and had set out to become a great, great journalist. The memory made him wince. How on earth could he ever have been so pathetically naïve? And now the calendar on the wall told him that in a fortnight's time he would be fifty. He had become an old man who had been nowhere and was going nowhere.

All those years ago he had dreamed of a career that was to have taken him from the *Dundee Post* to the *Glasgow Herald* and all the way to Fleet Street. Instead his career had taken him from the *Dundee Post* to the *Dumfries Enquirer* and then a non-negotiable full stop. His twenty years at the *Enquirer* had seen him rise from junior reporter to reporter to Editor. It had been twenty years of Gala Queens and residents complaining about landfill sites and controversial planning-applications and some women's group presenting a charity with a cheque for £73.26. It was all so endlessly tedious and mind-bendingly trivial. All anyone ever cared about was how many adverts they had sold for the next edition, how could they sell more. Have we tried him? Have you called them? Adverts, adverts, bloody adverts. Nobody gave a damn about the news any more.

The fact was that none of the readers ever thought about buying the paper for news. They bought it find out what was on at the week-end, to scour the small ads section for a bike for young Charlie, to see if they had printed any photos of Eileen from three doors down on her wedding day. News meant too much money. It was too much money because it meant paying decent reporters a decent salary to go out and find it, and if the paper were to find the money to pay for these decent reporters it would have to charge more for its advertising rates and it was already a bloody uphill task to sell the adverts. By the way did anyone try Donaldson's Chemists this week? So the least cost option was to forget the idea of spending money to dig out real news. Instead they hired junior reporters who would spend their days doing features on Gala Queens and planning-application controversies.

Bob checked his watch. Jesus. It seemed like he had been at his desk for thirteen years and it was still only two o'clock. The rest of the day seemed to stretch out in front of him like the Gobi desert.

A crash and a curse brought him awake from his reverie. He stood up slightly from his chair to get a view through the glass panel in his office door.

Wonderful. Absolutely bloody wonderful. It was Mandy. If there was one thing that was stone cold guaranteed to make him feel even older it was Mandy. As ever she had arrived back at the office like a pocket hurricane and she must have crashed into the metal table in the corridor in her haste to get to his office. Having completed her collision she must have dropped her bag and she was now in the process of collecting an unbelievable array of flotsam and jetsam off the floor.

Mandy was his new junior reporter. She was 21, fresh out of college and so full of dreams and ambition she could hardly contain it. She was one of those whirlwind people. Everything was fast, flustered. She talked fast, walked fast, drove fast. She lived her life in a constant state of chaos, an endlessly moving blur of wild red hair and freckles and baggy clothes. Her writing was nearly illegible. Her emails were full of totally bemusing abbreviations. Her sentences leapt from one thought to another without a breath ever being drawn.

She was bordering on being a complete basket-case and Bob Bennet couldn't help but like her because she seemed to be the last person on the planet who could stop him feeling so miserable all the time.

And that bag. That bloody stupid bag. Mandy's bag seemed to be the cause of endless drama. It was a huge old carpet bag that was permanently stuffed within an inch of its life. He often wondered what on earth she could possibly have in there. Wherever she was and whatever she was doing there always came a moment when she needed something out of the bag which would mean a major excavation accompanied by muttering and cursing. Whatever she wanted – glasses, pen, notebook, hair clip, chewing gum – it always seemed to be right at the bottom and could only be reached once the cursing and the rummaging had hit a fever pitch. And then whatever it was would be yanked out and she would clutch it triumphantly with a great grin.

As he watched her cramming all the gear back into her dropped bag, against all odds, he smiled. And then the smile faded to be replaced with a wary look. If she had been careering down his corridor with sufficient speed to spread the contents of the dreaded bag so far and wide it could only mean one thing. She had come up with another idea for "The Big Story".

No matter how many times he had tried to explain things, Mandy resolutely refused to get it. She didn't get it because she was out for the big one. That was why she was a journalist. She was ready to bowl into any situation without a shred of fear and expose a major corruption or blow away some dastardly plot. She was desperate to dig the dirt. For Mandy news was still pure. She was the journalistic equivalent of a young Jesuit priest. She had absolutely no concept of cynicism. No sense of the sad accounting reality of life. And she didn't give a shit about advertising.

Having finally gathered up her spillage Mandy burst into the office.

"Bob you have to listen to this. I know there have been times in the past and I know what you say and time and things but . . ."

"Hello Mandy."

" . . . But I promise you that this time I have found something that is really good. I mean big. I mean National News Bob. You see I have just been in Annan doing that story about the new car park that you wanted me to look at and I did it and anyway after that . . ."

"Hello Mandy."

" . . . well after that I went into this pub, not for a drink, just a coffee, I mean I wouldn't normally go into a pub it's just that the cafés all looked really . . ."

"MANDY! I said Hello!"

"What do you mean?"

"What I mean is that we have this ever so quaint custom in Scotland. It means that when we meet somebody either at their home or on the street or even in their office we take a small breath, smile, and say, 'Hello'. Maybe you could try it."

A blush. A bothered sort of look. "Oh yes, of course, absolutely, sorry Bob. That was rude. Hello. Hi. How are you and all that."

"Better Mandy. Very good. I am well. We call it the social niceties. Now why don't you sit down, slow down, take a deep breath, find a home for that amazing bag of yours and then maybe you could start again."

Still blushing, Mandy did as she was told and made a great show of taking two deep breaths before indicating to him that she was ready to start.

"Right Mandy. Much, much better. Now I gather that you have discovered the kind of story that will propel the *Dumfries Enquirer* into the limelight, and all of this is from a non alcoholic visit to a pub in Annan. So pray, do continue. Be succinct. Measure your words. Refer to notes in necessary."

As soon as he completed the sentence he regretted the last statement as Mandy immediately wrenched her bag up from the floor and entered into a frantic rummaging session that lasted for half a minute until she dragged out a note book.

"OK. Right. This is it. Now just you wait until you hear this. I met this guy at the bar and he was a lorry driver, well, he *is* a lorry driver, and anyway, he works for a haulage company over in Longtown. Now they don't just haul stuff, they deal in timber as well. And they are really big. Lots and lots of wagons, lots and lots of timber.

"Now. This is the good bit. Last November his boss got a phone call from the Ministry of Agriculture and they started asking him about the availability of railway sleepers. Now my driver didn't know exactly what they said, but it must have been something pretty definite because guess what?"

"Go on Mandy, I can't possibly guess what."

Now she grinned in triumph. "His boss went and bought a whole shipload of sleepers. I'm not talking about a metaphorical shipload Bob, I'm talking about a real one. A 25,000 tonne one! He spent over a million pounds! Now think about it. The Ministry rang this man up four months before the first reported case of Foot and Mouth disease and gave him the nod and the wink to go out and buy a million quid's worth of railway sleepers. And guess what!"

"I still can't Mandy. You're just going to have to tell me."

"He's sold them all to the Ministry already! To use for the bonfires to burn the cows. All of them. Every last one of them in three weeks and he has made millions of pounds out of it."

"Lucky guy."

"Never mind 'lucky guy' Bob, can't you see what this means? It means that the Government already knew last autumn that there was going to be a massive Foot and Mouth outbreak and they were already gearing themselves up to deal with it. They already knew! And they were covering it all up. It's a massive story. It could go all the way to the top."

"I'm quite sure that it could."

"Well we've got to run it. We have to. We may never have the chance to do something like this ever again. For God's sake Bob, it's all happening on our own doorstep. I can't believe it."

His heart sank because yet again it was down to him to puncture her balloon. The sad thing is that she was so right, he really should have been able to send this bundle of red-headed enthusiasm into the thick of the conspiracy, but he couldn't, and he wouldn't, and yet again he would have to tell her. It was his job to introduce her to cynicism, to realism, to all the miserable *-isms* that made growing up such a rotten idea. He slumped back in his chair and stared up at the ceiling.

"Yes Mandy, of course we should run it. But we won't. Now STOP, STOP, STOP. You're going to have to hear me out and you're not going to like it much. We won't run it for several reasons, all of which I am happy to explain. Firstly there is the paper. For you to go and investigate this story you would have to be away for at least three weeks. During that three weeks I would have to deal with a 33 percent reduction in the staff on the reporters desk. That would mean that I couldn't fill the next six editions of the paper, and I can assure you that the people who pay your wages and my wages wouldn't wear it.

"That's number one. Number two, I've been down this road before. Governments are always up to something dodgy. They always have. They always will. Now it doesn't matter how much proof you have, or how completely you build your case, they will always wheel out some smooth old Etonian type who will never stop smiling at you and will stone wall everything you ask. And as long as The Right Honourable Heathcote-Smythe keeps his act going, all that your story will ever amount to is a collection of 'unconfirmed rumours', and they are about as newsworthy as a sparrow building a nest in April."

And of course this made Mandy angry. "Oh come on Bob how can you possibly say that! How can you know? Nothing like this has ever happened before. They can't just stand there and deny it. This is Scotland. You can't do things like that here. The Press won't allow it."

"If that was the case it would all be very nice. But it isn't. That is the stuff for Election broadcasts Mandy. The reality is never the same. Thirty miles across the Solway from where we are sitting now there is a place called Sellafield. Before that it was Windscale. For twenty years I have heard stories about them making cock-ups. Leaks, accidents, hot cells. They are rumoured to have the highest levels of Leukaemia in the UK down there. We know it. They know it. But for nearly 50 years they have never admitted a thing. They just block it. Just like they will block this. Block you. Sorry Mandy, but that's how it is."

The wretched disappointment on her face made him feel even older. "So what the hell can we do Bob? Do we always have to just ignore everything? For ever? Is that the way it has to be?"

"For me, yes. Because I am old and past it. This is where I am and I'm not going anywhere else. For you Mandy it can be different. Keep your enthusiasm. Keep applying for everything. Try and get yourself into investigative television. Make yourself a name. Then go freelance. And one day if you get really, really lucky, you will be able to do these things. But not now. Not with the *Dumfries Enquirer*."

Mandy tried to smile but it didn't really work. He just wanted her to feel better. She deserved better.

"Look Mandy, it isn't all bad. There are things going to happen soon. Tell me, were you cold out today?"

"Yes. *Freezing*. I took the wrong coat."

"Have you thought about why?"

"No. 'Course not. I've been cold because it IS cold. It's February and it's windy and there's no sun. What are you on about Bob?" At times his eccentricities drove her nuts.

"What I am on about, Mandy, is an attempt to encourage the logical analytical side of your undoubted journalistic instincts. There is a very good reason why you have been so cold today. The reason is that the wind is blowing from the east. Now the wind doesn't often blow from the east in these parts, but when it does so in February it brings air all the way from Russia which is bloody cold.

"So, Mandy. A cold wind from the east. What does this mean? It means that the Foot and Mouth virus that is now on just about every farm in Longtown and Gretna is going to get blown straight here. Listen to what the vets are saying. The virus thrives in cold temperatures. If the wind keeps blowing in this direction, and the forecast says it will last at least five days, then you can bet your bottom dollar that there will be Foot and Mouth right here in Dumfries within a fortnight.

"Now this IS our kind of news Mandy, and I want you to get out there and cover it. Right now there are hundreds of local people who's liveliehoods are under threat and they are scared to death. So go out there and talk to them. What are they feeling? How are they trying to stop it? What will it mean to them if they get it.? By next week there will be fires burning all around our town and lots of good people will have to watch their lifetimes' work go up in black diesel smoke. And I want you to talk to them and find out what it is like, what it means, how they really feel."

He had her riveted, and strangely for Mandy, she actually looked a little bit afraid. He knew exactly why. He was asking her to intrude. To push herself forward at people at a bad time. It was nasty, embarrassing, not the right thing. Her brain was in overdrive. "Wow. Of course. Blimy. And you really want me to do this?"

"Yes Mandy, I do. You will be good at this and this will be good for you. It's going to be grim and depressing and miserable, but it is something that we need to do well, and we need to do it sensitively and I know that you can do it."

All of a sudden she felt almost tearful. "Thanks Bob. I really appreciate it. Honest. I really do. But, well, well . . . well, where do I start?"

"Why not start with your boyfriend. The one you introduced me to in the pub that night. What was he called. Bill or something wasn't it?"

Now she really blushed. The blush almost turned her face to the colour of her hair. "Will, actually."

"Ah, I sense a problem. Can I take it that you and Will are no longer an item?"

"No we're not. Haven't been for a while. It didn't work out."

"Was it cordial?"

"Not really. Not at all in fact. Bloody awful actually."

"What about his Dad. Jack. That's it. Jack Sinclair. I've met him a few times. He's a good guy. Did you get on with him?"

She brightened. "Oh yes, Jack is great. Actually sometimes Will would get cross because me and Jack would rabble on and on for ages at times. Sometimes I even thought he was a bit jealous. As if!"

"So there's your start. Go and talk to Jack. Let him point you in the right direction. If I know Jack he will be more than happy to."

"Yes. Yes of course I will. I'll go up this evening. After they've finished milking."

She reached down to the floor and hauled up the bag. "See you later Bob. And thanks again."

He stared at the door for a while after she had left. Maybe it wasn't all adverts after all. Maybe for once they could actually do something well, something good, something worthwhile. Maybe.

That same morning Jack Sinclair felt his heart sink seconds after his alarm clock delivered him into the day. The reason for this was that he immediately felt the cold that had seeped into his bedroom through the night. The cold meant the forecasters had been correct and the wind was already blowing from the east.

He shivered as he pulled his clothes on. His bedroom was bare and functional at best, downright bleak at worst. His wife Angela had left him seven years before, amidst a hail of insults and abuse. He hadn't turned out as she had expected. When they had first met and then married he had been a young, dashing officer in the Scots Guards who was also a landowner. She had seen him as glamorous and handsome and funny. Her father, who was a Colonel in the Regiment, had approved wholeheartedly.

But then things had changed. Started to slip. It hadn't taken long for their marriage to start sliding down the pan. Things had come to a head in 1993. His father had finally lost his battle against cancer and died. The Regiment had tried everything to persuade Jack to stay. He was one of their rising stars. But there really were no options. The only way he could stay in the Army was to sell the farm, there simply wasn't anybody else to run it. It was something that he just couldn't do. And so he had resigned his commission and returned to Dumfries.

By this time the whole of agriculture was easing its way into a state of permanent recession. Times were hard and they were only going to get harder. All of a sudden he was no longer the dashing officer and landowner, instead he was just another poor farmer breaking his back for thirteen hours a day to earn the dubious privilege of going further and further into debt.

From the moment they returned to the farm things had started to turn bad. Angela felt isolated and chronic bouts of depression soon followed. Their rows became daily affairs that were as regular to Jack as milking the cows every morning and night. Soon she started to spend more and more time away visiting her father wherever the regiment happened to be stationed. She said that she missed all of her friends and the well-regulated social life centred on the Officers Mess. She said that her father, a widower of many years standing, needed her to help him keep on the straight-and-narrow. She said that she felt caged by the routine of the farm and the drudgery of housework and the suffocating small 'c' conservatism of life in Dumfries.

Jack was at the stage where he didn't care much one way or the other. His Dad had let things go downhill in the last years as his illness had eaten away at him. Jack soon found that there was an unbelievable amount to do on the farm and never any money to do it. This meant he had to keep up with a constant DIY programme over and above the general running of the farm. He was tired all the time and, no matter what he did or how hard he worked, things just kept on getting worse. Soon it was just a relief to come into the house at the end of the day and not have to plunge into yet another vicious row with Angela.

In March 1994 it became apparent to him that the real reason for Angela's frequent visits to the regiment was to see Charles Hammerton-Smith. Now when it came to being a dashing officer and landowner Charles was very much the real deal. He carried all the airs and graces learnt during his time at Harrow and Oxford, and his family had owned half of Aberdeenshire for half of history. Charles and Jack had been contemporaries in the Guards and Jack had always loathed him. He always felt that Charles was the perfect man for the Regimental dinner, but a complete dead loss on the streets of Andersonstown and Ballymurphy. Not that it mattered much because Hammerton-Smith senior knew everyone there was to know, and the family had been grooming men who looked good on horses for the Guards for well over 200 years.

By the time she announced the news to Jack he was well past caring. If Hammerton-Smith wanted her, then he was welcome to her. Jack wasn't in the mood for arguing, he was ready to see the back of her. This of course only made things worse. She wanted her divorce, but she couldn't stomach the fact that Jack was so plainly happy and relieved to be rid of her. And so their fights got worse and worse until at last the lawyers finished their work and Angela departed his life, taking Will and most of their furniture.

The furniture never came back and somehow he never got round to replacing it. He always figured that at some stage another woman would come into his life and she would no doubt want to change everything anyway. So the house remained a strange, empty sort of a place. Not that it bothered Jack much. In the hours when he wasn't working he spent almost all of his time in his study which contained everything that he needed. To his way of thinking, the fact that most of the other rooms were more or less empty just made them easier to clean.

Although the furniture never came back, Will did – after seven months. Will had been twelve when the divorce was finalised and he missed just about everything when his mum took him back to the Regiment. He missed his friends from the surrounding farms and his school in Dumfries. He missed the farm work and driving tractors and quad bikes. And he missed his Dad with whom he had become accustomed to spending his days cutting silage, or feeding the sheep, or collecting the dairy cows for milking.

To make matters worse, Charles was hardly the ideal step-father. His family history more or less ensured that he was unlikely ever to take to a child who was not a biological carrier of the great Hammerton-Smith bloodline. At best he was off-hand and impatient, at worst he was downright cruel. It wasn't long before Will made his mother's life enough of a misery for her to admit defeat and let him return to his father.

Father and son soon fell into an easy and comfortable routine.

Whenever Will was not at school he worked on the farm. In the evenings they ate out of the microwave and watched sport on the TV. At weekends they both played rugby and golf. At first Jack had been worried that Will's schoolwork was going to suffer but his fears had been groundless. As each year passed Jack saw that Will had inherited a healthy portion of his own genes. The boy was hardy and self-reliant and nothing much knocked him back. His Parents Evenings were OK, although there were always bits and pieces of problems. Will was certainly never one to avoid a fight. By the time he was fourteen there was some talk of him keeping bad company; a couple of teachers in particular mentioned a boy called Ricky Macintosh.

This didn't overly concern Jack. Ricky was a frequent visitor to the farm in the holidays and, although he tended to be a bit wild, Jack never saw any real harm in him. He played scrum half in the same under-16's team that Will played in as a wing forward.

At the Parents Evening that followed a couple of months after Will's fifteenth birthday the warnings about Ricky grew darker. There was talk of truancy and the police. Jack had thought the comments of the teachers through carefully as he sat drinking coffee in his study long after Will had gone to bed. Finally he had decided that there was little point in him trying to intervene. Will was a free-spirited and independent boy and the more he was told not to do something the more likely he was to do it. He left it. Will was growing up fast. He would have to learn to make his own decisions, and stand or fall by them.

As the boy grew older it became perfectly clear that there was only ever going to be one career path that would interest him. Will was a born farmer. He loved everything about the job and he was ideally suited to it. He was naturally strong and he had terrific reserves of stamina. Crucially he was skilled at any task that was mechanical as well as having an instinctive affinity with the animals.

Jack never bothered trying very hard to persuade Will to stay on at school when he was sixteen. There seemed little point. The boy had set his heart on coming to work full time on the farm years before and he had never shown the remotest inclination to change his mind. This decision caused a brief resurgence in hostilities with Angela who was beside herself at the prospect of Will turning his back on all career prospects other than farming. All of her anger, tears and cajoling came to nothing. Will had inherited all of his dad's stubbornness and there was nothing she could do to make him change his mind.

In the late nineties farmers started giving up the ghost in droves. The recession that had moved seamlessly from salmonella to e coli to BSE just never seemed to end. One by one every sector of agriculture was hit, and none seemed to recover – eggs, chicken, pigs, sheep, beef cattle, cereals and finally milk. Will's decision to leave school and make the farming his life meant that they both had to plan the future of the business carefully. Somehow, by hook or by crook, they had to drag a living for two people out of their 200 rather ordinary acres. By the summer of 1999 the writing was really on the wall. They had absolutely flogged themselves through 1998 only to be informed by the accountant that the farm had generated a profit of £4,235. They were not alone. Every dairy farm in Britain was reeling with the collapse in the milk price. In former years his father had taught Jack that if one part of their farming enterprise was bad, the other parts tended to be good, and these would help to make good any shortfalls. If the price of lamb collapsed, the milk price would be good. If milk was bad, the beefers would probably do well.

As they looked through their books in the summer of 1999 it was clear that for the first time his dad's old theory had been shattered. The sheep side of the business had lost a fortune and the dairy enterprise had barely broken even. They had given up keeping beef cattle in the wake of the BSE crisis.

They had walked out of their accountant's office and straight into a pub. Over several pints they had made a decision. Every spare cost that they could think of had already been cut. There was just no way that they could see to make themselves more efficient. This meant that there was only one way forward, and halfway down their fourth pint they decided to take it. In poker terms, they decided to stake everything they had on a pair of Jacks.

This meant that they would take an almighty gamble on the future of milk quota. For fifteen years the amount of milk that any dairy farmer was allowed to produce had been governed by a quota set by the European Union in Brussels. If a farmer wanted to produce more milk, he would have to either buy or rent more quota. The cost of doing this was always high, and it tended to mean that it was very hard to make any money on the extra milk that came off the farm. However, any farmer who risked producing extra milk without acquiring the necessary quota faced a crippling fine at the end of the year.

Their gamble was a simple one. If the UK as a whole failed to reach its National Quota, then there would be no fines for any farm which had exceeded its own individual quota. Jack had seen many familiar faces depart the industry over the preceding eighteen months and he was convinced that the same story was going on all over the UK. Dairy farmers were selling up in huge numbers and there was no new blood coming into the industry to take their place. His hunch told him that there probably were no longer enough working dairy farms left to fill the National Quota. Which of course meant that there would be no more fines for farmers who went over their own quota. Which of course meant that the way forward was to gamble everything and expand.

Jack believed that if he pushed his bankers hard enough he could persuade them to increase the overdraft sufficiently for him to bring another 50 dairy cows into the herd and to build a new shed to house them in. Such a project would cost £100,000. He could get them to give him that. He knew it. To buy the required extra quota for these new cows would cost a further £90,000. He wouldn't be able to raise that. Not a cat in Hell's chance. The £90,000 was the pair of Jacks that they decided to stake their future on.

His hunch about his bankers was proved to be correct. It hadn't been easy but in the end he had prevailed and he took his overdraft to the new dizzy heights of £400,000. By the autumn of 2000 the herd at Hillside Farm had grown from 115 milk cows to 164 and a big new shed had been built and paid for. The extra work in building the shed and looking after the expanded herd had been killing, but there were very real signs that their gamble was about to pay off. At last the sheer numbers of farmers leaving the industry was beginning to take a toll. For months the UK had failed to fill its National Milk Quota. In fact there were early signs of a milk shortage and for the first time in years the price was beginning to ease upwards. There had been nothing in their plan that relied on an improvement in the amount they were paid for their milk. They had simply relied on upping their income by selling more of it at a low price. Any price increase for their much higher volume of milk would make an unbelievable difference. Suddenly there was cause for genuine optimism. An extra three pence a litre on the milk price would put them £30,000 a year ahead of their projections. A year before, a three pence per litre increase would have been an absolute pipe dream. Now it was beginning to look more than likely.

Everything should have been fantastic, but it wasn't. It wasn't because there was something horribly wrong with Will. As summer turned into autumn and autumn turned to winter every day seemed worse. Will became lethargic and seemed to lose all of his natural energy and stamina. It seemed to almost kill him to get out of bed. He started to make mistakes all the time and he had no patience. His mood swings became harder and harder to deal with. Some days he was like a zombie as he went through his daily tasks like an inefficient, slow-moving robot. Other days he was impossibly tetchy and he would fly off the handle over the slightest thing. These explosions would generally be followed by Will storming off in the Land Rover, sometimes to return late that night, sometimes the next morning.

For whatever reason everything in the boy's life seemed to be breaking down. It was obvious that he was getting no pleasure from the job of farming. He never worked with a smile on his face any more. They seldom talked. Jack couldn't get him to show any interest in planning for the future, and the fact that their big gamble was showing such signs of paying off handsomely was apparently of no consequence to him. When the new rugby season started he never showed up for training. Rather than eat together in front of the telly Will started taking his food to his room and soon Jack begun to wonder if he was eating at all as the weight seemed to be falling off him.

That autumn Jack had spent hours in his study wondering what on earth to do. He was finding the farm work almost crippling as on many occasions Will left him alone to look after their new expanded herd. No matter how hard he tried he couldn't seem to communicate with the boy. Everything that he said was always wrong. Every comment led to a blazing argument. He had never thought much about their relationship before. There had been no need. It had always come easily. Now he thought about it all the time and he couldn't come up with anything. He always told himself that it was just a phase. Will had managed to grow up without ever having much of a moody, sulky phase. Maybe he was just having it now at nineteen when most boys had got it all over and done with at fourteen and fifteen.

One of Jack's biggest problems was that he had nobody to talk to about it. All his friends were either fellow farmers or mates at the Rugby Club and the Golf Club. All these relationships were built around the price of lamb or Rangers' chances in the Champions League or what the bloody government was going to do next to kick the countryside. There was nobody he could talk to about what on earth was going on with his son. His mum and dad were both dead and buried. He had no brothers or sisters and his only two living relatives were two taciturn uncles who hid away in the hills and watched their sheep. His life on the farm and in the Guards had taught him to be self-reliant, to sort out his own problems, to shrug them off, to face them down. This inner core had never failed him before. Whatever life had thrown at him, whether it had been the tantrums of his wife or the collapse of his business or even the perils of the Turf Lodge Estate, he had always come through. But this was different.

Eventually the only person he could think of to talk to was Will's girlfriend Mandy. The two of them had been together for eighteen months and Jack had taken to her straight away. On the surface she was a loopy, dizzy, good-time girl who seemed to life her life in a whirl. But underneath Jack sensed a heart of gold. On several occasions, when Will had stormed off in the Land Rover or on the quad bike, Jack had been on the verge of calling Mandy at her office at the local newspaper. But it had just seemed all wrong for a man of his age to burden a 22 year-old girl with his problems. It was just a phase. It had to be. Will would snap out of it in time. All it needed was time, and until that time came, Jack would just have to manage.

In the end Mandy had come to him. She had come one evening

in November. Her eyes were red through with crying and she told him she just couldn't deal with it any more. She told him that she loved Will, she really did, but things had become impossible between them. As they talked, Jack realised that Mandy had been suffering the same moods and bouts of temper that he had suffered himself. What was worse was that Will had even been stealing from her. Her life had been turned into a small Hell.

Before she left she had given Jack a warning. It was a warning that he had been given before. The warning was Ricky Macintosh. Ricky was the poison, she said. Ricky was the cause. She had no idea what they were doing together, but she knew it was no good. So long as Will was spending time with Ricky things would only get worse. And then she left.

Jack had confronted Will that night. It had been awful. Shouting. Torrents of abuse. Foul language. What the hell was happening? What the hell was he doing? Couldn't he see that he was throwing everything away – Mandy, the farm, rugby, and for what? For whatever he was doing with Ricky. And Will had responded in kind. What right had Jack to preach at him? What made him so great? A man who had lost his wife, lost his precious place in the Guards, for what? What had he got to feel so big about? What was he? Just some sad old bastard living on his own, milking cows. It had nearly come to blows. Jack had only restrained himself from beating the living daylights out of his son by the slenderest of margins. As he sat taking deep breaths to calm himself Will had gone. There was the screeching sound of the Land Rover's tyres in the yard and then the sound of the engine screaming down the track, and then silence.

That had been December. Will had come back three days later but they had barely spoken. The silence lasted through the most miserable Christmas Jack had ever endured. The silence had lasted through the cold, dark rainy days of January and February. Some days Will got on with his tasks reasonably well. Others he just disappeared.

Their relationship, which had once been so close, was now as wrecked and as useless as a smoking, bombed-out city. And through those dark, wet days of January Jack felt himself slipping down. The work seemed to be endless. Fifteen hours a day. Seven days a week. Twelve months a year. He barely saw anybody. Only his son, 164 cows, 1,100 sheep, and the dwindling number of reps who called to eke out their skinny existence. He tried to dig deep and to hang on, but every day it got harder. The black mists of depression were closing in. The world was becoming a hard place to be in and there were even nights as he sat in his study in the creaking empty house as the rain lashed the window that he gave thought to leaving it. But in the end he still managed to tell himself that it was just a phase. It had to be. Be strong. Be patient. See it through. Things would turn. Soon it would be spring. Things could only get better. They simply had to.

As he pulled on his clothes and shivered he smiled sardonically to himself at that thought. That stupid, stupid thought. Things had to get better. Why? What great unwritten law was there that said that anything should ever get better for anyone? There wasn't one. There never had been and there never would be. Despite millions clinging on to their desperately naïve belief that it is everyone's God-given right to find themselves a Disney happy ending, earthquakes still happened, secret police forces still had their torture-chambers, and famine still stalked the earth.

Of course things could get worse, and they were just about to. Not just a bit worse. A whole lot worse. As bad as bad could be. The week before, the news stations had announced to a bemused nation that the Foot and Mouth virus had been found on a farm up by Hadrian's Wall in Northumbria. Foot and Mouth. Of all things. It seemed ridiculous, daft, something out of an episode of Monty Python. Foot and Mouth was one of those old diseases from History lessons in school. It was in there with Rickets and the Plague and Whooping Cough. Surely not now. Not in the United Kingdom in 2001. Surely not.

The problem was that the disease hadn't realised that it was supposed to have become a part of history, black and white images from 1967 along with those of Celtic winning the European Cup and the Marines hanging on for grim death in Khe Sahn. Now it was back with a bang, and within days it was jet-setting up and down the country with the speed and determination of desperate politicians in the week before an election.

Jack had watched the TV with a sense of dumb horror as the

virus had erupted in Northern Cumbria. It soon became apparent that infected sheep had been kept amongst thousands of others at the massive market at Longtown before being sent all over Britain. Within days of the outbreak the evening news carried the first ghastly images of hundreds of carcasses burning with their legs thrust stiffly into the air. One of the biggest of these infernos that so shocked the nation as it raged into the black night was on a large farm in Lockerbie, a mere fifteen miles away.

And yet there was still a thread of hope to cling to. Luckily Jack had switched his lambing time forward, and so he hadn't been to the auction at Longtown with his sheep for several weeks. This meant that the main danger was the wind. The virus could move many miles in a day when the weather conditions were right. This gave some hope, for the area of greatest infection was twenty miles due east of Hillside Farm. During the West Scottish winter, easterly winds were rare. The prevailing wind almost always blew from the west, sweeping over hundreds of miles, collecting moisture from the grey waters of the North Atlantic before dumping it on the hills of Galloway.

Normally he would have cursed this endless procession of depressions and low pressure. Normally he would have eagerly waited for a cold east wind to freeze the ground and dry out his sodden fields and give a better life for his flock of sheep. But not now. What he and all his neighbours hoped against hope for now was a month of mild, wet weather to be blown in from the west. If only the wind could stay in the west there just might be time for the culling policy to work and the disease to be stopped in its tracks at Gretna.

The previous night's weather forecast dashed these hopes. The cheery young presenter had swung her little stick from somewhere near Kiev, over the plains of the Ukraine and Poland, and all the way to Galloway. She had promised nice, crisp cold dry weather which with a bit of luck would enable everyone to get out and get themselves a bracing walk at the weekend. She wound up her summary with a big TV smile as she looked on fondly at the pictures of little yellow suns and arrows pointing from the East. For the farmers in and around Dumfries the little arrows of pointing at them from the east meant that disaster was on its way.

The enemy that was about to come at them was invisible. There were no trenches that they could dig. There were no real precautions that could be taken. There was absolutely nothing to do other than to keep pouring disinfectant on the pile of straw in the gateway to their tracks, and to avoid leaving the farm if at all possible. Jack was doing all of these things, but deep in his heart he knew there was no point. No matter what he did he couldn't stop the wind.

It had become part of his morning ritual to stand and bang away at Will's bedroom door until he received a bad-tempered grunt in reply. By the time his son would emerge Jack would have already have eaten his breakfast and brought the cows to the collecting yard ready for milking. Jack had given up shouting about this. Complaining only led to an escalating argument which in turn would only lead to the boy storming off with a torrent of curses. Better to say nothing. Better a moody, grim-faced fellow worker than none at all. It was only a phase. It would pass. It had to pass. Hell, in a couple of weeks it probably wouldn't matter anyway. In a couple of weeks their 164 dairy cows would probably just be a pile of ashes in the front field.

As he stepped out of the front door the wind hit him and cut straight through his coat and jumper. Hillside Farm lived up to its name. It sat 600 feet above sea level in the low-rolling hills that rose up above Dumfries and stretched all the way to the Clyde Estuary to the north. On a clear, crisp day the view from the yard was bordering on the breathtaking. The town of Dumfries sat either side of the river Nith four miles below him on a flat plain. The river then wound itself out to the Solway estuary that sparkled in the dawn sunshine. Beyond the band of water the peaks of the Lake District rose impressively into the deep blue of the morning sky.

The night had brought a hard frost to the fields and the world suddenly seemed wonderfully clear and clean. A mist hung in the valleys and the folds of the hills. Above him two buzzards were arcing across the sky in slow, majestic sweeps. Normally this was a time of high hope, of a feeling of awakening as the land sensed the spring. Not this morning. This morning the bone-hard frost created a landscape leaden with doom. He walked across the yard to the big new shed that they had completed a few months earlier.

THE CULL

Inside the cows were restlessly mooing their anticipation of getting their breakfast and having their udders emptied. Their breath swirled around in clouds of steam. Little did they know, thought Jack. Their big trusting eyes hadn't a clue of what was coming. A bolt-gun to the head, a set of chains around the legs, and then fire.

With an effort he shrugged himself out of his growing mood of black despair and started the morning milking.

Chapter 2
Breeding Ground

In the end, it was three days before the consignment of heroin at last resumed its delayed journey to Glasgow. This delay was only partly caused by the weather. The guy at the car park in the yellow waterproofs had been right to be pessimistic. The gale had not abated until the next afternoon and the first crossing from Larne was that evening. By this time the two men were back on the Belfast estate and waiting to get the nod to head off again. For a while it looked like they would be catching the midnight ferry. The Glasgow buyer had been on the phone on the hour, every hour, giving them a detailed opinion of exactly what he thought about the delay.

An hour before they were about to leave for the port, fate played the second of its cards. The house was suddenly thrown into a state of high alert as the news came in that one of their colleagues had been shot dead outside his house on the way to make a delivery. For a few hours all was pandemonium as intelligence was sought. Who had done it? Provos? Old IRA? New IRA? Real IRA? Or was it a faction from their own side? One of their rivals who had decided to break ranks and attack their turf? For the whole night the situation was unclear, and so long as it remained unclear, there was no way that the chief was going to allow two of his best men to go swanning off to Glasgow, no matter how pissed off the customer at the other end was getting. If someone was going to make a big move against them he would need every gun he could muster. No. Until the situation became clear they were going nowhere.

It did not become clear until the following lunchtime. It became clear thanks to a call from a public phone box from one of their contacts within the RUC. The police had found out a surprising amount of information in the first 24 hours of the investigation. Much to the disgust of the Chief, the police had found out things about his dead lieutenant that had never been brought to his attention. Apparently the man in question – Jimmy Neale – had been knocking off a bit on the side for over three years. Well that was fine. No problem with that. Why should there be?

The problem was the identity of the bit on the side that he was knocking-off, because this particular bit on the side was married to "Mad" Don McCall. "Mad Don" had earned his nickname over a period of many years. Now sometimes guys got the title "Mad" when it wasn't really warranted. They weren't really mad, just a bit hard, a bit off the rails, but not your actual grade-A mad. This wasn't the case with Don McCall. McCall was mad in every sense of the word. He was mad as in psychotic. Mad as in *as a hatter*. Mad as in absolute, raving, homicidal maniac. Don had always taken the greatest pleasure out of killing and causing pain. In another society in another era this tendency would have probably have been spotted early on whilst Don was little more than an excessively violent juvenile delinquent. With luck, and a following wind, he would have been packed off to some secure unit and filled with calming drugs before he got the chance to do any serious damage.

This hadn't happened in the Belfast streets of Don's wayward youth. The young prospective homicidal maniac was indeed spotted. He was spotted by a senior officer of the Ulster Volunteer Force and for eight years they had put him to maximum use in jobs that required knee-capping or beating and, on three occasions, murder. Don was the absolute dream ticket for the UVF. Just so long as they gave him a life of extreme violence to live he was as happy as a pig in muck. For eight years he built up the reputation as one of the meanest, maddest bastards ever to walk the streets of Belfast. He actually became quite famous, even to the extent that parents who were having problems with their wayward four-year-old children could bring them under instant control by threatening them with "Mad Don."

It couldn't go on of course, and eventually the RUC managed to catch him and much of the community breathed a huge sigh of relief when they heard that he had been sent to Long Kesh prison for a minimum of 30 years.

He had been in the Kesh for nine of these years when Jimmy Neale had sweet-talked his way into the bed of Don's wife. Jimmy had been emboldened by the sure and certain knowledge that there was no way that they would ever let Mad Don out. No way. Not Mad Don. He was more than your average terrorist. He was a raging nutter.

How wrong Jimmy had been. The kind of reasoned logic that he had been relying on had been left far behind in the euphoria of the Peace Process and the words of wiser heads were ignored. Mad Don had been let out the day before. It took him exactly six hours to steal a car and lay his hands on a Kalashnikov assault rifle. Eight hours after breathing the air of freedom for the first time in nine years Mad Don had left Jimmy Neale lying in an impressive pool of blood on the pavement outside his house.

The news came as a great relief to the Chief. Of course it was a shame about Jimmy, but when all was said and done Jimmy had always been a bit of tosser and if he was thick-headed enough to shag Mad Don McCall's wife then what the fuck did he expect? No. All-in-all it wasn't that bad. Jimmy was no great loss. Mad Don was safely banged up and back inside where there was little doubt that he would stay until Hell froze over and nobody was having a go at his operation after all.

He picked up the phone and called the Glasgow customer. He informed him that the two men would be catching the eight o' clock boat and they would be with him in the wee small hours. And the customer started yelling and bawling again! He couldn't believe it. Did the bloody man ever stop? At last his patience finally snapped and all the pent-up tension of the previous 24 hours came pouring out.

"Now listen you fucking Jock twat. The next time some mad bastard puts sixteen rounds into one of your men with a fucking Kalashnikov you will discover that it isn't business as fucking usual. So why don't you shut the fuck up before I come over the water and do it for you. They'll be there tonight. Now fuck off."

He crashed the phone down so hard that he split the plastic. The two delivery men looked on anxiously. He looked up. "So what are you two waiting for? Go on. Fuck off away with you. Take the Scottish bastard his smack before he has a fucking stroke."

The two men did as they were bid. This time they arrived in Larne to look out on a flat calm sea. This didn't fill them with any great joy. The Chief had ensured that there wouldn't be tea and biscuits waiting for them when they arrived in Glasgow in the wee small hours.

The Chief would have been somewhat surprised if he could have seen what was happening at the other end of the phone conversation. In his mind he was pretty well convinced that the abusive customer in Glasgow would have been sitting in a room similar to his own, a nondescript room in a nondescript council house in the middle of a the kind of sprawling estate that the police would always be reluctant to visit. Not the case at all. Instead the call had been taken in a very nicely appointed office seven floors up in a modern block in the centre of the city. The annual rent of the office would have paid twenty years of the rent for the kind of council dwelling that the Chief would have envisaged.

Similarly he would have been surprised by the look of the two men in the office. In his mind's eye he was talking to the very image of the Glasgow "hard man", about 45 or 50, very broad, tattoos probably, watched by two or three younger Glasgow hard men learning their trade. He couldn't have been much further from the truth. The man was indeed about 50 and he was certainly broad and very fit. However, he was wearing a particularly well cut and expensive suit along with a creaseless white shirt and a silk tie. He had actually been speaking into a microphone so that the whole conversation had been broadcast through speakers. This had enabled the man who was sitting behind a large mahogany desk by the window to listen in.

When the speaker announced that the caller had slammed the phone down both men chuckled. The caller said "Was that OK Mr Taylor? I didn't overdo it I hope." Most of the hard edges from the

Glasgow voice had gone, his voice was now softer, quieter.

The man behind the desk smiled. "No Briggs. That was fine. Perfect really."

"If you don't mind me asking Mr Taylor, why exactly did you want me to keep ringing and winding him up like that?"

"I don't mind you asking." Taylor spoke with no accent at all. His words were neat and precise, each one carefully chosen and dusted down before use. "There are a couple of reasons. Firstly, heroin supplies are not particularly abundant at the moment. We will not be alone in being short of material. This of course means that everyone will be pressurising their suppliers for delivery. We live in a rather nasty world when it is often the case that the only way to get what you want is to shout for it.

"Secondly it is what he expects. The Irish are really a rather unsophisticated people. They are very good at this sort of thing because they have had years of practice. Their gangs are tight knit and very loyal to each other. Thirty years of being chased about the place by the British Army have ensured it is so. They are also particularly violent. In his mind the gentlemen in Belfast will be confident that we will be cut from exactly the same cloth.

"Now this is ever so important because it means that he knows who he is dealing with and this makes him comfortable. Now if we had been polite and understanding about what has clearly been a wholly unavoidable delay he would have immediately smelt a rat. If he could see us right now, he would of course assume that we are a soft touch because in his eyes anyone who wears a suit and works from a nice office is exactly that. Now the last thing that we need is a gang of certified maniacs from Belfast coming over to try and muscle in on things. So you see, what you did was perfect. You did exactly what he would have done. You were coarse and rude and that will make him feel secure."

Briggs smiled. "OK. Got the drift."

The intercom buzzed from the secretary in the next office and Briggs picked up the phone. After listening for a moment he looked up to Taylor. "Phone call Mr Taylor. It's Zippo again. Do you want me to deal with it or would you like to speak to him?"

"I'll take it, but, Briggs, please try to remember to call him Macintosh. If he insists on using his ludicrous American nickname there is nothing we can do about it, but let us not join in. His name is Macintosh. Eric Macintosh. That is fine for me."

Taylor took the call.

"Good Morning Eric, and how are things in Dumfries on this fine and sunny day?"

There was a hesitation at the other end of the line. Social niceties obviously didn't play a major part in Macintosh's life. When he spoke, his voice was deep and his accent thick.

"Aye they're alright Mr Taylor, well, not really, you ken, we're getting fucking short here, I mean we're out. People are getting jumpy. When can I come and collect the stuff? You got any yet?"

"Not yet Eric, but soon. Tonight hopefully, late on. Our suppliers have had one or two problems with the delivery but they seem to be resolved now. Maybe you could come up and see us tomorrow night."

"Aye, OK then, nae bother. You know how it is when there's no gear about."

"Indeed I do Eric. I can take it that business is good."

The voice brightened. "Aye, fucking brilliant, more every day Mr Taylor."

"Well that is splendid. You try and calm them down Eric and all being well we will see you tomorrow evening."

"OK. Bye the now Mr Taylor."

"Yes, goodbye Eric."

Mandy left it to a little after 7.30 before she drove up to Hillside Farm. This gave plenty of time for Jack and Will to finish the job of evening milking. As she bumped her car up the track she fervently hoped that Will would have gone out. She hadn't seen him since Christmas and had no desire to see him now.

The yard seemed to be deserted and the only lights that she could see were in the house. She heaved her bag off the front seat and headed for the back door. She was halfway across the yard when an angry shout pulled her up short. She turned and saw Will walking fast towards her. He must have still been in the parlour washing out the milking equipment when she had arrived. Her heart sank.

"You! What the bloody hell do you think you're doing here?

Are you really that thick Mandy? Does nothing sink into that carrot-top mop of yours Mandy? You're not welcome here. So, piss off."

As he came close she saw that he had lost yet more weight. His face was bony and twisted with anger. Once upon a time it had been his smile that had attracted her. Will had always been smiling, a happy-go-lucky guy who didn't seem to have a care in the world. Not now. Now it looked like he hadn't smiled in months. His eyes held such hostility that she began to feel frightened.

"Don't worry Will. I haven't come to see you. I have no intention of seeing you again. In fact I was rather hoping you would be out."

His face twisted mockingly and he parroted her sentence in a wheedling, mocking voice. "I was rather hoping you'd be out."

"Yes I did. And I wish you were. I have come to talk to your father who I presume is in the house. So if you don't mind, please leave me alone and I will go and find him."

"Oh I see. Come to see Daddy have we. Oh well, that's fine then. You always did like your cosy little chats with Daddy didn't you Mandy? Had them all the time didn't you? I think you must have a thing for older men. Got fed-up with a young buck like me didn't you? Too uncouth for a sophisticated reporter like you. No, I wasn't good enough at all. But Daddy, oh well that's different isn't it? You've read all about it in your poxy magazines I bet. What's it like to get well and truly fucked by the older man. A man with a bit of experience . . ."

"Will! For God's sake . . ."

" . . . especially a widower. And a fine figure of a man too. A real old soldier. Bit of danger Mandy. Is that what turns you on? I hear that is what all you silly young girls want. Bit of danger. A bit of the dark side. I bet you would close your eyes and fantasise about him in his uniform on the Falls Road while he fucked you . . ."

She was livid and turned for the door. "That's enough. I have no idea what is the matter with you Will, but there is no need for all of this. Now leave me be, I'm going to find Jack."

She started to walk but he reached out and caught the hood of her coat and tugged hard. The surprise of it caught her off balance. She slipped and fell backwards. As her arms jerked up she unwittingly threw her bag and it spewed its contents out onto the cobbled yard. She landed badly and felt the wind driven out of her. He bent over her and pushed his face close to hers. He was shouting now and spittle splashed her cheeks as she tried to find her breath again.

"No I won't leave you alone you little whore. You've no business here. And if you think that I am going to let you come swanning up here to shake your little tail you've got another thing coming. So what you are going to do now you dirty little bitch, is leave. You're going to leave and you're not coming back . . ." He had hold of the hood again and he started to drag her towards her car. She still hadn't got her breath back and all she could do was flap her arms about weakly. Her zipped-up coat bit into her neck as he pulled her and she couldn't speak. " . . . and if you come back, bitch, if you come back I'm going to beat the living daylights out of you. Got that have you! I SAID HAVE YOU GOT THAT!"

"WILL!" The sound of Jack's voice cut across the cold winter air like a rifle shot. Mandy felt his grip on her hood ease and then release. She sank to the floor and gasped for air. Jack strode across the yard with a look of utter rage on his face.

"What in God's name do you think you are playing at? Who is this? Oh Jesus, it's you Mandy, are you OK?" He bent over and helped her to sit up. Will had slowly backed away. He was still boiling with anger but the look on his father's face was like ice-cold water. He started to walk towards the Land Rover. Jack looked up and noticed.

"No Will. No way. Not this time. I've let you get away with too much for too long. But not this time. Now get yourself over here."

Will never looked back. He sauntered over to the Land Rover and started to open the door. "Dad, why don't you just fuck off as well."

This enraged Jack and he started to rise to his feet. Something snapped. This was the last straw. This time there was going to be no more patience, no more biting of the tongue, this time he was going to give the bastard such a bloody hiding that . . . a tug on his trouser leg held him up. Mandy had at last got her breath and was able to speak.

"No Jack, don't. Leave it. Let him go. I'm fine. Really. Just a bit muddy that's all. No damage. Just let him go. You'll regret it. Just help me to my feet could you?"

Jack felt himself slowly freeze as Will leered at him, climbed into the Land Rover and sped out of the yard. He turned and helped Mandy to her feet. She started collecting up the clutter that had been thrown from her bag as tears welled up in her eyes. He helped her and when the bag was refilled they went inside.

When he saw her in the light of the kitchen he was appalled. There was an ugly red mark on her neck where the top of the zip had bitten in and her hair was soaked and filthy from the muck in the yard. Her clothes were similarly filthy and her dress was badly torn. Tears were pouring down her face and one of her cheeks was grazed and caked with muck. She attempted a small smile.

"You know what Jack, the main reason that I wanted to be a reporter was for the excitement. I don't know if I am so sure now."

"Oh God Mandy, what can I say. This is a nightmare. Look, let me get you a brandy and then you'd better go and clean yourself up a bit. I'll find you some sort of clothes and then I'll see to that cut on your face. Christ, when I get hold of that little bastard I'm going to wring his worthless neck, I'm . . ."

"Jack, calm down. I don't need a brandy. I'm driving. You go and pour yourself one whilst I make myself a coffee. The clothes would be very welcome and I could certainly do with cleaning up a bit. Stop worrying. I'm fine. I'm a big girl and I grew up with two older brothers who did this sort of thing more or less every day."

He saw straight through the brave words and the defiant smile. Her normally pale skin had turned chalk-white and she was trembling. He had seen enough cases of shock to know all the symptoms. But she was right. He needed to calm down. Raging away wasn't going to do anyone any good. He needed to get a grip and to find out what on earth had gone on in the yard. He took her advice on the brandy and knocked it back in one gulp. The strength of the liquor took the edge off his rage. He poured another one and joined her at the kitchen table as she shakily lit a cigarette.

"Mandy. What in God's name happened out there?"

"Honestly Jack, I haven't got a clue. I had just got out of the car and I was heading for the back door when Will came at me from the parlour. He was just raging. I hadn't even said a word. When I told him I was here to see you not him he just completely flipped. Jesus Jack, what is the matter with him? He was like a mad man out there and he looks terrible."

Jack slumped back on his chair. He suddenly felt overwhelmingly tired. "If only I could tell you Mandy. I just don't know and I can't find out. We had a huge bust-up before Christmas after the two of you split up and we have barely spoken since. He's like an unexploded bomb some of the time, some of the time he's just a zombie. Hell, you know well enough. You've seen it all. I keep trying to tell myself it's just a phase, but things just get worse and worse. To be honest I'm about at my wit's end."

She looked at the slumped figure and noticed that the lines on his weathered face were deeper than she had ever seen before. Jack always cut an impressive figure. He stood a hard-boned six foot three with hands like shovels and a shock of wiry blond hair which always seemed to have a life of its own. He was all sharp edges. Every bone in his face seemed oversized with leathery skin stretched over the top as tight as an African drum. All his wrinkle lines ran in the right directions. His face summed up his life. Lots of bad weather, lots of laughing. His eyes told the same story. Very green and a sense of mischief. But there was no mischief now. He looked tired, worn, close to breaking point.

He wasn't a man to show weakness, and for him to seem so broken she knew that he must be heading for the end of his tether. He made a visible effort to pull himself together and he straightened himself.

"Anyway Mandy. You said it was me that you wanted to see. To what do I owe this pleasure?"

Now she felt awful. It would seem so downright cheap to tell him the purpose of her visit. But what else could she say? There was no point in lying. "It seems awful now, after all this. My boss at the paper has asked me to cover the Foot and Mouth crisis as it spreads and hits the area. The human side of things, how it is affecting people, how they feel, what it means to their lives. He suggested that I should come to see you first. He said you would be a good man to talk to. But I can see that I shouldn't have, I mean it's a bad time, I should have thought, sorry Jack."

"Good lord woman, don't be sorry. Bob is absolutely right. We're going to get hit like we've never been hit before and the story has to be told. I never thought he had it in him. Of course you should do it. You're young, you're dedicated, you have sensitivity and you have talent. Of course I'll help. I'll be glad to. You go and get yourself a shower whilst I dig you out something to wear and then I will see what I can do for you."

Once she had cleaned up they sat at the table and talked. She admitted that she only had a vague grasp on many of the aspects of the disease and he helped to fill in the gaps. Once she realised that he was genuinely happy to help she started to fill in page after page of her notebook in big untidy handwriting.

"Tell me Jack, how bad is it going to be for the farmers who get it? How about you and Will. What will it actually mean?"

"It very much varies from farm to farm. For some farmers it will be the best thing that could ever happen, there's no point hiding it."

Her jaw dropped. "You're kidding."

"Not in the slightest. A lot of beef and sheep farmers have had a nightmare over the last few years. Their stock is worth next to nothing and their profits have been non-existent. For them the infection offers an escape. They are getting paid about three times the market price for their animals and the cheque that they are getting will enable them to pay off all their debts and escape the trap that they have been in. There are loads of farmers in their sixties who have been desperate to give up, but they just haven't been able to afford to do it. For them this will be an absolute Godsend."

"What about you Jack?"

"Oh, if only. No, we are in the other camp I'm afraid. For us it will be a bloody catastrophe."

"Why. Explain it to me."

He looked thoughtful for a moment and then nodded. "OK I will, but look this stuff is for you, not the paper. This is private stuff, understand?"

"Yes of course, but look, please don't tell me anything that you aren't comfortable with."

This made him laugh and for a moment the lines on his face didn't seem so deep any more. "Dear, oh dear Mandy. What on earth are we going to do with you!"

"What do you mean?" His laughter annoyed her.

"That, my girl, is not the thing for an aspiring reporter to say. It is the exact opposite. You are supposed to lull people into saying all the things that they aren't comfortable with."

She was a little flustered by this. "Oh I see. Well that just isn't me. I don't want to be that kind of reporter. And anyway you're not just people. You're a friend, well, you are aren't you?"

"Course I am. Sorry for teasing. And I don't mind at all. I know that you are discreet. Hell, a few months ago I was rather hopeful that you were all set to be my daughter-in-law."

This made her blush almost crimson. He mentally ticked himself off and hurried on.

"OK. The mess that is Hillside Farm. Last year we went to our accountants and he told us that we hadn't made any money again. So we had to do something. If we had stood still we would have gone slowly down the pan. Instead we decided to gamble. We put another 50 cows on and built a new shed. We were relying on enough farmers quitting the industry for Milk Quotas to not matter any more. And the bugger of it is that the plan was actually starting to work. We have put our income up and even the price of milk is rising whilst there is no sign of the country ever meeting quota again.

"The bad news is that to do all this we took our overdraft right up to £400,000. Now with income on the way up that would not have been too much of a problem. However, if we get culled it all changes. We will get a compensation cheque for about £280,000 which of course sounds like a stack of money. The trouble is that once we bank it we will still be left with an overdraft of £120,000 and we won't have any income for God knows how long, probably at least a year.

"This gives us a bunch of problems to deal with. Firstly it will cost us money to simply live. Secondly, the interest on the overdraft is ten grand a year. Thirdly, when we are at last allowed to re-stock, the price of beasts will probably have gone through the roof. This means that we will have no chance of building the herd up to today's levels for many years. Fourthly, there is the overdraft. Our bank had little choice than to let me take it up from £300,000 to £400,000. They could see that the only way that the business would ever be sufficiently viable to make the £300,000 they had already committed viable was to lend another £100,000. Once I stick my compensation cheque into the account my bank manager is going to breathe an almighty sigh of relief because he isn't so exposed any more. Now, I might be wrong, but my gut feeling tells me there is no way on earth that any bank is going to give us a facility much above £200,000.

"Now if I am right on this, by the time that we have paid our interest and lived we won't have much above £60,000 to spend on new stock. That means about 60 or 70 halfway decent cattle and no sheep. Today we have 164 cows and 1,100 sheep. And then there are the buildings."

"The buildings?"

"Yes. You see, in the last years when Dad was ill, he let a lot of the buildings go to rack and ruin. Now, it isn't the end of the world. We keep patching them up and by and large they keep the rain out. What is happening now on farms with the infection is that the Ministry men are condemning any buildings with rotten timber or poor brickwork. I reckon this will mean we will have to demolish at least three of our sheds and we only get a 20% grant towards replacing them. If we spent what was left of the compensation on this there would be nothing left to buy any animals at all.

'Anyway I don't suppose that the buildings really matter much because if we can only afford 60 cows we won't need any new buildings, and if we only have 60 cows to milk, we won't be able to make a living anyway. So, as you can see, we are more or less stuffed whichever way you look at it. The only real option will be for us to sell up, clear the overdraft, and go and find something else to do."

Although he ran through the scenario in a straightforward and matter-of-fact way she still found that her eyes were filling with tears. In her time with Will, before it had all gone so wrong, she had seen how hard they had both worked. She knew how much it must have hurt Jack to give up his career in the Army just when it was beginning to take off. By now he might even have been a Colonel. Instead he had come back to the land where generations of his family had toiled away in the wind and the rain. And now, because of a microscopic bug that nobody could either see or stop, they were going to lose it all. Will would represent the last generation of the Sinclair family to farm the fields of Hillside. It was all just so downright bloody miserable. No wonder the lines on Jack's face had got so deep, especially with all the worry about Will.

She tossed her notebook down and sighed. "Well I know more about all this than I did before, that's for sure. It's just awful. So very awful. I'm so, so sorry Jack. I really am."

He smiled. "I know you are. Knew you would be. There's nothing that can be done. Nothing that will work quickly enough anyway. Hopefully the farms twenty or thirty miles east of here will be OK. But I fear we've had it. And if we have, there is little point in collapsing in a heap and moaning about it. Que Sera Sera, whatever will be, will be. You just make sure that you write about it properly, do it well, and take your chance."

They fell into a sad sort of a silence. After a while she glanced at her watch and saw that it was past midnight. "I better be going. Thanks Jack, thanks for giving me so much help."

"On the contrary, it is me who should be thanking you. I needed to talk to someone, get it all off my chest a bit, it's helped. Now you get yourself home. I know you won't let us down."

Will crashed out of the end of the track and headed north. He stopped after a few miles and gazed blankly out of the window. What had he done? His mind was a nest of spiders. Images flashed through his mind like strobe lighting. He tried to breathe slowly and evenly to calm himself down. Every bit of his body felt bad. He wanted to be sick all the time. Waves of craving flowed through him. It was eating him alive as if he were full of evil wriggling maggots. It was like a pure torture. Hour after hour. A bright burning lightbulb that frazzed his eyeballs. He couldn't sleep, couldn't sit still, couldn't think. Just spiders crawling around his brain.

But what had he done? He forced himself to remember. It had only been a few minutes ago but already the overwhelming craving was brushing the memories aside. The craving made them unimportant, irrelevant, pointless. But there was a point. He knew he had to see the point. He had dragged Mandy through the mud of the yard. He had called her a bitch and a whore. He had screamed in her face. He had threatened to beat her.

"Oh Jesus fucking Christ Will, what have you done?"

He started to beat his head down on the steering wheel, softly at first, then harder and harder and harder. The pain began to grow. It was good pain. It threw all the spiders in his head around. It drove the craving back for a moment. Then it got too much and he had to stop and slump back in the seat.

He reached into his pocket and pulled out his mobile phone. He flashed the last dialled number onto the screen and hit enter. He felt no sense of hope for the call. It must have been the fiftieth time that he had tried the same number that day. Just like he had the day before. And the day before that. And every time he had suffered the neutral tones of the *Orange Answering Service* woman. He knew it would be the same again. But still he had to try. There was nothing else in his life that mattered any more. Only this one number. The number for salvation, for release, for peace.

"Yo, Will. How you doing?"

For a moment Will was too stunned to speak. There was actually a human voice on the other end and it took him completely off balance.

"Ricky, is that you Ricky?"

"Course it is. Who were you expecting, Posh fucking Spice?"

"Ricky, where the fuck have you been? I've been calling for days. Where have you been? I tried to find you yesterday. What's going on?"

"Oh you know, here and there, this and that, just chilling mainly. What about you bro'?"

"Where do you fucking think Ricky? On the farm. Where else? For fuck's sake Ricky, have you got anything yet?"

"No. Sorry mate. There's been some sort of hold-up, some sort of glitch in the chain, stuff has got really tight man, I mean really, seriously tight. The word is that there will be stuff coming in tomorrow night."

Will groaned. Tomorrow night. Tomorrow night felt like next century. Another 24 hours of this agony and spiders crawling through his brain.

"Jesus Ricky, I can't wait that long. I'm dying here. I mean really dying. What about you? You must have your own stash Ricky. You MUST have. Just let me have a little bit. Anything. A fiver's worth.

Anything. Come on man, we're mates. *Just a fiver bag.*"

"Sorry Will my man, no can do. I can't even do a five pence bag. I tell you, stuff is out, non-existent, the shelves are empty and all the shops are closed, you just have to hang tight my man, hang tight."

Will felt a tide of desperation washing over him. He felt tears building up in his eyes. His voice was beginning to crack. "Fuck it Ricky, I can't deal with this. You have to help me. We're mates remember. We've been mates for years. You can't leave me out to dry. Christ Ricky, you got me into this. Help me. For Christ's sake help me."

"Hey Will, keep yourself together. I will. As soon as I can, I will. Honest. Trust me. One more day. Just hang on. Look I've got to go. As soon as the stuff lands I'll call. Promise."

And the line was dead. Hope seemed dead. Somehow he was going to have to make it through to tomorrow night. And then he was going to have to do something. If he could just get sorted out for a while he could start to get his head together again. This time he was going to wean himself down. Every day he would cut it back. He would control it. Back a bit and back a bit and then he would kick it and get his life back.

A burst of clarity hit him. He saw what had happened in the yard as if it had been filmed under arc lights. He saw the fear on Mandy's face. He saw the hate in his father. Why had he done it? How could he have done it? The tears came again now. Helpless, miserable tears poured down his cheeks. They were the two people in the world that he loved more than any others. Why?

He knew why. It wasn't his fault. He had no control. He had a head full of spiders and his legs were full of maggots. He had no control any more. He was just a puppet that danced and danced and danced for as long as the puppeteer made it dance.

And the puppeteer was heroin.

Heroin. His god. His family. His church. His dictator. His jailer. His life.

He was past telling himself that it was OK, he was in control. He had done that for a while. Oh, I can handle it. I just use it when I'm out. I don't know what the big deal is. I like to take Ecstasy when I go clubbing, and I use a bit of smack to help me come back down. You have to use something. It's no big deal. I can take it or leave it. You just have to use a bit of common sense.

He had been through all the lies. And for a while it had been like that. He and Ricky would take off for Glasgow or Manchester on his weekends off. Then one time Ricky told him that smack was the best way to ease themselves down from the Ecstasy. No big deal. Everybody does it. Don't believe all the shite in the papers. The thing to remember is to avoid the needle. Only the dickheads jack it up. If you smoke it, it's cool. So long as you smoke it you're in control.

And for a while they had been in control. They would leave a club at five or six in the morning with their minds and bodies still burning and buzzing. They would drive out of town, park up in a quiet lay-by, and chase the dragon. A huge sense of contentment would wash through them. Their jagged nerves would be planed down. Just contentment. Perfect, perfect utter perfection as they would drive home. By the time he got back Will would be shattered after a straight 30 hours without sleep. He would exchange a few words with his dad who would ask where he had been and how was the night and tell him he was crackers. And then he would go and lie on his bed and sleep twelve hours straight.

The next morning he would wake with a raging hunger and thirst. Massive fry-up. Three pint-sized mugs of tea. Then out to milk the cows. That was how it had been. He had been in control. Surely he had. But then again maybe not. Maybe it had really only lasted a couple of weeks. Because it hadn't really been that long before the spiders had come. A month? Maybe six weeks? A month. Yes a month. And then there were spiders in his head. Not many of course, but they were there. They were there as he milked the cows, went round the sheep, cleaned out the troughs, fed the calves, mended machinery. They were there when he ate his breakfast or watched the match on tele or had a few pints with the lads after rugby training.

Every week brought a few more spiders. More little voices whispering at him. He couldn't seem to stop thinking about how good that moment of perfection was, how absolutely wonderful to feel the perfection spread all over his body and then contentment. Complete. Absolute. Wondrous. And then the rest of his life started to lose its brightness. Every day the other things were becoming second-best. Nights out with Mandy. Rugby. Golf. The farm. The match. None of it could compare. None of it was even halfway. It all seemed trivial when compared to that moment of perfection. All he could think about was the moment. The moment when everything else went away and he could float.

Sometimes he sensed it. He could see that the road ahead was fraught with danger. So he would stop. A week. Two weeks. Even a month. He told himself that this proved that it was OK. He could stop any time he wanted. No real junkie could stop for a month. So he wasn't a junkie. Of course he wasn't. He was smart, he only smoked. He didn't jack up. He would never jack up. That was for the dickheads.

He hadn't noticed because he hadn't wanted to. He hadn't noticed that all he had thought about for that month was the moment it was going to end. He hadn't noticed that he had bitten Mandy's head off just about every time they met. He hadn't noticed the silly arguments with his dad. He just told himself that he knew exactly what he was doing, and when the month was over he returned to his god. His sanctuary. His perfect world.

And then they had gone to *T in the Park*, a huge music festival. Him and Ricky. They had taken a tent and a bag full of drugs. Four days. Uppers every night followed by heroin every morning. And it had been fantastic. Brilliant. The absolute best time ever. When they got home they were shattered. But it was silage time. The forecast for the week was hot, hot and even more hot, and Hillside Farm had a massive crop of grass in the fields. There was no time to think of resting up, the crop had to be got in and that meant fourteen hours a day on the tractor.

He woke up each morning and took speed to fly him through the long, hot day. And at night he used heroin to slow his exhausted body back down again and send him into blissful, wonderful perfect sleep. And what a week it had been. Four days of mad, wild music and then a thousand tonnes of top-class, grade A silage in the barn. Life was good. Life couldn't be better. Work hard. Play hard. Find perfection. There were times in that long hot July when it seemed as good as it could get.

Now he knew different. Those eight days were the time when he had walked into the shadows, never to come out. Once the silage was all in and sealed up ready for the winter, life on the farm slowed down. His dad had gone away for three days with some friends from the golf club. And every day Will had smoked.

And so eight days with heroin every day became eleven days with heroin every day. When he stopped there were suddenly a whole lot more spiders in his brain. He tried all he could to ignore them. He threw himself into his work. He must have overdone it a bit. Well he had. Worth it though. Worth it for a week like that. Time to give it a rest for a while. No problem. He was well in control. He would leave it alone for a month again. Well. Maybe not that long. That would be going a bit overboard. No need to go over the top. What the hell for? A fortnight. That would do. A fortnight to wash the system out and prove he was in control.

He had lasted for three days.

For the first time the craving had really hurt. Before it had just been his mind as it dreamed of the moment of release, of floating away, of going back to that better world that he had found. But now it was physical as well. He felt so bloody sick. And he felt like he was being eaten alive. All day that first day he told himself that he was just being stupid and it was all in his head. He woke up on the morning of the second day feeling more miserable than he had ever felt before in his life. He was frightened. Almost desperate. He just felt so very ill. And things had gone wrong all day. First he had a huge bust-up with his dad. He had fed calf feed to the lambs by mistake. How could he have done that? It was such a stupid thing to do. And his dad had told him so. Calf feed has copper in it. Copper can kill lambs. Don't be so bloody careless. And his dad was right. It was careless. He knew full well that copper could kill lambs. But he had flown off the handle and they had yelled each other.

He was just so tensed up, wrapped tight, spiders behind his eye balls. He was angry and sick and suddenly so very frightened. Terrified. Out of control.

All he wanted in the whole wide world was to find help. He wanted to turn to his Dad. All his life his father had been there. Massive. Strong. Solid. Nothing bad would ever happen when his Dad was there. Dad was a warrior. He wanted to tell him. To confide in him. To get him to help. To get him to drive the demons away. Dad, I need to tell you something. I think that I'm becoming a junkie and I'm trying to get back in control but I don't know if I can and I am just so, so very frightened and I feel sick and I want to cry all the time and I'm so scared Dad. So scared Dad. So scared Dad. Help me Dad. Help me Dad. Please help me Dad. Oh Jesus, *please help me Dad*.

But he hadn't said any of this. He had forced it back inside. Fear had become rage. Instead of begging for help he had ranted and raged and stormed off in the Land Rover whilst his Dad had looked on in open astonishment.

That night he and Mandy had gone to the cinema. The spiders were getting worse. He couldn't concentrate on the film. He couldn't seem to sit still. The cinema seemed to be closing in on him. He was hot. Hot all over. Hotter than he had ever felt before. He had to get out. He told Mandy that he hated the film and he was going. He rushed outside. He needed some air, some space, the spiders were crawling all over him, he needed somewhere to hide, he needed someone to help. It was getting so hard. How could it be so hard? He was shaking and there was nowhere that he could go. Nowhere to run to, nowhere to hide. He couldn't believe that he wanted it so much, needed it so much, more than anything in the whole wide world, more than anything in history, more than anything that there had ever been, ever.

He had stopped by a wall and started to bang his head against it harder and harder and harder. He needed to drive the yearning away. He needed to punish himself for being such a fool. Stupid. Stupid. Stupid. Addict. Addict. Addict. *Junkie. Smackhead. Stupid.*

Then Mandy was there. Her face so full of concern, full of love, full of the hope of a better life. And that had been the moment. That was the very moment that he should have come clean. He should have told her. About the spiders and the craving and the yearning and how stupid he had been and how he was throwing his life away and how much, how very much, he wanted it back again. Turn back the clocks. Fresh start. Another chance. And it might not have been too late. Because Mandy would have helped him. Because Mandy loved him. And he loved Mandy. And together they might have done it, because he still could have found the strength somehow, and she would have given him the strength somehow, and that had been the moment.

The moment had passed.

The fear turned to anger, just like it had with his Dad. And he had turned on her. Taken it all out on her. He had been abusive and foul-mouthed. Part of him couldn't believe what the other half was saying. What was he doing? Why was he doing it? How could he be doing it? But he couldn't stop. The anger ate him whole. And he had ranted and yelled and hurled a bottle against a wall across the street and told her to get lost and fuck off and get out of his face.

She had tried. God bless her she had tried. She loved him and she was brave and stubborn but in the end the sheer heat of his anger had driven her away. And when she was gone he wanted her back. He needed her back. He needed someone. He rang but she slammed the phone down on him.

He hadn't slept that night. He had tossed and turned and thrown up three times. He felt more miserable and lonely than he had ever imagined possible. He didn't really know how he made it through the next day. His Dad had barely spoken a word to him. Even the animals seemed to stare at him accusingly.

That night he went into town and found Ricky. That night he bought more heroin. He was going to leave it alone for a fortnight. He lasted three days. Three days and his new master dragged him back.

From then on it was every day. He made promises to himself but they were never very serious. Of course he would knock it on the head for a month again. Of course he would. But not yet. Not now though. Maybe next month. Yeah next month would be a far better idea.

Then to his horror there were times when he never quite made it to his perfect world. It was like he was stuck in a lift, and the lift had a glass roof and when he looked through it he could see the beautiful blue sky above with fluffy white clouds and butterflies and skylarks, but the lift wouldn't go any further up. It wouldn't get him to the top any more. Hell, it was better being in the lift than in the lobby below, but he couldn't make it all the way to the top any more. He could look but not touch. So he would rush out and buy some more, and smoke some more, and that would kick-start the lift back into life, and it would go all the way up, and the door would slide open and there he would be in that perfect, beautiful place with warm blue skies and a gentle soft breeze.

Money had become a problem. It took a bit more every day. He stopped buying new clothes. He stopped going out. He stopped buying CDs. He cut back on everything but he never seemed to have quite enough. He was having to smoke more and more to make the lift go all the way to the top. He started taking coins from his father's pocket and Mandy's purse. He sold his CD player. He sold his golf clubs. Then Mandy had caught him nicking a fiver and they had a big argument and he hadn't seen her again for a month. And still he never had enough.

He begged Ricky to give him discount, to let him have a bit on account, go on Ricky, just till Friday, pay you back Friday, honest Ricky, come on man, we're mates, you can trust me Ricky, for fuck's sake, it's me Ricky. It's Will. Come on man, don't be a bastard, for God's sake man, *give me some!*

But Ricky had better advice. Only suckers smoke it Will. Suckers or rich bastards from Hollywood or pop stars. You can't get a proper hit if you smoke it. Not unless you smoke an absolute load. And you can't afford it Will. You can't keep coming round and begging. I know we're mates, of course we're mates, but this is business Will, and business is business, well isn't it?

And so he had started jacking-up. Just like a proper junkie.

Because he was a proper junkie.

Jacking-up sent him all the way to the top. He could get the whole trip for a tenner a day. Well fifteen. Sometimes twenty. Never any more than twenty-five. And soon there were times when he couldn't get the cash together and he would miss for a day, sometimes two days, and then the demons would close in all over him. And the spiders. And the maggots. And sometimes he simply couldn't control his rage. And Mandy went. And all of his friends went. And his life went. And any kind of relationship with his Dad went. And slowly but surely everything went until there was only heroin left.

One God. One Love. One life. One drug.

Heroin. Just heroin. Only heroin.

As long as there was heroin life was perfection. With no heroin it became a lingering nightmare. That was all there was. Get it. Find it. Afford it. Take it. Feel it. Love it. Adore it. Worship it. Crave it. Die for it. Find it. Take it. Steal for it. Beg for it. Do anything for it.

Anything at all. Because nothing else mattered. Only heroin mattered.

Life was heroin and heroin was life.

And now he had money burning a hole in his pocket and there was no heroin to buy. None until tomorrow. Until tomorrow night. It would seem like a hundred years with only the maggots and the spiders for company. But it would pass. He would get through it because at the end of the rainbow there was a needle and the needle was life itself.

As Will raged against his demons all the way through that long, cold February night he had absolutely no idea of the real reason for all his pain. If he had known it would probably sent him even more demented. The fact was that it was all down to "Mad" Don McCall. Mad Don had shot Jimmy Neale because Jimmy Neale had been sleeping with Mad Don's wife. And that act of psychotic revenge had held things up. And all over Scotland others like Will were paying the price with heads filled with spiders and legs filled with maggots

For a little while Ricky felt really quite bad about the phone call from his old friend. He had actually told Will a number of lies. The first of these lies was really not much more than a fairly harmless one. All the talk of places to go and things to do and ducking and diving was just flannel. He had said it all more or less out of habit. He definitely didn't want Will calling round in a right state, banging on the door and setting his Mum off.

His plans for the evening were far more mundane. Take a whacking great hit and watch the football.

The second lie was the one that bothered him a bit. There was no doubt that heroin supplies had completely dried up. He had spoken on the phone three times a day to Zippo for the last three days and in the end Zippo had got so fed up with it that he had warned him to fuck off phoning or he would plant him. In turn his own phone had rung and rung day and night as his customers had become increasingly desperate.

He had given up answering it the day before. He had got fed up with the begging and pleading and abuse. He just checked the number of the incoming call in case it was Zippo. When it wasn't he left it to the answering service. They all threatened to go and get their gear elsewhere but it really wasn't much of a threat at all. No matter who you bought your stuff off, in Dumfries all the suppliers were getting their stuff from Zippo. Zippo was the fountainhead. He controlled the market and he controlled what territory each of his pushers looked after.

There had been a couple of times when others had tried to freelance their way into the town, but not for long. Zippo soon sorted them out. Man, did he ever. Word got around pretty quick. It must have been two years since anyone had made a serious effort to muscle in on Zippo. Nobody had tried since. It has hard to imagine that anyone ever would. Not unless they were absolutely off their rockers.

No, the fact that there was not a gramme of smack to be had in the town was absolutely true. The lie had been in saying that he had none of his own. Now this was a lie. When he lifted up the floorboard under his bed he confirmed that he had four tenner bags left in his stash. He took one out and carefully shook the contents onto a spoon and heated it. Once he was happy, he added some lemon juice and mixed it around. He drew the mix into a needle through a pad of cotton wool and started to prepare a vein. Four bags. Well, three now. Three bags. He chuckled to himself. Baa Baa black sheep, have you any wool, yes sir, yes sir, three bags full. Three bags. Enough for two days. Three days even, at a push. Zippo had seemed pretty confident that there would be plenty more stuff tomorrow night. Maybe he really should give Will a call back. Maybe he should spare him a bag. After all they were mates. Best mates. Had been for years.

Actually, there was something he could try. It was a long shot, but what the hell. He decided to call Andrew Moncur. Moncur was the other Main Distributor in the organisation. Maybe he would have some. It wasn't very likely, but it was worth a try. He picked up his phone and scrolled through until he found the number. He dialled.

"Hello."

"Andrew. It's Ricky. How are you?"

"Pissed off. The phone never stops. Any word on the stuff yet?"

"Not really. They say maybe tomorrow night."

Moncur sighed. "For fuck's sake, what's going on?"

"No idea. Must be serious. That's why I'm calling. One of my mates is climbing the walls. He's really bad. I don't suppose you've got anything spare by any chance?"

"You must be kidding. I've been clean out for three days."

"I thought as much. It was just a long shot. Let's hope it all gets sorted tomorrow. Cheers Andrew."

"Aye, see you Ricky."

Well, he couldn't do any more. There was nowhere else to try. He'd done his bit. Nothing else to do. Will would just have to hang on.

He shot the heroin into his vein and slumped back onto his bed as a wave of ecstasy flowed all over him like a tropical sea. Baa, baa black sheep, have you any smack, no sir, no sir, I'll have to ring you back, none for the master and none for the dame, and none for Willy boy who's your best mate.

His rhyme delighted him and he laughed until he started coughing. Three bags. Three tickets to ride. Maybe it would be a bit risky to spare one after all. Zippo had seemed confident, but Zippo could be wrong. After all it was clear that circumstances were out of Zippo's control. No. Better not. Better safe than sorry. He would really kick himself if he let Will have a bag and there was another delay. No, sorry pal, but no.

He put the spoon away with the three bags and replaced the floorboard. He then switched on the TV and lit up a cigarette. He pushed the thought of Will out of his brain. Nothing he could do about it. He savoured the feeling of the smoke as it went down and down into his lungs and tried to concentrate on what the pundits were saying about the match that was due to start.

He felt a marvellous sense of absolute well-being. He really couldn't quite believe just how amazingly well life was turning out. For almost all of his nineteen years everyone had been telling him that it would end in tears. His Dad, his Mum, grandparents, teachers, coppers, social workers, all of them. After a while it was like the record had got stuck. You're a bad one Ricky. You're a wrong one Ricky. Rotten apple. Black sheep. Always in trouble. Never listens. Won't do as he's told.

He hadn't really meant it, not to start with anyway. He just liked a laugh, that was all. It just always seemed to go wrong on him. Hell, it was only ever a bit of fun. But his teachers hadn't seen it that way. And both his headmasters hadn't seen it that way. And his Dad certainly hadn't seen it that way. No son of mine . . . *whack*. I'll shape you up you little . . . *whack*. If you ever even think of . . . *whack*.

And word had soon got round. Ricky Macintosh is a bad one. Ricky Macintosh is a wrong one. Ricky Macintosh will come to no good, just you wait and see. And parents told their children that they would be grounded for a very, very long time indeed if they were caught playing with that Ricky Macintosh. They were to have nothing to do with that Ricky Macintosh.

And so he had never been asked round for tea. He never got invitations for birthday parties. He never got taken on days out. And it made him angry because it was only ever a bit of fun. He didn't mean any real harm. He was only a kid, only eleven. But minds were already made up. A right wrong one that Ricky Macintosh. He'll come to no good. Just you wait and see.

Half the time when he got into bother at school it wasn't even him. The teachers just picked him out and whoever had really done it never owned-up. And so he would wind up in the headmaster's office again. And of course he wouldn't split on whoever had done it. Course he wouldn't. So he just took it. And then he would have to go home and take it again.

Didn't I warn you Ricky . . . *whack*. You can't say that I didn't Ricky . . . *whack*. This will keep happening until you bloody well learn you little shit . . . *whack*.

By the time he was twelve he had had enough. One time when he had yet again been in trouble and the headmaster had yet again rang his father he decided that he wasn't having it any more. The last two times his Dad had beaten him it had been worse than before. His Dad had been made redundant from ICI after he had worked there for 26 years. It had made him bitter and angry and he just couldn't find work no matter how he tried. Soon he was drinking every day and his temper got worse and worse. He started hitting Ricky's Mum. And when Ricky was in trouble at school he beat him without mercy.

Instead of going home that afternoon he had gone round to his Uncle Eric's place. Ever since he had been young he had always liked his uncle Eric. Uncle Eric was the black sheep of the family. His dad had always hated his brother-in-law with seething contempt. He would rage away over the dinner table about the big idle bastard who had never done a day's work in his life. Uncle Eric was a typical, no-good scrounger, a dole cheat, a loafer. Conversations were often dominated by whatever Uncle Eric had done now, who he had battered, how he had been caught, how he would really be for it if they caught him again.

Ricky had never really taken any of it seriously. To him his Uncle Eric was great. He was a huge bear of a man who always had time for young Ricky. Young Ricky was alright by him. Bit of a lad. But who didn't get in bother at school? And why not? Teachers! Complete tossers the lot of them. Uncle Eric played football with Ricky and his mates and kicked lumps off all of them but nobody cared because Uncle Eric was well cool.

His Mum and Dad would have huge rows about it. He's not going round there again and that's final. I'm not having him getting poisoned by that no-good bastard. Now you just wait a minute. That no-good bastard is my brother and he loves Ricky and that is good enough for me . . . *whack*.

Sadly, Uncle Eric wasn't around all the time. He kept disappearing off for stretches inside, first Dumfries for three months, then Dumfries again for six months and then Shotts for a year. He had only been out for a week that afternoon when Ricky called. His Dad had knocked him about a couple of days before and he had a black eye. Uncle Eric wanted to know who had done it, and when he found out he went straight round and put his Dad into hospital for three weeks. If his Dad had reported it Uncle Eric would have gone down for at least another two years. But Dad hadn't. He kept it to himself and said he'd fallen down the stairs.

Ricky was never bothered by his Dad again. In fact after he got back from the infirmary all the pride seemed to have gone out of him. He gave up all hope of ever working again and quietly drank away his life in front of endless hours of daytime TV. He had died when Ricky was fourteen. Technically it had been cancer. In reality he had just given up. Ricky often wondered who was the more to blame, ICI or Uncle Eric. He favoured ICI.

With no Dad any more, there was nobody for the school to ring. In almost every aspect Ricky's life took a turn for the better. He no longer lived in fear of going home, and without the prospect of getting leathered by his Dad, there was little that the teachers could do to threaten him. He started going to school less and less and the school was really quite happy to do without him. He spent his days messing around with fellow truants, shoplifting, sometimes sniffing glue. He also spent a lot of time with his Uncle Eric.

After they had buried his Dad he was surprised at how badly his Mum had taken it. He had figured that she would have been as glad as he was to see the back of him. She wasn't. She pined and suddenly seemed to get a lot older. The doctor kept giving her pills and she kept taking them. She took her husband's place in the big chair in front of the TV and disappeared into a numb, anti-depressant world of talk shows and soaps. Most of the time she hardly seemed to realise that Ricky was even alive.

They would have certainly got into all kinds of financial problems but for Uncle Eric. Uncle Eric always made sure that they had electric cards and phone cards and enough money for a fish supper.

Then another great thing happened to Ricky. For the first time in his life he found a friend. His friend was Will. In many ways they were like chalk and cheese. Will was the tall, strapping lad from the countryside who was great at sport and chased by all the girls. Ricky was the skinny lad from Sunnybank Estate who wore shiny trousers that were too short. None of this mattered because they just clicked. They both had a completely happy-go-lucky view of life and they weren't inclined to let anyone talk them out of it. What was really great was that Will's Dad didn't seem to have anything against Ricky. Jack never listened to any of the gossip and anyway he lived out in the middle of nowhere. Will said that his Mum had left them and now they were on their own, running the farm, eating out of the microwave, watching the match.

In the holidays Ricky would sometimes stay up at the farm for weeks at a time, He soon got to enjoying the work. Jack was great. He let him drive the tractors and the quad bikes and everything.

The friendship came at just the right time because when he was fourteen his life was hit by a meteor. Uncle Eric had been caught breaking into an off-licence, and to make matters worse he had thumped a policeman. He was sent down for four years and this time it was H.M. Prison Barlinnie: the dreaded "Bar L".

Without Will, Ricky would have been lost. As it was, he spent most of that summer on the farm helping out. By September he had grown two inches, filled out and had acquired a golden tan. When he returned to school that autumn he found to his delight that Will wasn't the only one to be chased by the girls.

That October he scraped together every penny he could find and one weekend him and Will took off on a great adventure. They took the train from Dumfries Station and headed off to visit Uncle Eric in Barlinnie Prison. Ricky acted with great bravado all the way there as they guzzled away at cans of Tennants that Will had pinched out of his Dad's stock. In reality he was nervous and a little afraid. Barlinnie had a fearsome reputation and the idea of actually going there filled him with dread.

It turned out fine. Uncle Eric was in tremendous spirits. He said that life in Bar L was a piece of cake. Nae bother. He'd be home in no time. How was his Mum? Was she keeping OK? Nobody giving her any bother, because if they were there were ways that he could sort it. And money? Good. And he was really impressed by the way Ricky had grown and filled out and how he was turning into a real man.

And the best bit was when they were leaving and Uncle Eric told them about all the contacts that he had been making and how good things were going to be when he got out and how Ricky would be a part of it all because Ricky was family and Ricky was all right. And after all that, when he and Will had got up to leave, and he had said "See you soon Uncle Eric, we'll come back before Christmas Uncle Eric", his uncle had taken him by the shoulders and grinned at him.

"Don't you think you're getting a wee bit old to call me Uncle Eric the now Ricky. Look at you. You're nearly a man. It's time you called me Zippo. All my mates call me Zippo. Everyone calls me

Zippo, even the fucking Polis. So from now on it's Zippo. OK?"

"OK . . . Zippo."

He felt ten feet tall. It was a rite of passage. As he walked out of the great gates of Barlinnie he felt like a man.

Zippo was home two years later having served three out of four. This time everything was different. He was like a new man. Soon he was joined by two mates that he had met inside.

There was Tommy. Tommy Banks. Tommy was about 40 and it seemed like he was all tattoos. He had long, shiny black hair that he slicked back behind his ears and a black moustache. He wasn't very tall, no more than five foot ten, and he was thin and wiry. He was a big, big Glasgow Rangers fan and, whenever he had had one too many, he would break into all manner of UDA songs and seek out a fight with any Fenian fucker that he could find. He never went anywhere without his favourite Stanley knife in his pocket. He loved that knife. Every time he used it on someone he would commemorate the occasion with a small notch next to the Rangers badge that he had stuck on the metal. Tommy took a bit of a shine to Ricky, but Ricky never really reciprocated. Ricky once watched Tommy take a long slice of some guy's cheek because the guy had accidentally collided in the pub whilst Tommy was watching the match. When Tommy had done this his thin face had contorted with rage and he had screamed like a madman. So when Tommy would jape about with Ricky and punch him on the shoulder and shadow-box with him Ricky would laugh a little nervously. Tommy always made him nervous. In fact, Tommy scared the living shite out of him.

And then there was Wee Kenny. Wee Kenny was one of those silly joke names along much the same lines as Little John. They nicknamed Kenny "Wee" in Barlinnie for the simple reason that he was a giant. Wee Kenny wasn't just big, he was big all over. He stood six and a half feet tall and weighed well in excess of twenty stone. But Wee Kenny was really rather a sad case. He had been brought up on a small sheep farm in the Perthshire hills. His mother had died young which left his Dad to try and do the best that he could. School was a nightmare of teasing and being the class dunce. He made no friends and had the piss taken out of him every minute of his school life.

It was soon apparent that Kenny was rather simple. A bit slow. Backward. A sandwich short of the picnic. Though not enough to warrant an institution. Everyone concerned agreed that the small farm in the hills was the best place for him. As he grew older, he grew enormous. The work on the farm gave him huge strength. One afternoon three kids from Dundee came onto the farm with the intention of stealing whatever they could find. They had watched Kenny's Dad drive away and thought the place to be deserted. Kenny got really mad when he saw what they were trying to do. He got so mad that he buried an axe six inches deep into the head of one of the intruders. The other two scarpered and only began to get over the incident years later after prolonged counselling.

When his Dad brought the police in, Kenny went quietly. He explained things as best as he could, but he didn't find it easy. He managed to convey enough for the police to only charge him with manslaughter. His Dad bankrupted their meagre farm in his efforts to pay for a decent defence for his son. It had all been to no avail. Kenny had been sentenced to ten years in Barlinnie, and his Dad had found himself at the mercy of Perth City Council, who duly housed him, but only for a couple of years because that was how long it took him to die of a broken heart.

All of this left poor Kenny banged up in Barlinnie in an environment that he found totally confusing. More than anything he was frightened that it would be like school, and that the merciless teasing would start up again. He need not have concerned himself. The word was soon out about Kenny's prodigious feat with the axe, and so all his fellow cons gave him a very wide berth indeed

For six years he got his head down, did everything he was told to do, never spoke to a soul, and dreaded the day that they would let him out into a world where he had no farm, no sheep and no Dad.

The big change in Kenny's life came on an otherwise uneventful day in March. It was a week after Zippo had started his stretch at Barlinnie. A few Glasgow cons had decided that they didn't much like the cut of his jib. He was too full of himself. Too cocky. They felt it was time that they brought him down a peg or two. They didn't like the idea of anyone from a small hick place in the country coming and playing the "hard man" on their patch.

THE CULL

Zippo got jumped in the yard by six of them. They soon realised that they had underestimated their target. Two were put down quickly, one with a crunching kick in the balls, and the other with a stiff forefinger that had sunk deep into his eye socket and caused a prolonged stay in the infirmary and 50 percent blindness for the rest of his life. That still left four-to-one, and despite Zippo's desperate viciousness, the discerning crowd that had gathered to watch could see that there would only be one result.

Then Wee Kenny intervened. There was only one reason that he had done so and thereby broke cover after six years. The reason was that three times in his first week in Barlinnie, Zippo had greeted Kenny at the breakfast table with a smile and "How're you doing Wee Kenny, you alright!" It wasn't much, but in six years nobody else had bothered. Kenny's intervention was every bit as effective as the Americans picking a side in a twentieth-century war. It was decisive and involved massive force. He grabbed two of the assailants by their collars and crashed their heads together with a crunch that even made the hardened convict audience wince. He tossed a third man against a brick wall whilst Zippo finished off the fourth with what many connoisseurs considered to be the finest and best-timed head butt they had ever seen.

The wardens crashed onto the scene seconds after the field had been won and both men wound up in solitary for a month. After this it was almost natural that Zippo would adopt Wee Kenny. They were never apart. Kenny was a bit like a big dog. He had made his mind up that Zippo was his master, which meant that Zippo had his loyalty for life. The luck of the draw had it that Kenny was released a month after Zippo who duly picked him up at the gates and took him to his new home in Dumfries.

There was nothing overtly violent about Wee Kenny. He was very quiet and, unbelievably, spent much of his free time bird-watching, a boyhood passion that he had never grown out of. He seldom got involved in any of the punishment duties that they were forced to undertake every now and then. That was always carried out by Zippo himself and Tommy Banks. But he was always there. Always at Zippo's side, wherever he went. If anyone was going to have a go at Zippo, they would have to go through Wee Kenny first, and for that they would need a JCB.

Ricky had wondered what his uncle had meant when he had told him about his "plans" the day he and Will had gone to see him in prison. It soon became clear, and Ricky was amazed. His uncle suddenly had such purpose and drive. He was still the same old Zippo, but not aimless any more. He brought two of his old mates into his team and then, with a brilliantly effective campaign of relentless violence, they assumed control of the growing Dumfries drug market.

That had been three years ago and it had coincided with Ricky leaving school, an event that was a blessed relief to institution and pupil alike. Zippo had been true to his word and had immediately installed Ricky as one of his main distributors. "Distributor" had been a word that his uncle had picked up in prison. He had picked up lots of these words and he used them often as he set about his new business – words like "product" and "network" and "territory" and "command structure" and "vertical integration". It was almost as if he had taken a three year course in business management.

Ricky loved it all. He was a "main distributor" which meant that he not only "serviced" his own clients, but he could also recruit "secondary distributors" within his "designated territory". They stocked a more or less complete range of drugs, but it was always made clear that heroin was to be the key product in their range. Recreational drugs were all well and good, but they only meant a few quid at the weekend. Heroin was the "cash cow". Heroin was where the real profits were to be had. Zippo had explained this quite carefully to his nephew. Once a punter was introduced fully to heroin they could look forward to having a customer for life, as hardly anyone managed to kick the drug. The average expenditure for one of these customers was £15 a day. Zippo ran through the maths with evident relish.

"Think about it Ricky. £15 a day. £105 a week. That's just over £5,000 a year. We need to look on our clients as five year customers. That's £25,000. OK? Now think about it. You get forty customers and that's a million quid in five years. Now as a main distributor you get to buy a tenner bag for £6. Let's assume you sell half the product direct and half through your secondary distributors. You will make an average profit of 30 percent I don't know what your maths is like Ricky boy, but 30 percent of a million quid is £300,000. Think about that."

And by God Ricky had thought about it. It was unbelievable. He soon learned that he was a born salesman. Over the next three years he had developed a superb sales ledger. He currently was servicing 43 direct accounts, and three secondary distributors who held 58 accounts between them. This gave him the unbelievable income of about £150,000 a year.

As the heroin gently flowed through his body, a big contented smile spread across his face as he thought of his Dad and all the teachers and social workers and gossiping neighbours who had got it so very wrong. He was earning seven times more than any of them, hell, he was earning four times more that his bastard headmaster. And he got paid cash, no tax, no National Insurance. Not bad for a wrong one. Not bad for the bad apple.

He loved to see the look on their faces as he strode about Sunnybank estate in a grand's worth of clothes talking away on his mobile phone. He loved to see the envy in their eyes as they clocked yet another few hundred quid's worth of jewellery around his girlfriend's neck.

Never come to any good that Ricky Macintosh they had said. You just watch, he'll get his come uppance. Oh yeah. Well fuck the lot of them. Sometimes he would walk past all the solicitors and accountants on Castle Street and Buccleuch Street and savour the knowledge that there wasn't a single person inside those fancy offices that earned as much as him.

Yet even though he was filled with a sense of almost complete well-being, there was still a small black cloud hovering on the edge of the skyline. Will. He felt bad about Will. It had pained him to see his best friend get such a chronic addiction. It never really occurred to Ricky that his own habit was every bit as severe. It just didn't seem that way. It was easier for him because he had money to burn and getting enough gear was never a problem. He could conduct his life and business without any worry about where the next score was coming from.

Not Will. For Will, every score was a nightmare of scraping and stealing. And when he had no money, he had to do without. And when he did without he caved in. His uncle had always been very firm about nobody ever getting any favours. Business was business. You never drop the price, you never give it away, you never give credit, cash up front or no deal, simple. If I find anyone breaking our price structure they're out, even if it's only by 50p a bag. We set the price, we control the price, that's final, even for you Ricky.

And he had done it. He had often ignored his old friend as he had begged and pleaded. Well, no more. He was going to make an exception and his Uncle would never know. Just like his Uncle had no idea that he took the stuff himself. As soon as the gear landed tomorrow he would get Will sorted straight away, and from then on he would see him right.

Once this decision was made, he felt great. All would then be well in his world. He sank back into the pillows, lit another cigarette, and watched the footballers darting around the giant screen of his new £1,200 television.

Once the game had finished Ricky drifted off into a deep sleep of happy dreams.

Andrew Moncur certainly wasn't sleeping. He was fuming. For two days his phone had never stopped ringing. Andrew's customers were entirely different to Ricky's. By and large, Ricky looked after the estates. These were people who were close to Zippo and his operation. There was no way that they would dare to moan and kick up a fuss. They knew better.

Andrew dealt with customers from the countryside and the leafy suburbs. By and large they were better off. They had been brought up to complain loudly in restaurants and to expect fawning service in shops. This meant that they weren't taking the shortage well. Not well at all. They expected Andrew to offer the same kind of customer service as they would find in Boots or their hair salon or Next. So for three days he had been putting up with their anger and outrage. And he was thoroughly pissed off with it.

He was 24 and he had been dealing drugs of one kind or another for five years. He had always been something of a golden boy. His Dad owned a highly successful building business and he had been elected to the town council a few years previously. As a boy, Andrew had always been one of those children for whom everything seemed to come easily. His parents had spoiled him from a very early age. He had always been a bright boy, and so he had been able to breeze through school, doing well at everything with minimal effort. Not only was he good academically, he had always been a natural sportsman. He played football and golf, but rugby had always been his forte. He was a full-back and he had everything; speed, vision, handling ability, a laser-accurate kick. He had represented the South West of Scotland at every junior level. From the age of ten he had been talked about. They had all said that he could go all the way.

When he finished school he had easily gained the grades that he needed to study law at Edinburgh. University was much the same as school. He made the university rugby team in his first year and he was soon able to cut a dash around the campus. He was a tall, lean boy with thick dark hair and looks that ensured constant female attention.

There was only one thing lacking. Money. His father was a typical old-fashioned builder. He was far from convinced by the worth of university. After all, he'd done all right for himself and he hadn't had to go poncing around for three years with a load of toffee-nosed gits. His father would have been a great deal happier if Andrew had left school and gone straight into the family business. One thing was for certain, if his son wanted to ponce about like a toff, he could pay for it himself. There was no way he was going to bank-roll him for three years. He would just have to get a job washing-up in a restaurant like anyone else.

Andrew never fancied the idea of washing-up much. He didn't consider himself a washing-up sort of person. He was moving in affluent circles but he never had any money. He decided that it would have to change. It didn't take him long to discover that he could make more or less as much money as he could spend from selling drugs. There was a booming drugs scene within the university and he found that he had a natural ability in the field. By the end of his first year all was rosy in the garden. He was a fixture in the rugby side, he was getting invited to all the right parties, he spent weekends away in big fancy houses, and his pockets were always stuffed with cash. All was well with the world.

It lasted until the November of his second year. The university authorities smelt a rat. There had been whispers. They discreetly passed on the information to the police and Andrew was caught with far, far more than could possibly be put down to personal use. He was sentenced to eight weeks community service and thrown out of the university.

He returned to Dumfries under the very darkest of clouds. His father had been incandescent with rage. He told him that he had disgraced the family and he had embarrassed him personally. How did he think it looked? Had he not considered that he was a town councillor? He told Andrew that he would have to start at the bottom in the business. He would have to go out and work on the sites as a common labourer and work his way up slowly. It was all that he deserved.

Andrew in turn had told his father where he could stick it. He had no more wish to be a hod carrier than he had to be a washer-up. He sniffed around, he asked about. It took him a couple of weeks to discover the name of Ricky Macintosh. Soon he was buying stuff from Ricky and selling it into the circles where Ricky would never move. After a few months he became a main distributor in his own right. He had worked hard for eighteen months and now he was reaping the rewards. Business was booming and he was making well over a hundred thousand pounds a year. He drove a brand-new sports car, he had a beautifully appointed flat and he always wore the best designer clothes that the boutiques of Glasgow and Edinburgh could offer. His father couldn't understand it. He couldn't understand it at all. Andrew told him that he was into computer work, websites and software design. More money in it than bricks and mortar. Silly old sod, he bought every word of it.

Edinburgh had taught Andrew a big lesson. He was careful now. Really careful. He never carried more stuff than he had to. One drop's worth. Two at most. If he got pulled again, there was no way that they could ever pin him as a dealer. No way in hell.

He now had a superb sales ledger. The money was guaranteed. It had been hard graft, but worth every minute. He couldn't go wrong now. He was made. The only problem was when the bloody supply dried up. Then it meant a tonne of grief and hassle. Maybe Ricky was right. Maybe it would be tomorrow night. He hoped to hell that it would be.

THE CULL

He looked at his watch. It was after one. He switched off his phone and turned in for the night. He slept like a log. He always slept like a log.

That was more than could be said for others. Mandy tossed and turned and kept wanting to cry. In the end she got up and made a start on her first Foot and Mouth story. She may as well not have bothered, she couldn't seem to focus on it at all. Will shivered his way through the cold night in the Land Rover as the spiders crawled all over his brain. Exhaustion eventually overtook him a little before five, and he slept fitfully for two hours until he woke to a dawn more grey and miserable than any he had ever known before.

Jack's phone rang half an hour after he had watched Mandy drive away. It was John Dawson from the farm next door.

"Hello Jack, John Dawson here. Sorry to call you so late."

"Don't worry about it, it's fine, I was up anyway. What can I do for you John."

"Nothing Jack. There's nothing anyone can do. I just thought I should call. Better me than the Ministry. I've got it Jack. Tested positive today. They're coming to cull tomorrow . . ."

The line fell silent as Dawson fought to control the emotion in his voice.

" . . . you know what that means."

Jack felt so very empty. "Yes John. I know. Next-door farm. Contiguous cull. I'll be next."

"Sorry to have to tell you . . . well . . . you know . . . just sorry."

"I know John. I'm sorry too. Thanks for ringing. I appreciate it."

He sat up all night. Mostly he just stared into space. It wasn't a surprise. He had known it in his heart. But now it had really happened it was hard to deal with. So this was the end of the road. This was the bottom. The lower depths. The end of the line. At least he couldn't sink any further.

Little did he know.

Poor bastard.

Chapter 3
Nemesis

Fate tossed its fourth card onto the table at quarter-to-one in the morning four miles north of Girvan on the Ayrshire coast road to Glasgow. The two men from Belfast had enjoyed a calm crossing on the ferry from Larne, and had disembarked into the deserted streets of Stranraer without incident. They looked forward to quiet roads all the way to Glasgow where they could at last complete their business. There was no reason why anything should disrupt their plans and, for 40 minutes, nothing did.

Then fate intervened. The temperature gauge shot up and the engine started to go to hell. A mile later they were in a lay-by watching smoke pour out of the engine into the cold night air. Thankfully there was perfect reception for the mobile phone and they were able to ring the Chief in Belfast.

"Oh for fuck's sake. I don't fucking believe this. OK. OK. Let's think. Right. You have to stash the gear as quickly as you can. The last thing we need is some bored copper pulled up and clocking your accents. Where are you again? Describe it. OK. Get into the field and stash the stuff under the hedge, and for fuck's sake make sure you mark the spot. Then ring the RAC, all the details are in the glove compartment. You'll have to find a B&B or something. Hire a car first thing, pick up the stuff, and get to Glasgow. I'll call them and fill them in."

The Chief then endured another dose of abuse on the phone and this time he felt he had to take it. A head gasket wasn't nearly as impressive a reason for a delay as Mad Don and his Kalashnikov. What the hell. Surely nothing else could go wrong. The delivery would be completed tomorrow and surely things could get back to normal again.

The next morning Zippo awoke, stretched, lit a Benson & Hedges without consciously thinking about it, and gazed around the room appreciatively. The room was big, the furniture antique, and the carpet deep enough to sink your toes into. It was one of the finest hotels in Glasgow and he had become a regular. It was now part of his routine. Whenever he was making a collection, he would drive up the night before and enjoy the endless pleasure of staying in a suite at the Excelsior.

Four hundred quid a night! He still couldn't really believe it. Who would have ever thought that he, Eric Macintosh, he, Zippo, would every month spend a night in a four hundred quid a night suite at the Excelsior. It was not just the fact that he was actually staying there, it was the fact that the staff actually knew him now, *Well hello again Mr Macintosh, how very nice to see you again Mr. Macintosh, and how are you Mrs Macintosh, looking as lovely as ever I must say. Will you be wanting to avail yourself of the facilities in the beauty parlour this evening Mrs Macintosh, oh splendid, please leave it all to me, I will arrange everything.*

It had been a bit different the first time of course with him feeling uncomfortable in his new Armani suit and Tina clattering across the marble floor to the desk, clumsy in her unaccustomed high-heels. Then the tone had been a little off, slightly condescending, a message that had been subtle, but clear, we're not for your type Mr Macintosh, we will put on our fixed smiles and do our jobs, but we will let you know that we really don't want you or your little tart.

But he had soon learned. Zippo made a habit of learning. Picking it up. Cottoning-on. The assistant manager was young and smooth with film-star good looks. Yet there was sometime about him that made Zippo recognise a kindred spirit, the sharp line of the jaw, the hungry eyes, the hint of a tattoo peeking out from under his cuff. Zippo sensed the estates, sensed a fellow traveller. He collared him in early on their first evening and got him to sit down at a table in the lobby.

"Listen pal, I'm not used to places like this. But I've come into a bit of money recently, Uncle died in Canada, and I will be coming up to Glasgow every few weeks. I don't want to stand out here. Need a lift pal, if you know what I mean." He slid a napkin across the table. The assistant manager looked at the contents covertly. Inside were four fifty-pound notes. "Just help me out a bit pal. What to wear, where to buy it, the right luggage, same with Tina, you know what I mean."

The assistant manager had grinned eagerly. "Of course Mr Macintosh, I know precisely what you mean and I would only be too pleased to assist in any way that I can. Your Uncle, I gather he was really rather comfortable?"

"Aye, he was one seriously rich fucker."

"Good. This is the first thing. The main thing. You need to behave like one of the real high rollers that we have stay with us. That means that you should always tip a tenner. Don't make a big deal about it. Just be casual, make like it is nothing, trivial, now that's class. Once the waiters and porters see that, they will see you as class. You will be amazed at the difference."

Zippo grinned and casually flipped a ten-pound note across the table. "Nae bother Pal. But there's just one thing. I don't have to make out that it's nothing. You know why? Because it is nothing. Fuck all."

So that had been that. Young Richard Gregson had taken them under his wing and the Excelsior had become their second home. Having arrived in Glasgow and checked in he would always make a real evening of it. He would lose Tina early. She had taken to every beauty-enhancing facility the hotel had to offer like a duck to water. Swim, sauna, steam room, massage, facial, manicure, make-up, hair, and the whole routine would take about five hours. He would spend this time touring around pubs in a taxi that would wait outside. Over several pints of heavy he would catch up with old mates from Shotts and Barlinnie, all of them suitably agape at his flash suits and gold jewellery. And he would throw a bit of money around, lots of big rounds, a fifty lent here, a hundred there, cheers Zippo, you know how it is, times are hard. He didn't mind. It was part of the game. Mates from prison were like family. He would always see them right.

Then he would return to the hotel for nine and meet Tina in the bar. By that time she would be dolled to the nines, and in his eyes she could have walked straight out of *OK* magazine. They would eat in the restaurant and drink champagne till they staggered up to their suite.

He looked at her now on the other side of the huge bed. He tugged slowly at the duvet so that it slid away from her nude body without waking her. He drank in her thin nakedness hungrily. His life had become one long story of having things he had never dreamed could possibly be his. Buckets of money, respect, power, control, but most of all Tina. All of his life, ever since adolescence, he had wanted a Tina. When he had been in school the Tinas were always out of reach. He was fine with the lads. He always stood out. He stood out because he was hard. He had been hard for as long as he could remember. He had battered lads in infant school. The playground had been his kingdom. Lots of lads had tried it. Sometimes on their own. Sometimes in twos and threes, but the result was always the same. Zippo always did them. Maybe not at first, but always in the end.

The reason for this was one that he had never properly realised. The reason was quite simple: Zippo had always been ever so slightly mad. There were a couple of key components seemingly missing from his brain. One was a sense of compassion. The vast majority of men would stop short of pushing their forefinger into another man's eye as hard as they could. It was a step too far. Beyond the pale. Not Zippo. He would do whatever it took. Not because he particularly enjoyed it. He wasn't a sadist. He just did it because it got the job done. Second was knowing when he was beaten. Zippo didn't. He would fight until the end. Once the fighting madness took him he would never give up, no matter how badly hurt he was or how much punishment he took. Slowly this would erode the self-belief of whoever his opponent happened to be, and then they would hesitate, make a small mistake, get a finger in their eye socket, and then it would be over.

Through his school days his hardness brought him respect among the lads. He could talk the talk in the playground, and then in pubs and the night clubs. But it all dried up with girls. He became tongue-tied and clumsy and shy. His amorous life had been restricted to drunken gropes in alleys with girls who his mates later mocked him for. Dogs. Slags. Slappers. And later, in his times between prison, the girls became women. Hard-faced women from the estates who smoked like chimneys and drank Bacardi and coke and were there to be had for the price of ten of them. But there were never any Tinas. Never the really pretty ones.

That had changed two years ago. He had been round at the flat of one of his main distributors, Sammy Bland. Tina had come to the door and she had started begging and pleading. She had no money and she was desperate. She was fifteen and she had been a user for eighteen months. To most men she wouldn't have looked very pretty that day. Her thin face was pale and contorted with desperation. There were patches of grey under her eyes, her clothes were creased and dirty, and her straight blond hair was lank and greasy. But Zippo saw beyond the addict and saw the girl in the playground in the short skirt with the flirty eyes who had never given him a second glance.

And so he had taken her. It was a match made in heaven. She was what he had always wanted. And he was the man who had what she needed. Had as much as she liked.

She was seventeen now and the filthy addict girl was a thing of the past. Money had changed her. Expensive clothes and hair and make-up. Of course she could never wear sleeveless dresses, and sure, she was getting skinnier all the time, but to him, she was a knock-out. She was a justification. Because when he had her on his arm he was somebody. She turned heads, made people think, how the hell has that hard looking bastard got a girl like that. Well, let them think.

He finished his cigarette and gave her a smack on her bottom.

"Come on you lazy bitch. Get up. I want a cup of tea."

"Oh fuck off Zippo I'm tired. Get it yourself."

"Get me a cup of tea or I'll smack you harder."

"Oh fucking hell"

She eased herself up and rubbed the sleep from her eyes.

"You're a right bastard you are Zippo."

"Aye but don't you just love me, hen?"

"Yeah, yeah." She started to run her newly manicured hand down his belly toward his crotch.

"No. Cup of tea first. I'm gagging. That champagne always gives me a right fucking thirst in the morning."

She got out of the bed and started to pull on a silk dressing gown. "Oi! Take that fucking thing off."

"Oh come on Zippo, it's fucking freezing."

"Freezing my arse. It's boiling in here. They've got the central heating on full. Don't be so fucking soft."

He loved making her walk around naked. He loved the power. The control. It turned him on something rotten. She moodily boiled the kettle and made a play of crashing his cup onto a saucer. Tough shit. He propped himself against the pillows, lit another cigarette and greedily drank in her white angular limbs.

"Here you are bastard." She pouted as she plonked the tea down on the bedside table.

"That's better. Now come here."

"Hang on a bit. I'm just going to get fixed up." He sipped his tea as she rummaged in her bag and started pulling out the necessary for her morning heroin breakfast.

Heroin. It had been heroin that had changed his life. Before heroin he had been just another loser. In school being the hard man had been more or less enough. He never got anywhere from an educational point of view but that never caused him to lose sleep. He couldn't abide the teachers and they couldn't abide him. The feeling was entirely mutual and both sides knew full well that he had absolutely no intention of doing any school work whatsoever from the age of eleven.

Being the king of the playground was enough. He bullied boys out of things that he wanted, starting with Kit-Kats and peanut butter sandwiches in primary school, working gradually up to money and cigarettes in high school. The big shock came when he hit sixteen and walked light-heartedly through the school gates for the last time. He was happy to be entering the real world where he would sign-on, and hang around in the pub, and get involved in some serious nicking, and have lots of cash in his pockets, and get a really fit girlfriend.

It didn't work out. He never seemed to have any money whatsoever. The dole money never lasted longer than halfway through Friday night. His first efforts as a criminal were little less than pathetic. He soon found that nicking stuff to try and sell was a different proposition to simply nicking stuff that he wanted for himself. He still got into fights. There were plenty of vicious little skirmishes outside pubs and night clubs in rainy late-night streets, and his reputation for being hard steadily grew. Eventually he did start getting noticed. He got occasional jobs as a bouncer, and on two occasions, he got paid a nice bonus for collecting a couple of debts. It was at about this time that he bought himself an old-fashioned Zippo lighter which he loved to use with a flourish. It wasn't long before Zippo became his adopted name. He was delighted with this. He had always been a sucker for any American gangster film and Zippo seemed to embody the very image that he coveted.

He was convinced that his big moment had arrived when he was asked along on a robbery. The target was a Post Office on the outskirts of Kilmarnock. They went in with baseball bats and stockings over their heads. It all went great. The guy behind the counter couldn't wait to hand over every penny that was in the till, and they were away and clear. But not for long. The guy who was driving the getaway car had been watching the same kind of films as Zippo, and his belief in his ability to drive like Steve McQueen wasn't matched by the reality of his talent. He put the car into a lamp-post within half a mile and they piled out and legged it. Zippo actually managed to get away only to be picked up later that evening by the Dumfries Police. The driver had come apart at the seams and given the police every name he could think of. Zippo's lawyer did a hell of a job and played every card he could think of – disrupted home, first offence, good lad at heart, bad influences. The judge didn't buy all of it, but he bought enough to let Zippo away with three years. He wound up serving two.

Once out, it was more of the same until he was arrested having almost killed a lad from Gretna in a night club. The lawyer tried his best again but this time it didn't wash quite as well. This time it was three and a half years and he got out after two and a half. Another mundane period of life followed until he got caught trying to break into a garage. Another stretch, this time in Shotts. By the time he got out he was 35. His life was just draining away. All of his contemporaries had been married, most divorced, several had kids. Some had real jobs, some had settled down, some grimly continued a life of signing on and petty crime. There was no glamour in it. The same old tawdry pubs. The same old thin, embittered faces. The same hard-faced women, just older, rougher, under thicker make-up, more desperate. The off-licence robbery was almost halfheartedly pathetic. It was almost as if he wanted to be caught. The fact was that he had almost come to like prison. Prison was a bit like school. If you were hard enough, inside you could be somebody. Inside he could command respect. Men moved aside when he wanted to sit down, they passed over their steamed pudding if he gave them the nod, they paid in cigarettes to avoid being beaten up in the showers.

When the sentence was four years he was almost glad. When he found out it was to be Barlinnie he felt a surge of excitement. Bar L was the big league. If he could make his mark there, surely something would start to happen in his life.

How right he was. For the first week he was pumped full of adrenalin. They would come. Somebody. He hadn't a clue who, and he hadn't a clue when, but he knew they would come. When they did he felt as ready as he had ever been. What he hadn't counted on was that there would be six of them. Six big ones. Six hard men like himself. He went quite berserk but this time is wasn't going to be enough. This time, for the first time in his life, he was going to go down. And then the giant figure of Wee Kenny had intervened.

Once he had finished his month in solitary he was passed the word that Taylor wanted to see him. He could tell by the way that he was given this message that seeing Taylor was a big deal. He had no idea why. In fact he didn't know Taylor from Adam. He looked out a mate that he knew from Shotts and quizzed him. Taylor was a lawyer. He worked for the big men in Glasgow. The really big men. He handled things for them. Got them off when they got caught. Taylor himself had been arrested for tax fraud and he had found out just how much the police valued his scalp when he was given eighteen months in Barlinnie. The cops had obviously held the fervent hope that a year and a half in the Victorian jail amongst the worst that the streets of Glasgow had to offer would be a living hell for the lawyer. They were wrong.

Taylor's employers were grateful to him. He had kept his mouth shut and had stonewalled the cops for hour after hour. It was the kind of thing they appreciated. They all made absolutely sure that his time inside would be as comfortable as possible. This all meant that he was the best connected con in Barlinnie. He was like royalty in his cell. Nobody would dare lay a finger on him. That was the word. Taylor was to be left alone. Taylor had backing. Taylor was a main man.

Zippo was amazed when he was taken to Taylor's cell that evening. In all his time in three Scottish prisons he had never come across a con quite like Jeremy Taylor. He was a small, slender man in his late forties. Most of his hair had gone and he wore scholarly metal glasses. He was working away at his desk when Zippo entered, and when he turned to greet his visitor, Zippo was astonished to see that he was wearing a tie. He was so out of place amongst the rest of the hard-nosed inhabitants of the wing that it was almost laughable.

At the sight of Zippo his face lit up into a warm, welcoming smile. "Ah Eric, you are Eric aren't you? Yes. Yes of course. Now please, do sit down Eric. Wait. Just a moment. Let me just clear some of these papers. There. That's better. Please, have a seat. So jolly cramped in here I'm afraid. Now, I'm Jeremy. I have so looked forward to having the opportunity to have a little chat."

He held out a hand and Zippo, feeling like he was in some kind of totally weird dream, dutifully shook it and sat on the small cleared area of the bottom bunk. The top bunk was completely filled with cardboard boxes filled with papers. Every spare centimetre of the cell was filled with boxes overflowing with papers.

Normally he wouldn't have given this man the time of day. For as long as he could remember he had hated these kind of twats with their suits and smooth manners. Teachers and solicitors and dole office managers, twats, the sodding lot of them. But this time it was different because this time he had been given the word that if Mr Taylor wanted to have a chat, then you went for a chat, because he had backing. Real backing. The sort of backing that meant that you would get absolutely planted if you didn't tow the line. So he sat quietly as Taylor fussed over the tea.

THE CULL

The man was just so relaxed. It was bloody ridiculous. Here he was in one of the hardest jails in Scotland and it was like home from home. At last he had the tea poured and he sat facing Zippo.

"Now then Eric. Let's get cracking shall we." Zippo was itching to tell him that his name wasn't fucking Eric, his name was fucking Zippo, but the cat had got his tongue so he just nodded.

"I don't know how much you know about me so I will fill you in a bit. I'm a lawyer, and even though I say it myself, I've always been a rather good one. Over the years I have had some success in sorting out difficulties for a very particular clientele in Glasgow. I had other clients of course, many of them, but there were a number of very special clients who were my main concern. I think you know the kind of clients that I refer to?"

Zippo nodded.

"Good. Now. Unfortunately the Glasgow police developed a rather negative view of my work over the years and certain members of that force made it their goal to bring me down. They found it particularly frustrating that so much of their work was being undone when I exposed the weaknesses of their cases in court. Quite understandable of course, I bear them no grudges, had our roles been reversed I would have felt exactly the same.

"I was stupid and careless in allowing my accountant to take unnecessary liberties with my tax returns. This gave the police their chance and they took it. I believe that the term is a 'Fair cop'. I do feel that they were a little underhand in pulling strings to put me into Barlinnie but, as you can see, it isn't a very great hardship. My friends have done all that they can to ensure that my stay here is as comfortable as possible. I can't complain. I really can't. Oh by the way, could I offer you a biscuit. No. Quite sure? OK.

"Now, where was I? Of course. Where I am now: in prison! You will no doubt be aware that a prison term has many regrettable consequences for a lawyer, the main one of which is that I am now disbarred and I won't be able to practise any more. This means that I am having to spend my time here making plans for how I can earn a crust once I am released.

"I actually believed that I would have endless time on my hands but as you can see from all these blessed papers that is hardly the case. There are so many colleagues in here in need of sound legal advice and I still do a lot of work in an advisory role for my special clients in Glasgow. However, I am digressing, and I fear I am in danger of boring you and that wouldn't do at all.

"In short, over these last few months I have made some definite decisions about the direction that my career will take after my release and I must say that I find the opportunities really quite exciting. Now, where shall I start? Well, I can see that you are a man of the world so I might as well get straight to the point.

"Much of the work that I have undertaken over the last few years has been in defending my clients from cases brought against them for the sale and distribution of drugs. It has been impossible not to be impressed by what a wonderfully lucrative business this has become. Do you know, Eric, that sales of illegal narcotics now represent almost ten percent of the whole of World Trade. Absolutely remarkable. It is an exiting and rewarding field. In short, it has become the fastest growing and most profitable trade on earth and one that I am eager to join.

"Of course I would never in a million years want to tread on the toes of any of my friends in Glasgow and Edinburgh. That would be rude, foolish and ultimately suicidal, and I can assure you Eric that I have no wish to commit suicide. I have spent some time discussing my aspirations with these friends and basically we have come to a deal. As long as I am willing to offer my services in an unofficial, purely advisory capacity to them, then they are more than happy to help me establish myself in the drugs business.

"So Eric, why am I boring you with all this? Well, I ask for a little patience and I promise all will become clear. My friends have pointed out that there are wonderful opportunities to be found in many of the smaller Scottish towns. These offer an ideal market place and their potential is largely untapped. Of course drugs are available in these towns, but as yet, the trade is small and poorly organised. In short, it is amateurish. There is vast potential in these areas for sales to be increased and new customers to be found. Nobody is even scratching the surface of this potential. Conditions are perfect. The countryside has gone through a rotten time over the last few years. Farming is a mess, tourism is shrinking and many of the old industries are in chronic decline. This means that there is lots of unemployment and lots of despair. Once upon a time these conditions meant that the victims would drown their sorrows in the pub. This is beginning to change. The Government is taxing alcohol so heavily that drinking is becoming a very expensive pastime.

"Not so drugs. Drugs are duty free and they offer far better value. They offer a complete escape at an affordable price. Rural Scotland is a wonderful and more or less untapped market for these products.

"Now let us move on and look at the second exciting feature of this market – guaranteed customer loyalty. This is what really thrills me, I can't tell you how much. If one were to start marketing a product such as electric kettles there are many pitfalls. You may start with an excellent product which you can sell at a competitive price and still make a handsome return. But then things soon start to go wrong. One, your customers don't buy a kettle every week, and the market is quickly flooded. Two, your competitors will soon copy the best bits of your design, and then they will undercut your price, which in turn eats into your profits. You are still burdened with all of your overheads whilst your sales decline and your profit margins fall. It is called Free Trade and there is nothing anybody can do about it.

'Now these rules simply don't apply in the drugs trade. Because it is illegal, there is no interference from the Monopolies and Mergers commission. If one is able to take complete control of a market one need have no fear of competitors eroding the profit margins. You can also retain complete control of the pricing structure. But even that isn't the best part. The best part is the kind of relationship that you can build up with your customer. You see, Eric, this is absolutely the most important point and I can't emphasise it strongly enough. IF through clever sales and marketing you can persuade a customer to start using heroin, and IF you are able to achieve absolute control of your market place, then you have the perfect trading situation. You see, selling heroin isn't like selling electric kettles. The customer needs that heroin every single day. Not just weekends and bank holidays. Not just for parties and special occasions. Every single day, seven days a week, 365 days a year.

"Statistics show that only about one in four users ever manage to kick the habit no matter how desperately they may wish to. So once you establish your clientele your levels of income and profits are more or less assured. Fantastic really. With me so far Eric?"

Zippo was utterly mesmerised. But he certainly was with him. With him every step of the way. He was riveted. Fascinated. He had never, ever heard anyone talk so cleverly, so clearly. This man was amazing.

"Aye I'm with you Mr Taylor. Nae bother. Just keep going."

"Good. Splendid. More tea? Sure? Fine. Now where was I? That's right. The market. So we have established that there is a wonderful opportunity and we have established that there are undreamed-of profits and rewards waiting for anyone who can take it. Once I had got my head around this I settled down to the task of finding a method to take these opportunities and I believe that I have found an ideal mechanism. Basically I am copying the concept of franchising. Are you familiar with the mechanics of franchising Eric?"

"No. Not really. Not at all."

"Don't worry, that's quite understandable. It is a very specific field. Let's take McDonalds as a prime example. They are a tremendously successful company as we all know. How do they do it? Simple. They have a tried and trusted plan and they stick to it. I'll take you through it if you like.

"They find a town where they don't have a restaurant. They then acquire a plot of land at a reasonable price and build a restaurant. Once this is done, they put the rest of the land for sale. Now before McDonalds this land was almost worthless, but once there is a McDonalds restaurant there, lots of companies are desperate to be next door to them, and so they can sell the balance of the land off for a fortune and they make a killing. What they do next is sell the right to use the restaurant and this is called a franchise. There is never a shortage of takers for these franchises even though they cost hundreds of thousands of pounds. The banks are more than happy to lend money to someone wanting to buy a McDonalds franchise because the restaurant is more or less a guaranteed success. McDonalds do everything to ensure this. They supply the uniforms, train the staff, spend millions on advertising to promote the brand, and they supply everything that the franchisee needs to run his business – food, drinks, free little toys, napkins, menus, takeaway boxes, the lot, and of course they make money out of every item.

"Now think about it Eric. What they are doing is exploiting an opportunity to cash in on a monopoly, just like the one we have identified in the drugs business. Of course the law of the land insists that any town can have as many burger restaurants as it likes, but McDonaldscan guarantee that only one of these will sell their brand. This means that whoever buys the franchise has a guaranteed monopoly to sell McDonalds products in his given territory. He makes a fortune. They make a fortune. Everybody is happy. All they have to do is to ensure that they put enough money back into marketing and advertising to ensure that they retain their status as the world's favourite burger seller.

"Now, I'm sure you can see that McDonalds offer us a superb example to follow and imitate. Let's see how we can translate what they are doing in the field of burgers to what we want to do in the field of drugs. What are the key aspects to setting up and running a successful drugs business? We'll list them. First there is the product. Whoever is offering the franchise must have an excellent product ready to supply and be able to give assurances that this supply will be consistent. That is what I am working on and I am confident of achieving this. I have excellent contacts and I am lucky to have plenty of funds available to finance the operation.

"Next we need to assess what kind of qualities we need for our franchisee. Well, I have looked at this long and hard and I have come to the conclusion that there is one quality that is overwhelmingly important. Can you guess Eric? No? Then I will tell you. It is the ability to perform acts of absolute and extreme violence without any qualm, or second thoughts, or conscience. That is how we achieve our monopoly. We win our trading territory through terror and fear. Anyone who attempts to trade in any of our franchised areas will be dealt with. They will be dealt with maximum force. They will be dealt with in such a way that other competitors would hesitate long and hard before ever considering muscling in on our trade.

"Now this means that I need choose my franchisees with great care. They cannot be ordinary men. On the contrary they must be *extra*ordinary men. Men who will do absolutely anything that it takes to claim their territories and to hold them. Men like you Eric. I watched you the other day and I was impressed. Impressed enough to make enquiries, and everything I found out made me even more impressed.

"Basically Eric, I see you as a perfect candidate to become one of my franchisees. You have never, ever backed down, and I don't believe you ever will. In addition to this I believe that your home town of Dumfries represents exactly the kind of untapped market that we are looking for.

"I have drawn up a hit list of favoured towns to seek out franchisees and Dumfries is in the top five. I am sure that you can see now why Barlinnie makes such a perfect base for this kind of venture. One of the major tasks for anyone setting up a franchise operation is to identify and recruit suitable franchisees. It tends to be a long and expensive operation. Not so for me. The police bring all the potential candidates right here to me. Thus far I have recruited four. I rather hope that you will be the fifth, Eric.

"To conclude, I will quickly take you through the structure we will create. I will sell you all the drugs that you require at an agreed wholesale price. We will take heroin as an example as heroin will always be our cash cow. The standard trade in heroin is the £10 bag. I will sell you the equivalent of a £10 bag of 40 percent pure heroin for £7. Once you take possession of the drug you will then 'cut' it to twenty percent pure heroin, thereby reducing your cost to £3.50 a bag. You will then sell this on to your main distributors for £6 a bag. They then have the option of selling direct to the customer for a £4 a bag profit, or selling to a secondary distributor for a £2 a bag profit.

"How do these numbers pan out? Well, Dumfries has a population of about 50,000 and my research has shown that with a properly managed supply chain and slick marketing it is quite usual to expect two percent of population to become customers – in the case of Dumfries that would be 1,000 heroin users. They will purchase an average of £15 a day's worth of the product. In a nutshell you can aspire to sell 1,500 £10 bags a day, giving you a profit of £3,750. That is about £120,000 a month. That is a profit of about one and a half million pounds a year. Impressive, don't you think?"

Zippo was stone-cold astounded. He could barely get his head around it. He could barely breathe. He certainly couldn't speak. He just nodded.

"The beauty of the system is that this wealth filters down. Your main distributors will earn well in excess of £100,000 a year and the secondary distributors in excess of £50,000 a year. This kind of money makes them loyal to you, ties them to you, makes them hungry for more. Not that they have much choice because you will be the only person who can supply the products in the town because you control the market in the way you know best.

"Now I will be offering other services to my franchisees. The first of these is obviously one of training. There is a lot to learn about how to set up a successful operation. You will need to acquire one or two new skills – how to 'cut' the product, how to recruit the right kind of distributors, and some basic business management techniques. We can undertake all of these tasks during our stay here in Barlinnie.

"Secondly, should you experience problems either in winning your territory or in holding it later on, I will ensure that we can hire you back-up teams as and when required. These are sub-contractors that I have already recruited. They are good professional men, all of whom are ex-soldiers. Similarly should you require any hardware, namely weaponry, to control your territory, I can again arrange supply. Payments for these services will be spread over a sensible period so that you can repay the monies owing out of your ongoing income.

"Thirdly, and probably most important of all, I will offer a full money-laundering service. This is vital. Think about it. You are going to have well over £100,000 of hard cash in your possession every month. That is an awful lot of money and you can't simply wander into town and put it into a building society. The authorities are always trying to chase this cash. It is one of the best methods they have of catching the main players in the trade. Cleaning this money by feeding it through legitimate businesses is a highly skilled operation and one in which I am lucky enough to have developed some expertise.

"Basically I will buy back your money. I will pay you £80 for every £100 that you give me and I will pay this money into a bank in Switzerland where only you can gain access. This service is not optional. I cannot afford to invest time and effort into my franchisees only to see their operations fall apart because the police nail them via the money.

"So that, Eric, is that. I am delighted to offer you the opportunity to take up the franchise to distribute my drugs in your town. Give it some thought. Let me know as soon as you have made your mind up, and we will start the training programme."

Zippo hadn't needed to think about it for very long at all. He went back to Taylor the next day and signed on the dotted line. And from that moment he started to surprise himself. Everyone had always told him that he was thick for as long as he could remember. They had told him this so many times that it never crossed his mind to disbelieve it. What did it matter anyway? He had no need to be clever. He just needed to be hard.

It wasn't long before he began to realise that this was not the case at all. He thrived on the training that Taylor gave him. He picked things up easily and he loved all the business terms that his mentor used. Taylor was impressed and encouraging. He suggested that Zippo should try attending the business studies classes. He did. And he passed the exam. He actually passed an exam. He could barely believe it.

When Zippo was released from Barlinnie three years later he was a changed man. Ironically enough, one of the main reasons that the prison authorities had agreed his early release was that they were so impressed with the effort that he had put into his studies. Little did they know!

He took Tommy and Wee Kenny with him back to Dumfries and started work on his franchise. Using a start-up loan supplied by Taylor he bought a council house in the middle of Sunnybank estate. He also rented a small isolated cottage eleven miles west of the town. He used the cottage to store the drugs. It was ideal for this purpose as it could only be reached down a semi-overgrown track that ran half a mile from a small country road. It was surrounded on two sides by thick woodland. Fifty yards into the woods they dug a hole and buried a large metal safe to store the product.

He had given great thought as to who he would recruit to complete his main team, and eventually he had decided on the

King brothers. Mike and Terry King had been in the class below Zippo in school. He had known them for years. Like Zippo they had done their share of time, and like Zippo they were hard – proper hard men. They knew their way around the town.

Eradicating the opposition had been almost ridiculously easy. There was no serious organisation, just a collection of small gangs and one-man bands. Taylor had recommended that he should develop a trademark punishment. It needed to be something fairly dramatic, something to be whispered about, a terrifying deterrent like the IRA's kneecapping or the ANC's necklacing. He created the Zippo treatment. He would tie his victim onto an old wooden chair in the cottage and get Wee Kenny to hold the head still. Having explained to the victim exactly what he was going to do, he would hold his favourite Zippo lighter under the victim's nostril, and light it. The pain was beyond belief and the victim would walk around for weeks later with a heavily bandaged nose. Word of the Zippo Treatment soon spread.

It was not something that had to happen on a regular basis. By and large he was simply able to convert the existing dealers into his own main distributors. It suited them down to the ground. Zippo had an excellent supply and his gear was first rate. Who wanted to be chasing off to Glasgow and Liverpool when it could be delivered to them? Once they agreed to switch to his operation they were given sales targets. To start with they were all given the opportunity to be main distributors which gave them the right to buy at £6 a bag. If they hit their targets, they continued to enjoy these terms. If they missed their targets, they were reduced to being secondary distributors, and they could only buy in at £8 a bag.

Zippo insisted on three things from all of his distributors. The main distributors could only retain their status by achieving targets. Nobody was ever allowed to drop the agreed price. Nobody was ever allowed to offer credit. Deliveries were made to the main distributors once a week. The location would be agreed over mobile phones which were changed regularly. Tommy and the King brothers handled all the deliveries. They would collect the drugs from the cottage and meet the distributor at a prearranged location somewhere out in the country.

Once a month Zippo and Wee Kenny would make the trip to Glasgow to collect the next month's supply of drugs. They would travel in two cars. On arrival in the city Zippo would spend a couple of hours with Taylor paying for the new batch and selling back the previous month's cash for laundering, whilst Kenny would be taken to a rendezvous to make the collection. A car would then escort Kenny back to meet Zippo and the two of them would drive in convoy to the cottage to stash the drugs.

These journeys started as day trips, but as the business established itself, Zippo started to make an evening of it, especially once he discovered the Excelsior. He would travel up the afternoon before the day the collection was due and enjoy himself. Every now and then Taylor would take him for lunch at his golf club on the Ayrshire coast. It was all very civilised. A proper business meeting between two men who had found their way into the most lucrative trade on the planet.

Tina sank back into the ornate hotel armchair and a slow smile spread over her face as the drug she had injected washed its way into her system. The sight of her pale naked frame in the middle of the ornate suite was beginning to arouse Zippo hugely when his mobile phone rang.

"Morning Eric. Jeremy here."

"Morning Mr Taylor. You well?" He could never get out of the habit of calling him Mr Taylor.

"Yes thank you Eric. Fine and dandy. However, there have been one or two small glitches through the night. We won't be in a position to make the delivery until mid-afternoon so I was wondering if you and that delightful young lady of yours would care to join me for lunch once we have done our bit of business."

"No Mr Taylor. Not this time."

"Oh dear. Is there a problem?"

"Aye there is. You're always taking us out. It's about time I did the honours. Why don't you come and join us here at the Excelsior?"

"Well of course I would be delighted. How very generous. Are you in your usual suite?"

"Aye."

"Then I will be around at about eleven-thirty. Briggs will take Wee Kenny to collect the product. That all sounds splendid."

Zippo put the phone back down on the bedside table and leered over at the blissfully happy figure of Tina.

"Hey you. You've had your breakfast. Now get yourself over here."

Taylor felt a glow of satisfaction as he strode down the hotel corridor later that morning and tapped on Zippo's door. He now had ten franchises and business was booming. What had seemed an excellent plan in Barlinnie had worked to perfection in practice. Every one of his franchises was working well, but Dumfries and Eric had always been his jewel in the crown. All of the men that he had recruited in Barlinnie had one thing in common: an ability to undertake any act of absolute violence that was required to acquire and hold their turf. Taylor had identified this as his number one priority. However some were much harder work to deal with than others. Sometimes the money went to their heads. Sometimes the violence went to their heads. Sometimes the idiots started taking the stuff themselves and that certainly went to their heads.

The more successful his enterprise became the more difficulties there seemed to be. He seemed to spend more and more time keeping them in line, cracking the whip. It had been necessary to send out Briggs and his team of ex-soldiers three times in the last two months to bring franchisees back into line. They were becoming greedy, intoxicated by their success and new-found wealth. In the end most of them were just plain stupid. They couldn't see that without him and his operation they would never have amounted to a thing. They were starting to haggle over the price and threatening to find supplies elsewhere.

None of this was much of a surprise. He had known that it would happen and it had. It only meant that he appreciated Zippo more. From very early on in Barlinnie he had recognised that Zippo had been different. For him the time spent studying and preparing had been like an awakening. He had taken to everything and taken to it quickly, obviously amazed at his own ability to do so. The Dumfries operation had reflected this. There was never any trouble. It ran like clockwork and made a living fortune.

Had all ten of his franchises been like Dumfries he might have been tempted to break with his original plan and give it a couple of more years. But all ten were not like Dumfries. There was Dumfries which was great. There were three towns which were more or less OK. There were four towns which were becoming an increasing headache and there were two which were a nightmare.

No. Enough was enough. Luckily he had always guessed that the business would become harder and harder to manage. With this in mind he had set himself a target on the day that he had walked out of Barlinnie. The target was £20,000,000 in his account in the discreet little bank down the cobbled back street in Geneva. Today the total in that account stood at £19,651,000. He was nearly there. As soon as the account hit the magic twenty million he would be away to the magnificent villa he had picked up the year before on Grand Cayman.

Once Zippo had let him in the two men sorted out business whilst Tina made herself up in the bathroom.

"Right Eric. Let's go through things. This delivery first. £100,000 worth, am I correct, and £10,000 for the other bits and pieces?"

"Aye."

Zippo passed over 110 rolls of notes.

"Splendid. And how much do you have for me to sort out this month?"

"Good month Mr Taylor. Hundred and twenty grand." He passed over a further batch of notes."

"A good month indeed. Now let's see. Eighty percent of £120,000 means that I will transfer £96,000 into your account in Switzerland and that means, assuming that my records are correct, and I have no doubt that they are, that you now have a little over £1,500,000 in the bank Eric. A very tidy nest egg. A very tidy nest egg indeed. It shows that hard work and good management will always be rewarded."

Taylor carefully placed all the money into a briefcase and held it out to the man who had come in with him and had taken up a station by the door.

"Here you are Harris. Take this away for me please. Thank you."

The man left without a word. Taylor and Zippo chatted over coffee whilst Tina tried to make herself look like one of the girls in *Vogue*. Both men spoke eagerly of the future, but this was only skin deep. In the back of Taylor's mind was an image of the palm trees and white beaches and his beautiful white villa. In the back of Zippo's mind was how much he was looking forward to impressing Taylor over lunch when he saw how all the waiters knew him.

And there was also an image of blue skies and sunshine in Zippo's mind. He had taken Tina to Spain a few months earlier and he had spent many hours in a small bar run by a lad he had known from Shotts. The mate had rung him three weeks ago. He had more or less made his mind up to sell up. Was Zippo interested? And Zippo was interested. In fact he had more or less made his mind up. He had plenty of money now. Plenty for about six lifetimes in Spain. Once the idea had been sown in his mind he couldn't get away from thinking about it. He thought of the sun and the great food and the kind of place with its own swimming pool that he could buy and Tina lying naked and golden on the verandah and, yes, he was going to it. Soon. Before the winter.

So both men talked of their future together whilst they dreamed of escape. Later, when they had finished a slow leisurely lunch, Briggs came into the restaurant and told his boss that the material was loaded and they were waiting with Wee Kenny in a car park a couple of streets away. Taylor leant over to Zippo and spoke quietly.

"Eric, I have some rather good news. As you are no doubt aware we have experienced one or two problems with this delivery. In fact, the gentlemen who were bringing it into town only made it a couple of hours ago. They had some kind of car trouble. Anyway, the upshot of this is that we haven't had time to cut it. This of course is jolly good news for you Eric because you can cut it twice. A rather tidy bonus wouldn't you say. About £50,000. Well merited I would say. You deserve it Eric. Now, time is moving on I'm afraid. I must be off. Thanks ever so much for the lunch, it was wonderful. I will see you next month."

He patted Zippo lightly on the shoulder, kissed Tina's manicured hand decorously, and left. As Zippo sat back and sipped his brandy, fate played its next card. Zippo felt full of good food and wine and very contented. Across the table Tina looked so bloody good that he just wanted to take her upstairs and fuck her there and then. And why not, he thought. Why should he rush back? He had just been given a £50,000 bonus out of the blue, so why not celebrate? There was no reason why not. Who would ever have thought it. Thought that he, Zippo, would decide to take another night in his £400 a night suite at the Excelsior because he had just got himself a fifty grand windfall. And so he made his mind up. He would call Kenny and tell him to come back and park the car up in the hotel car park. The gear would be fine. The hotel had great security. He would then go and shag Tina within an inch of her life, have a kip, have a sauna and a soak in the Jacuzzi, and then? Then whatever. Whatever he fucking liked. Dumfries could wait.

There was little of the usual bounce in Mandy's step that morning. The long sleepless hours of the night had left her feeling edgy and depressed. The short drive to work did little to lift her spirits. The news on the local radio was all bad. There were now six confirmed cases of Foot and Mouth in the district. She hadn't needed the radio to find this out. Plumes of black smoke were already drifting up into the clear winter sky from the hills to the east of the town. The cull was under way. As she made her way to the office she passed several Army Land Rovers. So it was starting. The soldiers had arrived. Now the killing that they had all watched with such horror on the TV had come to the hills and valleys of Dumfries.

She thought of Jack and Will and the appalling mess that they had got themselves into. What would happen now? Will had been in a bad enough state before all of this. What effect would the culling of all their animals have on his fragile state of mind? The thought made her shudder.

The normally sleepy office was buzzing. Suddenly after years of utter obscurity the town was on the map. The name of Dumfries was suddenly appearing every night on the evening news. It was amazing. She would never have believed that this little town where nothing ever happened could possibly be the centre of national attention.

She had only been at her desk for five minutes when Bob Bennet called her into his office. As soon as she sat down he noticed the graze on her cheek.

"Bloody hell Mandy. You look like you've been in the wars. What happened?"

"Oh nothing really. It was stupid. You know how fast I walk, well I slipped and fell in Jack Sinclair's yard last night. Clumsy old cow."

"You sure you're OK?"

"Course I am. Fine. It's nothing."

"Was Jack in?"

"Yes. Yes he was. He was really helpful. He brought me right up to speed with everything. I feel a lot more confident now."

Bennet nodded approvingly. "Excellent. Thought he would. Good man, Sinclair. How are things with them?"

"Terrible. He's worried sick. The wind is the worst thing that could have happened. You were right about that Bob. I saw the smoke from the fires this morning. They seemed terribly close to Hillside. It's not looking good."

"No. It couldn't be looking a whole lot worse really. Anyway it's happening and we have to report it. They are setting up a command post in Loreburne Hall. Calling it 'The Bunker'. Bit dramatic, but there you go. The Ministry and the Army. Everything is going to be co-ordinated from there. They will be having a press conference at eleven o'clock. Get yourself down there and cover it. There is a rumour that one of the Edinburgh ministers is hitting town today. Get on the phone. Chase it up. If you confirm it, cover that as well. If you have any time over, get yourself out to the farms where they are culling. They won't let you in but try and talk to people at the gates – Ministry, soldiers, relatives, anyone. Start painting the picture. OK? Off you go. I need a story by no later than three tomorrow afternoon so off you pop."

She had been waiting for this for so long. A real story. A story that had everything, drama, human interest, tragedy, the lot. It was her chance. A chance to really prove that she had what it took. She should have been bouncing, but instead she just felt flat and miserable. She couldn't feel happy that her chance had only come about because so many people were going to have their lives wrecked. But then that was what the job was all about. Not much big news was good news. There certainly wasn't much good news to be found in Dumfries that morning.

NEMESIS

If Mandy woke up feeling flat and jaded that morning, Will was about 700 times worse. He had finally managed to fall asleep in the Land Rover a little before five. As he had slept, the night had moved from cold to freezing and by the time he woke up he couldn't see out of the windows for frost. He had barely been eating for days and he had no resistance to the cold. Whilst he slept the cold had eaten away into the marrow of his bones. He shivered uncontrollably and he couldn't stop his teeth chattering.

He reached into the back and pulled out some old sacks which he used as makeshift blankets whilst the engine slowly began to warm up. Slowly the ice on the windows began to melt, revealing a beautiful early-morning world. He was in a lay-by on a road that wound its way up into the hills. As he looked, out glittering white frosted fields spread all the way down to the town of Dumfries below. The first burning red of the sun was tinting the sky to the east. In the fields sheep huddled together and their breath swirled idly above them in small clouds.

It was the kind of morning that he had always loved. Getting out of bed had never been a problem for Will. It had come easy. He loved to get out of the back door on crisp winter's morning like this. He loved the feel of the biting-cold on his face and the way that the reds and oranges of the dawn sun would tint the frozen fields.

That had been then. Now look at me he thought. He turned the rear-view mirror around to study his reflection. He grimaced at the sight that met him. There were black smudges under his eyes and his skin was chalk white. His hair was lank and greasy and for the first time in his life he had acne. His teeth were yellow and felt like they were coated in mould spores. He looked like he felt. A complete state.

As the heater began to get going he felt the nausea begin to build up. It was like this every morning when he had no heroin. Soon he was forced to lean out of the window and retch. There was nothing in his stomach to bring up, which meant that the convulsions cramped his stomach. When the nausea at last retreated he felt shattered. The bouts of vomiting seemed to drain all the energy from him.

He felt washed out and cold and drained. More than anything, he felt as if he were about to drown in a black sea of depression. He couldn't believe how quickly his life had come to this. Soon the tears started to come again. Tears of despair. Tears of wanting. Tears of regret. So very much regret. More regret than he could ever begin to handle. His mind was a little clearer than it had been and it replayed the events of the night before over and over and over. The more he remembered, the more the tears flowed, until he found himself racked with sobs. Part of him said stop, get a grip, don't be soft, stop blubbing, grow up, take it like a man. But it was only a small part. A much bigger part just wanted to give in, to cry and cry and cry.

It had never been this bad before. He had never felt as low as this. He was so ashamed, so sorry for what had happened, so distraught at what he had done. What the hell had possessed him? How could he have spoken like that to Mandy? Mandy, who was so good, so loving, so full of life and hope and everything.

And there was his Dad. He respected his Dad more than anyone in the world. And he loved him. They had been so close, more like brothers than father and son. And when they had been together they had faced the world down. It had never mattered how bad and how hard things had got because he had always known that they would come through. Because they were strong. Because they would never admit defeat. Because they would stick with each other no matter what. That was how it had been. And what had he done? He had done everything he could to destroy it and smash it and break it into a million pieces. The more guilty and miserable and ashamed he had felt, the more he had taken it out on his Dad with his tantrums and sulks.

Why? Why the fuck was he doing this? Why couldn't he get some control of his life? Heroin. Bastard fucking heroin. And it was still there. That great empty place in the middle of his soul that only heroin could fill. It wouldn't go away. The brain might clear a bit and the nausea might back off, but the endless, permanent agonising yearning would never go away.

And suddenly he knew that he had to stop. He had to stop running and he had to face it. Surely he was young enough. Surely he could find the strength from somewhere. Others did it, so why not him? But he also knew he could never do it alone. He would have to have help. He would have to come out of hiding. He only had one person to turn to and that was his Dad.

He made his decision. He would go back and he would tell him. He would tell him everything. And he would apologise. Apologise for everything. And maybe his Dad wouldn't understand, wouldn't want to understand, wouldn't care. Maybe he had already pushed him too far. Maybe last night had been the final straw. Well, it was a risk he was just going to have to take. If his Dad turned his back on him and sent him away then there was nothing he could do. It was time for truth. He just hoped and prayed with all his heart that Jack would forgive him. That he would have enough love left to save him. To get him out of the nightmare. To get him his life back.

He decided to go into town and find somewhere to clean himself up a bit and to try and force down some food. And then he would go home and face up to telling the truth. It was time. It had to be.

Jack could barely face the prospect of getting out of bed that morning. He had sat long into the night after getting the call from his neighbour. How much sleep had he managed to get? Two hours? Maybe three? Not much anyway. He had more or less finished the bottle of brandy and he felt sick. Really sick. In fact he was going to be sick. He lurched into the bathroom and just hung on long enough to throw up into the toilet. It went on and on and when he was finished he felt drained and dizzy. He sloshed ice-cold water into his face and tried to pull himself together.

He banged on Will's door without much optimism. After a minute or so he looked into the room to find the bed empty. He hadn't expected anything else. How long would the boy be away for this time? A day? Two days? Part of him hoped it would be a while. He had no idea what was eating away at his son but he felt pretty sure that watching their animals being slaughtered and burned would hardly help. Yes, better he should stay away. Nobody should have to live through this.

He wearily made himself a mug of tea and grimly chewed his way through three slices of plain bread that were rather stale. It slowly began to settle his stomach. He tossed the near-empty brandy bottle in the bin feeling angry at himself for being so pathetic and weak. The second cup of extra sweet tea started to revive him. What if Will did come back? He didn't think that he would, but what if he did? He just couldn't face another row. He couldn't face the look of contempt and loathing on his son's face. Not now. Not today. Not with all this.

He had to find a way of dealing with it better. He had to stop being such a damned soldier. Maybe he should show some weakness. Maybe he should climb down a bit, try and meet the boy halfway, whatever was eating him must be serious. Oh God, it was so difficult. He was no good at these things. It should have been Angela. Why wasn't she there for the boy to turn to? The lousy bitch. Off hunting with that cowardly toffee-nosed git Hammerton-Smith.

There was only him. Jack. Jack the father. And he simply had to do better. He had to let Will know that he was there for him and that he would help him no matter what it was, because he loved him. Somehow he had to find a way of saying it. Why was it so damned hard to get away from the old stiff upper lip. That damned, bleak Scottish reserve. Was it really that ingrained? Surely not. It couldn't be. He wouldn't allow it to be. Somehow he would get through. Let the boy know he would always be there for him. Surely he could manage that much.

Feeling slightly more human, he heaved on his coat and went outside to milk the cows. The sight of them waiting in the shed nearly broke his heart. As soon as they saw him they started to moo enthusiastically. Time for food. Time to get milked. And then a nice trough of fresh silage. Such simple pleasures. They were so content. So happy with their great big brown eyes.

As he started to open the cold steel gates to guide them into the collecting yard the younger ones pushed their heads through the fence to lick at his jacket. The mooing was louder now as they collectively relished emptying their udders. He noticed number 92 was not in her usual place. Where was she? Oh yes, there. Way back. She must be getting ready for the bull. He would see to that later.

But then he realised that he wouldn't. He wouldn't because number 92 would never be having a calf again. Not number 92, or number 27, or number 113. Not any of them, because tomorrow, or the next day, or even the day after that, they would all be dead. All of them. Every cow, every heifer, his two bulls, all the calves, all the ewes, all the lambs. It was impossible to comprehend. All of them. No exceptions. Not even one. And when it was all over there would be nothing alive at Hillside except for his two dogs.

These thoughts made the work almost impossibly hard. What was the point? Why bother feeding and mucking out? For what? They would all be dead tomorrow or the day after that. But he carried on like a robot. Methodical. Mechanical. He did all the jobs one by one for the simple reason that they were there to be done. There was no way that he would make his animals go without feed or forage. It wasn't their fault. There was no reason for them to suffer. Besides, what the hell else was he going to do? Sit around and mope? Go back on the brandy? No way. If it was going to happen, then there was bugger-all he could do about it. All he could do was to try and stay professional, to try and stay dignified.

By ten he had finished his chores and gone back inside in real need of more hot, sweet tea to re-hydrate and build his blood sugars back up. There was a message waiting on the answering machine. It was the Ministry. They wanted him to call back as soon as possible. He made the call. And they told him. Basically they told him what he already knew. There were diagnosed Foot and Mouth cases on the farm next door. This meant that they would have to slaughter all the animals at Hillside Farm as part of the agreed policy of contiguous culling. There were things that he needed to do. Would he please ring the valuer. Here was the number. He had a choice. He could either have the valuer come and assess his stock on an individual basis or he could accept the set valuations that they had given for the various classes of stock. So long as he was not keeping pedigree animals the latter course would probably be preferable. Better for him. More money that way. Better for them too. The quicker they could cull, the quicker they would halt the march of the disease.

They would be coming the next morning. Could he get things ready please. Could he round up the sheep into one place. A contained area. Somewhere where they could be fed through in a line for the slaughter men. Good. And did he have a cattle crush? Good. They would want to lead the cows and young stock through the crush. Could he move the crush? Somewhere out of sight of the main shed. So that the rest couldn't see. He could? Excellent. Thank you so much for your co-operation Mr Sinclair. We really appreciate it Mr Sinclair. We really do. Hopefully all will go to plan tomorrow. But we have a lot on. We hope you understand. We will do all we can. Goodbye Mr Sinclair. And once again, thank you Mr Sinclair.

He was beginning to become numb. He was sliding into a familiar combat mode. Feelings were pushed aside. No point thinking about what will happen afterwards. Just think about the now. Concentrate on the next few hours, concentrate on the battle, the fire fight. And if one of you men goes down you don't think about it. You check if he is alive, and if he's not you just forget it and move forward. Don't think about his Mum and his Dad and his young fiancée and how he did that amazing imitation of the Brigadier when he had had a few, you don't think about any of it, you just keep going forward, gain ground, work out fields of fire, liaise with artillery, keep the NCOs moving. You just do the job. Then when it's finished, well, then you think about it. Pick up the pieces. Realise who has gone. Work out what you are going to say when you ring their family. That was all for later. Now the coldness set in. It all had to be done and he would see it through. It would be done right. No bodge jobs. If they were going to kill his animals they would do it properly. God help them if they didn't.

He called the valuer. It was a short conversation. No, he didn't have any pedigree stock. Yes, he would agree to accept the standard values. Yes, he would sign the form.

And then the soldiers came.

He heard their Jeep as it came up the track in the stillness of the morning. He walked out to the yard expecting it to be Will's Land Rover. But it wasn't. It was an Army Land Rover. A sergeant and a private climbed out. He clocked the uniform. King's Own Borderers.

The sergeant came across the yard. "Good morning sir, Mr Sinclair is it sir? Mr Jack Sinclair?"

"Aye it is." The combat instinct that was again taking a hold of him. It led him into half-forgotten banter. "Well this is just bloody marvellous isn't it? I mean what do the silly bastards think they're doing? This bloody job is going to be bad enough without them sending me a bunch of ponces to help out."

The sergeant's face clouded. "Excuse me sir?"

"You heard me lad. Ponces. You lot. All of you. King's Own Borderers. You couldn't fight your way out of a wet paper bag."

Now the soldier's face really did cloud over. "Now I know this must be a bad time sir, and I appreciate that, but there is no need for . . ."

Jack's laughter stopped him short. "OK. OK. Don't get your knickers in a twist. I'm only pulling your leg. I used to be Scots Guards. Old habits die hard. That's all."

The sergeant looked relieved. "Oh, right. Got you. You had me going there for a minute. When was that sir?"

"'77 to '93. Came out as a Major."

"Hang on a minute. Sinclair. Jack Sinclair. Yeah, that's it. Fuck me. Are you Jack Sinclair as in Liam Kelly?"

"Aye. That's me. You must be as old as me to remember that bit of ancient history."

"Not the sort of thing as gets forgotten in a hurry that sir. Bloody tremendous it was. I wish we'd met under different circumstances. I'd buy you a drink. Still will. Once this is done."

"On the subject of a drink do you lads want a brew?"

They did. Jack took them into the kitchen. They explained their role. They were to co-ordinate everything that had to be done. They had a contractor coming in that afternoon to look at where to put the pyre to burn the slaughtered animals. Once he had picked his spot they would arrange for lorry loads of coal and diesel and timber to be delivered. They would make sure that the slaughter men had all they needed. In short, they would make sure that none of the civvy bastards made a bollocks of the job and if they needed to bang heads together they would bang them: hard.

They promised that they would see him right. They promised that it was the least that they could do for an old army man, especially the old army man who took down Liam Kelly. Whilst they were talking the back door opened and Will came in.

He shrank back in shock as he saw the soldiers. He had cleaned himself up. He was freshly shaved and he had combed his greasy hair back. He suddenly looked so very young. So vulnerable with the fear in his face.

When he spoke his voice was quiet, nervous, afraid. "Hi Dad. What is it? What's going on?"

Jack turned to the soldiers. "You'll just give me a few minutes with my lad will you? Just help yourselves to tea and biscuits. There's bread and stuff in the fridge. Just dig in. I won't be long."

Father and son walked out into the yard. They sat on the wall by the top field and stared down the hillside to the valley below. From their vantage point there were now five clearly visible pillars of smoke climbing into the blue sky.

"I'm afraid it's happened Will. They've got positive cases next door. Confirmed last night. It means that they will be slaughtering all of our stock. Contiguous cull. They are coming tomorrow. That's why the soldiers are here. They co-ordinate everything. There's a lot to get ready. Well, I'm sure you can imagine."

The boy seemed to shrink further into himself. Jack wanted to reach out to him. To pull him close and comfort him. Like he used to do when he was eight when he had fallen off his bike or tripped in the yard. But he wasn't eight any more.

Will pulled out a crumpled pack of cigarettes and lit one with a shaky hand.

"Here, give me one of those will you. Sod it." Jack had given up years earlier. What the hell. Why not. If ever there was a time to have a fag, this was it.

"Didn't know you smoked Dad?"

"Used to. Like a bloody chimney. And it suddenly seems like a good idea to start again." He took a long, hard pull and the unaccustomed nicotine hit sent him dizzy for a moment. "Jesus H Christ. How good is that! Wow. It's worth giving up for fifteen years just to really enjoy one as much as this."

Will looked at the goofy grin on his father's face in wonder. And then Jack became more serious. "Listen Will, there is something I want to say. Now just hear me out. It won't take long. Promise."

Jack was half expecting an eruption. There wasn't one. Will faintly nodded and then bowed his head and stared at his boots.

"OK. Good. Now I know things haven't been so good of late. I don't know why and I don't understand. I have tried to understand but, well, I suppose I'm not that good at these things. I'm a gruff old bastard. Always have been, and I dare say I always will be.

But don't get me wrong. I do care Will. I care a lot. I just don't seem to be able to show it.

"The next two or three days are going to be Hell. No point pussyfooting around it. It is going to be a complete nightmare. Christ knows what it is going to do to us, but somehow we'll have to see it through. And then when it's done, there will be just about nothing to do. No milking, no sheep, no silage, no nothing. Just a clean up and disinfectant job.

"Let's see if we can use the time Will. We've been flogging our guts out for as long as I can remember. Let's try and find a positive out of this lousy business. Whatever the problem is Will, anything, it doesn't matter what, I'll try and help. If you don't want to tell me about it, fine. If you do, fine. Somehow we'll come out of this nightmare. And then, well who knows. Maybe it will have been the best thing that has ever happened. Maybe we'll do something completely different. I don't know. Keep ostriches or set up a paint ball course or a mountain bike trail, whatever.

"The main thing is that you know that I'm with you. Always will be. What has gone, has gone. No point in looking back and worrying about it. Think it over."

Will looked up at his father. Jack was shocked to see that tears were cascading down his cheeks.

"I had already decided Dad. This morning. I made up my mind. To come to you. To ask for help. You see, I really need help. You're right though. Not now. Let's get this business over and then I'll tell you. All of it. Promise."

His eyes shone with the tears that continued to pour out. "Oh Jesus Dad". He collapsed into the strong grasp of his father who held him as he sobbed and sobbed. They sat like that for several minutes, quiet, on a wall overlooking the fires, reunited, strong again. At last Will pulled himself away and wiped his face roughly with his sleeve.

"OK. Enough of that. I'm better now. Got it off the chest. What shall I do?"

"I was hoping that you could spend the afternoon gathering all the sheep. We need to bring them all down to the small field by the Top Farm. It'll take you a while, but you should manage it. I'll get the crush moved ready for the cattle. There will be more people coming, I think they will want to start laying some hardcore in the field, so that the wagons can drive out there to tip the timber and the coal for the fire."

"Fine. No problem. I'd rather be away from all this anyway. Better in the hills. Well, until tomorrow. I'll get started. See you later."

"Aye. Just come back down if you need a hand with anything."

Will jumped on the quad bike and whistled the two sheep dogs who eagerly leapt on the back. They had always called it the Top Farm. Its real name was actually Upper Hillside Farm. Up to fifteen years ago it had been completely separate from Hillside Farm, although the only way to get up to it was to follow a track that ran through the Hillside yard. When the old farmer who had owned it had died, Jack's father had bought the farm at auction. It wasn't much of a place and he hadn't paid much of a price for it. It comprised 120 acres of rough moorland and they used it exclusively for sheep. The house was rather run down but it had always proved useful as a dwelling when they had been able to employ farm workers. Once they had been forced to lay-off the last of their hands they had made lots of plans for the Top Farm. The house and courtyard were built from old stone and they would have converted into three magnificent holiday homes. But the conversion would have cost a fortune and they never had sufficient time or money to make it happen.

Jack's father had built an excellent large sheep shed in the late eighties which offered superb conditions at lambing time. All in all, it had proved a useful purchase and it provided an ideal centre for their sheep business.

It took Will ten minutes to drive up the two-mile track and when he got to the yard he turned the quad bike to face out into the view. The view was always truly stunning. Top Farm was 200 feet higher than the main farm, and below, the landscape of Dumfriesshire and Cumbria opened out in a magnificent vista in the crystal-clear winter air.

He smoked another cigarette. He still felt desperately ill and washed out and the cold was eating through him, but for the first time in months and months he felt a faint glimmer of hope. No matter how bad he felt he was determined to see the next two days through. Then . . . well, then was then. Maybe he would take more smack once Ricky was back with stuff to sell. But it wouldn't be for long. No way. Because enough was enough. It was time he got his life back.

He worked like a madman that afternoon. The day drifted slowly into evening as the light drew in and the hard winter night descended. By six he had worked for an hour in the dark but he was confident that every one of their 1,100 sheep was in the small field. He tossed far more hay into the field than he would ever normally have done and he sat for a while watching the ghostly white shapes eat hungrily in the darkness. The last supper. Enjoy it while it lasts. Poor bastards.

By the time he took the quad bike back down to the lower farm real exhaustion was beginning to set in. Big lights had been set up in the field at the front of the house and a large digger was spreading out hardcore into a makeshift track. Another digger was in the process of digging the bonfire pit. Will found Jack talking to one of the contractors.

"That's all the sheep gathered up top. Anything else needs doing?"

Jack could see that his son was almost at the end of his tether. There wasn't much to be done anyway. The cows were all milked and the stock had been fed and bedded down for the night. The main work was now in the field and that was being handled by the contractors. They were waiting on another three loads of hardcore and they hoped to have the track finished that night. Ten loads of coal and three loads of timber were due the next morning. As long as there were no delays they would have the pyre ready for the following evening.

"No, apart from these lads, we're all done down here. Get yourself inside and warm up. If you can find the energy, stick a pan of stew on the hob."

"Sure."

As the warmth of the kitchen hit him the tiredness really kicked-in. He dumped his wellies by the door and hung up his coat. For some reason the warmth set off another vicious bout of craving. He shook his head and squeezed his eyes tight shut for a moment as he tried to fight it. Slowly it eased slightly, and he forced himself to start peeling and chopping vegetables. He gave the task his full concentration to take his mind away from the desperate yearning inside. Potatoes, carrots, swedes, barley, lamb, tinned tomatoes. It seemed to take him for ever but at last the pan was bubbling on the hob. He took a can of coke out of the fridge and collapsed into the big old armchair by the Aga. Seconds later he was fast asleep.

He had no concept of how long he had been out when the ringing of the phone dragged him back to consciousness. He felt dizzy and disorientated and it took several rings for him to pull himself together.

"Hello."

There was silence at the other end. His own voice sounded thick and groggy.

"Hello. Anyone there?"

More silence then. "Is that you Will?"

"Yes. Speaking."

"It's Mandy, Will."

This time it was his turn for silence. He struggled to bring his brain into gear. "Oh. Right. Jesus. Just give me a minute can you Mandy?"

"I don't much feel like giving you anything right at this moment Will."

"No. I don't suppose you do. I don't really know what to say. Not a lot I can say really is there. Just sorry. Really sorry. But that probably isn't good enough."

More silence, then. "Well, it would be a start."

"You have no idea just how sorry I am Mandy. Truly. I don't seem have any control any more. I do these things and I just can't stop myself. Part of me can see how wrong it all is but that part doesn't seem to be able to do anything about it. It's like I'm driven. Nothing I can do to stop it. Then, when it's all over, everything comes back and I can't believe what I've done. And then I want more than anything in the world to undo it, but it's too late. But last night was the worst. Last night was too much."

"You're not kidding you bastard. You should see my face."

He groaned. "Christ Mandy, what can I say?"

"Actually you're doing OK. This is the first time that you've been halfway civil to me in months. But I really think that you owe the bigger apology to Jack. I at least had the luxury of being able to dump you. Poor Jack has been stuck with you week in, week out. Can't you see what you are doing to him? Can't you see the pain? Jack is a very strong man, but you are breaking him down piece by piece."

Her words bit deep. There was a harshness to her tone. He could feel the anger starting to rise up in him and it made him feel panicky. Again he screwed his eyes shut and fought for control. Not this time. No way. A huge wave of craving swept through him that made him gasp aloud.

"Will. Will are you still there? Are you OK?" She had allowed the hard note to slip out of her voice. Instead it was the old Mandy, warm, caring, concerned. The rage eased back.

"Yes. I'm here. Sorry. I'm just trying to get a hold of myself. I put the temper back in its kennel. Sometimes I feel like I am a madman."

"Well you've certainly been acting like one. Look Will, I know this may get you mad again, because it has always made you mad before, but for God's sake I have to keep asking, surely you can see that . . . Will . . . what is it? What has happened? Where is the cause? Where did the boy I used to know go? There must be something. Please Will, try and tell me. I'm still here you know. You may have been a complete rotter but I've not gone away. Please don't get mad this time. Just try. Try and talk."

"It's OK Mandy. I won't get mad. Not this time." He thought for a moment. Was this the time? Maybe it was. If he was going to find a way back into his life he had to start somewhere. So why not here? Why not now?

"Will?"

"Still here Mandy. Are you sure you really want to know? After all, you have managed to get rid of me. You might be well advised to leave it that way."

"I want to know. And the day I get rid of you is the day that I go all day without thinking about you and worrying about you and wishing that the old Will would come back. And that isn't today. So yes, I want to know."

"I'm a junkie Mandy."

"What!"

"You heard. I'm a heroin addict. A Smackhead. I inject heroin. Jack it up. When I have smack I'm OK. When I don't, I'm not

OK. Not OK at all. I haven't had any in four days now. There's some kind of problem with supplies. And it's eating me alive. That's why I was so awful last night. I didn't want to be, I just couldn't stop myself, I just . . ." He couldn't keep going. He felt such appalling shame at the words. He was crying again. Just like he had with his Dad. And all of a sudden he knew why he got so mad and lost control. It was just a defence mechanism. It was the only way he could stop himself from breaking down and crying. And he had never wanted anyone to see him like this, so broken, so full of despair and loneliness and regret. He had never wanted that. So he had kept it locked away. Instead of showing the gaping open wounds that were slowly but surely breaking him up, he had shown burning rage instead. And now that he had started to cry he just couldn't seem to stop. Slowly her voice fought its way through his desperate sobbing.

"Will . . . Will . . . Will. Please Will. It's OK. Honestly Will it's OK. Really OK. I promise. You've told me and now I understand. All I ever wanted was to understand."

"I thought that you would hate me. Despise me. Never want to see me again. Same with Dad. I couldn't stand it. Not this. Not having to admit that I'm a junkie."

"Will, when are you ever going to get it into that great thick head of yours that I love you. So does Jack. We both do Will. We wouldn't just desert you. You must be kidding. But why now? Why have you decided to tell me now?"

"Because of last night. I decided this morning. I decided to tell Dad and ask for help, and if he hated me for it, well, that was a risk I had to take. The way I behaved last night was too much. I couldn't believe what I had done, and to you Mandy, how could I do that to you? To say all of those things to you?"

"Does that mean that you want to kick it?"

"Yes."

"Is that real Will? Or is it just remorse?"

"I think it's real. I want it to be real. I can't go on like this."

"No you can't. If it is real Will, I am here for you. All the way. You must know that. I don't care how messy it gets or how ugly. I can deal with it. I'm stubborn. And if Jack starts kicking up he will have me to deal with. But I don't for a minute think that he will. I know we will both be with you, every step of the way. Thank God I know what the hell this has all been about. Now talk to me. Tell me about it. Everything. How you started? How long? How much? You've held it back for long enough. I refuse to be kept in the dark any more. So speak."

And he did. Once he started he couldn't stop. It felt like lancing an agonising boil and squeezing out the stinking pus that had caused such pain for so long. Mandy never interrupted. Only once. Once to say "Ricky! I knew it. I knew it would all be down to that runtish little shit."

Whilst they were talking, the back door opened and Jack stuck his head in. He saw Will hunched over the phone and was about to speak when he heard him say "Mandy". He smiled and closed the door behind him quietly.

After two hours another huge surge of exhaustion hit him and his eyes began to close. "Mandy. I'm going to have to go. I'm shattered. I just can't keep my eyes open any more. The brain wants to talk all night but the body won't play ball. I have to get a decent night's sleep before, well, you know, before tomorrow."

"What do you mean before tomorrow?"

"What, you don't know? Well I don't suppose you do. They're coming tomorrow to kill the animals. We're a contiguous cull."

"Oh Jesus no. That is why I called. I was going to find out from Jack how things were. So soon. I can't believe it."

"They're in a big hurry. The quicker they can kill, the quicker they stop the bloody thing I suppose."

"Will you be OK?"

He laughed. "No. But somehow I'll manage. I've left Dad enough over these last months. I can't leave him alone with this. It's a couple of days and then it's over. I'll make it."

They said their goodbyes and he sank back into the chair. He was asleep in seconds. Jack came in half an hour later and decided it would be kinder to throw a blanket over his son rather than waking him to go upstairs. He took a bowl of stew out of the pan and watched Will as he slept. He sensed that there was something a little less desperate about the boy. Thank God he had spoken to Mandy. Jack had checked the door twice more and knew that they had been on the line together for almost a couple hours. Surely it was a good sign. Maybe things could at last begin to get better. The next two days promised to be as bad as any in his life, but they would end. Everything came to an end. And once it was all over, and the fire had burnt out, they would all have a chance to start again. Maybe this time they could make a better job of things.

He idly contemplated pouring himself a scotch but dumped the idea almost as soon as it had come into his head. He was tired. Dog tired. He wearily climbed up the stairs and collapsed into his cold bed. Like his son before him he was asleep in seconds.

That night they both slept the sleep of the dead on a farm where death was due to arrive the next morning at 7.30 sharp.

Will felt crushing disappointment when he awoke that morning. It was day five. He had vainly hoped that the craving may have eased a little. He was wrong. If anything the long rest seemed to have refreshed and restored the demons. It was worse than ever. He tried to force down a hot cup of tea but he immediately threw it up. His exertions in gathering in the sheep the previous afternoon had taken a huge amount out of him. His limbs and bones felt like stone and he felt a blackness all through him.

Jack looked worried when he came into the kitchen at 6.30. "You alright there lad?"

"Yeah, not so bad. Bit off-colour that's all. I'll be OK."

They started to arrive after seven. The soldiers. The man from the Ministry. The contractors. Three loads of coal and one of timber. The yard was soon a hive of activity. And then the slaughtermen came. Four of them. The Ministry man doled out overalls and everybody pulled them on. The weather had turned in the night. There was no cold crisp air that morning. A strong wind from the west swept in rain from Ireland.

Men looked sinister in the white overalls and yellow boots as they huddled out of the rain and cupped their cigarettes to keep them from getting wet. Jack and Will had to milk the cows. They would only be more agitated if they had to spend the day with full udders. It was a heartbreaking task. A feeling of desperate panic was rising in Will's throat. He couldn't do this. He couldn't face it. The soft brown eyes of the cows seemed to stare into his soul. The utter horror of what was about to happen made him feel even sicker.

Once the cows were milked they were returned to the shed and given silage.

Then it started.

Jack and Will led the cows out one by one to the place where Jack had moved the cattle crush the day before. They pushed and cajoled each animal into the crush then, bang. One of the slaughtermen would place a bolt-gun to the side of the animal's head and bang. Death was instant. It was as humane as possible and thankfully it was hidden from the view of the rest of the herd.

But animals can always sense death. And soon there was death in the air. More death with every slain beast. The noise in the shed was growing and it became a little harder for Jack and Will to guide the animals into the crush. The dead cows had chains attached to their legs and they were dragged away and dumped in front of the silage pit. As the morning wore on the pile grew. It was a slow mechanical horror. Time seemed to slow to nothing. There was no past and no future. Only now. Only the endless conveyor belt of slaughter.

Will felt as if he was disintegrating. All the horrors in the world seemed to be crawling all over him. Everything was closing in. He could hardly breathe. He couldn't deal with it. He was trapped.

How many? How many so far? He looked over to the growing pile of corpses. It seemed as if there were thousands. Millions even. But there weren't. There must have been 30. Maybe 40. So many more to go. And when all the cows were dead it would be the calves, and then the bulls, and then the sheep. Oh Christ, the sheep. Eleven hundred of them. So much more death. So many more corpses. What were they doing? What crime were they committing? Would they ever be forgiven? No. Never. Not for this. They would never be forgiven for this.

He was so light-headed. He had barely eaten for days. Barely slept either. And the desperate need for heroin and the horror of the slaughter were sending his mind spinning out of control. It took every ounce of determination to keep going, keep in control, he could do it, he had to, he couldn't let his Dad down again, not again, somehow he would keep on. But every time the bolt-gun crashed through another cow's skull it took another chunk out of him, weakened him, consumed him in horror.

Jack was like a machine. The hard lines of his hard face were locked. Everything was battened down. Buried. He was cold steel. He wouldn't break. It had to be done and he was going to do it. No matter what. But he was starting to worry more and more about his son. There was a wild look in his eyes. Oh he was trying, giving it all he had, he could see that, but he was losing. Jack had seen it before, seen it in young men on the estates in Belfast, their first time under fire, frozen stiff with fear behind a two-foot garden wall. He didn't know how much more the boy would take. He tried to keep the fear at bay. He gave him small pats on the shoulder and muttered encouragement. "It's OK lad. Just keep going. Won't be long now."

And then the mobile phone in Will's pocket started to ring. They had just shoved yet another cow into the crush. *Bang*. The slaughter men started to attach the chains. Jack nodded. "Go on, you take the call. We're alright for a minute here."

Will walked away a few yards.

"Hello."

"Yo! Will my man! It's Ricky. We're back in business. I tell you what brother, I've just called in a tonne of favours for you."

The call had taken Will by surprise. He was disorientated. "Tonne of favours?"

"You bet. The stuff got delayed again. Can you believe it? Anyway I heard that it was heading into town an hour ago. It normally takes ages for them to sort it out and bag it off. So I called. Told them I needed a favour. Got them to give me a bit before it got taken away for processing. And they agreed. So, when you're ready my man, I'm ready."

Zippo hadn't been quite as amenable as Ricky made out. In fact he had given him a real mouthful and told him that there was absolutely no fucking chance. But then Ricky had told him it was for Will. He told him that Will was in a complete fucking state. Honest. And Zippo remembered Will. He remembered the young lad who had looked as if he was scared out of his wits when he had come to Barlinnie with Ricky all those years before. He had liked Will. He had been a good mate to Ricky. So OK. So just this once. Meet me and I'll give you a bit to keep him going. But don't dare make a habit of this. Don't think I'm getting fucking soft, cos

I'm not. And so he had met Ricky and quickly passed him a tenner bag. And Ricky had been able to call Will. And it made Ricky feel a bit better about the other night. He had done his bit. Gone out of the way for his mate. Because that was what mates did.

And so the heroin neared the end of a journey that had started many weeks earlier in the dusty mountains of Afghanistan. Of course there had been one or two hiccups, namely an Irish Sea storm, a jealous Loyalist psychopath and a blown head gasket. But in the end it had made it all the way to the outskirts of Dumfries. Another tenner bag. Delivery complete. Poppy to needle. Thank you for using our service. We hope you will travel with us again.

And yet the little tenner bag that Zippo passed out of the car window to Ricky wasn't the usual tenner bag. In was in fact very unusual. What made it so unusual was that due to the benevolence of both Taylor and Zippo it had missed two of its usual cuts. It was still 80 percent pure.

The news was too much for Will. Any of the resolve that he had been digging out from anywhere he could find was now gone. It was the appalling horror of the cull. It was the sad brown eyes, and the increasingly desperate sounds from the shed, and the awful growing heap of corpses, and the endless, agonising, gnawing need for heroin. He just couldn't take it. He couldn't. He was all done. No more. He wanted out and Ricky had the way out. All ready for him just ten minutes down the road. He had to go. Had to escape. No more need. No more death. No more killing. Go. Go. Go now.

"Usual car park. Ten minutes. I'm coming now."

He hit the end button on his phone and turned to his father who was looking at him questioningly. " Dad. I'm sorry. I mean . . . it's just . . . I can't . . . I just can't . . . no more. I can't take any more. No more. I just can't. You have to believe me. Sorry Dad. So sorry. I just can't . . ."

And then he was running. Running to the Land Rover. Nothing in the world would stop him. One day he would break it. He would. He really would. But not this day. He was too weak. Too broken. Too much death. The Ministry men shot out of the shed when he heard the ignition fire up.

"Hey! What the hell do you think you're doing? Stop. Stop now! You can't leave. It's illegal. You're quarantined! You can't leave the farm until I give you a licence . . ."

He stopped the shouting. He was only shouting at the back of a Land Rover that was speeding away down the track. He turned to Jack, raging, livid.

"This is outrageous Mr Sinclair. Surely he knows full well about the quarantine restrictions. I warn you that this is a very serious offence. There will be consequences I can assure you. We cannot afford this, this . . . this kind of gross irresponsibility if we are going to . . ."

"Oh for the love of God man will you shut up!"

"Now you listen here Mr Sinclair, I will not tolerate this kind of . . ."

"No you jumped up little pratt, you listen. You listen or I might just knock you into next week. Watching animals being slaughtered like this probably doesn't mean much to you. Why should it? They are just statistics for you to take back to your poxy little office and stick on your beloved graphs. For that boy it is different. He was there when most of these cows were born. He's fed them as calves and heifers. He's milked them and brought them in from the field and helped them have their first calves themselves. And now he is watching them being slaughtered. All of them. One by one. And put on a pile. And guess what? He can't deal with it because he is really not much more than a boy. And if you are such a beaurocratic insensitive bastard that you can't understand that, then I pity you, I really do. But I warn you, you better get right out of my face this very minute before I get properly mad!"

The Ministry man looked around edgily. A small group had gathered to watch. The soldiers, the slaughter men, a couple of the contractors. They stared hard at him, accusing, threatening. Their emotions were already rubbed raw by the grisly task they were undertaking. He swallowed, but his throat was dry. Better leave it. Report it to his superior later. He turned and walked to his car where he made a show of pulling papers out of his briefcase.

Will was flying with his foot down to the floor. The window was open and the rain was pouring in and soaking him. He didn't care. He didn't notice. Because all he knew was that he had escaped. He had left the horror and the killing far behind. With each mile he covered he was closer to his salvation, closer to that wonderful, magical, orgasmic, perfect moment when the needle hit the vein, and all the nightmares would go away. Closer and closer. He felt exultant. Joyous. So near now. Two more junctions. Now one. And there was the car park. And there was Ricky.

He screeched to a halt and threw open the door.

"Come on Ricky, get in."

"Well I was actually just going to . . ."

"Get in! Get in! IN! IN! IN!"

Ricky got in, and the Land Rover was moving before he had chance to shut the door. The sight of Will scared him. He was filthy dirty. His face was chalk-white but his eyes burned and blazed.

"Fuck's sake Ricky. Get on with it. Get it out. Get it ready. I need it Ricky. Christ you'll never know how much. We'll never be forgiven for what we've done. Can't you see? Never. No way. Not just a few. It was hundreds. Thousands. Millions. Oh God. Gun to the head; BANG. Gun to the head: BANG. Gun to the head; BANG. Come on Ricky don't fuck about. Get on with it. There's somewhere to park up there. Come on!"

"Will for Christ's sake calm down. And slow down. What's up man!" Will was beginning to frighten him now as he babbled on and on with spittle frothing out of his mouth.

"Slow down! What's up! Are you fucking kidding or what? You should have seen their eyes Ricky. Oh fuck you should have seen their eyes. They knew. They all knew. Knew what we were doing. They trusted us, all of them, trusted us. Oh no, we won't be forgiven. That it Ricky? Ready is it? Yeah? Yeah? Give it here." He swung the Land Rover into a gateway into a field. Ricky looked about anxiously. They were only about 50 yards from houses.

"No man. Don't be crazy. Not here, there's people everywhere. Let's get out a bit more."

But Will had already dragged his coat off and pulled up his sleeve and prepared a vein. "No. Here. Now. Give it. FUCKING GIVE IT!!"

He wrenched the needle off Ricky and pushed it into his arm. Within seconds the 80 percent pure heroin erupted into his system. His eyes rolled back into his head and the horrors were melted away. The spiders, the maggots, the big brown eyes, the vast piles of bodies, the sound of the bolt going through the skull, all away, all gone. Nothing to be frightened of any more. He closed his eyes and felt the wonderful, beautiful feeling seep all over his body and caress his soul. And he was drifting, drifting away on a warm summer's breeze, and the elevator shot to the top, and the doors opened, and outside were thousands and thousands of miles of gorgeous green fields filled with buttercups. And there were the skylarks darting in tight circles. And the grass was so soft, so warm, like the best bed that anyone had ever made, and he lay down, and at last he could rest his head, rest properly, because he was so tired, so very tired, and he needed to sleep on this perfect bed with daisies all around him, and the warm breeze slid over his cheeks like satin, and sleep was coming. Beautiful, perfect, endless sleep.

The uncut heroin was four times stronger than he had ever taken before. It was four hits in one go. And it was four hits in one go after four days of nothing. The drug erupted into his system like a SWAT team. It raced around the veins and arteries and caused total system overload. The messages to the brain were euphoric. Elsewhere the results were catastrophic. His body was too run-down and malnourished to have a chance of coping with the shock. His heart just stopped. And his life faded away.

It took less than two minutes.

Part Two
Cull

"August 1968. Kurtz staged Operation Archangel
with combined local forces. It was rated a major success.
He received no official clearance.
He just thought it up and did it. What balls.
They were going to nail his arse
to the floorboards until the Press got hold of it.
Then they had to promote him to full Colonel.
Oh man, the bullshit piled up so fast in Vietnam
you needed wings to stay above it."

Apocalypse Now

Chapter 4
Killing Fields

"Will! For fuck's sake Will come on! We can't just sit here, get it together man, let's go."

Ricky leant across and shook him, gently at first, then harder. "Come on. Wake up you bastard. Let's move it."

Will's head was tipped right back and his eyes were closed. There was a slight smile of contentment on his lips. Then Ricky noticed that his pale skin was taking on a slight blue tinge. And he started to get scared. Really scared. He shook him harder and slapped his face. Nothing. Pulse? He should take his pulse. How the fuck do you take a pulse? He tried sticking his thumb all over Will's limp wrist. Nothing. Was that because there was no pulse, or was it because he didn't know how to find it? He tried the neck. Nothing. Oh Christ what was he supposed to do? Will's face was getting bluer. He was so still. He couldn't be dead. No way. Not so quick. Unconscious. Had to be. Ring an ambulance. That was it.

He pulled his phone out of his pocket then hesitated. They always had a record of whose phone it was. No. He had a Pay-as You-Go phone. They couldn't track that. Or could they? Better play safe. He patted the pockets of Will's coat until he found his phone.

"Emergency Services . . ."

He confirmed that the phone belonged to William Sinclair. No it wasn't William Sinclair speaking. William Sinclair was unconscious. William Sinclair was turning blue. William Sinclair was dying. He described the Land Rover and gave the location. Then he started to get out. No, not yet. He grabbed a bit of rag out of the back and tried to wipe every surface that he may have touched. Will was really blue now. So still. So very still. Ricky couldn't bear to look at him. He's dead. He's fucking dead. Oh Christ. Oh shit. What had happened? He was really freaked now. He had to go. Quick. Before they arrived. Maybe he was just unconscious. Maybe there was a pulse there somewhere. Surely there had to be. People couldn't just die as quick as that. Could they? Oh fuck.

He darted over the gate and ran across the field. He made his way across two more fields and hid himself in a small cluster of trees a 150 yards away. The ambulance arrived five minutes later. He couldn't really see properly. The ambulance men were leaning through the door. Then they pulled Will out and put him on a stretcher. They were doing something. He couldn't tell. The body was twitching. He was alive! Thank God. Must have been some sort of electric shock to get the heart going. Thank God he'd called in time.

But now the body was still again. The ambulance men didn't seem to be in so much of a hurry now. Why not! Come on! He wanted to scream at them. Get the stretcher inside. Get him to hospital. But they didn't. One shook his head. Lit a cigarette. Leant on the gate. Shook his head again, shoulders slumped. The other got a blanket. He covered Will. Covered his head. Covered all of him. Oh Jesus no. No. No. No.

He started to breathe in short, shallow breaths as the realisation hit him. Dead. Will was dead. An overdose. His best friend was dead. The only real friend he had ever had. Gone. His fault. Ricky Macintosh's fault. Don't play with that Ricky Macintosh. He's a bad one that one. He's evil. He's poison. If you play with Ricky Macintosh you'll die. Your face will turn blue and you'll die.

There were tears now. He started to run. And he kept running through nettles and brambles, all withered and dead from the long months of winter. And he ran through big puddles in the wet fields and slipped in the muddy patches by the gates. And he ripped his jacket on barbed wire. And still he ran. Wet, covered in muck, soaked by the teeming rain.

After twenty minutes he stopped and gasped for air. Where was he? He looked about and found landmarks. He had to calm down.

He knew where he was. He was on the edge of town. Not far from home. He took deep breaths. He calmed himself and got a grip. He walked home.

His Mum was out. He ran to his bedroom and pulled off his filthy clothes and stuffed them in a carrier bag. He would throw them away later. He didn't want any questions from his Mum. He showered and got some clean stuff on. He smoked cigarette after cigarette then reached under the floorboard. He needed a hit. That would help. Get a hit and he would be calm. He prepared the needle with shaking hands and then fear hit him. What if he died too? What if the stuff was wrong? No. That didn't make sense. This was the old stuff. Different from the stuff Will had taken. But still. He stared at the needle for several minutes then pushed it back into the place under the floorboard. He would deal with it without smack.

He had to be together. They couldn't find out anything. He took himself back through what had happened. He had wiped everything. He had used Will's phone. They couldn't know. He was fine.

Or was he? There was something. What? Yes. That was it. Will's phone. They would check it. Last number received. His number. Fuck. But he could sort that. It was a Pay-as-You-Go phone. He would ditch it. Get another.

Zippo. He had to call Zippo. He had to tell him. They had a bad batch. Christ he had to tell him now before they sold any more. Christ they could be killing people right, left and centre. There would be bodies all over Dumfries.

"Yeah."

"Zippo, it's Ricky. We've got bad news Zippo. Really bad news."

"What?"

"It's Will. He took that bag you gave me and he's dead."

"What!! How do you know?"

"I was there man. With him. He was desperate. Like I told you. We got in the Land Rover and drove to a lay-by and he took it straight away. And then . . . he just went. Just like that. Turned blue. I didn't know if he was dead or just out cold. I called an ambulance and watched them. They tried to get him back but they couldn't. They put a blanket over him. Covered his face. He's gone Zippo. There must be something wrong with the batch. We can't sell any more man. We need to check it."

There was a long groan down the phone. "Oh fuck. FUCK. FUCK. FUCK."

"What? What is it?"

Zippo paused. "Look Ricky. There wasn't anything wrong with the smack. Well in a way there was. It was a rush job when I picked it up. They let me have it uncut. I was chuffed to bits. I can cut it twice you see. More profit. But I never got the chance you see. I hadn't touched it when I saw you. It had never been fucking cut at all. It was 80 percent pure."

"You're kidding."

"No. No I'm not. He just took 80 percent pure stuff. It must have been too much. Well it would have been. It was like four hits in one go. Shite. I never thought. Look Ricky we need to talk, soon, now. I'll pick you up. We have to be fucking careful here. I need to check you've covered your tracks. I'll pick you up outside the Spar in ten minutes. Be there."

"That means we killed him Zippo."

"Like fuck it does. He's dead because he was a fucking junkie. Every junkie knows the score. You use it, you take the risk. Simple as that. Now get your arse in gear. I want this wrapped up tighter than a duck's arse."

Roger Philips felt world weary. He felt that way most of the time these days. It hadn't always been the case. Once upon a time he had loved his job. Everything about it. He had wanted to be a copper for as long as he could remember. And being a copper was every bit as good as he had expected. Good mates. A job that was always interesting. Decent pay. Some moaned about the hours and the paperwork but not Roger. He did it because he loved it. And he was a bloody good copper too.

He had moved up quickly from the beat to CID. Maybe he had never been the brightest. Not like the lads they were fast-tracking from the universities. But he always made up for that. He could work harder than anyone. He was dogged. He was stubborn. And he knew his town. Sometimes it took him a while but he always got there in the end. And he always did it right. His procedure was always right. His paperwork was always right. When they took one of his cases to court there were never any loopholes. He nicked villains and they got sent down. Simple as that.

He got to Detective Inspector quickly and now he had a reputation. He nailed his cases down hard. No errors. No mistakes. He did the job properly.

He made a name for himself. He was a good copper. A really good copper. One of the best they had. He was the man to sort out the really tough cases and nine times out of ten he cracked them. The harder the case, the harder he worked. If it meant not going home he didn't go home. He hammered away until he got his result. Good copper, old Philips.

So two years ago they had moved him over to the Drugs Squad. A promotion. More money. The best place for him because this was where they really needed a result.

Dumfries was fast becoming a "heroin town". The stuff was taking off. And once it took root it was like cancer. The users needed at least £15 a day and they would do more or less anything to get it. Once any town became a "heroin town" a whole host of problems would follow as surely as night followed day. More shoplifting, more car crime, more break-ins, more hold-ups in small stores and post offices. Then there were the blazing domestics. Father knocks ten bells out of his junkie son who has been stealing from his pocket, junkie son smashes in his sister's face because she point-blank refuses to lend him another tenner. There were always so many little, nasty crimes that sprouted from the same dung heap. Heroin.

He had been delighted with the promotion. This was real police work. The best. Right there in the front line. He had seen what the growth of heroin users was doing to the town. They all had. Now he got the chance to stop it. This was something he could really get his teeth into. They believed that he was the right man for the problem and they were bloody well right.

He had thrown himself into it just like he had thrown himself to every bit of police work he had ever been given. But this time it was different. He soon found that the harder he threw himself at the brick wall, it just meant that it hurt more. He got more and more bruised, but the wall was always fine. All that he could do was prise out the occasional brick, and that would be replaced almost straight away.

The problem was that they were so damned well organised. All he could ever seem to do was lift the small-time guys. Intelligence would take for ever, and in the end they would pull a lad with slightly too much on him for his brief to be able to argue that it was for personal use. He would get them into court and then it would all come out. Deprived childhood. His Dad left the home when he was six. Never been able to get a job. He's a really nice lad at heart. Just bad influences. The court should consider carefully before they ruin this young man's future.

And nobody ever seemed to ask the real questions, like if this really nice lad at heart is so bloody deprived how the hell has he come up with the cash to pay for such a fancy lawyer? Oh no. Never that. The top guys paid for the best lawyers they could hire when any of their people were caught. The briefs did their job. Earned their money. After hours and hours of patient, careful police work, the little toe rags would be away with a few hours of community service or a suspended sentence or at worst three or four months inside.

It was no deterrent. None whatsoever. Not when the little bastards could earn the kind of money that was available. The courts were a joke. Bit of community service! So bloody what. That was hardly going to put them off. Not when they could earn £1,000 a week for doing next to bugger-all.

There was another problem. A massive one. The only way he could see that they could ever get close to someone at the top was to get one of the small-time lads to talk. If all they were facing was scrubbing graffiti off walls for a fortnight or so, they were pretty damned unlikely to do this. Even if he could threaten them with something worse, they still would never talk. They would never talk because there would never be anything that he would be able to threaten them with that would remotely compare with what Zippo would do when he got to them.

Philips knew everything about Zippo. He knew that if any dealer threatened to implicate him in any way he would hold that bloody lighter of his under their nostril and light it. It had become legend. There was no way anyone would ever risk it. Who in their right mind would?

Zippo. Eric bastard Macintosh. Zippo. How the hell had that big hard bastard from Sunnybank ever got this big? Roger had spent hours with his files. For 40 years he had just been another two-bit nuisance. Bit of a nutter, but no big deal. Attempted robberies, assault and battery, drunk and disorderly, nothing much, run of the mill, just another big bloody nuisance. Always make sure there are at least four of you when you go to lift him. But small time. Always small time.

Then, within a few months of coming out of Barlinnie, all of the sudden he had become "the man". And ever since the streets had been awash with heroin. Somehow he had made some unbelievable contacts in Bar L. Someone really big. Really sophisticated. Certainly not Wee Kenny or Tommy Banks or the King brothers. They were just the muscle. More or less psychotic, but muscle all the same. For two years Philips had lived and breathed Eric Zippo Macintosh. He had tried everything. And he had got absolutely nowhere.

When they raided the Sunnybank house there was nothing there. When they picked him up there was nothing on him. When they demanded where the hell he got the money for his fancy clothes and cars he could always pull out a bookies' slip. Got lucky didn't I, Mr Philips. Hell of a tip from this lad down the pub. Came in. £200 at sixteen to one. Lovely job. Look. Here's the slip. Go and check it if you like. And he had. Surprise, surprise. There it all was in the books. £3,200 paid out on a £200 stake at sixteen to one. Fat chance. Oh, Zippo would have given the £200 alright, but the bookie had never paid him a penny. He just put it through the books, reduced his tax bill.

Trying to catch Zippo was like getting hold of soap in a bath. It was beginning to get to him. At every meeting his colleagues pointed out how much crime was drugs-related. Heroin-related. How could they hope stop it? These addicts would do anything for their next fix. How are things going in the Drugs Squad? Are we any nearer to Zippo Macintosh? Why?

Why? Why? Why?

He knew the answer but he never told them. He had known the answer for eighteen months. They were no nearer Zippo than they had ever been because Zippo was too good for him. Whoever had taught him in Barlinnie had done a hell of a job. Zippo's operation was superb, real Premiership class. He ran things with an iron fist and everyone was absolutely shit-scared of him. There were no cracks. No chinks in the armour. All Roger could do was to work and work and work some more. He would make sure that he knew everything there was to know, and then one day when the big hard bastard at last made a mistake, he would be there waiting.

In the meantime he was weary. Weary as hell. He looked at his watch. Ten to one. Sod it. He pushed the pile of papers to one side and pulled on his jacket. He needed some air. A stroll and a sandwich. Clear the head a bit. As he was making his way to the front door of the station the desk sergeant called over to him.

"DI Philips. Hang on a sec. I think this is one for you."

He crossed over to the desk. "What is it?"

"Hospital sir. A and E. They've just had a Dead on Arrival. Looks like he OD'd. They found the needle on the floor of the car. Well, Land Rover actually. Parked in a gate out by the Glasgow Road. Someone used his mobile to call it in."

Another. Another victim. Another young life. Would it ever stop?

"Do they know who it is?"

"Yeah. He had a wallet on him. Sinclair. William Frederick Sinclair of Hillside Farm . . ."

"Oh no. Oh Jesus, surely not."

"You know him Sir?"

"Yes. Yes I know him. It's Jack Sinclair's lad. They both play at my Golf Club. Will. A good lad. Oh Christ, I don't believe it."

"Do you want to handle it sir?"

Are you kidding! He wanted to scream. Do you think I want to be the one to go and tell Jack that his only son is dead on the slab! He didn't of course. He just muttered. "Aye. Aye I better had. Better someone Jack knows. I'll go to the infirmary. Keep it tight for an hour or two. Best he hears it from me."

Heroin. Always heroin. The cancer. And Zippo fucking Macintosh was probably laughing his socks off.

How many now? Jack had lost count. It shouldn't have been that hard. It wasn't as if they were killing them at breakneck speed. It was steady, mechanical. He couldn't really face trying to judge from the pile of corpses. It seemed enormous now. Almost unbearable to look at. He judged from the cows left in the shed. It wasn't easy as they were moving around now. Agitated. Uneasy. Sniffing the air. Frightened. He reckoned there must have been about 60 left in there. It seemed like they had been at it for ever and yet there were still sixty left. Then there were the calves and the heifers and the bulls and then the sheep. Christ it was hard.

He decided which cow was to be next. Number 63. He was about to go in to guide her out when the sergeant called over to him.

"Mr Sinclair. Someone here to see you."

Jack made his way out of the shed. The sergeant spoke. "There's a bit of bother I'm afraid sir. It's a copper. My private stopped him down the track and told him that nobody was allowed in. He insisted. Said he had to talk to you. We didn't really know what to do. Well, it seemed important so I gave him some wellies and a suit and decided to let him in. I'm afraid the Ministry man is playing holy fuck. Sorry about all of this."

"It's all right. I'll sort it."

He saw them by the main gate. He recognised Roger Philips looking awkward and ill at ease in the white overalls. The Ministry man was agitated and was flapping his arms about. As Jack drew closer he could hear him.

" . . . I don't care how urgent it is and I don't care if you are a policeman, the rules are very specific. Nobody, and I mean nobody, comes onto an infected farm. Can't you see what is happening here? There's a cull going on for Christ's sake. Now I ask you again. Will you please leave immediately before I am forced to take further measures."

"Afternoon Roger" said Jack.

The Ministry man spun around. "Please stay out of this Mr Sinclair. I am dealing with the situation."

Jack completely ignored him and spoke again to Philips. "Sorry about all this Roger. As you can see, it's not a very good time."

Philips was appalled. He had been dreading this task, but now it was even worse. He had no idea that there was a cull in progress at Hillside Farm. The horror of the situation had become apparent when the soldier had stopped him halfway up the track. Across the yard he could see the corpses of the cows in front of the silage pit. Jesus what a sight. And Jack looked terrible too. What a bloody nightmare.

"Need a word Jack. Could we walk over there. Somewhere quiet."

"Sure."

Again the Ministry man intervened. " I'm afraid that you are not going to be walking over anywhere. This situation is becoming intolerable. There are rules and it is my job so see that they are enforced. Now I insist this man leaves the premises immediately."

Jack turned on him angrily. "Look sunshine, I'm starting to get a little bit tired of you. If Roger says it's important, it's important. So I suggest you get yourself out of my face in about ten seconds flat. OK?"

Jack stood six inches taller than the man and he frightened him. He began to speak again then thought better of it. It was outrageous. He had a job to do. Again he looked over to the sergeant for support, but he saw there would be no help there. Bloody soldiers. They come in throwing their weight about and wouldn't lift a finger. For the second time that day he stormed off to his car.

Jack and Philips walked over to the far corner of the yard and stared out over the fields. Philips pulled out his cigarettes and lit one.

"Give me one of those could you Roger."

"Didn't know you used them."

"I don't. Well didn't. All of this you know. Just seem to have started again."

Philips took a deep breath. It was always the worst job in the world. They all hated it. But it had never been this bad before.

"Brace yourself Jack. I have terrible news."

The words were like ice cold water down Jack's spine. "Jesus Roger. What is it?"

"It's Will. He's dead Jack."

Jack's knees gave and he almost fell over. He should have guessed. Why hadn't he guessed? He should have seen it in the man's face. Should have known. Known because he'd done the same job himself. In the Army. But it couldn't be true. Will had barely been gone. What time was it now? Two. Maybe half past.

He had been here at eleven.

"Can't be. He was here all morning. Can't be."

"I'm afraid there's no doubt Jack. I saw him myself."

"How. The Land Rover? A crash?"

Oh why oh why did he have to tell him. Why did he have to tell anyone.

"No. Sorry Jack. It was an overdose."

"A what!!"

"An overdose. Heroin."

Jack went very, very still. Heroin. Had he said heroin? He had. And this was real. He wasn't about to wake up in his cold bare bedroom. It was here. It was now. And he had said heroin. Dead. Overdose. Surely not here. Surely not Will. That was something on the TV. A news item. A *Panorama* documentary. Not here. But it was here. It had been the same with the parents he had told. Shot whilst on patrol. A nice morning. The flowers in the small gardens showing the first colours of spring. The sound of morning radio in the kitchens. A couple of dogs chasing each other around the place. And then the sound of a shot and a another young lad from some small town would have lost half his face. And those parents must have thought that it was just for the TV too. Not their boy. No way. He didn't join the Army to get his head blown in half on an estate in Belfast. He wanted to learn to ski. He wanted to see the jungle. Not this.

And now it was him. He stared ahead blankly. So much was sinking in so fast. This had been why. This explained everything. No wonder the lad had been in such a state. And he could help now. But he couldn't. There was no chance ever to help again. He was gone. Gone.

He screwed his eyes shut and fought for control. Massive waves of despair were starting to crash over him. He was losing it. It was too much. He tried to drag himself back. Had to. He forced himself to focus on Philips who was now talking to him.

" . . . I can't tell you how sorry I am Jack. I really don't know what to do here. Normally I would ask you to come and officially identify the body, but with all this, I don't know, I suppose you could come later. I don't know."

"I'll come. I'll come now."

"Really Jack, you don't have to. I can sort something out."

"It's OK Roger. I'll come. Give me a minute to change please." He looked over to where the sergeant was watching them. "Got a minute Sarge?"

The soldier came over to where they were standing. Jack forced himself to stand straight. Dragged himself back into control. Shoulders back. Chest out. Breathe Jack. Come on man, breathe. Better. Show some bottle. Be an officer. At last control was coming. It was a habit as old and well worn as the rocky crags above the Top Farm.

"Yes sir?"

"I've had bad news Sarge. The worst. My son Will. He's dead."

"Oh Christ sir, I'm so sorry."

"Thanks Sarge. I have to go now. Have to identify the body. Don't know when I'll be back. Will you watch things for me?"

"Of course sir. Just leave it. We'll make sure everything here is as it should be."

"Thanks. Appreciate it."

He walked to the house. Back straight. Good. And breathe, Jack, breathe. You've been here before. Never this bad, sure, but you've been here. So deal with it. He allowed a coldness to come into him. He couldn't face being open. If he allowed his emotions to take over he would come apart. And that wasn't going to happen. It had never happened before. It wasn't going to happen now. Cold. Mechanical. A machine.

Be the machine Jack. Clear the brain of any thought it doesn't need. No fear. No memories. No day dreams. The top window of number 32. Did that curtain move? Stop the patrol, hand signal, down boys, alert boys, nothing else matters but the window of number 32. Did the curtain move? Sniper? No, there she is. Cleaning the window sill. Get them back up. Move the patrol on. Get the mind wiped clear. Feel for the danger. Be cold. Be a machine.

He was mechanical as he changed. Trousers. Shirt. Tie. Jacket. Wallet? In pocket. Handkerchief? No. Get one. Shoes clean? Not really. Quick wipe. Mirror. Not bad. Hair a state, but it always was. His eyes had died. No sparkle. No laughter. Just cold. Bleak. Empty. A machine.

He went back into the yard. The Ministry man was back out of his car, arguing again. Arguing with Roger Philips. Arguing with the sergeant. He saw Jack. Saw he was changed. No more Wellington boots. No more white overalls.

" . . . Mr Sinclair, I cannot tell you how sorry I am to hear of your tragic news. Terrible. Truly terrible. Particularly at a time like this. But I am afraid that it doesn't change the rules. You are simply not allowed to leave the farm. There is a quarantine in place. I really must insist Mr Sinclair."

Jack looked at the man calmly. "Please move out of the way. I am going to see my son."

"Mr Sinclair, even in these circumstances I still . . ."

"I said please move out of the way. I am going to see my son."

"I'm afraid I can't do that, I . . ."

He never saw the punch. It came without warning. Hard and brutal into his stomach. It knocked the wind clean out of him. He fell to the ground in a kind of slow motion. Jack stepped round him and walked away. "Roger, I am going to your car."

He made his way down the track to where Philips had left his car. Back straight Jack. March. Show them nothing. Give them nothing. You know they are all watching. Behind the curtains, in the gardens, coming down the pavement with their shopping, watching. Always watching your every move. Watching and hating. Watching for a weakness. Any weakness. Doesn't matter how small. They would sense it and log it away until Saturday night down the club and a few rum-and-blacks. Hey, a word. Just a quiet word. We've noticed something. Its about that new officer on the estate. The big one. A Jock. Blond hair. Well . . . and they would pass the weakness on to the men who would know what to do about it. So he wouldn't show one. Not a glimmer. Not a crack. Stand tall. March Jack. March. Give them nothing.

The Ministry man was trying to get up from the wet muddy floor. He suddenly vomited. All down his front. All over the white suit. He tried to speak. His eyes fixed on Philips.

"You . . . you saw that . . . you're a policeman for Christ's sake. Arrest him. Do it man! Assault. I'll have him for this."

It was the sergeant who spoke as he helped pull the man to his feet. "Now then sir why don't you calm down a bit. No damage done. Amazing how a fall like that can wind you a bit. Lucky you've got your suit on isn't it. We can soon change that can't we? Plenty more where that came from. New suit. Nice cup of hot tea. You'll be as good as new. Come along now sir."

He started to guide the man toward the house by his arm. The Ministry man wrenched his arm free and spun round.

"Fall! That was no fall! You saw it damn you. Both of you. He hit me. It was assault!"

The sergeant shook his head, looking confused. "Assault? No. Never saw anything like that. Strange how a fall can leave you disorientated isn't it? That and the pressure. Lots of pressure with this job sir. It can wear you down. Get you confused. No. All I saw was a fall. Isn't that right Mr Philips?" Philips nodded after a moment's hesitation. "There you go sir, you ARE confused. And I'm certain that my private there will have seen you fall too, especially after I've had a little word with him. So that's three of us. And there are only three of us here. Just a fall. So best we don't have any nonsense. Let's get you inside. Nice cup of tea and a fresh suit and then we'll get on. Lots still to do here."

There were tears of pain and frustration in the man's eyes now. But there was nothing he could do. These were the type of men he had never met before. They were laughing at him. Making him small. But what could he do? Three against one. Two soldiers and a police officer. Everyone would believe them. He was helpless. He turned and went through the back door.

The sergeant nodded to Philips. "Thanks sir. I think Mr Sinclair has enough on his plate don't you? I'll sort this officious little twat out. Don't worry. There will be no more come of it. You get yourself off."

Philips headed away and the sergeant lit a cigarette and looked thoughtfully down the track to where the policeman's car was parked. He had seen the way Sinclair had put the man down and just walked away. Tall. Unbroken. What a fucking show. Something to tell the lads in the pub. Jack Sinclair. The man who took down Liam Kelly. What a fucking show.

Jack was already in the passenger seat when Philips got in. He was sitting very still. Staring out through the raindrops on the windscreen.

"Don't worry about that business Jack. It's covered. The

sergeant sorted it all out. You won't hear any more."

"What did he do?"

"Told the little bastard that he fell. Told him that we all saw him fall. I certainly saw him fall."

"Thanks Roger. Appreciated. What happens now?"

"We go to the hospital. You identify the body. There are a few formalities. Not many. That's it really. Best to just get it done."

"Yes. Let's get it done."

The next couple of hours were strange. He was fully detached now. He had almost stepped out of his body. The whole world had a kind of dreamlike quality. He felt as if he wasn't really there. It was as if he was watching the whole thing on the TV. The drive to town. Parking up. The corridors of the hospital. The quiet room. The sheet being pulled back. And yes it was Will. No doubt. No doubt at all. That was Will. His only son. Laid out with his eyes closed and a faint smile playing on his lips. He was so intact. This wasn't one of the boys from the patrol with half his face missing or a gaping hole in his stomach. He was perfectly intact. So very still. That slight smile. And gone. Gone far, far away, never to return.

Jack was in complete control now. Every step. Every gesture. Every movement. Philips found it almost frightening. The man was like a machine. He worked through what he had to do. Filled in the forms. Signed where he had to sign. Barely spoke. Like a machine.

When they were finished at the hospital Jack asked to be dropped in town near his solicitor's office. Before he got out of the car he turned in his seat and laid a hand on Philip's arm.

"Thanks Roger. Really. I know what it's like. Done it myself. Northern Ireland. Shit job isn't it?"

"The worst."

"I need to sort things out now. Official things. I'm not going back to the farm. Not for a while. They don't need me there. I'll find a hotel. Leave it until it's over. I want to know about this, Roger. As much as you can tell me. I need to know. Will you meet me tomorrow night? Tell me over a few pints. I need it."

"Sure Jack. I'll do that. Call me. I'll pick you up."

For the next few hours the dream continued. His solicitor saw him straight away and agreed to take control of all the details. The funeral office next. Time and place. Would there be a post mortem?

Probably. Fine. They would liaise with the hospital. Burial or cremation? Burial. Next to his Grandad. They would arrange the day and the time as soon as the hospital could release the body.

Back to the solicitors. Jack explained that he wouldn't be going back to the farm. Not until after the cull. Not until they had killed everything and the fire had burnt down. He would stay away till then. He needed to use a phone. He had some calls he needed to make.

The solicitor quite understood. He lent him an office for as long as he needed it. The first call was the worst. Angela. She went berserk. She was screaming and swearing. Why had she ever left the boy him? How could it have happened? Let him run wild didn't you? Let him take heroin and you never even noticed did you? You bastard. You killed him you bastard. It was you, you bastard. Jack gritted his teeth and took it. He wasn't willing to consider what she was saying. He couldn't afford to. Not yet. Not now. He had enough little voices in his own head saying the same thing.

Your fault Jack. Let him have his head didn't you? You didn't look hard enough. You thought it was just a phase. You didn't try hard enough. If you had tried he would be alive now. He would be fine. The same old smiling Will. But you didn't. You just felt sorry for yourself and left him be. And now he's dead. Dead, dead, dead, and you killed him Jack. You. You, you, YOU.

He screwed his eyes shut and drove the voices away. Breathe Jack, breathe. And it was no longer Angela on the other end of the line. It was her father. The Colonel. "Jack. Jack are you there?"

"Yes sir. I'm here."

"So sorry Jack. So very sorry. Don't listen to her. She's just distraught. You know how it is. Shock. Best if you speak to me from now on. About the arrangements and things. OK?"

"That's fine sir."

"Better go Jack. I better see to Angela. Bye."

He left the office and did some shopping. He tried to focus on simple tasks. Washing gear. Go to *Boots*. Shaving cream, razor, toothbrush, paste, bag to keep it all in. He bought spare underwear and socks and two shirts. He bought a litre bottle of scotch and checked into a bed-and-breakfast.

How long would he be staying? Oh, a few days probably. Well that's fine. No problem with rooms at the moment, February is always quiet, but what with all this Foot and Mouth, and all the terrible pictures of them burning the animals, well, well who would want to come and visit Dumfries at the moment?

And then at last he was in his room. It was quite small and completely ghastly. Orange nylon sheets and a cheap framed print of Victorian children playing with a dog. Four walls of his very own private Hell. Hell for £14 a night, and breakfast from eight till nine. He put his washing gear by the sink, hung up the shirts, put the socks and underwear in the bedside drawer. He hung his jacket on the back of the door. He took a glass and filled it with scotch and took a big swig. Through the window the grey skies were breaking up with the arrival of the evening. Out on the hills he could see four columns of black smoke drifting upwards.

The night ahead seemed as if it would last for ever. And when the night was at last over there would be tomorrow. And then there was the rest of his life. He kicked the thought away. One hour at a time. Each game as it comes.

Get drunk. Find oblivion. Pretend there is no tomorrow.

Chapter 5
Jack's Spider

Bob Bennet picked up the news of Will's death when he made his regular afternoon call to the police station. At first it was the overdose part of the report that registered with him. So many of the nasty, nitty-gritty bits of local news seemed to revolve around drugs. There was no doubt that it was getting worse. When he had joined the paper, drugs were very much a rarity in the area. Not so now. They had become endemic, particularly heroin, the town's drug of choice.

Yet another sickening statistic. Another family thrown into turmoil. Another young life tossed away.

Then the name registered. Sinclair. William Sinclair, nineteen, of Hillside Farm. Christ, that was Jack's lad. The same lad who had been courting Mandy. Oh no.

He checked his watch. Nearly four. Mandy was due back any minute with her story. He began to brace himself. He was pretty sure that the relationship had been over for a while but it would still hit her hard. His mind started coming up with reasons why it really wasn't his job to break the news. When all was said and done she wasn't family. Maybe he could just leave it. Let her find out somewhere else. But that wouldn't be fair. And anyway, he could hardly ignore it. It was news. Not unique. Not earth-shattering. But things had not yet gone that far down the pan that a young lad dying of a heroin overdose wasn't news.

She came bounding into his office a few minutes later clutching her first Foot and Mouth story. Why was it always like this? It seemed that every time she burst through his office door brimful of enthusiasm it was his task to smack her down.

"Here you are Bob. On time as promised. I think I got everything. I got a quick interview with the Minister and I had a quick word with the senior army officer in the bunker and then I met a few people at the end of the track at two of the farms where . . ."

His expression pulled her up short. "What is it Bob? Are you feeling OK?"

He shook his head. "You better sit down Mandy."

She sat slowly. "Oh God. What is it Bob?"

"I just heard from the police. The daily report. I'm afraid there is some rather awful news. It's your friend,. Will Sinclair. He died of a heroin overdose this morning."

Time stood still for a moment and then she seemed to totally collapse. It was as if all the bones in her body turned to soft clay. Her limbs seemed to melt. Instantly the tears started. Completely desperate tears. She made no effort to control or contain herself, she just let the instant appalling grief pour out.

A couple of faces appeared at the window in his office door. Bennet shook his head and waved them away. He got up and walked around his desk to crouch down in front of her. He laid a hand on her shoulder and she collapsed into him, clinging on as if he were a life-raft in the midst of mountainous grey waves.

He felt awkward as she clung to him as the great sobs racked her body. He could feel the moisture of her tears on his cheek. She pushed her head into his shoulder as hard as she could. It was awful. What could he do?

In the end he eased her away and spoke gently. "It's OK Mandy. It will be OK. Let me get you a cup of tea. Here. Here's a hanky. Here."

He felt utterly useless. He had no experience in anything like this. He hopelessly went through the motions of making tea and eventually handed her a cup. She was coming round a little now. She put the cup down on the desk and started wiping the tears away.

"I spoke to him last night. First time in ages. He had been so horrible to me and I couldn't stand it any more and I told him to go away and I never wanted to see him again. And then when I called last night to speak to Jack he answered the phone and we talked for hours and he told me. He told me all about it Bob. About his addiction and the heroin and how he felt so bad about the way he had behaved and how he was really going to try. And I said I would be there for him and I would help him and now he's gone and I can never help him again and I really loved him you know, I really did, but it's too late now, he's gone, really gone . . . "

The sobs once again took over.

"I don't know what to say Mandy. I don't know what to do. Can I run you somewhere? Take you home?"

"No. No thank you Bob. I'll . . . I don't know . . . I'll just . . . I'll just go now. If that's all right. Here's my story. I'll go. I better go and see Jack. Oh God, poor Jack. That poor, poor man. I must go and see him. I'll be in in the morning. Sorry Bob. I have to go."

And then she was gone. He felt ashamed of himself and empty and drained. What else could he have done? He picked up her story out of habit and started reading. It barely needed editing at all. It was the best thing she had ever done. Poor Mandy.

She had to sit at the wheel of the car for a few moments until she trusted herself to drive. When she did at last get going she was unusually slow. The tears poured down her cheeks and she didn't bother to wipe them. It took her 25 minutes to get to Hillside farm instead of the normal fifteen. She was stopped halfway up the track by a soldier who had been sitting in a Land Rover.

As Mandy pulled up he got out and walked around to the driver's door. A soldier. What was happening? She wound down the window. He bent so that he could speak to her face-to-face.

"Sorry Miss. I'm afraid you won't be able to come any further. There's a cull in progress. Only required personnel allowed." He noticed her tear-stained cheeks and red-raw eyes. "Are you OK Miss?"

"Yes . . . Well no, actually . . . But yes. Fine. I must see Jack. Something terrible has happened. It's Will. Will's dead. I must see Jack."

"I'm afraid Mr Sinclair isn't here. He had to go with the policeman. To the hospital. I don't think he's coming back Miss. We heard he would be staying in town. Don't blame him. Better away from here. From all this."

"Oh. Oh I see. Well thank you. He didn't say where he was going at all?"

"Sorry Miss. No idea. Maybe the policeman would know. Philips he was called. Seemed like they knew each other. Like they were friends. Are you quite sure you're all right Miss?"

She wiped her face again. "Yes honestly, I'll be OK. It's a terrible shock. He . . . I mean Will . . . he was my boyfriend. Used to be. Must go. You've been really helpful. Thanks again."

She quickly reversed down the track before the tears got hold of her again. At the bottom she had to sit for nearly quarter of an hour before she was sufficiently composed to drive. How could she have forgotten about the cull? How awful. How unimaginably awful. So much death. Poor Jack. She had to find him. She headed for the police station.

Philips was about to leave when the front desk buzzed him to tell him he had a visitor. He remembered Mandy. He had seen her with Will a time or two at the Golf Club. And then she had interviewed him twice in a professional capacity. Nice kid. One look at her told him that she was taking it badly. Really badly.

He took her into a small interview room.

"I'm so sorry Mandy. I really am."

"I know. Everyone is sorry. But it doesn't mean he isn't gone. Oh God, I'm finding it so hard to deal with."

Unlike Bennet, the policeman was all too used to these situations. He knew what to do. He had learned from long and miserable practice. He was calm, slightly detached.

"What can I do for you Mandy?"

"It's Jack. I feel I must see Jack. They told me he has left the farm. Staying in the town they said. Do you know where he is?"

"I'm afraid I don't Mandy. But I will be seeing him tomorrow. I will tell him that you want to see him. If you give me a number I will pass it on."

She scribbled on a scrap of paper. "Here. It's my mobile. Tell him any time. Doesn't matter how late."

"Fine. I'll make sure I do that for you. Now I think it best if you got yourself home. Can I drive you?"

"No. Thank you. I'm OK. I'll go now. Thanks for your help." She was rising to her feet when her face seemed to change and harden. For a moment the desperate grief was replaced by a kind of cold rage. "One name Mr Philips. One name. Macintosh. Ricky Macintosh. He's the little shit who did this. Make sure you get him."

Ricky at that very minute was sitting in his Uncle's living-room in the house on Sunnybank. Zippo had gone over what had happened time and time again. Ricky felt himself sweating. He felt as if he were on trial. All the time Wee Kenny sat in a corner flicking through the pages of one of his bird-watching books. At last Zippo felt happier. Ricky certainly wasn't himself. But fuck it, who would be, he'd just watched his best mate die in the seat next to him.

"OK Ricky. Enough. We're OK. Nothing to lead them here. You did well. Wiping the Land Rover clean was good thinking. It's done. Tommy and the King boys are cutting the gear now. We'll be ready to roll again in the morning. I'll call you then. You can make the pick-from Tommy. Got the cash now?"

"Yeah." Ricky counted out the payment for his next batch of heroin. He would have to be together tomorrow. Lots of calls to make. Lots of desperate people. And by tomorrow the word would be all over the streets about Will. There would be questions asked. Lots of questions. People would be scared.

"What do I tell people? They'll be nervous."

"Tell them he hadn't had any for ages. Say he'd been clean for weeks. Must have been the shock. Tell them he must have had a weak heart. Hell, what the fuck does it matter anyway, nobody's going to say no are they? No one is likely to say actually this has given me second thoughts about the whole thing. They're junkies and we're the only people in town with the gear. If they start to get lippy just tell them to fuck right off and get it somewhere else. That'll soon shut them up. Tossers."

"Yeah. Suppose so."

Zippo was slightly worried about Ricky. "Look lad, I know this must be hard for you. He was a mate and all that. If you don't feel up to it for a while I could sort something out. You could get away if you like. Somewhere hot for a couple of weeks. Get pissed up. Do a bit of shagging. Cheer yourself up. I'll sort something out. Your mobile will still work in Spain. Mine did. Take the orders over the phone and ring them in to me. I'll fix up someone else to make the drops."

Spain. Sunshine. It sounded good. Really good. And why the hell not? He could afford it. It was what he needed. Get clear away from Dumfries for a while. Get the whole thing out of his head. When he came back it would all have blown over.

"I'll do that Zippo. Definitely. Get away for a while. Get my head right. I'll go tomorrow."

And so he went. In the end he stayed for a month. He got a tan and his acne dried up and went away. Heroin was no problem to find and he cruised along on two bags a day. He bought designer clothes and threw his money around. In fact, he had the time of his life. Thoughts of Will soon left his mind. Luck of the draw. Wasn't his fault. If he hadn't got the stuff from Ricky he would have got it somewhere else. And he never knew it was 80 percent pure. Course he fucking didn't. He wouldn't have let him do it if he had known. And it wasn't Zippo's fault either. Zippo was just trying to do a favour. Zippo couldn't think of everything. He was a busy man. He had a business to run.

When Roger Philips knocked on his door two days later he was already on the beach halfway through the fifth bottle of San Miguel that day. His mother answered the door. It was three in the afternoon and she was still in her bed clothes. She stared out with eyes dulled from years of valium.

"Who the fuck are you?"

"DI Philips. I would like to speak to Ricky."

"Well you fucking can't. Not here is he?"

"Will he be back?"

"How should I know. Doesn't tell me anything does he? He's gone. Gone away. Gone to Spain. Go there if you want to find him."

The ash from the cigarette between her lips suddenly became dislodged and fell onto her dressing gown. She flapped at it angrily and the gown came open. One of her breasts came dislodged from the loose nightie underneath. She pushed it back in.

"Keep your fucking eyes to yourself you."

Philips took a deep breath. The woman was somewhere in cloud cuckoo land. Maybe it was worth a try.

"Maybe you could let me take a quick look at his room?"

This made her cackle. A harsh, dry sound. "You fucking kidding? What do you think I am? Fucking stupid or something. Go on. Fuck off and get a warrant. I've had enough of this."

She slammed the door in his face. Same old story. Another brick wall. He knew he had about as much chance of getting a warrant as banana trees growing on Sunnybank estate. He would track the lad down when he got back from Spain. And then it would be the same story all over again. The lad would be arrogant and cocky and he would say nothing. Philips knew all about Ricky Macintosh. He had a file on him. He was one of the main pushers in the town. But knowing was one thing. Catching the little shit was quite another.

For Jack the hours drifted by without definition. He had no idea when he fell asleep that night. When he awoke a grey dawn had broken. He was still in his shirt and trousers. The whisky bottle was nearly empty. For the second time in three days he lurched to the toilet to vomit. He collapsed back onto the bed. His head was thumping without mercy. He forced himself up and tried to ignore the dizziness and nausea. He managed to make a cup of tea and gulped it down. Then another.

His mind felt like a filthy sponge and his body felt weak all over. The thought of doing anything at all made him feel exhausted. He took a shower, but it did little good. He switched on the TV and watched the silly smiling faces as they skipped jauntily through the morning news.

Somehow he found his way through the day. He had thought that there would be a huge amount to do. There had to be. But there wasn't really. He collected the Land Rover from the police, having filled in a few forms. There was another hour with the funeral director where he gave a list of people to be sent details. They also agreed to handle the announcement in the papers. Then nothing.

The lethargy was still strong. For a while he considered going back to the B&B and trying to sleep but he couldn't face the room. The prospect of simply burying himself in a pub and getting blind drunk again appealed, but he wanted as clear a head as possible when he met Philips later on.

And so he walked.

Mile after mile, going nowhere in particular. He walked until the muscles in his legs were sore.

All the time his mind was empty. There seemed no topic he could bear to think about. His whole world had completely collapsed in a matter of hours. Wherever he looked there was only pain. Instead he concentrated on the simplicity of walking. He walked quickly, eating up mile after mile, not allowing himself to stop. After several hours he was almost surprised to find himself in Castle Douglas and he realised that he had walked twenty miles. It was a little after six. The afternoon had melted away.

He called Philips and arranged to be picked up and then he found a Spar shop and wolfed down four sandwiches as hunger finally hit him. When Philips collected him from the main car park they drove a few miles and found a quiet pub devoid of customers. They took their pints to a small table in a corner. Philips offered a cigarette and Jack took it. It was good. Really good. He dug in his pocket for change and went to buy some from the machine.

"I don't know what you want Jack. I'll help of course. But you must understand I can't tell you anything detailed."

"I know Roger. I just can't understand. Can't believe it. I mean I'm not completely naïve. I knew we had drugs here in Dumfries, it's just . . . well I thought . . ."

"You thought that it was just on the estates. Just the down-and-outs and the unemployed. Yeah?"

Jack took a sip of beer and nodded. "I suppose so."

"You're not on your own. Most people think the same. The fact is that heroin is Dumfries's best-kept secret. Not surprising really. We keep trying to find ways to attract more tourists. Having one of the worst heroin problems per head of population in Scotland is hardly going to bring in the coach parties.

"So to cover it up we comfort ourselves with stereotypes. We tell ourselves that it is just a few kids. The ones from the estates who had always been in bother and never did any good in school and were always bound to slide down the slippery slope into addiction. Well it's bullshit Jack. We reckon that there are over a thousand addicts here in Dumfries. There are young people, middle-aged people, unemployed, professionals, mothers, businessmen, the whole spectrum."

"You're joking. How could people do their jobs?"

"Without much difficulty. Being on heroin isn't like being pissed. You are still quite lucid, quite able to undertake all your usual tasks. In fact, so long as you have a fairly decent quality supply and you are sensible about how you go about taking it, there is little reason why you can't take heroin all your life and die of old age."

Jack was astounded. "I can't buy that. So why do so many people get so fucked up?"

"Money basically. A normal heroin habit will cost you anywhere between £10 and £30 a day. Now if you are a solicitor, finding £150 a week after all your other expenses is by no means impossible. You can get your stuff, get decent clean needles, and you can just chug along. You hit problems when you either can't afford it or you can't get it. People by and large are absolutely fine to go along with their daily lives as long as they have had their fix. The shit hits the fan when they miss it for a day or two. That is where the bad symptoms kick in.

"So what happens? Performance at work falls off, maybe they lose their job, maybe they buy cheaper stuff, maybe they can't get decent needles, maybe they get arrested for stealing to try and finance the habit, all sorts. There are lots of different types of addict. By and large those who can afford it manage their lives OK. Those who can't fall into the pit."

Jack got up and bought another round. He was wary with his next question.

"What about Will. Did you know?"

"No. Course not. We are completely under-resourced. To be honest we spend no time at all worrying about users. It's the dealers that we focus on. As far as we know there was no way that Will was a dealer."

"How could it have happened? How could he have started?"

"On Christ Jack, that is some question. I wouldn't usually answer it at all. Not my job. I'm just a copper, not a sociologist. But I'll take a stab. A big reason among kids is basically that it's a game of dare. You know the kind of thing. Go on, don't be so soft, are you scared, all that lot. Peer pressure. Try it or you can't be in the gang. Only with heroin it is rather more evil.

"As I said before, Smack is expensive. Once you have a £15-a-day habit the cash takes a bit of finding, especially if you are 15 or 16. Stealing is always the first route. Family first, then shops. But you soon learn a better way. If you can persuade three or four other kids to start using, then you can more or less finance your own habit by selling them their stuff. So the game of dare has a big ulterior motive. Lots of these kids are actively looking for new customers for themselves."

Jack shook his head. "Jesus, it's like pyramid selling."

"Exactly like pyramid selling. However, knowing Will I doubt if that was the reason he got started. He was a big lad, knew how to look after himself, somehow I couldn't see anyone taking the piss out of him. I would guess he took the Ecstasy route."

"The Ecstasy route?"

"Did he go off at weekends? Raves, all-nighters?"

"Yes. Yes he did."

"Then almost certainly he would have been taking Ecstasy. They all do. It is a party drug that puts you on a huge high for hours on end. It has become a culture. Thousands of kids at a rave dance all night and they are all flying on Ecstasy. It is a fairly new drug and nobody really knows yet whether it does a great deal of harm. If there is harm it seems as it will be a long-term damage rather than short-term. There is certainly a stack of it being used. When the customs boys intercept a shipment there are literally hundreds and thousands of pills.

"The main problem with ecstasy is that it sends you so high that it is really hard to get back down again. Now that isn't the end of the world if you don't have anything to do the next day, but if you have a job to go to, you need to find something to help you come back down. This is where lots of kids start using heroin. I know, it is hard to believe they could be so stupid, that is what every parent can't understand. Why on earth would they start taking the most addictive drug on the planet to come down off a drug that is barely addictive at all?"

Jack nodded. "Sure. Exactly my thoughts."

Philips drained his glass. "It's a selling job Jack. This is where the dealer can secure another long-term customer. A simple lie. Basically they say that smoking heroin or 'chasing the dragon' is cool. They say that all the bad stuff that you hear about is when you start injecting or 'jacking up'. In a way they are right. You are unlikely to do yourself much physical damage smoking the stuff. But it still gets you hooked. And it doesn't take very long to do that."

"So why start jacking-up?"

"Money. Once you have a habit it is really hard to feed it by smoking. Too much is lost. Basically it is a very inefficient way of getting smack into the system. People soon find that they are having to spend more and more to get enough of a hit. And that is where the ever-helpful dealer comes in again. He is their friend, their adviser, he can see that they are struggling, and so he helps them. Inject it, he tells them. It costs lots less and the high is so much higher. And once he gets them to do it he has them just where he has always wanted them. Another intravenous drug user. An almost guaranteed customer for life. I would guess that was how it was for Will."

This time Philips got up to get more drinks. Jack felt almost shell-shocked. It was a world he had barely realised had existed. He had been blindly milking his cows and feeding his sheep whilst his son had been sucked into this world. In hindsight the pieces of the jig-saw were falling into place. Money must have been a nightmare for the boy. They had both agreed to take token salaries until their big gamble showed any signs of coming off. They both had been taking a wage of £100 a week which he had always figured would have been plenty. After all, the boy had no mortgage, no rates, no heating bill, no groceries to pay for. £100 a week was for clothes and going out. Not a fortune, but surely enough.

Not enough for a £15-a-day habit. Not nearly enough. He remembered how Mandy had caught him stealing from her bag. He remembered the days when he was convinced he should have had more cash in his pocket than he did. The days when the boy had been such a nightmare to live with must have been the days when he couldn't find the money to buy his drugs.

Philips sat back down. Jack knew what his next question had to be. No doubt Philips did too. "So why the overdose? Was it poisoned heroin?"

"Probably quite the opposite. Tell me, how was Will over the few days before the overdose. How was his behaviour?"

"He was a nightmare. Angry, touchy, bad-tempered, even violent."

"That figures. There has been a big shortage over the last week. Not just here, there have been several other towns in Scotland the same. We have no idea why. There must have been some kind of supply glitch. He must have been getting more and more desperate. What happens when there is a delay is that things get rushed when the stuff at last arrives. It's understandable. Everyone is under pressure. All the users are in the same state as Will was. They give their dealers ear-ache and it gets passed all the way up the chain. This sometimes means that the heroin isn't cut properly."

"Cut?"

"Yes, cut. Every way down the line the drug is cut. They use all sorts. Icing sugar is a favourite. Obviously the more you cut it, the more money you can make. By the time it gets to street level it is usually only about 20 percent pure. So that is what people are accustomed to. Now if there is a rush job on, and somewhere along the line someone doesn't get the chance to make their usual cut, you suddenly get 40 percent pure stuff arriving. Now if the user takes the usual dose, and remember they have probably been without for a few days, in reality this is a double dose. This can be such a massive shock to the system that everything just closes down. So as you see, it isn't that the drug is bad, it is just too good. And there is absolutely no way the user knows what he is taking. I could very well be wrong about this Jack, but I doubt it. Will's autopsy will show the presence of unusually pure heroin in the system."

Once again Jack was rocked. "Poor bastards. Basically they're playing Russian Roulette every time they take it."

"That's about it. It looks like white powder and there is more or less no way of telling. You just take it and hope for the best. Your life is literally in the hands of your supplier."

"Jesus."

Both men were silent for a few moments. At last Jack looked up. "And the suppliers. Who are they?"

"It's big business Jack. One of the biggest businesses on the planet. Illegal drugs now make up close on ten percent of world trade. There are hardly any commodities that even come close – grain, oil, not much else. Drugs will be far and away the biggest business in our little town. The boys at the top of the chain will be earning way more than any of the solicitors or doctors or businessmen. Think about it. A thousand users is a very conservative estimate. Let's say they average £15 a day each, that's fifteen grand a day, 450 grand an month, five and a half million a year. Serious, serious money, and as I said these are very conservative figures."

"Christ. Who is making it? Lots of little dealers?"

"Nope. Just the one. One guy controls this town and he pushes the stuff down through his network. Nobody else dares come near him. He's a proper grade 'A' nutter you see and he surrounds himself with more of the same. Anyone who dares come near his turf is punished. These are very, very violent men."

"So if you know all this why the hell do you let it go on?"

Philips laughed sarcastically. "Come on Jack, don't be so bloody naïve. You were in Ireland weren't you, when you were in the army?"

"Yes."

"So tell me. What happened when you started a tour? You got briefed. Yes? By the Military Intelligence and the RUC, yes?"

"Yes, they did."

"And they told you the names and addresses of all the players in your sector, yes?"

"Mostly. Pretty much all of them."

"So Jack, why did it go on? How come you lads didn't just take them out? Hell, you knew who they were."

"You know full well why not. It was the bloody law. The bloody politicians. We were fighting with our hands tied behind our backs. Hell, if we could have taken the gloves off we would have finished the business in three months flat."

"There you go. You said the magic word. The law. We are in just the same position here as you boys were in the Province. Hell, it's even worse for us. If you managed to make a collar when one of those lads was involved in a shooting or planting a bomb or something you had him by the short and curlies. He knew full well that he was heading straight for a ten-year stretch in Long Kesh prison. No 'ifs'. No 'buts'. No telling the judge that it was his first time and he deserved lenient treatment. They went down and they went down hard. Full stop.

"That meant that you at least had a bit of leverage. If you could get them to spill the beans on their comrades they would get off, get a new identity, get spirited out of the country. And budget was never a problem. The Government threw money at it. If it cost a quarter of a million to give a Supergrass a new ID, then who gave a shit. It was small change.

"Even then, you only managed to turn about one in five because they were all so shit-scared about what would happen if the Boyos ever caught up with them.

"Now try comparing that with what I have to work with. We're undermanned as hell, so it takes all of our resources to mount a surveillance operation on any of the dealers. If we get lucky we catch him. But they never carry much. Just enough to make two drops at the most. The days of them hanging around on the street and trying to sell to passers-by are long gone. The buyers place their orders to a mobile phone – Pay-as-You-Go and untraceable – and the dealer will only ever carry enough for two customers.

"So let's say we nick him in the act. I get him back to the station. Now straight away he knows two things. One, his boss will hire the best lawyer money can buy, and two, even if he does go down, it will only ever be for three or four months at the most. So how the hell can I persuade him to spill the beans about the others in the network? I've got no budget to give him a new identity. Basically Jack I have absolutely fuck-all chance. And if by some miracle one of them did turn into a grass, he would face punishment every bit as bad as that faced by the touts you guys turned.

"I tell you Jack, these are really, really violent individuals. Anyone who crosses them gets absolutely filled in. Everyone knows this. Nobody crosses them. And why the hell would they? What would you do? Community service or a couple of months inside or risk major bodily harm?"

Jack again shook his head. "Amazing. It's just Ireland all over again. So long as they are tight-knit and well enough organised and they have the ability to scare the living shit out of the community where they live, then they are more or less fireproof. It must eat you up."

"Oh yes. Every bastard day of my life. God alone knows how we will ever stop it, certainly not so long as we are always the ones working with both hands tied behind our backs. It is wrecking morale you know. Over two-thirds of the crime we have to deal with is drug-related. We see it every day, but we have just about no hope of ever stopping it. It makes me sick. Really sick."

Again they were quiet for a while. Philips glanced at his watch. It was just after nine. "I'll have to be moving Jack. Sheila will kill me. I'll drop you back in town shall I?"

"Thanks. That would be good."

"By the way. There was a girl looking for you at the station yesterday. She was in a bit of a state. Mandy. Will's girl. She gave me a mobile number. Asked me to pass it on. Said to ring any time."

"Oh Christ, Mandy. I should have called her. Just give me a sec will you?"

He dialled her number and spoke very briefly. "Sorry I never called Mandy. I can't speak right now. I'm with someone. But I will call back. I promise." Jack folded the piece of paper and put it in his breast pocket. They were mainly silent on the journey back to Dumfries. As they approached the outskirts of the town Philips spoke. "I really don't know what to say Jack. You can see that the whole drugs business is more or less out of control. I hope you can understand a bit how Will got involved. Don't eat yourself up about it. I promise you, you're not on your own. There are hundreds and thousands of parents like you out there. I know it is tempting to blame it on yourself. You shouldn't. Even if you had known, there probably wouldn't have been anything you could have done. Try and forget it if you can. All of it. Remember Will as he was before all this. Anything else will just eat you up. Life will go on. It always does."

"I'll try. It seems impossible at the moment, but you're right I suppose. It has helped though. Really. At least I know now. At least I have some idea."

Philips dropped him off by the river. It was a fairly fine night and he had little wish to go back to his room. He found a bench and sat down. He pulled his phone out of his pocket and rang Mandy.

"Hello." Her voice sounded dull. Flat.

"Hello Mandy, it's Jack."

"Oh thank God you called. How are you? I tried to see you at the farm, but, well, well you know."

"I know. I'm OK I suppose."

"Can I come and see you Jack?"

"Yes. Yes of course, but maybe not for a day or two. I'm not very good company right now. I have to find a way of dealing with this. Best on my own for a while."

She sounded disappointed. "Of course. Whatever you think is best. We talked you know, talked for ages, the night before he . . ." She couldn't finish the sentence.

"Yes I know. I heard you. I kept popping into the kitchen and then leaving again. I'm glad you did."

"Will told me everything Jack. And he was going to tell you. He was waiting until after the cull. Then he was going to talk to you, to ask for your help, he was desperate to kick it Jack, he really was. You must know that. You must know how much he loved you and how bad he felt about everything that had happened."

Jack felt a choking sensation. He forced it back. "Why didn't he come sooner? I wouldn't have cared. Why didn't he know that?"

"He was ashamed Jack. You were his hero. He could never bear letting you down. He felt as if he had betrayed you. He couldn't stand it. What I don't know is how he came to take stuff that morning. He told me why he had been in such a state, there was a shortage, no heroin to be had anywhere. He had been off it long enough to see what it was doing to him. Where the hell did he find it?"

"He got a call. In the morning. He got a call and he was gone. It must have been his dealer, ringing to tell him that he had stuff again. He may have thought he could do without the night before. But it must have been different in the morning. He wasn't good Mandy. Christ, he was trying, really trying, but the cull was destroying him little by little. I'm not surprised. It was destroying me. When the phone rang and he had to leave I kind of figured that it must have been you. I was glad to see him go. I don't think he could have taken much more."

"It wasn't me. It must have been Ricky."

"Ricky?"

"Oh yes, it would have been Ricky all right. I just know that he was the little bastard that got Will into it. I just know it."

Jack was shocked by this. "You're joking. He hadn't seen Ricky in ages."

"That's what he would have wanted you to think. He saw Ricky all the time. Of course he did. Ricky was his dealer. I never realised it at the time but I can see it now."

"Surely not, Mandy. I know that Ricky was always a bit of a handful, but he was a good enough lad at heart. He used to stay up at the farm for weeks at a time when he was younger. Ricky a drug dealer? No. No, I can't believe that."

Mandy sighed in exasperation. "When was the last time you saw Ricky, Jack?"

"God, I don't know. Ages ago."

"Well the loveable little rascal is long gone. You should see him now. Flash designer clothes, sporty car, bimbo on the arm all decked out in gold, thinks he's some kind of pop star."

For Jack it was almost the last straw. Ricky. The cheeky lad who everyone had warned him against. "Just a quiet word Mr Sinclair, we are a little worried about the kind of company Will is keeping, one boy in particular, Ricky Macintosh, Will would be better staying clear of him. He's trouble that one".

And Jack had hated them for it. The casual way that they branded the lad just because they had given up trying to find ways to get through to him. There had been lots of Rickys in the Army. Little tough guys who joined up because nobody else would have them. But the Army knew what to do with them. It had worked it out over hundreds of years. Hard discipline was part of it of course. But a much bigger part was showing them how to be part of a team, giving them a real family that they could trust and rely on, taking them in so they were no longer outcasts.

And it had worked. He had seen it time and again. And these lads usually went on to make great soldiers. He had been convinced that Ricky was just the same. He was damned if he was going to listen to warnings from teachers who had absolutely no right to write boys off. And this was how it had turned out. All those voices had been right all along. Ricky Macintosh is bad news, they had said. Really bad news. The very worst kind of news. He had killed his son. Jack had welcomed him in and opened up the doors of his home for him. And in turn Ricky had turned Will into a junkie and now he was dead.

"Jack. Jack are you still there?"

"Yes I am. Sorry Mandy. Just lost in thought, that's all. I think I'll have to go now. I will see you at the funeral I suppose."

"I'll be there."

"Bye Mandy."

"Bye."

Hearing about Ricky was more than he could stand. He had fought back his emotions for a day and a half. Now he had nothing left to fight with. Everywhere he looked there was only despair. The tears came. They came slowly at first and then faster and harder. He let them come. He sat for many hours that cold night on the bench by the river and the tears came and came and came.

When at last they stopped he knew that he wouldn't cry again.

Grief was about to harden into rage.

It rained for the funeral. A stinging, cold February rain. The mourners huddled under umbrellas and shivered. It was a fine turn-out. Well over a hundred. But Jack was alone. His only family were the two uncles from the hills and they were hardly close. There were friends and acquaintances from school and golf and rugby. There were a few neighbouring farmers, but not many. Most didn't dare venture away from their farms in case they were to bring back the dreaded virus. There had been a disinfectant mat at the gates of the cemetery and all the vehicles had their wheels sprayed.

And there was Angela. Angela with the Colonel and Hammerton-Smith. Both men were resplendent in their full dress uniforms. When they had arrived the Colonel had spoken with Jack and gone over details for the day. Angela had refused to come near. Hammerton-Smith had nodded curtly.

The church service was over. Now all that was left was to lay the body into the ground in the little graveyard in the hills. The cars were parked and the mourners followed the coffin. When they reached the grave-side Jack was alone. All day people had been nervous around him. They were embarrassed. They didn't know what to say. If Will had died in a car accident it would have been different. They would still have found it hard, but they would have known what to do. But he hadn't died in a car accident. He had died from a massive overdose of heroin. The autopsy had shown the heroin in his system had been a staggering

80 percent pure. He had never stood a chance. They estimated that death would have been more or less instantaneous.

That was why everyone was keeping their distance. They had all known his son in different ways. Some as a farmer, some as a useful golfer, some as a tireless wing forward. They had known the laughing Will, the handsome Will, the happy-go-lucky Will. And now they had to come to terms with the fact that the very same Will had been a junkie. He had lived as a junkie and he had died as a junkie. It was inconceivable. He wasn't some delinquent kid from the estates, he was one of them, and he had been a junkie.

So they stayed clear. Jack got small nods and quick condolences with eyes averted. He had sat alone in the church and now he was alone at the grave-side. A tall figure, stiff as a board. The rain teemed down, but he wore no hat and carried no umbrella. He was immune to it. His hair was plastered to his skull, making his hard face look almost demonic. Nobody saw any flicker of expression cross his face all through that day. He was like stone. Like ice. A machine. They kept their distance.

And then as the vicar was talking, Jack felt a small touch at his side. It was Mandy. She pushed her hand through the crook of his arm and stood with him. Faces turned to look at them. A strange couple. He so very tall and straight. She so much smaller, so much younger. Yet like him she was hatless and cared nothing about the rain. She had seen how they stayed clear of Jack. She had seen the unmasked hatred in his ex-wife's eyes. She had seen how alone he was. And so she went to stand with him. The hell with them. All of them.

When it was all over, they had a small reception in the Cairndale Hotel. Jack gritted his teeth and fought his way through the polite condolences. He tried to ignore the looks, the murmured conversations, the shaking of heads. It would pass. Just another couple of hours and it would pass.

Then Angela was there. She came from nowhere. Immediately Jack saw that she had been drinking. Hammerton-Smith was vainly trying to hold her back but she was having none of it. She half-dragged him across the room to where Jack was standing.

Once she arrived she tossed a full glass of whisky into his face.

"You bastard Jack. Look at you. No expression. No remorse. You're just a fucking machine. How could you have done it? How could you have not known? You didn't care did you? He was just cheap labour for your beloved farm wasn't he . . ."

Hammerton-Smith was becoming desperate. "Angela please. This really isn't the time. Please. Let's go now."

She thrust him away. "Get your hands off me! I don't care whether it is the time or not. My son is dead! Dead damn it! Do you think I give a shit about what people think!"

This time she hit Jack. The punch smacked into his face and the watching audience gasped. He never moved. Not a muscle. Not a flicker. She hit him again. And again. Harder each time. Still nothing. He was like a statue. Nothing. He just stared back with empty eyes. Hammerton-Smith again tried to pull her back but again she pulled herself free. She was ready to strike again when Mandy was between her and Jack. Mandy slapped her hard across the face. Very hard. Hard enough to freeze her in shock.

Mandy's voice was low and venomous. "How dare you? How dare you come back here with your accusations? You left them. You tried to take Will with you but he hated being with you. So he came back to his father. And his father loved him. And I loved him. So don't you dare come with your accusations. You weren't there for him. We were. Now go away."

The slap had knocked all the anger out of Angela. She suddenly felt sober and terribly embarrassed. Everyone was looking. Her cheek stung and it made her want to cry. She had to get away. Her father was with her now. He took her arm firmly. He looked to Jack. "Sorry Jack. Very sorry. We'd best go I think."

Jack gave a small nod. There was complete silence in the room as the Colonel and his daughter and Charles Hammerton-Smith made their exit. Finally Jack cleared his throat and spoke. He only spoke quietly. There was no need to raise his voice.

"I think, ladies and gentlemen, that this is probably an appropriate time to wind things up. I would like to thank you all for coming, and I can only apologise if you have been embarrassed. You must understand that it is a difficult time for all of us."

He turned and left the room. Mandy followed him. Everyone else stared on in disbelief. William Sinclair's funeral was to be a talking point for quite a few days.

Once they were outside on the pavement Jack turned to Mandy.

"Thanks for that. You have been as good a friend to me as you were to Will. We will sit down soon. Talk. I promise. Maybe up at the farm. Once it's all over and they've all gone. But I need to be alone now. I'll see you soon."

She watched him walk away and wondered where he was going. It was past five now. Too late for any more work. She didn't feel like it anyway. Tomorrow it would be time to start over and get stuck back into the Foot and Mouth story. The disease was raging all around the town now. The Bunker had become frenzied, and it seemed there were Army vehicles everywhere. Columns of smoke rose up all around the skyline. A bath and a good long night's sleep she decided. And then back into the fray. What else was there to do?

Jack walked again. The funeral had been so bad that it defied belief. There was no way that burying his only son could ever have been anything but bad, but the way everything had turned out had been a lingering nightmare. Where he should have been filled with grief and able to bid his final farewell to Will, he had instead been consumed by a growing rage. What right had they all to sit in judgement? He didn't care if they wanted to judge him. That made no odds. But he had sensed them judging Will. Will had let the side down. They didn't want to hear about heroin. They didn't want to know that it could encroach beyond the estates and into their lives. In their memories he had already become the one who was a junkie. The one who hung around with that boy from Sunnybank. The one who crossed the tracks to play.

Bastards.

He didn't even want to think about Angela. If the scene made her feel better, then so be it. She was really gone now. He knew he would never see her again in his life and he was glad. Hammerton-Smith was welcome to her.

There was nothing to do but walk. Will was buried now. The formalities were complete. Nothing else to take care of. He had spoken to the sergeant up at the farm earlier in the day, and things were more or less complete up there as well.

Everything was dead. Only the two dogs were left. The sergeant had been feeding them. All the corpses were now on the pyre and it was alight. It would probably burn for three days. A new man from the Ministry had been given the farm. He would need to talk to Jack at some stage about the clean-up job. No hurry. Whenever he was ready.

This time he walked south. He took the road that ran through New Abbey and out to the coast. After an hour or so he came to the entrance to Mabie Forest. Mabie Forest comprised hundreds of acres of pine trees blanketed over several low hills. It was criss-crossed by a network of footpaths and it was a popular walking spot for the people of Dumfries. The gates were closed now, and a sign said that they would be so for the duration of the crisis. Jack ignored the sign and vaulted the gate.

It was very dark now and the rain was still pouring down. He had to walk slowly, feeling his way in the dark. He came to the car park and managed to find the place where the trails started. It was difficult work to find his way. No stars. No moon. Simply staying on the path took all his concentration. After a while he had climbed high and there was a bench looking down onto the Nith valley and the town of Dumfries. The rain had stopped now, and there were some jagged breaks in the cloud. He sat for a while staring down on the orange street lamps clustered below.

He later described this as his spider moment.

At the time he had no such realisation. There were no thoughts of Robert the Bruce hiding in his cave in Annandale weighed down by his futility. History tells us that this was the moment of maximum despair for the old Scottish king. Like Jack that night, he was no doubt freezing cold and soaking wet. Like Jack, he had nowhere to go. His life had come to its darkest moment. What seemed like the end of the line. And then he started to watch the efforts of an eager spider spinning its web. If that little creature can show so much determination, then why not me, he had thought. And so it was that he pulled himself together and the rest, of course, is history. Nice story. Maybe it's true. Maybe not. It doesn't matter much either way. It is folklore now.

Jack was certainly pretty well at rock-bottom that evening as he stared out into the void. He was aimless. Not really thinking about anything. His thoughts were gently rolling around his brain in much the same way as shopping that has spilled out of a carrier bag on the floor of the car boot.

Then, for absolutely no reason, thoughts began to click together. Foot and Mouth disease. A virus. A virus that was spreading at dangerous speed. A virus that had to be stopped quickly before they lost the chance to bring it under control. And how could it be stopped? By killing. Killing every animal in its path so that there would be no live bodies to provide it with a road to travel down.

Find the disease. Recognise the disease. Destroy the disease by the use of maximum force.

Heroin was a disease. Like Foot and Mouth, it had come into the area invisibly, undetectable in tiny polythene bags. And it too was spreading out of control. How do you stop a disease that is in danger of getting out of control? Maximum force.

Maximum force. Doing what was necessary. If it meant the culling policy then so be it. If it meant culling millions of animals in brutal conditions, then so be it. They had taken off the gloves. It was happening live on prime time TV.

Take off the gloves. Untie the hands. Let slip the dogs of war.

He thought about Philips. A good man. A man who was desperate to stamp out the disease. But he couldn't. He couldn't because the law that he was trained and paid to uphold wouldn't let him. The law had tied his hands behind his back and the carriers of the disease just laughed at him.

Carriers. That was all they were. They weren't supermen. They weren't anything special. They were simply men who had the knack of violence who knew there was no way they would ever be caught because they could hide behind the law. How many were there? Not many probably. If the whole lot of them were to come up against a company of his men from The Guards in a fire fight the whole thing would be over in seconds. Without the law to protect them these men were nothing. The only way they could make their operation work was the absolute certainty that the law would look after them, give them an open field to play on, to keep them from harm.

This took his mind back to Ireland. Philips had been so right. He had completed three tours in the Province. Twice their sectors had been urban, once they had been on the border. Each time they had been fully briefed on their arrival. Names, addresses, photos.

They knew almost all the main players. What they were. Who they were. Where they were. What they never knew was what they were going to do next and where they were going to do it. The whole operation was about trying to catch them in the act. And while they waited, they patrolled.

Hour after hour. Day after day. Weaving up and down the streets of the bleak estates. Presenting a daily target to the snipers. Trying to provoke some action. Sacrificing the occasional dead soldier to flush out a player, get him in the open, shoot him down as long as he had shot first.

He remembered watching an old black and white French movie about the Battle for Algiers in the early sixties. The terrorists had got so out of hand that the Paris Government had sent in their Paratroops and allowed them to take the gloves off. What they did was so very simple. They mirrored the behaviour of the terrorists. They too became monsters. They pulled in the guys at the bottom of the chain and tortured them until they found out who was next up the ladder. Then they pulled him and did the same. Mechanically they worked their way to the top, leaving pools of blood on the concrete as they went. It only took a couple of months and all the leaders were away.

With the law to protect them the terrorists had grown stronger every day no matter what security measures the government took. Without the law they were history in weeks. They had often discussed the film in the barracks. What would happen if Whitehall let them do the same job in the Province? Opinions were split. Some felt it was the ideal solution. Clear out the men of violence from both sides, then look to negotiate a sensible peace with the those who were left. If they could rip away the threat of violence the communities would have the chance of sorting things out.

Others disagreed. All they would do would be to create martyrs. There would be a short lull, and then there would be another generation come through, because in the end the people by and large supported the men of violence, be they orange or green. The exercise would achieve much the same results as mowing brambles and nettles. They would only come back the next year thicker and stronger than ever. Just like they had in Algiers. The French had been kicked out two years later.

But it wasn't always the case. The only way brambles would come back was if they had a breeding ground. Sometimes when you got rid of them other, better plants would quickly take root and leave no room for the brambles to return. Brambles could only come back if the field wanted them. So when tyrants and dictators were overthrown they were gone for good. Once their violent grip was prised open they had no way back. They were gone. Gone for good.

The logic fascinated him.

There was no way back for a new Hitler or a new Mussolini because the people were fed up with them. They didn't want them any more. But take away the top command structure of the Belfast Brigade of the IRA and it would be replaced within months because, to the people of Ballymurphy and Andytown and Turf Lodge, these men were their heroes, their protectors.

So what about these people and their tight heroin network? Surely they were ultimately vulnerable. They had absolutely no popular support at all. If they were to be taken down, nobody would shed a tear. And would they be replaced? That would depend on the public. For as soon as they were gone the public would be empowered. Would they use this power? Would they stamp on each new nettle before it got the chance to grow more than an inch tall?

Maybe. Maybe they would. It would depend on how things were done.

He was sitting up now. His mind had started to race. He could suddenly see with crystal clarity that the men who had been responsible for the death of his son were vulnerable. Really vulnerable. He also realised that he had the skill to exploit it. The British taxpayers had spent thousands and thousands of pounds to train him. He had done his three stints in the Province. He could do it. He could plan and he could execute. He knew about real violence. The murderous, professional violence of a trained soldier, not like their violence, the bully-in-the-playground violence, small-time violence.

Oh yes. He could take them. No rules of engagement. No boundaries. No guidelines to adhere to. He could take them.

Only an hour before, all there had been before him was a gaping void. His future had offered nothing more than a million acres of emptiness and despair. No matter how hard he tried he could not find a way to face it.

Now it was different. Now the future was bright. Now he knew with complete certainty what he was going to do. He was going to take the bastards down. He was going to take them down so hard that they wouldn't get up for a very long time.

Already he knew exactly what he was going to do. Now there was merely the matter of how he was going to do it. Two images jumped into his head. First was a picture of French Paras dragging a man out of a door in a dusty North African alley. Second was the face of Ricky Macintosh. He had a place to start. That was all he needed.

And then another image came and he suddenly thought he knew much more about how it could be done. It was a face. A face with a slight, almost mocking smile where there should have been terror there.

The face belonged to Liam Kelly.

Chapter 6
Liam

I many ways the Liam Kelly affair represented the high point of Jack's life. The Regiment had headed back to the Province in 1989 for Jack's third tour. This time they were given the sprawling estates of Turf Lodge and Ballymurphy as their sector. Jack had been promoted to Major the year before, and so for the first time he was heavily involved in all the intelligence briefings. There was a unanimity about the main task the Regiment faced: to apprehend Liam Kelly.

Kelly was very much the IRA's rising star. According to their records, he had been recruited as a teenager. Not surprising really. Two dramatic events had pushed Liam into the arms of the Provisionals. When he was thirteen the UDA had gunned his father down outside their front door. Then, when he was fifteen, soldiers from the Queen's Lancashire Regiment had smashed down the very same door and ripped their house to pieces as part of one of their Sweeps. His mother had tried to intervene, only to be thrown to the floor. The fall had been heavy enough to rupture her spleen and her health had never really recovered.

Liam was never destined to be one of the really hard men. He was a quiet boy at school. He worked hard in his lessons and kept himself to himself at break time. There had been one occasion when he had been bullied by Jimmy Nelson. It only happened once. That night somebody had rung the local Army hotline giving his name as Jimmy Nelson. The caller had said that he had

155

information for them. A Saracen had pulled up outside the Nelson house that evening, and the soldiers couldn't understand why the boy knew nothing about anything. Later that night all the windows were put through and someone spray-painted "Fucking Tout Bastard" on the wall. It took Nelson a while to prove that he really had known nothing about it. He had no idea how this terrible thing could have happened until Liam had a quiet word in the playground. Stay away from me Jimmy. Stay away or it will be worse next time.

His chemistry teacher had picked out talent for the Organisation for years. Liam stood out. A quiet boy, but bright. Really bright. The teacher had seen Jimmy Nelson beat up Liam in the lunch hour. He had seen the Saracen arrive at the Nelson house. He put two and two together. He kept it to himself, but started to keep young Liam back after lessons. He would talk around the subject of the Troubles carefully, watching the boy's every move. He saw the hatred blaze in Liam's eyes when he mentioned the Brits. He took him in. Made the introductions.

The Belfast Brigade were smart enough to realise that Liam was worth far more than mere cannon-fodder. They nurtured him carefully, making sure that he finished school and went on to university. When he finished his studies he got a job with a bank. To the world he was the same old quiet Liam. However, behind the façade he was being groomed, nurtured, prepared.

In 1980 he informed the bank that an uncle who had emigrated to Canada years before had finally died and left him a little something. He requested a year's sabbatical to go and see a bit of the world. They gave it to him. In fact he only saw one bit of the world: a training camp in Libya. He had stayed there for a gruelling nine months and he had graduated with honours. When he returned to Belfast he had acquired expertise in weapons handling and explosives. Much more importantly, he had spent many hours under the tutelage of Major Reinhart Hoffman of the East German Stasi.

Hoffman was a class act. One of the best in his field. Getting one-to-one tuition in the arts of terrorism from Reinhart Hoffman was much akin to having Seve Ballasteros work on your eight-iron approach shots. The German saw real potential in Liam and he worked hard with him. He taught him many skills. There were techniques in the gathering of intelligence. New methods of putting a terrorist organisation into tight, self-sufficient cells. All the various disciplines required to successfully plan and stage terrorist operations. Finally, and most crucially, he learnt the art of interrogation.

The Chief of the Belfast Brigade was presented a full report from Hoffman and he was suitably impressed. Liam was soon rising through the ranks. When he planned an operation it seldom went wrong. He always did the groundwork. Always covered all eventualities. Always chose the right men for the task and trained them carefully in every detail.

By the mid-eighties he was heavily involved in modernising the command structures of the Brigade. It was the era of the Supergrass and the Brigade was in danger of falling apart. The Brits were trying everything from SAS hit squads to paid bounty hunters. Morale was collapsing. Paranoia was setting in. Liam helped tighten things back up. They needed to look at every one of their active soldiers. Nobody was to be trusted any more. Liam did the interrogations. Liam built the dossiers. Liam rooted out the bad apples. The command council was delighted with the effectiveness of Liam's interrogations. More often than not he didn't need to resort to physical torture. Hoffman had taught him how to torture the mind and the soul.

This gave the Brigade a new tactic. They started lifting known members of the UDA and handing them over to Liam. After a few days he would bleed them dry. Soon the intelligence that he collected was turned into several superbly successful operations. Morale started to pick up. Liam was fast becoming a star. He was promoted again, this time getting a command role. His patch included Ballymurphy and Turf Lodge. Soon the British Regiments given the job of patrolling these estates started to suffer. Four sodiers were killed in a matter of months. The Army, Military Intelligence, MI5 and the RUC all gave the area top priority.

Intelligence reports kept coming back with the same name. Liam Kelly. Liam Kelly of number 32, Marlborough Rd. Liam Kelly, an under manager at the Royal Ulster Bank. Liam Kelly who was 33 and was married with two young kids. Liam Kelly who was five foot seven, weighed just over ten stone, and had light sandy hair. Liam Kelly who wore John Lennon spectacles, dressed in a grey *Marks and Spencers* suit every day, and caught a bus to work with his sandwiches and a copy of the *Guardian*. Liam Kelly who didn't look like he would harm a fly.

They tried everything. They raided his house. They tapped his phone. They mounted surveillance. They even put up a £100,000 bounty for information leading to his conviction.

And they got nowhere. The man was as slippery as an eel. He danced around them. He mocked them. And soldiers kept dying on patrol in Turf Lodge and Ballymurphy.

Jack lost a man on patrol during the second week of the tour. It was a sucker punch. Stupid. Utterly stupid. They had briefed and briefed and briefed again. Beware of anything that is unusual. Absolutely anything. Anything out of place means danger. Anything that isn't how it should be means danger.

It had been a purse.

An ordinary, common-or-garden ladies purse. It was lying in the gutter, dropped by accident by someone hurrying to get their shopping out of the rain. It was the kind of thing that should have set alarm bells ringing. But no matter how many times the men were briefed, it didn't mean that patrolling would ever be anything more than mind-numbingly boring.

Private Walter Haslam had been bored. He was only eighteen and he was cold and bored. The grinding routine of Belfast was already getting to him. He had been going through the motions. Stop. Crouch. Check 360 degrees. Let the men behind you move ahead. Check again. Move. Find cover. Crouch. Check 360 degrees. He was doing all of this. But his mind was elsewhere. He was thinking about the girl who was waiting for him back in Stirling. He was thinking about what they would do together when he got home for his next leave. He was miles away. So when he saw the purse he never thought twice. He just picked it up. The purse was lying a foot up from a drain. A piece of cotton ran from the purse and through the grid of the drain to an explosive device. As soon as he lifted the purse the cotton triggered the device and Private Walter Haslam never did get to do all the things he had day-dreamed about with the girl waiting in Stirling.

Immediately the doors had flown open and the women and their children were there, wildly cheering. From being empty and deserted it was suddenly a carnival. Jack secured their position and gritted his teeth in the face of the gleeful taunts. A Saracen arrived and the medics picked up what was left of Private Haslam and took him away.

Jack was seething. Enraged. Two weeks. Two bloody weeks and he had lost a man. After all the training. Christ how could they have fallen for such an obvious sucker punch? Stupid. Stupid. Stupid.

Haslam's death made it personal for Jack. The purse bomb was classic Kelly. Simple and deadly. No danger to his side. No risk of losses. If the soldiers had spotted the purse and defused it, then so what? What would have been lost? A few grammes of Semtex. But if they fell for it, well then it was a result. Another enemy soldier blown away in broad daylight watched through the net curtains. Something to celebrate. Something to shout about. Something to weaken the resolve of the occupying forces.

The Regiment's response was the same as it always was. They made a Sweep of the area at three o' clock the next morning. Lights. Voices through the tannoy. Smash the front doors in if they weren't answered in 30 seconds. Break some ornaments. Push the bastards about a bit.

Jack hated the Sweeps. They were crude. Completely unsubtle. They used the same men who had endured the cheering and the taunting as the medics had scraped what was left of Walter Haslam from the pavement. The men were wild for revenge. So they went in heavy. Smashing and swearing.

And what did it achieve? Nothing. Worse than nothing. Everyone knew the Sweep would happen. They would find no weapons, no Semtex, nothing. All they would achieve would be to create more hatred. They would appear like monsters as they swore in the faces of mothers whilst their young children watched in terror. And those same young children would grow into the next generation of players. And so it would all go on and on for ever. Jack had argued against the Sweep as hard as he could. But his attempts at reason had fallen on deaf ears. When we lose one, we do a Sweep. We let them know who is in charge. We let them know we mean business. That is the policy. We do the Sweep.

Jack was moving up and down the street, trying to keep the men under control. There was a commotion coming from inside

Number nineteen. Number nineteen? He searched his memory. Neale. Helen Neale. Wife of Patrick Neale. Patrick Neale. Implicated in a bombing on the Falls Road in 1979. Patrick Neale serving a ten in Long Kesh.

He heard a woman's voice loud and angry. Then he heard screaming. He went in. Helen Neale was down. Corporal McDonald was leaning over her. "We'll teach you, you stinking fucking Taig bitch. Give us lip will you? WILL YOU! So who's going to look after you now bitch? Not fucking hubby. Hubby's in the Kesh isn't he, bitch? Hubby's away on a tenner . . ."

He was hitting her, hard, with his big fist clenched white with anger. Her nose was bleeding and her nightclothes were already stained red.

Jack's voice stopped him. "McDonald. Back off. Get outside. Report to Sergeant Wilson immediately. You're on a charge. Now all of you. Out. Now."

"But sir we was only . . ."

"NOW!"

The three men filed out. Jack picked her up and radioed for a medic. He sat her down. She was in a woeful state. He fetched a wet face-cloth from the bathroom and started to wipe away the blood. She was silent, shaking, like a young rabbit under the murderous gaze of a cat. And as he wiped the pale face and pushed her hair back he saw to his surprise that she was beautiful. Astonishingly beautiful.

He made tea in the kitchen whilst the medic attended to her. "Not as bad as it looks sir. Nothing broken. She'll patch up all right."

She sipped her tea and stared ahead into space. What a life, he thought. Cooped up and all alone with her man away for a decade in Long Kesh. He supposed that the Brigade would look after her. But still, what a nightmare existence. At last she seemed to come round a little. She fixed him with her large green eyes.

"Thank you. You're a good man. There aren't many good men. Not round here. Not anymore."

"I can't begin to tell you how sorry I am about the way my men behaved. Corporal McDonald will be severely punished for this. You have my word on it."

"I understand you know. I know why. They watched their mate

get blown to pieces and all the kids danced and cheered. I can see why. Everyone turns into monsters round here. Your lot. Our lot. All the same. Monsters."

He left her and wound up the Sweep. They found nothing. Surprise, surprise. He called in the next morning whilst his men held station in the street outside. She looked better. Much better. Fantastic in fact.

She smiled as she opened the door. "Morning Major. Will you come in a moment?"

He nodded. Stepped inside. "I can't stay. We're on patrol, well, you can see. I just wanted to see if you are OK?"

"I'm fine. Used to it you know. Paddy used to do worse than that every Friday night when he was worse for the drink. I'll mend Major. Always have, always will."

"The soldier involved is on a charge. You should know that."

"I should?"

"Well. Yes. I thought so. We won't tolerate that kind of outrage. Not in the British Army."

She laughed. "That's where you're wrong I'm afraid Major. The British Army has tolerated exactly that kind of outrage for 400 years and more. That's why we're all in such a mess here. It's not the Army who won't tolerate it. It's you. And for that, I thank you."

Her smile was confusing him. She was confusing him. She was extraordinary.

"Yes, well, that may be so, anyway, I really must go. Glad you're OK."

"Major. Could I ask a favour. A huge favour."

"Well, yes. Yes, of course."

"My man has been in the Kesh for three years now. Nobody comes near me because if they do they'll lose their kneecaps. And I'm lonely Major. So very lonely. Would you hold me. Just for a minute. Would you?"

What the hell was he to do? Was it some sort of trap? It didn't feel like one. Even the Provos wouldn't try anything so blatant. Or would they? Or was it simply true? Surely not. But it might be. Maybe she really was just reaching out. What the hell. He stepped to her and took her in his arms. She fell into him and he sensed her silently sobbing. Trap? If it was she deserved an Oscar. At last he eased her away.

"Sorry. I must go."

"I know what you're thinking. You think it's a trap. Of course you do. This bastard place fills everyone's mind with poison. You'll think that no matter what I say. But I speak true. It really is this simple. I'm just a lonely woman with nobody to talk to, nobody to hold. That's all."

He felt awkward as he left the house. He tried to clear his mind. No matter how much he concentrated on the details of the patrol he couldn't get her out of his mind. What had just happened? Surely it had to be a trap. But maybe not. Maybe it was actually true. And then an idea hit him hard enough to make him pull up fast.

All around him his men went down instantly and started to scan the street through their gunsights.

"What is it sir? Something up?"

"No. Nothing. Carry on Sarge."

He let the idea grow in his mind all that evening and in the morning he took it to his superior officer.

" . . . I know it sounds daft sir, but I really think she fancies me."

The Colonel chuckled. "Well stranger things have happened Jack, though it is quite beyond me what any woman in their right mind would see in a big clumsy bugger like you. I hope you feel suitably flattered."

"No, no sir. I haven't made things clear."

"Well, not to me you haven't."

Jack forced himself to speak carefully. "What has got me thinking is a scrap of intelligence they gave us when we got our initial briefing. They told all officers to be extra vigilant because they had received a tip-off that the Brigade were desperate to lift an officer for Kelly to interrogate."

"Yes I remember that."

"OK. Well let's assume that Helen Neale does fancy me, or maybe it is in fact a trap, it doesn't much matter which. I start calling round there. At first I do it when we're on patrol. Assuming she is happy to see me I stay a little bit longer each time. Then I start calling in my civvies, when we're off-duty. You can guess what will happen."

Now the Colonel was very fully engaged. "It will be noticed. Reported."

"Correct. Then the thing would be to make a pattern out of the visits. Make them regular. Predictable."

"I see now where you are going. It would all be reported to Kelly and he would almost certainly arrange to have you lifted."

Jack grinned. "Lifted and taken straight to him for questioning."

"Marvellous. Then you get tortured, questioned, shot and dumped back on the streets somewhere."

"Well obviously, that wasn't quite what I had in mind."

The Colonel chuckled "I should hope not. What are you thinking then?"

"The only way this works is if our spook friends have a suitable homing device. They could bury it in the sole of my shoe somewhere. It would need to be possible for a team of SAS to follow the signal from a distance of a couple of miles. Once I get lifted, they follow the signal, and when the signal stops for a reasonable period, wham, Liam Kelly is in the bag."

It was a very simple plan, but the Army and the security forces agonised over it for several days. Jack patiently carried on with his normal duties and waited. In the end it was given a green light. He was introduced to three dishevelled characters from the SAS. One was from Birmingham, one from East London and one from the outskirts of Adelaide. They wore jeans and casual shirts and trainers on their feet. Their hair was long and the Aussie didn't seem to have any love of shaving. They looked more like three blokes in the queue at the dole office than elite soldiers.

When Jack entered the room the Australian, who was called Terry, greeted him with enthusiasm. "Bloody hell lads, here he is. How are you mate? Tell me, is it right that you're clean off your bloody rocker?"

Jack smiled. "Course I am. I'm Scottish. What else would you expect?"

"Thought so. Wanna beer mate? Here you go. I'm Terry. This is Phil and this is Steve. We're the wankers who've got the job of keeping tabs on you."

The meeting was informal. All banter. They agreed that when

the signal showed that he had been in one place for more than two hours they would make their move. If he was just in transit, then so be it. They couldn't risk leaving it any longer. When they had finished their business Terry said, "Well good on you mate. Don't worry. We might look a right bunch of tossers but we'll get you home all right. No worries."

No worries. Nice.

The operation, which some wag christened Operation Troy in honour of another dazzling Helen, started the next day.

For a week Jack knocked on Helen Neale's door every morning. She was always in and she was always glad to see him. He stayed a little longer each day. Outside number nineteen the squaddies muttered to each other about their randy Major, and how they didn't blame him either, and how they would give her one if they got half a chance.

On the ninth day he called round in the evening for the first time. He wore slacks and a jacket. Astonishment showed on her face as she opened the door. But she let him in. Curtains twitched in several houses on Marlborough Sreet.

"Bloody hell Major, are you mad? What the hell do you think you're playing at?"

"Night off. Nothing much to do in the barracks. Thought I'd pop round for a cup of tea. Nothing wrong in that is there?"

She laughed. "What do you mean you daft bugger. This is bloody Turf Lodge estate. You can't just come and knock the door and beg a cup of tea. You're an officer in the bloody British Army for crying out loud."

"So do I get kicked out?"

"No. Course not. I wouldn't do that. Don't want to do that." She blushed a little.

"Good. Then I'll put the kettle on. You'll be OK will you? They won't do anything to you?"

"Oh they won't like it, but stuff that. They won't bother me much. They owe me. My man's doing a hard ten in the Kesh. They'll grump and moan but that will be all. Sod the lot of them."

He paused at the kitchen door. He knew that the powers above him would be livid if they knew what he was going to say next. Well tough, he thought. "Helen. You should know I'm married.

Got a son. I'm not here for what you may think. Just company, you said you wanted company. That OK?"

"Jesus Jack you should have been born 150 years ago. Course it's OK. Make the bloody tea will you?"

And so Operation Troy was under way. He built up the routine. The morning visits stopped but he called in the evening every Tuesday and Thursday. Each time he found the tension was getting harder to deal with. What if the intelligence had been wrong? What if the bit about Kelly wanting to pull in a Brit officer was just a red herring?

If it was, he was dead meat. There would be no snatch team, just a couple of balaclavas and a gun to the head. Bang. Bye bye Jack.

It took just about everything he had to try and stay natural and relaxed during his visits. After the third visit Helen made a habit of cooking and he would take a bottle of wine. The whole thing was surreal. She was a good cook and she would put a candle on the table with the curtains drawn tight. They would talk about everything and anything and she was good company. They got on. Their time was an island of sanity amidst the hate and madness all around them.

On the surface he was relaxed, happy-go-lucky. Underneath he was being eaten alive by the coursing adrenalin. Tensed. Waiting for the back door to crash in any second. Soon he found it hard to sleep at nights. He was more and more jumpy on patrol. By the fourth week he wondered how much more he could take.

And then they came.

They came in just how he had known they would. It was a little after nine when the back door flew open. Three of them. Two anoraks, one demin jacket, three black balaclavas. Slow motion. Guns.

How was Helen? Ballistic. Wild. Demented. Not a trap then. Or was it? One of them knocked her to the floor. Hard with the butt of his rifle. She was out cold. Jesus, he might havecracked her skull. Jack lunged at the man. Hit him. Knocked him to the floor. Then he stopped. A circle of metal was being pushed into his skull a little above his right ear.

"Now you calm down Mr British fucking officer. We're going for a little drive. But one move and it's lights out. Got it?"

"Yes." Jack spoke through gritted teeth.

They wrapped thick insulation tape across his mouth. They used the same tape to tie his wrists behind his back. Then they pushed him forward with a thrust of a gun to his back.

Out of the back door now. Through the tiny back garden. Through the wooden gate. Into the alley. There was a van there. The back door was opened and he was pushed inside. Driving. Lots of corners. The three men in the back were quiet. Wound up. If it was a set-up, then the ambush would come soon. It didn't. Five minutes. Ten minutes. They relaxed a little. Cigarettes were lit. Twenty minutes. Banter now.

"You know what? You really are one seriously stupid British bastard. What the fuck did you think you were doing? Jesus. I mean I've heard about the dick ruling the head but this is fucking ridiculous."

Forty minutes now. They must be out of the city. The intelligence men had wondered about this. Where would he be taken? A safe house in Belfast, or out somewhere in the countryside. Forty-five minutes now. Maybe fifty. They had left the main road. He was sure of it. They were winding round tight bends now. The driver was working the gearbox hard. Now the van was bumping along. Bad road surface? No way. Not this bad. A track. A rough track. Where to? Isolated cottage? Farm?

They were stopped now. A cloth bag was pulled over his head and he was dragged out. Walking was difficult. Uneven surface. He nearly tripped and fell twice. Now there was a step. A door. Inside now. The gun was still pushed hard into his back. He hit something. A chair. Wooden chair.

"Sit down please Major."

He manoeuvred his way around the chair and sat down. The hood was removed. He was sitting at an old wooden table. Nothing fancy. MFI probably. A man in a balaclava sat the other side, smoking. On the table was a chipped ashtray with six docked cigarettes in it. He could see two other men sitting in the corners of the room. Then there were the three who had lifted him. Six in all. All of them were armed except the man on the other side of the table. The light was harsh. One bulb hanging from the ceiling. No shade. This was it. He had arrived.

"Major Jack Sinclair, you have to be the most stupid officer the

British Army has ever produced. Now I know that Helen Neale is a lovely woman. A very lovely woman. Lovely person too. But for heaven's sake, on Turf Lodge! Take the tape off now please."

The tape was ripped from Jack's face. He shook his head to clear the pain.

The man pulled off his balaclava and smoothed down his hair. Light sandy hair. He put on his glasses. Metal. John Lennon style. It was Liam Kelly.

"You know who I am of course."

"No."

"Oh come on Jack. Let's not start the silliness straight away shall we. The Scots Guards landed three weeks ago. All officers underwent two days of intelligence briefings in Lisburn Barracks. Same operational procedure as always. Now please don't try and tell me that nobody out there had the first clue of who was in charge of your sector. You know who I am. Yes?"

"Yes."

"And I am?"

"You're Kelly. Liam Kelly."

Liam smiled and carefully lit another cigarette. "That's right. Very good Major. I'm Liam Kelly. And you are Major Jack Sinclair. And I promise you that we are going to get to know each other very well indeed over the next few days. I think I should talk about this a bit."

The voice was soft. Melodic. Almost seductive. There had been much discussion about how Jack should be in his two hours. Should he tough it out, spit in faces, scream abuse? Should he resort to name, rank and number and clam up? Or should he be scared, panicked, subservient? They had decided on the latter. It would probably be the most realistic. It was also going to be the easiest approach because Jack was scared half out of his wits. His voice was almost a croak.

"Look. Mr Kelly. I'll tell you everything you want. Everything. Really. They told us you see. At the briefings. About you. How you interrogated people. They said . . . well they said . . ."

"What did they say Jack?"

"They said that everyone always talks. Always talks."

"And they were right. Well, they have done so thus far. I

suppose there will have to be a first at some stage. But not yet. You're not going to be the first then Jack?"

"No. I'm not stupid. You won't have to hurt me. Please don't do that Mr Kelly. I don't want you to that. Please Mr Kelly."

Liam shook his head sadly. "Well Jack I can't really promise you that. I'll have to hurt you. You see, even if you tell me everything that you know in the whole world, I will still have to hurt you to make sure that you tell me the same story when you're hurting. If you see what I mean."

"Oh Christ. Oh dear Christ no. Not that. Not torture. You don't need to. I promise. I promise on my mother's grave . . ." They had talked about this too. It had been Terry's suggestion. Tell you what mate, piss yourself, adds authenticity. Beg and plead and piss yourself. Promise I won't tell. So Jack pissed himself and begged. The hot urine ran down the inside of his thighs and into a small pool on the floor. Liam sniffed and glanced under the table.

"Oh dear, oh dear Jack. Look what's happened now. You know, I've tried to find out about this in books from the library. Why on earth is it that we lose all control of our bladders when we are frightened? Don't worry, there's nothing to be ashamed of, you all do it. Every last one of you. I would never interrogate anyone on the carpet in my front room that's for sure."

Liam reached down and pulled a pad of A4 paper from the briefcase at his side.

"We've spent days wondering about you Jack. Hours and hours. Can it be real, we wondered? Surely nobody could ever be that stupid? At first I was dead against the whole thing. No way I said. It's a set-up. Has to be. Nobody could possibly be that stupid. But then I got to thinking, well, maybe they could. We men do the absolute stupidest things when it comes to women. We always have. I suppose we always will. Cigarette? You'll have to keep it in your mouth. I'm not undoing your hands. Here."

He leant over the table and placed the lit cigarette between Jack's lips then carried on.

"And if a man was going to be stupid, then Helen Neale is exactly the woman to cause it. All alone, vulnerable, lonely, and so, so very beautiful. A tragic blooming rose in the midst of a dung heap. So I thought maybe it might be true. Maybe you were living some fantasy about being a knight in shining armour. The damsel in distress is sorely tempting to any man.

"So I decided to look at it. I really wasn't convinced, but we've been wanting to get ourselves a live British officer for such a long time. Well it all seemed OK. All the troops were tucked up in the barracks. So why not? I warned the boys of course. I told them it was a bit like a game of chess. No matter how long and how hard you look at the board there are times you just can't see what your opponent is going to do next. I told them it was their decision. If it was an elaborate trap and we couldn't see where it was coming from they would be the ones looking at a ten in the Kesh. Well they decided to give it a go. And lo-and-behold. Here we are Jack. It seems that you really were that stupid."

"I love her."

"I'm sure you must. But love can get you into bother Jack. Ask Romeo."

Jack bowed his head and sucked at the cigarette.

"Oh dear Jack. It's all a bit sad isn't it? A real Friday night weepy. Two people find each other in the midst of this nasty little war of ours and all they want is love. Make love not war, isn't that what they say Jack? Jack?"

"Yes."

"The trouble is that we can't get away from the war. I would love to turn a blind eye and leave you be. Course I would. There is far too much hate. Hate is everywhere. We breathe it in every day of our lives like a contagion. But you must understand that I can't just forget it. Like you, I'm just a soldier, although it would appear that I am a rather better one than you. I don't particularly like doing most of the things that I have to do. Who does? Only the real nutters. But war is war. We all have to do what is required. What my army requires of me is that I find out everything you know. I will find out about your tactics and strategy. I will find out the detailed layout of every barracks you have ever stayed in. I will find out about what training methods you are using. But more important than all of these things, I will find out what you know about us.

"You see Jack, knowledge is power, and when I take your knowledge it will give my army more power. For you it will be a miserable experience. I can promise that it will give me no pleasure either. But in the end, it will mean that fewer of my people will be gunned down or sent to rot for years on end in Long Kesh prison. War Jack. War. You are my enemy. Love doesn't come into it I'm afraid."

Jack started to cry. He couldn't believe it was happening to him. He had been ready for this moment. Every nerve in his brain had been prepared. He was ready for pain. He was ready for abuse, for the feeling of saliva in his face. What he hadn't been ready for was the soft Irish voice. He felt almost hypnotised. Kelly was right. It was all so sad. So totally, stupidly, hopelessly sad.

Why were they enemies? Anywhere else he could have met this man and they would have shared a few beers. They shared the same passport, spoke the same language, they both believed in what they did. Not here though. Four hundred stupid, brutal years had brought them both to this. Two ordinary, decent men who would go to the well of violence because that was what was expected of them. So bloody sad. And tears poured down his cheeks. Fear and grief.

"I think, Jack, we should maybe get started. We'll start with the easy stuff. Get to know each other. I want you to tell me about yourself. Who are you Jack? Where do you come from? Your Mum. Your Dad. Your dreams. How was your childhood. Why the army? Lets get used to each other shall we. You call me Liam. I call you Jack. We're only men. Men from different sides of the tracks in a silly, endless little war. Let's try and be as civilised as we can. So, where shall we start? Tell me about your first day at school, when you were a little boy, when you were five . . ."

He had used this method several times before. At first he had thought Hoffman was crazy. Hoffman said that this was the way with the really hard ones. The professionals. Lay the cards on the table. Don't try and con them. Be honest. Be straight. Just talk. You are both soldiers. Get them into the habit of talking. Get them to talk about something that there is no point lying about. Take your time. Take days if you like. There is no rush. Your war has already lasted hundreds of years. A few more days won't matter.

And Jack started to talk. He allowed his mind to wander all the way back to the small village school in the early sixties. Hard wooden benches. Short pants on cold frosty days. The cane if you got your maths wrong. A two-mile walk from the farm down small country lanes. Liam periodically pushed a cigarette between his lips for him. The men in the corners quietly read their newspapers. The slow hours of the night drifted by as Liam jotted occasional notes in his pad.

Then the lights went out.

And Jack's brain seemed to cave in.

Somewhere he registered noise. Huge, massive noise. Darkness. BANG BANG. Pause. BANG BANG. Pause. BANG BANG . . . BANG BANG. Pause. BANG BANG. His brain was clearing. Two shot bursts. Trademark SAS. Double tap. Double tap. How long had it been? Seconds. Maybe ten seconds. Maybe less.

There was a torch now. A monstrous figure in night vision goggles was standing with a snub-nosed gun at Kelly's head. The men in the corners were down. Pools of blood were spreading over the floor.

"All right mate. You OK?"

Jack tried to shake the noise of the stun grenades out of his head. "Yes. Yes I'm fine thanks Terry."

Liam had laid his hands on the table and a small smile played on his lips. "So Jack. It was a trap after all. You are a very brave man Major Jack Sinclair. I salute you."

Jack held his eyes. "One thing Liam. Just one. Helen? Was she a set-up?"

Kelly smiled a sad smile. "No. No she wasn't. It was all as it seemed. Just another sad lonely lady with her man gone away."

"What will happen to her?"

"Nothing Jack. I will make sure of that. She did nothing wrong. She just didn't want to be alone. I'll make sure she's OK."

"Thanks Liam."

"None needed. We're not all monsters you know."

"I know that."

There was the sound of a helicopter now. Vehicles were pulling up outside. Voices. Orders. Soldiers came into the room. Terry patted Jack on the shoulder.

"We'll be off now mate. Bloody good effort. See you around."

Then the SAS men were gone. Hands released the tape on his

wrists. Across the table Liam was standing now with his hands on his head. A soldier handcuffed him and pushed him toward the door. He gave a last glance to Jack, the smile still on his lips.

"Maybe we will meet again one day Major Sinclair. Maybe when all this is over. Maybe in happier times."

"I'd like that Liam."

"See you around, Major."

They took him out. Hands helped Jack to his feet. He still felt dizzy and disorientated from the blast. He should have felt elated. It was a triumph. A great victory. But he felt like shit. Absolute utter shit.

They took him out of the Province the next day. There was no future for him there. He was the most marked man in the British Army. He kicked his heels at the barracks until the Regiment finished its tour. He was awarded the Military Cross. He was a star. Major Jack Sinclair, the one who took down Liam Kelly. He should have been on top of the world. But it never seemed that way. Just another nasty incident in a nasty little war that would probably never end.

He never returned to the Province again.

Liam Kelly was sent to Long Kesh prison for twenty years.

Four days had passed since the funeral. Jack had returned to Hillside Farm. It was a ghostly, empty place. He couldn't get used to almost complete lack of noise. Instead of the sound of over 200 animals there was only the sound of the wind whistling through the empty sheds. The replacement Ministry man had been clearly nervous when he parked up and crossed the yard. The man was on tenterhooks. He obviously knew all about what had happened with his predecessor. Jack tried to put him at ease.

"Look, I know things got a little out of hand last week. I'm sure you heard all about it. It was a bad day. A really bad day. Maybe you can imagine. It's all done now. You don't have to worry. I won't bite."

The man, who was called Roger, breathed a visible sigh of relief. Maybe this wouldn't be so bad after all. They went through what had to be done all that afternoon. There were several more compensation issues to be resolved – feed and silage to be thrown away, medicines that would go out of date, sheds which were unfit to be cleaned and would have to come down.

"What would you like to do about the cleaning, Mr Sinclair? You have a choice. You can either organise it yourself or we can arrange for a team to come in and do the job. We will pay you £10 an hour and cover the costs of any machinery you need to hire if you choose to take on the job. We supply the overalls and the chemicals that you need. Either way, I will come in on a weekly basis to audit the work."

"I'll handle it myself. I will want to bring in some more help of course. You cover the cost of them as well, I presume?"

"Yes. So long as it's within reason. No more than three men I would suggest. Four of you in total. You keep a record of hours worked and machinery hired and invoice us. So long as I am happy with the job you will be fully reimbursed."

Jack nodded. This was perfect. Only one more hurdle now.

"I've been giving some thought to the clean-up job. I would like to get the top farm done first. It's smaller, and I think I will be wanting to restock with a few sheep before I get dairy cows. Is that OK?"

"Fine. According to the official records the two farms are entirely separate entities. You can do the top farm and, so long as I am happy, I can get you a licence to clear that before you start on things down here. There is another track that can be used for access I believe."

"Yes. It hasn't been used in years. It comes down from the road up there." Jack pointed up to where a single-track lane wound around the edge of the hill. "It won't take much to open it up again. Half a day on the digger should do it."

"I would ask you to block off the track from here. Keep it completely separate. Then everything will be in order."

"Excellent. That is just what I was hoping." It took Roger another two hours to go through the work required in every shed in detail. It was going to be a mammoth task. Two months at least. Maybe even three. That suited Jack down to the ground.

Filling in all the various compensation forms took him the best part of two days. Then he was away and clear. He left the farm early on a fine Friday morning and drove along the coast to

Stranraer. He left the Land Rover in the car park and bought a return ticket for the Seacat to Belfast. It was a wonderful clear day and he could easily see the Ulster coast across the water.

He spent the whole of the crossing on the deck staring down into the churning waves thrown up by the fast catamaran. How long had it been? Eleven years. Eleven long years since he had crossed the same grey waters to start his third tour. How much had changed in that time. Angela was gone. His Army career was gone. And now his only son and all his animals were gone too.

The last time he had arrived in Belfast he had been thirty-two and on his way up. He had been ambitious as Hell and had set his sights on a high rank. He never considered that the Army wasn't going to be his life's work. So much had changed.

Now here he was again. 43 now. Lines on his face and scars all over his soul. The Army had never been the same after the night with Liam. He had started to question things more and more. He did as he was told and did it well. But the passion was gone. He had looked war in the face and found it to be ugly and deceitful. There was no place for honour.

He could not escape the fact that his life had been more or less downhill all the way from that night when they had taken down Liam Kelly. And now everything had gone. Absolutely everything. His life was a blank sheet of paper. No more responsibilities. No more family to provide for. No soldiers to train and organise. No more animals to feed and tend.

Nothing. Just himself. And his quest.

After an hour and a half they slipped into the moorings in the centre of Belfast. Jack found a taxi and got in.

"The Shamrock Bar please mate. Up on Turf Lodge."

The driver half-turned in his seat and looked enquiringly at the tall passenger in the wax jacket.

"You sure about this?"

"Quite sure."

"Fair enough. You're the punter."

The city seemed different. The road blocks and the checkpoints were all gone. The Crumlin Road prison was derelict and overgrown with weeds. The city seemed busier, more vibrant. More pedestrians, fewer soldiers. There was barely a soldier to be seen. They passed the old barracks. They were all boarded up and deserted. A relic from another era.

Turf Lodge hadn't changed much. The maisonettes were merely a little older, a little more tawdry. There were still the murals of men in balaclavas with their AK47 rifles. There were still the Irish tricolour flags. There was still the grinding poverty. He passed number nineteen Marlborough Road. Helen. What had become of her? It all seemed so long ago.

The taxi pulled up outside a modern one-storey bar that stood alone by overgrown playing fields. All the windows were protected by wire mesh and the pebbledashed walls were covered in graffiti.

"Seven quid mate."

Jack handed the cabbie a ten-pound note. "Thanks. Keep the change."

The man gave him a last quizzical look and he was gone. Jack stood for a moment and stared down the empty streets where he and his men had once patrolled every morning. It was all so bloody bleak. What on earth had possessed them to fight so hard and so long over wretched places like these? He sighed and went inside.

There was no natural light in the bar. The windows were small and absolutely filthy. He had been in before. They had sometimes stormed in on a Saturday night. They would kill the music and line all the men up against the wall whilst the women swore at them from the seats. They never found anything. It had just been a charade designed to antagonise. So much hate. Always so much hate.

Lunchtime trade was slow. There were only twelve customers in, all men, six of them sitting along the bar making their half-pints last as long as they could. A TV was switched up loud. A game show. Silly white teeth and a moronic audience. They all stopped talking when he walked in. All stared. Malevolent stares. Strangers weren't welcome.

Jack walked to the counter and the barman came to him reluctantly.

"Aye."

"Pint of Guinness. And change for the cigarette machine."

"You sure you're in the right place?"

"Quite sure."

THE CULL

The man stared at him for a moment, then shrugged his shoulders and started to pour the drink. Still nobody spoke. They just stared. Thin grey faces. Too many fags. Too much carbohydrate. Not enough fresh air. The barman banged down the pint, making it splash. The change followed. A pound coin rolled off the counter onto to the floor. Jack stooped to pick it up.

"I'd like you to pass on a message for me."

"I'm not a call centre. Find someone else."

Jack ignored the hostility. He kept his voice friendly.

"It's for Liam Kelly."

"Never heard of him."

"Then you must be new around here. Find somebody that does, and pass on a message. Tell him it's Jack Sinclair. Tell him I'm here. Waiting."

"You could be waiting a long time."

"I'm in no hurry. I think you will find it a very bad idea not to pass the message on. Mr Kelly wouldn't be at all amused if you didn't. And we don't want that now do we?"

The man scowled then lumbered into a back room. Jack took his pint, got a packet of cigarettes from the machine, and sat down at a table in the corner to wait.

Over the years he had heard little snippets of news about Kelly. In the weeks after he had been taken, the rumours floated back from the Province. Kelly had never said a word to his interrogators. Not one word. He just sat and smiled at them. The trial had been a formality. There were some who had thought he would get more than twenty years. But twenty was enough. Twenty was a result. Things got easier for the Regiments who had the job of patrolling Ballymurphy and Turf Lodge.

Then there was nothing. As the years went by Jack would often find himself thinking about Kelly. As time passed and he watched his son grow up Liam Kelly was holed up in Long Kesh. How was he taking it? Would he break? Would he ever come out? Then one day in 1999 Jack saw his name in the paper. He was out, released as part of the Peace Process. Jack had wondered what on earth freedom had meant for him. His whole adult life had been dedicated to the Cause. How would he adjust to peace? There had been family. A wife. Two kids. Had they waited? Was there a home for him to go back to?

He sat for two hours. The ashtray filled up slowly. The first pint was followed by another, this time accompanied by a bag of crisps, which were stale. At last the door swung open and Liam came in. He surveyed the room until he spotted Jack at his corner table. When he saw him he shook his head and smiled.

"Well, well. I'll be buggered. Major Jack Sinclair. It really is you? You always did enjoy your little one-man visits to Turf Lodge. Old habits die hard I see. What are you drinking?"

"Guinness please Liam. Pint."

Jack watched him at the bar. Much of his hair had gone and he was slightly stooped. The ten years had aged him twenty, but the smile was still the same. The small smile and the soft melodic voice. He joined Jack at the table and passed over his pint.

"Well, Major, cheers."

"Aye. Cheers."

Liam reached into his pocket and pulled out a packet of cigarettes, passed one to Jack, then lit them both.

"I'll let you use your hands this time Jack."

"That's good of you."

"I have to say it Jack, even if it sounds like a stuck record, but you are one seriously mad bastard coming up here alone."

Jack smiled. "Thought there was peace."

"Aye, fat chance. Don't you realise that you sent me down for ten years of my life in Long Kesh prison. A man can get to feeling bitter about a thing like that. You know that I could just give the nod and that would be it. One nod and you'd never make it out of Turf Lodge."

"Let's say I'm taking an educated risk."

Liam laughed. "Hell of a risk. I don't suppose there are any SAS men lurking about the place. They've been gone a while now. Thank Christ. So please, enlighten me, what makes your risk educated?"

Jack took a drink. "You, I suppose Liam. You're a soldier at heart. You told me as much once. It was a war. We did what was expected of us. Some skirmishes you win. Other you lose. I happened to win ours. It wasn't personal. It was war."

"It still might be."

"Not for you Liam. You were always one of the establishment in the Movement. Top brass. Senior officer. You're not the type to run with the madmen in the Real IRA. If the word from Sinn Fein HQ is no more killing, you will carry out your orders, revenge or no revenge. Besides, what would be the point, I may have won the skirmish but you won the war."

"Oh did we now, sorry if my eyesight is poor, but I don't see a United Ireland out there."

"No. Not yet. But Belfast will soon be more or less all green. The Orangemen are moving out to the countryside and the Republicans are taking over. You're winning Belfast by human settlement. The power of demographics. And Belfast was always your war Liam."

Kelly was thoughtful. "So, you've been keeping up. And you'r e right of course. Right about almost all of it. I'm out now. There's not much left of the old Brigade. We're all reservists now. And you're right about the Real IRA. Bloody idiots the lot of them. They're more interested in their drugs business than anything else. Bloody nuisance. What about you Jack? Made Colonel yet?"

"No. I left the Guards in '93. My Dad died and I had to go back and look after the farm."

"Not a soldier any more then. I was wondering if this was some kind of weird approach from some elements in British Intelligence."

This made Jack laugh. "Christ no. I left the establishment years ago. I'm just a nobody now."

"Now I'm really intrigued. What the hell are you here for? Reliving the golden days of your youth?"

"Hardly. No, it's business. Strictly business. I have a proposition Liam. Something I think you'll rather enjoy. What are you doing these days?"

"I work in an accountancy firm. I'm very junior. It isn't much, but it keeps a roof over my head."

"How are the family?"

"Oh they're long gone. My wife never knew, you know. We met at university. She had never grown up with the worst of the troubles. She used to feel that I was being unjustly victimised when you lot would storm about the house every couple of weeks. When it all came out at the trial, she discovered that I was the bogey man. She took the kids away. Over the water. Manchester. I haven't seen them since."

"I'm sorry to hear that."

Kelly nodded slowly. "And you Jack? Your family?"

"Angela left me a few months after I left the Army. She couldn't adjust to life on the farm. She moved in with one of my fellow officers. My son Will . . . well, that's why I'm here Liam. Let me get a couple more pints."

The experience at the bar was very different this time. The barman placed the glasses down carefully and none of the contents spilled. He even muttered "Thanks" as Jack handed him the money. So this was it. Time to make his pitch.

When he sat back down at the table Liam said. "So, you were saying. Your son."

Show time.

"I had a bad day a couple of weeks ago. A really bad day. They slaughtered all the animals on the farm as part of the culling process, and my son Will died from a heroin overdose. He was nineteen."

Liam stopped lifting his glass to his lips when it was halfway up from the table. "Jesus Jack. I'm sorry. That's hard."

"Hard. Yes. Very hard. At first I more or less came apart at the seams. All of a sudden everything was gone. But not now. I'm back on track now. And I'm here."

Now Liam was very intrigued. "Go on."

"Did you ever watch a film called 'The Battle for Algiers' Liam?"

"Of course I did. Compulsory viewing for any serious terrorist."

"What did you make of it?"

"I was bloody glad that you bastards never did the same thing as the French over here."

"Would it have worked?"

"In the short term, yes. It would have been a bloody nightmare. Not in the long run though. Torturing and killing your enemy only gives him more and more martyrs. In the end he will come back stronger and in the end he will win. Look at the French, they were packed and gone two years later. That was one of our problems here, you Brits were bastards, but never quite big enough bastards for us to mobilise the whole population. Anyway, for Christ's sake Jack, what's the Battle of Algiers got to with anything?"

THE CULL

Jack looked him right in the eyes. "Everything Liam. Absolutely everything. It is my template. I have found out from a mate of mine in the Drug Squad that in Dumfries the whole of the heroin trade is controlled by one gang, one man. They try to operate just like any terrorist organisation. They have a tight structure and anyone who tries to step out and threaten them is wasted.

"I'm going to take them down Liam. All of them. I'm going to start at the bottom rung and work all the way up to the top. Just like the French did."

"Fuck me."

Jack ploughed on. Keep going. Make it sound like sanity, not madness.

"It will need a small team of professionals. Four men. Myself. Two foot-soldiers. One interrogator. And I need someone to help me put it all together. All my experience has been in working as part of an Army. I am used to platoons and companies and artillery support and air strikes on demand. I need someone who knows how to work a plan like this. So I thought that the best thing would be to come and talk to the best in the business. You Liam."

Liam was quiet for a moment and he glanced about to make sure nobody could be listening.

"This work. Not charity work is it Jack?"

"Sometime in the next couple of months I will be getting a compensation cheque for £280,000 from the Ministry of Agriculture. I am offering you £150,000 for your services and those of two men. The farm has to be fully disinfected. The job will take about three months for a team of four men. It pays £600 a week and it would offer perfect cover for you and your guys. I have an empty farmhouse with plenty of rooms. Five months for the whole operation."

Liam became all business. "Right. Tell me the plan as you have it so far. All of it. Every detail."

Jack ran through his embryonic plan for ten minutes. When he explained the final phase Liam nearly spat Guinness all down his front. His laughter caused cautious glances from the men at the bar.

"Brilliant. Absolutely bloody brilliant. Hell Jack, you were wasted in that boring old Army of yours. You're a born terrorist. I love that last bit. That's a bit of class. Brilliant."

LIAM

"So?"

Jack's question hung in the air between them for a few seconds. Then Liam spoke. "I'm in. Course I'm bloody well in. Do you seriously think I would choose to frig around doing end-of-year tax returns for plumbers with this offer on the table. Besides, I have other reasons. Good reasons."

He held his hand out across the table and Jack shook it. The gesture was noticed by every customer in the pub. An electrical charge of excitement fizzed around the room. They had absolutely no idea what the handshake signified, and they knew they probably never would have. The big Scotsman had come to Turf Lodge with something. And whatever that something was, Liam Kelly had picked it up and taken it.

It meant that Liam Kelly was back in business. About time too.

"Jack, I'm going now. I need to think. My brain feels like it's about to pop. I'll pick you up here tomorrow at about one. We'll take a drive out to the country. I'll have a full proposal for you. Jesus, who would ever have thought it. You never know what contacts you make when you lift a Brit Major for questioning."

"Before you go Liam, there is one other thing."

"Yes?"

"Helen Neale. Was she OK?"

Liam smiled. "She was fine. She left. Went south. She's in Dublin now. Doing well I hear. You can chalk that one off your conscience Jack."

Jack nodded. One less item of baggage to carry about. The slate was nearly clean. He was combat-ready.

Chapter 7
Onslaught

Jack found a small hotel on the edge of the city centre and checked in. He felt elated. All his instincts had told him that Liam would sign up to his scheme but it was a huge relief nonetheless. It had only been as his taxi had headed out of Turf Lodge and back into town that he had realised just what a risk he had taken.

Why had the danger not really occurred to him? He pondered the question that evening as he strolled around the city centre. He had always had courage, but it had never been something that he thought about much. It was just there. But he hadn't needed any courage to make the trip to Turf Lodge. The answer was elusive. It finally came as he stood in the soft rain staring at the derelict shell that had once been the Crumlin Road Prison. There had been so much misery within those stark walls for so many years. Lives that were broken never to heal. Beatings. Brutality. Endless awfulness. And now nothing. Just another building with no purpose any more.

That was what filled him. Nothing. There were no real consequences any more. Without consequences there was nothing to create fear. If Liam had taken the opportunity to organise a bullet for the back of his head then so what? He wouldn't have cared much either way. One way to go was the path of revenge. The other was peace and quiet.

Revenge. It was a strange emotion. There was no fire in him. He was cold. Detached. Dispassionate. He just felt cold. Cold all the way through.

THE CULL

The city seemed so strange. He found it hard to believe that it was really Belfast at all. The old Belfast seemed light-years way. Now there were wine bars, theme pubs, boutiques, busy streets. The old air of threat was gone. No road blocks. No young soldiers on patrol. All gone. A nasty, vicious little war consigned to the history books.

He had left part of himself behind on these streets and estates. Something had died in him. Faith? Patriotism? Nothing so tangible. Just something. He had carried a sadness ever since the night when the SAS squad had gunned down five men and taken Liam to Long Kesh prison. And now there was an even bigger hole. A chasm. He felt like a man without a soul. A machine. Fully serviced. Topped up with oil. Ready to work. A machine doesn't work out of love or belief or passion or fervour. The only reason that it works is because it has been switched on. And it stops working when it is switched off.

That's me then, he realised. Switched on. Ready to do a job of work. Capable of doing it. All a bullet in the head would have meant was that I would have been switched off.

So be it.

The next day he again caught a cab to Turf Lodge. Somehow the streets were no longer threatening. Now it was just another grindingly poor estate in a north British town. There were no demons. No ghosts. He was a part of it now. He was with Liam. That made him part of it.

Liam collected him in an old Ford Escort and they headed straight out of town. They drove for 40 minutes then parked up and walked. They climbed a small hill and sat on a rock at the top. Liam was fighting hard for his breath.

"Christ I'm in bad nick. That is what being locked down 23 hours a day with nothing much to do other than read and smoke does for you. I keep promising to try and get fit. Can't seem to get round to it. I suppose this clean-up job on the farm will help.

"How was it? The Kesh?"

"Terrible to start with. It really was like a concentration camp you know. The wardens were the most brutal bastards I have ever come across. But it got better in time. Once it was obvious that peace was round the corner they eased off. In the end it was just boring." As his breathing had returned to somewhere near normal he lit a cigarette. "OK. I've given things a lot of thought and there are a few issues."

"Fire-away."

"Right. The way I am looking at this is that me and my lads are the hired hands. It's your contract Jack. Your fight. This means the plan has to be tailored to what you want. There is one big hole. Not a hole that affects any operational issues. It's one that affects you and I'm not sure that you have thought it through. What is the end game Jack?"

"End game?"

"Yes. Where is it that you want to be once we complete the final phase? For me and the lads it is easy. We just come back across the water and melt away. You are different. Out of the £280,000 you are getting as compensation you are paying us £150,000. I estimate that we will spend at least another £30,000 on operational expenses. It doesn't leave you with a fortune.

"Now you have to realise that they will soon find out that it was all down to you. The police aren't daft you know. Who is there out there who has a grievance about drugs? Check the records. Look boss, this one's interesting. His son died of a heroin OD whilst all his animals were being culled, ex-Major in the Army, worth checking wouldn't you say boss? Get my drift?"

Jack nodded slowly. Liam was right. This was indeed the part that he hadn't thought through. Liam continued.

"So where do you go Jack? Basically you either give up or you're on the run."

Two choices. Give up, or go on the run. No way was he giving up. That wasn't part of the programme at all. "On the run."

"OK fine. I thought as much. The next question is how do you want to be on the run? Do you want to disappear, get out of the country and start over? Or do you want to continue the fight that you have started?"

"Continue I suppose, though I can't for the life of me see how."

Liam laughed. "That's because you are a soldier at heart Jack. You don't think like a terrorist. Not yet. There will be ways. Lots of ways. You just can't see them yet. Your mind works in a conventional way. All you can see is finishing the job and wait till they give you another one. You never had to think of the future when you were in the Army. They always told you what was next. They always told you what to do. What happened when you had lifted me?"

"They took me back to the barracks. Got me out of the Province as quickly as they could. I just had to kick my heels until the Regiment completed its tour of duty."

"Exactly my point. You waited to be told what to do. Now you are on the other side of the fence. When this thing is over you will be on your own and every move will be down to you. That's why it needs careful planning. I have some ideas. I bet you haven't even thought about the media."

Jack shook his head. Now he was confused. "The media? No. Why should I?"

"A soldier again. You have never had to think about the consequences of your actions. It wasn't your job. You were just a paid soldier and you followed orders. You didn't do the things you did in Ireland because of any burning belief. You did it because it was a day's work. You were given your rules and guidelines and objectives. What the world thought about the things you were doing was not your concern. That was Whitehall's job. They handled the PR.

"We were different of course. We were fighting for a cause. We were fighting against 400 years of non stop shit from you lot and your Orangemen lackeys. The reason behind just about every one of our actions was to generate publicity and get the world to listen to our message. Sometimes it worked. After Bobby Sands and the hunger strikers the whole world was with us. Sometimes it didn't. After Enniskillen the whole world hated us. The publicity was the end game of just about every operation I ever planned. What did we want to achieve? Boost the morale of our people? Erode the morale of the occupying forces? Make sure the world never got the chance to forget that we were still in there fighting? Publicity is the life-blood of any terrorist. You can't get anyone to listen to your message by standing in a soapbox and shouting at the top of your voice. You have to do something dramatic. Dramatic enough for the media to say 'Why?' 'How?' 'What for?' and when they ask these questions you can give them your answers. And the answer is your cause. Your message. And that is how people get to hear about it."

"Jesus Liam, you're way ahead of me here. I hadn't even considered any of this."

"Well that's what you pay me for. So think, Jack. What is the cause? Do you simply want to take a few Dumfries pushers to the cleaners and exact revenge for what happened to your son? Or do you want to go further? Do you want to take the fight to all of them, all the pushers, all the gangs, not just in Dumfries, but everywhere?"

"Everywhere I suppose, but this is daft, it's all hypothetical, there's only me, I'm not in an Army any more."

"That's where you're wrong. If we get this right you will lead an army of millions. Every worried father, every terrified mother, every jaded policeman, every shallow politician waiting for the right bandwagon. They can all be yours Jack. But publicity will be the key. What we are going to do will generate publicity. Of course it will. Lots of it. That's why I like it so much. But publicity is a fire that needs feeding. If you feed it right it grows into an inferno that nobody can put out. And I think I know how you can do it Jack. Interested?"

"Of course."

"Then we need to take a little fortnight trip to New York. I will introduce you to someone, someone who will show you just how to make it happen. Right. That's covered. Just a couple of other things. I've been thinking about the timescale. Once we lift more than three or four of these guys the others will start to smell a rat. Time will be everything. Once we start we have to move fast. Really fast."

Jack had thought much the same. "Yes, I realise that."

"It means that we can't tip-toe around these guys. We will have to break them quickly. It isn't going to be pleasant. You'll be going to a bad place Jack. One of the worst. I used to think of it as Hell's Kitchen. Are you ready for that? Are you strong enough?"

"Oh I'm ready Liam. Don't worry about that."

Liam looked into the eyes that had died. He had thought as much. It was something he had seen so many times before in the eyes of his recruits. Some wanted the action and the glory and getting the girls on a Saturday night. They would never be any good. He had never taken them on. Others came to the Organisation because there was nowhere else to go. They came because they had been hurt. A brother thrown in the Kesh, an uncle gunned down by the UVF, a niece put into a coma by a British Army plastic bullet. These were the ones whose souls were torn. These were the ones who would do what was necessary. He could always tell them. They were the ones with the dead eyes. Just like Jack Sinclair.

"Last thing. You have total say during all stages of putting the plan together. It is your show Jack. But once it's done, I'm in charge. Command is non-negotiable. You act on my orders until the thing is done. Is that acceptable?"

"Yes. I agree on that. The command structure has to be clear. Anything else?"

"Actually one more thing. After New York we need to take a detour. I want to fly back via the Cayman Islands. I want to open a bank account for me and the boys. If we get any heat the money will have to be well hidden. All the flights are your expense Jack I'm afraid. I'm broke."

"Fine by me. A bit of sunshine won't go amiss. So what next?"

"You go back. We travel to New York separately. We'll meet there in a week. As soon as we get back I'll bring the boys over and we'll get on with cleaning your bloody farm up."

Six weeks later the clean-up was well under way. Liam had arrived with his men a week after they had returned from the Cayman Islands. He had known both of the men for years. Jack only had to take one look at them to know that they were perfect. They were both big men in their early 40s. And quiet. Very quiet.

John Doyle had joined up in 1976. He had been throwing stones and bottles at British Soldiers on Ballymurphy since the age of nine. At that time his Dad was serving fifteen years in Long Kesh after he had been stopped at a road block carrying explosives. His little brother had been shot dead in street-fighting when he had only just turned thirteen. The Cause was a family affair for the Doyle family. Doyle had served under Liam for eight years and had never been anything but steady and reliable. He had finally been caught stashing weapons in 1993 and had joined his old leader inside for five years before being released.

Once out he had found work in the building trade which was showing signs of booming in the wake of peace. He had never married and he had few friends. His social life revolved around Saturday nights with old comrades reminiscing about the old days. He had never been entirely convinced that they had won. Now he was in reserve. When the call came he would always be ready. Until then he had been more than happy to join up again with his old boss.

Declan O'Hara was cut from similar cloth. He was a Turf Lodge boy and he had joined up after a British Para had spat in his mother's face one night in 1973 during a Sweep. His career had been similar to John Doyle's. He had been another steady one. Always cool under fire, never over-excitable. He had made it all the way to the Peace without being caught. Peace left him unfulfilled. He had married young but it hadn't worked. She had gone back to her mother's when he was 25. He hadn't bothered again. For three years he had been driving a truck up and down the road to Dublin. He hadn't had to think for long before saying yes.

The job of cleaning the top farm was more tedious than back-breaking. Using the power washers that Jack had hired in, they had to spray, blast and disinfect every square inch of all the buildings and the yard. Every time that Jack was convinced that it was impossible to get a particular area any cleaner, the Ministry man or one of the government vets would always find a cranny with some muck in it. Most of the work was done by himself, O'Hara and Doyle as Liam was away from the farm much of the time collecting the various items they would need to launch the operation.

The three Irishmen moved into the farmhouse which Jack and Will had once ear-marked for tourists. These were strange tourists indeed, thought Jack. The three and a half weeks it took to eventually get the nod from the Ministry that the farm was clean were useful. It gave the four men time to get to know each other and to start to forge themselves into a tight unit. In the evenings they sat around the old kitchen table where they worked the plan again and again until it started to become watertight.

After the first week, O'Hara and Doyle began surveillance on Ricky Macintosh. Across the road from his house on Sunnybank there was a small play area ringed by a hedge. From behind the hedge a man could easily stay concealed and watch the house. Once Ricky would leave the house, the watcher would radio his colleague, who would get out of the car he had been waiting in a couple of streets away and tail him. After two weeks a pattern had emerged. Most evenings Ricky would at some stage call in at the Wheatsheaf pub. His stays in the pub varied. Sometimes he would stay until closing time, playing pool and drinking heavily. Other nights he would leave after a quick couple of drinks with his friends. On these nights he generally made the half-mile walk across the edge of town to visit his girlfriend's flat. This walk involved a shortcut over a large open piece of ground with seven football pitches. Perfect.

As soon as the Ministry had issued a licence to Jack confirming that the top farm was clean, they started building. Most of the sheds up there were old and small. In fact most of them hadn't been used for years as they were no longer suitable for the demands of modern farming.

The only building that had been used in more than five years was the new sheep-shed that Jack's father had built. It was a large shed, 100 feet long by 80 feet wide. The floor was concreted and in excellent condition. The sides were only cladded to halfway down, which left an opening to allow air to circulate freely inside in order to keep the animals healthy. Usually at this time of the year they would bring the ewes down from the higher fields and put them in pens as they were ready to lamb. Part of the clean-up operation had entailed taking all of the pens outside to the yard where they had blasted them clean. Without the pens the floor area was completely clear.

They started to build right in the centre of the shed. The unit that they constructed was oblong-shaped, 60 feet long and 27 feet wide. The entrance was at the back end of the shed. Once through the main door there was a wide corridor with ten doors up each side. At the end of the corridor was a large room which was twenty feet by fifteen. This was covered with a ceiling of plywood and lit by a simple bulb hanging from the centre. Behind the twenty doors in the corridor were small rooms which were eight feet long by four feet wide. Instead of plywood, these rooms were topped by sheets of thick, clear Perspex. Over the Perspex they fitted strong halogen lamps which shone brightly down into the rooms below. Above the lamps was a ceiling of thin hardboard. They painted these rooms a brilliant white which covered the door, the walls, the floor, and the thin sheets over the lights. The white paint had the effect of magnifying the bright light that shone down from above.

The doors were a heavy-duty hardwood. They took two cuts out of each door. In lower one they fitted a hatch just above floor level. In the other, which was at the top of the door, they fitted an audio speaker. This was protected on the inside of the door by a wire mesh. The final addition to each door was a peephole on the outside which looked in.

The work took them three weeks. John Doyle, the builder, worked on it full time. One man would help him through the day whilst the others started on the task of cleaning the main farm. They all mucked in in the evenings.

When it was done, Liam inspected his creation carefully. The thing made him shudder. After ten years in hated H Blocks of Long Kesh, the sight of the cells gave him goosebumps. The stark white cells that they had created were worse than anything that even the Kesh had offered. But then again, the inmates of these cells were only going to be incarcerated for a matter of days, not ten and twenty years. It was fine. It was perfect. They had brought a small piece of Hell to the Scottish hills.

April had drifted into May and the weather had warmed up. All around Hillside Farm the world was exploding into green. Normally Jack would have been watching the fields and trying to guess at what point there might be enough grass to take his first cut of silage. Not this year. Not next either. Probably never again. Fields which would normally be grazed down by hundreds of animals were now filled with daisies and dandelions. He could sense the land going to sleep.

On the day that they completed the cell-block Jack wheeled out the old cut-in-half oil drum that he used as a barbeque. It was a perfectly still spring evening. All around there was the sound of birds, and high above the buzzards soared in their lazy circles. The men ate steaks and drank beer as the sun turned the sky umpteen colours of red and orange. Far below them the street lights of the town of Dumfries slowly started to twinkle as the light faded to black.

They sat out until after midnight that night talking quietly, and eventually they exchanged their beers for mugs of coffee. They had all known combat. They were all familiar with the sensation of knowing that an operation would start the next day. They had all learnt their trade in the estates and mean streets of North and West Belfast. Now they were about to ply their trade in another northern town. Smaller. Sleepier. Far away from the headlines and the gaze of the world media.

Before the Foot and Mouth outbreak nothing much of any note had happened in Dumfries for 700 years when Robert the Bruce had slain John Comyn in the Greyfriars Monastery and had thereby set out his stall for the Scottish throne. By now the epidemic seemed to have been stopped. There had been no new cases of the disease in the Dumfries and Galloway region for some time. The soldiers had packed up their gear and moved down to North Yorkshire and Cumbria where the disease was still raging. The reporters and the TV crews had disappeared. Burning cattle was not particularly big news any more. The novelty value had worn off. Dumfries was once again left alone again to disappear out of view in its sleepy corner of south west Scotland.

But the town was damaged. Probably damaged beyond repair. For years the collapse of agriculture had been pushing the town down. Twenty years before it had been a booming place as it serviced the needs of hundreds and hundreds of thriving farms. It had also had industry of its own. On market days the streets were teeming. But slowly it had all collapsed. The factories had been closed down, the farmers had been ground into the dust and the tourists went where the sun shone and their currency bought them more. Even before Foot and Mouth the decline was almost terminal.

Now it was really terminal. Just about every business relied in one way or another on the region's twin economic pillars of tourism and agriculture. Now they were both all shot to hell. The streets had emptied out and the businesses of Dumfries could do no more than grit their teeth and batten down the hatches to face a long recession. Once the fires had gone out and the slaughter-men had moved on nobody seemed to care much. The eyes of the nation moved on to other news. Dumfries settled down to another 700 years of obscurity. Its fifteen minutes of fame were over.

Little could anyone have known on that balmy spring evening that this small Scottish town was about to be catapulted into the very epi-centre of world media attention by a group of 40 year-old men sipping their coffee high up in the hills.

The next day the operation began.

Ricky hadn't thought about Will for some weeks now. During his time in Spain he had wiped his mind clear of any remorse for what had happened to his friend. There was no point in brooding about it. It hadn't been anyone's fault. It was just an accident. Nothing else. They had only been trying to do him a favour. The heroin supply had settled down again and business was booming. He had actually passed over a few of his direct retail customers to a couple of his better secondary distributors. He had more money in his pocket than he could spend. Why work himself to death? There was no reason. He decided to take it easy.

One consequence of his six weeks in the sun was that he had moved up to two, sometimes three bags of heroin a day. It wasn't much of a problem. He always had plenty and he could easily afford ten bags a day if he wanted. In fact over the last couple of weeks it definitely had been three bags a day. Maybe it was getting a little too much. Not that it bothered him particularly. The stuff was clean and he knew what he was doing. He wasn't thick. He used clean needles and he took care. As long as you could afford your stuff, and you didn't do anything stupid, smack would do you no harm. It was a litany that he had often repeated to his customers. Take it properly and you'll be fine. No problems. Cancer will get you first. Just as long as you can afford it. And money was no problem to Ricky Macintosh. No problem at all.

He looked at himself in the mirror appreciatively. All the clothes that he had just put on had come from expensive boutiques in Spain. How much cash did these clothes represent? He worked it out. Just under two grand's worth, 2,000 quid! On clothes! Who would ever have guessed it. His face was still tanned. Ever since getting home he had made regular trips to the sunbed. He liked himself tanned. So did the girls. They were no problem now. Not now he had his clothes and a pocket full of cash. To complete his image he put on a pair of designer sunglasses that had set him back £200.

Never come to any good that Ricky Macintosh. That is what they had all said. Well who was laughing now?

He could sense the curtains twitching as he strutted through the estate to the pub. Behind the curtains were all the sad bastards who had told their kids not to play with him. And where were they now? Drawing what they could from the Social. Scratching round the second-hand shops to get a bed with their measily allowance cheque. Sitting in the pub looking miserable as fuck and trying to make a half-pint last until nine o'clock. He knew they all hated him. They hated him when he would casually toss a 50-pound note on the bar to pay for drinks for him and his mates. They hated him when he paraded his girls and draped them in jewellery. They hated him when he lit up his fag with his Cartier lighter. And stuff them. Stuff the lot of them. What goes around comes around bastards. Maybe you should have invited me round for tea after all. If you had, maybe you could have asked for a sub to get you through to Friday. Maybe.

It was a beautiful night. He decided he would just have a couple of quick drinks and then go round to his girlfriend's. He called her on the mobile and told her he'd be there in an hour or so. He had two pints and played a couple of games of pool. He smiled as he sensed the envious looks as he walked out of the Wheatsheaf. He had 500 quid in his wallet and everyone who was sitting at the bar always saw it as he paid for his drinks. Nobody else would have dared walk about Sunnybank at night with that kind of money on them. But he was OK. Nobody would dare lay a finger on him. They all knew what would happen. He was Zippo's nephew. He was untouchable. He was royalty.

"OK Ricky. Stand very still. Now turn around."

Where the hell had he come from? Big man. Balaclava. And a gun. A very, very real gun. Pushed hard into his chest. He was on the playing fields now. Not far, just a few yards, but a hedge hid him from the houses on the edge of the estate. Where had he come from? And now suddenly there was tape over his mouth. How? Another one. Another one behind him. And his hands were in handcuffs behind his back. So fast. Who the hell were these guys?

ONSLAUGHT

They had come from nowhere. Fear now. Real fear. Blinding fear. The accent. He knew the accent. What was the accent? Oh shit. Oh fuck. Oh Christ. He knew the accent. Belfast. Fucking Belfast. They were pushing him forward now. Through a gap in the hedge where the young kids did tricks on their mountain bikes. A van. A black van. Side door opening. A push. Inside. Head on the floor. Cheeks pressed down into the metal. Someone was pulling up his sleeve. A prick. Christ an injection. A needle. What the fuck . . . blackness. Great waves of blackness. Somewhere seventeen million miles away there was the noise of an engine and the van was moving. Then there was nothing. Just a black void.

He awoke to light and noise.

The light was unbelievable. It seemed to burn through his eyeballs. He screwed his eyes shut, unable to face it. Then slowly he opened them again. Jesus it was bright. So bright it seemed to scorch. He realised he was cold. Terribly, terribly cold. He was naked. He was lying on a cold concrete floor that was all painted white. He looked about frantically. Everything was white.

White walls. White door. White ceiling except for the lights. He reached out and touched the wall. Cold. Cold and white and concrete. And there was noise. It rammed into his ears. He couldn't think. What was it? What kind of a noise was this? He closed his eyes and tried to separate the noise. There were different things. There were children singing their times-tables to different tunes, there was a voice repeating lines in some foreign language. What? What was it? Russian maybe. And there was the speaking clock, and there were other things. But it was loud, louder than anything he had ever heard before. It was appalling. Unbearable. He dragged himself to his feet and went to the door.

And he started screaming. He screamed and screamed and screamed and beat the door with his fists. Nothing. Absolutely nothing. Just the barrage of sound and the terrible light. He was panicking now. Really panicking. What the hell was happening? Where the hell was he? It was a nightmare. That's it. A nightmare. He would wake up now. Once he realised that it was a nightmare he would wake up. He closed his eyes and willed himself to wake up. Just like he had always woken up before. He opened them again. Still the same. Light and noise. Light and noise.

He attacked the door again, this time with more desperation. Nothing. His hands hurt from hitting the unyielding wood. Nothing. Was there anyone out there? There had to be. Did there? Or had he suddenly gone mad. Had the drugs suddenly completely fried his brain? It must be some kind of hallucination. Again he screwed his eyes shut. Snap out of it Ricky. This can't be real. You're imagining it. Get it out. Get rid of it. But no. It wouldn't go away. He couldn't escape.

He realised that he had been screaming all the time. It was strange because the noise was so loud that he couldn't seem to force the noise out of his mouth. His throat hurt now. He had screamed it raw. And he was cold. So bloody cold. He tried to sit down and wrap his arms around himself for warmth but the floor and the walls were like ice. So he stood again and beat at the door and the walls but his hands hurt. They were bleeding now.

He crouched in the middle of the cell and hugged himself. And now the tears came. Terrible, terrible tears of fear and panic. What was happening to him? Who was doing this to him? Why were they doing this to him? And then a memory slid down his back like iced water. The voice. The black balaclava. The accent. Belfast. Oh Christ. Oh sweet Christ no. Why? Why him? Why would anyone from Belfast want him? But he knew. He didn't want to know, but he knew. It was the drugs. The heroin. They were moving in. Men from Belfast. Men with guns. Oh Christ no. No, no, no, no, no.

Please no. Not me. Please not me. Please God no.

And then there was another horrible awakening. It was only small but it was there. He needed a fix. How long had he been out? Couldn't say. Not that long. The yearning wasn't bad. Not yet. But it was there. A small wispy cloud miles out on the horizon. But the cloud would get bigger. And soon the little cloud would cover the whole sky. And the sky would blacken and the storm would rage. He needed smack. He didn't have any smack. He wasn't going to get any smack. He was locked up in the noise and the brightness and there was no smack.

He couldn't face it. He curled up on the concrete floor and wept. He couldn't take this. He couldn't take it now. And how long had he been awake. Fifteen minutes? Maybe half an hour. How long would they keep him here? Days? Weeks? Months? Oh Christ, please help me Christ, please. Please, please, please, please.

There was no time. Time didn't exist in this place. Every second was a year. Every minute was a decade. Every hour a lifetime. There was only now. Now was noise. Now was cold. Now was light. Now was terror.

What was that? Something. A movement. A movement in the door. The whiteness had moved and there was an eye. A human eye. Looking in. Looking at him. He jumped to his feet and flew at the door. He begged and pleaded and cried and then the eye was gone. There was only whiteness again. He collapsed down and wept.

But now there was another sound. A new sound. It wasn't coming from the speaker with the rest of the sound. It was coming from outside. Outside the door. He could barely hear it but it was there. He pushed his ear against the wood and searched for the new sound. And he found it. Screaming. Terrible screaming. Pain. Agony. All the pain in the world. Someone was screaming out there. Why? What was happening? What were they doing to them? Who was it? Was he alone? Were there others? What was happening?

Torture. It was torture. Someone was being tortured. Screaming. Terrible pain. No. Please no. They would come for him. That was what was next. No. Please no. Not torture. Please not torture. What would they do? What could they possibly be doing to whoever was screaming? Pain. Terrible pain. All the pain in the world. He retreated to the back of the cell and held his hands over his ears. Make the sound go away. Please let it go away.

Please . . .   Please . . .   Please . . .

Liam walked down the track to the main farm where he joined Jack in the kitchen. Jack poured coffee. They lit cigarettes.

"How is he?" asked Jack

"Oh he's all over the place. No strength to him at all. It won't take long. Did you notice his arms? Full of needle marks. He's main-lining. A lot I would guess. We'll give him another eighteen hours. The craving will be eating him alive by then."

"OK."

"Do you want to sit in on it?"

"Yes."

Liam nodded slightly. "OK. Fine."

How long? How long had it been now? No idea. Impossible to tell. A lifetime. And the craving was really eating him now. It was getting so bad he could almost touch it. He curled up into a ball and hung on. Hung on to what? There was nothing. Only noise. Only the killing cold. Only the need. The burning need.

Suddenly there was movement. The door. The door was opening. He scrambled up. Two of them. Huge. Like great black monsters in their balaclavas. They had him by his arms. He tried to struggle but it was pointless. Their hands on his arms were like vices. Christ this was it. It was his turn now. His turn to scream with the terrible pain.

"Come on now Ricky. No point in making it hard on yourself."

That voice again. That accent. Terror.

Out in the corridor now. He wasn't going. No. He tried to hold them back but they just dragged his bare feet along the concrete floor, grazing all his toes. More doors either side. How many others were there? Was Zippo behind one of these doors? Now they were going through another door. Much darker now. And quiet. Thank God the noise was out of his head.

One low-wattage bulb. Two more men. A table. One man behind the table. The other in the corner. Both wearing balaclava hats. Sinister. Frightening. A nightmare. The first two men were pushing him into a chair. A strange chair. Only deep enough for half his buttocks. They pulled his arms behind his back and taped them tight onto a pole so that they pulled the sockets. They pulled his legs apart and taped them to the front legs of the chair. It was wider than most chairs forcing his legs wide apart.

And then they were done. He tried to move but all his limbs were bound far too tight. His breathing was shallow and fast. Terror was climbing up his throat. In front of him, across the table, the man lit a cigarette and arranged a pad and two pens neatly in front of him. He looked up. The eyes bore into Ricky.

Oh God.

Oh no.

Oh Jesus. He had thought that he had just spoken in his head, but then he realised that he was muttering aloud. There was spit around his lips. On his chin.

"So Ricky. Welcome to Hell. Be nice. Be polite. Say hello. You can call me Freddy. Say hello, Freddy."

Ricky gulped. It came out as a whisper. "Hello Freddy."

"Good. Splendid. Outstanding. That is a truly promising start. Because Ricky, the next hours of your life are all about making choices. Choices about how things are going to go. They can either be quite bearable or completely unbearable. Do you understand where I am coming from Ricky?"

"Yes."

"Yes Freddy."

"Sorry, yes Freddy."

"Good. So Ricky, where shall we start? This all must be a bit of a shock. One minute you are off to see that lovely girl of yours and then, bang, you're here. Here with us. Tell me Ricky, do you recognise my accent by any chance."

Ricky nodded. Please him. He had to please him. He had just noticed all the places on the floor around the chair where the concrete was stained with blood. " Yes Freddy. Ireland. Northern Ireland. Belfast."

"Wonderful. Ten out of ten Ricky. I'm delighted to find such a knowledge of dialects in one so young. Now I dare say that you must be aware that we have had our share of troubles over the water for a while. Four hundred years to be exact. Now by nature we Irish are lovely fellas. We like a drink. We like a sing-song. We like a flutter on the horses. But the Troubles have hardened us. We fought a long war against everything the British Army could throw at us. So we had to be hard. Really hard. Not like the amateur hard men you might have come across Ricky. I mean really hard. Bullet in the back of the head hard. Knee-caps off hard. Do you understand what I am saying Ricky?"

A whisper now. "Yes Freddy."

"And we learnt that when we needed to find something out from someone we never got very far by asking nicely. It was sad, but that was the case. We needed information from men who were every bit as hard as we were, boys from the UVF and the UDA. Well they hated us didn't they? So they weren't going to tell us anything, of course they wouldn't, we were their sworn enemies.

"So you see, Ricky, we had to persuade them. And we got good at it. Me in particular. It was my job Ricky. What I trained for. What I studied and thought about long into the night. How to get them to tell. Even the hardest. The maddest. The most fanatical. And do you know what Ricky? They always told. All of them. Every last one of them. Oh, I grant you there were times when it was messy. Very messy. It still can be. I'm sure you could hear in your cell, even though we try to play a bit of music for you to try and mask it. Did you hear, Ricky?"

"Yes Freddy. I heard."

"Well I'm sorry if it frightened you. What you must know, Ricky, is that I don't enjoy any of this. I'm not a psycho. I'm not a sadist. I rather dislike it all to be honest. But it has to be done. What I have found is that it is always worth having a little talk first. Get to know each other. Talk things through like adults. In short, let you know exactly what your options are before the nasty stuff gets started. Options Ricky. You understand the concept of options do you?"

"Yes Freddy."

"Splendid. You've made a good start Ricky. Very polite. You deserve a reward. Would you like a smoke?"

"Yes please Freddy."

Liam got up, lit a cigarette, and put it between Ricky's lips.

From his corner seat Jack winced. He had been in this position himself all those years before. And he had been a trained soldier. The boy looked so pathetic. His face was a mask of fear and his skinny, spread-eagled nakedness made him totally vulnerable. Liam had warned him. He had told him. Don't get soft now Jack. Be the machine. This boy was responsible for Will's death. This is Hell's Kitchen. You called it. You created it. You paid for it. You deal with it.

Liam stood by Ricky with an ashtray. "Don't worry about the ash Ricky. I'm here. I'll catch it. Wouldn't want you to burn your bollocks would we now?"

Ricky closed his eyes and pulled hard on the cigarette.

"So. Where were we? Oh yes. Options. Where things can go from here. Now let's face it Ricky, your situation isn't very good is it? You've been cooped up for hours in that nasty cold room with all that noise and all that light. And you don't know what is happening. And you don't know why it is happening. And you can hear screaming. And I guess you must be rather frightened. Are you frightened Ricky?"

"Yes."

"Are you very frightened Ricky?"

"Yes."

"Are you terrified Ricky?"

"Yes."

"YES FREDDY!!!!!" Liam screamed it. Close. Right into the boy's ear.

"Yes, Freddy."

"Well of course you are. No shame in that. Anyone would be." The voice was back to its normal gentle rhythm. Tears were streaming down Ricky's cheeks, onto his chin, down his chest, into his crotch. Liam paused a moment and pulled out a handkerchief. He gently wiped Ricky's face. "Now, now, I know. It's horrible isn't it?"

A snuffle "Yes Freddy."

Liam took the cigarette from Ricky's lips, docked it and sat back down.

"Options Ricky. Options. I'm going to start with the bad side. The place where you really don't want to go. The worst place in the world. The land of the nightmares. I apologise in advance for upsetting you, but it is only fair. You must know your options.

"You may have been wondering about the chair. Have you been wondering about this strange chair Ricky?"

"Yes Freddy."

"Well, believe it or not, this odd-looking chair is the result of years of research Ricky. In fact I'm rather proud of it. There is a lot more than you may think to asking people questions that they don't want to answer. To start off with we weaken you. We don't let you sleep with light and noise. And we strip you naked. Take away the comfort and protection of your clothes. Make you cold. Make you miserable. And then we bring you in here and strap you into this odd chair. And it's tight, isn't it Ricky? Really tight?"

"Yes Freddy."

"And you can't move at all. Not even an inch. You are completely trapped. And of course your legs are pulled right apart and your genitals are all exposed and hanging free. Aren't they Ricky?"

"Yes Freddy."

"And no matter what happens there is nothing you can do to protect your genitals is there Ricky?"

"No Freddy."

"And this is the clever bit. The deeply-thought-out psychology that has gone into the making of this chair. You see Ricky, all of us men have a thing about our genitals. It is where we are most vulnerable. Our weakest of weak points. So it is hard to imagine what could possibly be worse than being strapped bollock-naked to a chair with your genitals just dangling free waiting for whatever I might want to do to them Would you like to see some of the things I might do to them?"

"No! No please. Please . . ."

"Calm down, calm down. I'm not saying I'm about to do it, I'm saying I will show you what I might do. OK. First up. This is a little invention of mine. It's simple. It's easy to make. The materials are cheap. And it is superbly effective. Look. We have two six-inch pieces of wood and at each end they are attached by a nut and bolt. Now as you can see it is quite a long bolt. Now you are going to have to use your imagination here whilst I demonstrate how it works."

Liam rooted in a briefcase on the floor by his side. "OK. What do we have here? Two plums. One Safeway carrier bag. Now I'm going to pop the plums into the bag, and this is where you need to use that imagination. What you have to pretend is that the plumbs are your testicles and the bag is your scrotum. And the whole package is hanging down off the edge of the strange chair. Now look. I am fitting the plumbs into the space between the pieces of wood just like this. OK? And now I can start tightening the wing-nuts.

"Now think, Ricky. Think of those times at school when someone kicked a football into your knackers. Remember how much that hurt? Terrible wasn't it? But that was nothing. Just imagine this. Just imagine me reaching down and tightening and tightening and tightening."

"Oh God no, you don't have to, I'll tell you anything . . ."

"Quiet please Ricky. Don't interrupt my flow. I hate it when people do that. Now where was I? Oh yes. Now let's just assume that you pass the first test. Even when I squeeze your bollocks nearly flat you still come through. What then? Well that would tell me something. It would tell me that you have a high ability pain to resist pain. So what next?"

Liam held up the bag with the pieces of wood clamped tight onto the plumbs inside. The inside of the plastic was stained where the fruit had burst. "Well there has to be more pain. Worse pain. So we move to a new level. A real test."

Liam reached into his pocket and took out a lighter. "Now this isn't sophisticated at all. Rather crude really. But let's face it Ricky, there is nothing that hurts quite as much as being burned. You know how it is when you burn your finger with a match. And it doesn't just hurt a bit. It hurts a lot. Hurts like hell. And that is just one little burn for half a second. Now just imagine this."

Liam lit the lighter and held it under the burst fruit. There was a rank smell of burning plastic. The bag caught quickly and the melted plastic dripped to the floor until the fruit burst free and splatted onto the concrete. Liam pushed his face in close. Ricky was moaning now. Blubbering. His eyes were clamped shut. "Imagine it Ricky. Imagine just how much that would hurt. Try Ricky. TRY!!!"

Ricky twisted his head away and screwed his eyes tighter shut. "NO! NO! PLEASE! NO! . . ."

Liam bent down and gently patted the bottom of Ricky's scrotum. The boys eyes shot open wide and he screamed with everything he had. Jack felt sick to his stomach. It was foul. Disgusting. He had to stop this. No. He took a breath. No Jack. You started all this. You knew how it would be. See it through.

It seemed as if Ricky's eyes were about to come clean out of the sockets. He thrashed and writhed and screamed and screamed until his throat couldn't take any more, leaving him covered in a sheen of sweat and gasping for breath.

"Here Ricky. Another cigarette. Here. Take it. It will calm you. Nicotine soothes. Nicotine calms. There. Take a hard pull. There. That's better isn't it Ricky?"

"Yes Freddy." Less than a whisper. Almost inaudible.

"This is why I like to discuss options. It is a nasty business. Very nasty. Best avoided. Trust me Ricky. It really is. So instead of all the pain and the unpleasantness you can choose the better option. And that is of course to talk with me. We can put all this behind us and talk like civilised men should. I ask you a question. You give me an answer. Nothing hard. No mathematical teasers. No philosophy or physics or genetics. Just questions that you know all the answers to. I ask, you answer. Now what could be more simple? That is simple isn't it Ricky?"

"Yes Freddy."

"And it gets better. Oh yes, much better. Because if I am happy that you really are doing the very best that you can to tell me the truth I will reward you. Effort deserves reward. And each reward will make life so much better. First you will get a blanket for your cell. Then a mattress to lie on. Then something warm to eat. Then some jogging pants and a sweat-shirt and then the best of all. Can you guess what the best thing of all is Ricky? Can you?"

Ricky shook his head.

"I guessed, you see. It wasn't all that hard. Not when we took off all those expensive clothes and saw what a dreadful mess you have made of your arms. It wasn't hard to guess. Wasn't hard to figure out what would be the best treat in the whole world for young Ricky Macintosh."

Liam reached into his briefcase and pulled out a full syringe. "There Ricky. Look at that. Have you ever seen anything more beautiful. Heroin. Lovely, lovely 40 percent pure, sweet heroin. Imagine that, Ricky. Imagine how good things could be. Some clothes, a blanket, a nice mattress, food, and all that wonderful lovely heroin flowing through your body . . ."

"Anything Freddy. I promise. You don't need to hurt me. I swear it. I swear. Just ask me. Please ask me. I won't lie. I promise."

"Well you mustn't lie Ricky. Because what is given can be taken away. If I find you telling one single lie it will all be taken away, no matter how much truth you have already told me. And then I will hurt you. I will have to. You would deserve that. Can you see that Ricky?"

"Yes. Yes. No lies. Only the truth. All truth."

"Because I will know Ricky. I will know if you're lying. I'll know straight away. I'm an expert you see. You know that don't you Ricky?"

"I know Freddy. I won't lie. Honest. I promise. I won't lie Freddy. Never."

And he didn't. Liam sat patiently writing notes in his pad for the next six hours. One by one Ricky received his rewards. In the end he was sitting in a tracksuit with his arms and legs free. Liam's questions were fast and he moved quickly from point to point. As the hours wore on, he went over each question at least ten times, always probing for any discrepancies.

There were none. The boy had him told everything that he knew. Just as Liam had known he would. And now he had the lot. Zippo, Wee Kenny, Tommy Banks, the King brothers, Tina, the secondary distributors. He knew who they were, where they lived, where they went out, when they went out, who they went out with. He knew about houses and hobbies and routines and families and habits. He knew what kind of people they were, how they acted, what they were like. And he knew exactly how the heroin made its way along the chain, how much it cost, what mark-up was added, how rendezvous were arranged on mobile phones. It took six hours.

And Liam Kelly had it all.

By the end of day two the operation was way ahead of schedule.

"OK Ricky. Here you are."

Liam passed the needle and a piece of cloth. Ricky dragged up his sleeve, prepared a vein. His eyes rolled with ecstasy as the drug hit his bloodstream.

"Back to your room now Ricky. Sleep tight. No more music now. And we'll switch the lights down. There will be more work for you tomorrow, and if you're a good boy, as good as you have been today, there will be another one of these." Liam wagged a syringe in front of Ricky's eyes. "Sleep tight now."

Doyle and O'Hara led him out of the door and back down the corridor. He fell onto his mattress and wrapped the blanket tight around him. The cell was only lit by a soft, dim light. He realised that he had betrayed absolutely everything that there was to betray. And he didn't care. He didn't care because there was no more sound and no more light and no more cold and no more chair.

THE CULL

And there was smack. Wonderful, wonderful smack surging through his veins.

Chapter 8
The Block

Liam joined the others in the kitchen of the main farmhouse a little after 10.30 that night. He had spent a couple of hours checking over the video they had taken of the interrogation and organising his notes. He had then walked up to the fields at the very top of the farm and had spent a while sitting staring out into space.

Jack noticed that his features were tight and drawn as he came in. He looked drained.

"Some curry in the pot, boss" said O'Hara.

"Cheers Declan."

Liam ladled out a portion of curry, took a can of lager from the fridge and joined them at the table. He gave Jack a tight grin. "So Major. Your instincts were right. These guys are rank amateurs. No need for 'The Battle of Algiers' after all. Five more interrogations and that will be that."

"Five?"

"Yes. Andrew Moncur, who seems to be the only main distributor other than Ricky who has secondary distributors. Tommy Banks and the King brothers. We don't need to find anything out from them, but we will need to break them, and big boss-man Zippo. Then I believe there will be one more. But that will be your call Jack."

"Who?"

"The Glasgow man. Whoever it was that Zippo met in Barlinnie. The fountainhead. I know we said we would stop in

Dumfries, but my gut feeling tells me that he will be there on a plate for us."

Jack thought about this as Liam dug into his curry. Liam continued on. "I just can't believe how soft their organisation is. Jesus Jack, if we had been like that you lads would been through us like a dose of salts by 1972. They're wide open."

"They aren't terrorists. It is a corporate model. It's like a bloody franchise. They are so confident. They pin everything on the law. As long as the law has no real teeth they know they are fire-proof. I kept thinking how different Ricky would have been in a police cell. He would have said bugger-all until his solicitor turned up and he would have said bugger-all then." Jack paused for a moment. "Not with you though Liam. Jesus."

Liam grimaced. "I told you it wouldn't be nice. But remember Jack, that boy doesn't have a single scratch on him. Not a scratch."

"I suppose not, I just couldn't help thinking . . ." The sentence tailed off.

"You just couldn't help thinking about the time when you were in that chair, yes?"

"Yes. I don't know how I would have been."

"Nobody does. Not until it happens."

"How often did it get nasty Liam?"

"Not often. Only twice. Both of them real head-bangers from the UVF. Psychos. Real fanatics. It wasn't very nice. But they talked in the end. Everybody does."

Jack stared down at his can of beer. Liam smiled. "Come on Major, spit it out. I know what you are thinking."

"What?"

"What would you have been like? Am I right?"

"I suppose so."

"I think you would have been a nightmare. You have that bloody stubborn streak. And you were a believer then. For you the British Army could do no wrong. You were on the side of the angels. Saving the world from itself. It would have been nasty I think. Very nasty. Lucky it never happened."

Jack couldn't help but shudder. "I remember that night you mentioned a name. Hoffman. Who was Hoffman?"

"He was an officer in the East German Stasi. He was my guru

at the terrorist school in Libya. His speciality was interrogation. He had been tutored by the best: ex-Gestapo officers, KGB, the real deal. But he was subtle. He knew that if you could build enough fear then there was seldom a need for the pain."

"What about you Liam? How could you take it? I can see in your face how much you hate it."

Liam sighed. "You lot really could never understand us. You still can't. That's why you could never win. You used to think it was just propaganda when we said it was a war. It is impossible for you to imagine. You don't know what it's like to have foreign soldiers on your streets who kick your door down in the middle of the night and trash your house and spit in your Ma's face. You can't imagine how it is to be scared shitless if you walk too close to the wrong bit of town. And the Kesh. I bet you never set foot inside the Kesh did you Jack? None of the soldiers did. I bet you all laughed at the daft things we used to say about it? You know, all the stuff about it being a concentration camp. Just propaganda, nothing more. Well, did you ever go Jack."

Jack bowed his head slightly. "No."

"None of you did. You all thought it couldn't be the case because this is Britain and we don't do things like that. Well, not any more. You did of course, you invented the bloody concentration camp in 1902. You killed 25,000 Boer women and kids in your camps. And then you built more in the fifties for the Mau Mau in Kenya. Christ alone knows how many you killed there. And you did it again in Long Kesh Prison. None of you could bear to face up to the fact that what we were saying was the truth. None of the soldiers believed us. Nobody on the mainland believed us. The media never believed us. So it was war. A war where we were out-gunned and out-numbered. We had to do anything we could to hang on in there. Anything. Intelligence was my job. I didn't like it. But I was good at it. And I did it."

Jack shook his head. "I can see that. But why now? Why again? I can't believe it is just money."

Now Liam was quiet. He had finished the curry and lit a cigarette. "Shame Jack. Something I am ashamed of. A debt. It was in the mid-eighties. We had a major meeting in the Brigade. The UDA had set up a major drugs operation in the Shankhill. They were coining it in. Our Chief wanted to do the same. It was too good an opportunity to pass-up. We needed the money. Funds from the States were drying up. I was against it. All we had was the support of our people. Our communities. This would erode that support. Always before we had sorted problems out for our people. If there were thieves, or sex-offenders or kids going wild, we were the ones that our people turned to. We sorted it. Not the RUC. It gave us our legitimacy. Now they wanted to peddle poison to our own people to raise a few quid. It was wrong. I knew it was wrong. But they wouldn't listen. So we became drug-dealers. Some still are. And there are boys in Belfast who are like your son. I bear responsibility for that Jack. So I suppose this is war too."

"Now I can understand. And that is why you want phase three of the plan."

"That's correct." Liam was tight-lipped. He felt bad that he hadn't been honest with Jack from the start. He couldn't really understand why he hadn't been. Jack chuckled. "Does that mean I'm going to get a refund."

"Does it buggery. Anyway, how can you get a refund? We've not had a penny yet."

"Not yet, but you will in a couple of days. I got a call this evening. The cheque is in the post. Anyway, what about the plan. Have things changed?"

"Yes. Yes I think they have. Completely. It seems to me that we know more-or-less all we need to about their operation. The Algiers concept was that we should start at the bottom and work our way up until we found who was at the top. No need now. We know who is at the top. We know who they are, what they are and where they are. Now these are the guys who are the main threat. If we start pulling in the lower people they will start to smell a rat. Better that we take them first. The others can wait, they are much less of a threat. I think we go in fast and we go in hard. Let's get them picked up as soon as possible."

Jack had thought on exactly the same lines. "Fine by me. When?"

"Tomorrow night. We take Moncur first. Ricky will help set that up. Then we take Banks as he is leaving the pub. Then we do the King brothers. Late. About three o'clock. And then we take Zippo. We go in the hour before dawn. But I am worried about this Wee Kenny character. Everything about him is wrong. He sounds as if he is huge, and as loyal to Zippo as a big dog. He will be nothing but trouble. Bad to deal with. Difficult to handle. And to be honest it doesn't really sound as if he is actually one of the bad guys. I think we leave him. Immobilise him and leave him. OK with you Jack?"

"Fine by me."

"Then we all better get some sleep. Big day tomorrow."

Things had really started to fly for Andrew Moncur. He had been expanding his operation dramatically. He had set on three new secondary distributors. He now had a total of six. His new outlets were out of town. The first had been in Castle Douglas, a small town eighteen miles to the west of Dumfries. Andrew had known the boy from playing rugby. He had always been the star of the Castle Douglas team from when Andrew had started playing at the age of nine. Tony McDonald had been a stand-off with magic in his boots. There had always been talk that he could make it all the way to the Scotland team one day. In fact he had been picked for his country at the under-fifteen level. Then he had disappeared from the scene at the age of eighteen.

Andrew had asked about. Drugs he was told. McDonald had a habit. He was shot. Couldn't play rugby now. Bloody shame. So much talent. What a waste.

Andrew had looked him up. He had found Tony McDonald in a right state. It had been no problem to enlist him as a secondary distributor, and once the boy had settled himself down onto a more regular supply of heroin, he had shown as much flair as a dealer as he once had on the rugby field. He had given Andrew two more excellent contacts, both in small towns along the coast. Kirkudbright and Dalbeattie. And now business was booming.

He was confident that he had to be the number one outlet in Zippo's operation now. Maybe he should ask for better terms. After all, he was moving a tonne of stuff for them. It was tempting. Seriously tempting. But he knew he wasn't dealing with the most rational of people. He had always sensed their resentment. To them he would always be the posh kid from the nice house with a Councillor for a father. Maybe it was a matter best left alone.

THE CULL

He was on his way to meet Ricky Macintosh. He wondered what it was all about. They never had much to do with each other. Ricky serviced customers on the estates, whilst most of Andrew's business came from the suburbs and the countryside. They had no problem with each other. Both of them were loaded, and both of them were only going to get more loaded. There was nothing to fall out about.

Ricky had called that morning. He wanted to meet up for a chat. Nothing particular. Just this and that. They arranged to meet in a pub on the edge of town. Andrew parked up in the car park at the back of the pub. He pressed the button to set the alarm and felt something in his back. He turned. What the hell? A man. Balaclava. Gun. Jesus. What was happening? He was being pushed now. A black van. Where the hell had that come from? The floor. An injection. Darkness.

It was one of those unlikely things. Across the road a man was decorating a first-floor bedroom. He was on his day off. He had stopped for a cup of tea and he was gazing out of the window thinking of nothing in particular. He noticed Andrew's new convertible BMW as it pulled onto the car park. Lucky little bastard. Not yet twenty and driving about in forty grand's worth of car. The man knew Andrew. He was the lock forward who scrummed down next him every Saturday.

What happened next made him rub his eyes in disbelief. Was the man wearing a balaclava? Was Andrew forced into the van? No. Surely not. It was all so quick. And then the van was gone. What should he do about it? No. It couldn't be anything serious. Sod it. He wasn't going to waste his day off. The car. That was the key. If the car was still there the next morning he would ring the Councillor and tell him. It probably wasn't anything. He would only make himself look a prat.

Tommy Banks had had a few when he left the pub that night. There was nothing unusual about this. He had a few every night. Always had. Ever since he was fourteen. The only time that he didn't have a few was when he was inside. Tommy was pissed off. There had been green and white shirts everywhere he had looked in the pub. They all stayed clear of course. They knew better than to get too close. But he was sick of the sight of their grinning faces. Celtic had just completed the treble, and Martin O'Neal was being hailed as the greatest thing since the bloody Pope. He felt like battering the lot of them. But there were limits. He had cut one of the Fenian bastards a few months before and Zippo had gone ballistic. He couldn't understand what Zippo's problem was. He wasn't the man that Tommy had known in Barlinnie. He fancied himself as some kind of fancy businessman now. When Tommy had first come down to Dumfries the two of them had spent time together, mainly in the pub. Not any more. Zippo never fancied the pub much any more. All he wanted to do was to take his little tart to fancy restaurants. Yeah, pissed off. Really pissed off. He was getting sick of Dumfries. A small town full of wankers. And there was nowhere to drink that wasn't full of smirking twats in their green and white shirts.

Maybe it was time to move on. Go back to Glasgow. Back to proper bubs with pictures of the Queen on the walls where any Fenian bastard would be kicked to shit ten seconds after walking through the door. Maybe it was time.

"Don't move Tommy."

Who the fuck . . .

A van. Shit. He reached for the knife in his pocket.

"No knife Tommy."

He could feel the shape of a gun pushed into his neck. He stopped his hand. He was already breaking into a cold sweat. He knew that voice. That was Belfast. His head hit the floor of the van hard. Someone had their knee in the small of his back. Maybe it would be OK. Maybe they were UDA. If they were UDA he would reason with them.

"Welcome to Hell you Orange bastard."

A prick. And then darkness. But before darkness the horrible realisation set in. Orange bastard. The voice had said Orange Bastard. Not UDA. Not UDA at all. Holy shit.

The King brothers had decided on a big night in. They had planned it for a while. They had made a call to a mate of Zippo's who had arranged for two of his best girls to take the train down to Dumfries from Glasgow. They had collected the girls from the station a little after six and they had them in bed before seven. They were due back on the nine o'clock train the next morning and the brothers were determined to get the best value for their investment. The night was costing them £500 each. Already they had both decided that the money had been well spent. Both girls were gorgeous and eighteen. Just like Zippo's mate had said, they were up for anything. Anything at all.

Their exertions meant that neither man was in any state to resist when their bedroom doors flew in a little after two that morning. Before they had chance to do anything other than register absolute shock at the black-clothed monsters, they were held by strong hands, and needles were jabbed into their arms. Then blackness.

The girls presented a problem. Liam thought about it whilst O'Hara kept them on the bed at gunpoint. He glanced down at the two unconscious bodies of the 40 year-old King brothers. They were hardly the most handsome of men. The girls, on the other hand were gorgeous. They also didn't seem overly concerned at their nakedness. The penny dropped.

"You're working girls, yes?"

They nodded.

"Where from?"

"Glasgow."

"Then you know the score. Here. Here's a couple of hundred. Ring a taxi. Get back there. You don't want the fuss. You don't want any part of this. OK?"

"OK."

Two big men heaved up the unconscious bodies of the King brothers and carried them out over their shoulders. Liam tossed the notes onto the bed. Easy come, easy go. He had filled his pocket from Andrew Moncur's wallet a few hours earlier. You had to take the chance to pick up day-to-day expenses whenever you could.

"Good evening ladies."

One of the girls picked up the money and nodded. She knew that accent. Belfast. She had no intention of playing with fire. What the hell. A taxi beat the train and the pair of them had been bloody animals anyway. They got back to their flat a little before dawn. They never said a word. Why should they?

THE BLOCK

4 a.m. One more collection. They pulled the van up in the back yard behind Zippo's house. Ricky had given them all the details that they needed to know about the house. There was no alarm. No need. Nobody in their right mind would ever dream of breaking into Zippo's house. The lights were out in the bedrooms. Good. The only light was on the landing. They could see the dull glow through a window. They went in through the back door. The big bastard hadn't even bothered to lock it. Doyle found the switchboard and killed the power.

Up the stairs now. Slow. Very slow. Hand-signals on the landing. They all wore night vision goggles. The landing was a ghostly green. Two men to one door. Two men to the other door. Liam held up his hand. Made a fist. Go,

O'Hara kicked in the door. Jack swung into the doorway. He saw the massive figure of Wee Kenny rising in his bed. He levelled his rifle. Fired. The tranquilliser dart hit him square in the chest. A look of utter surprise filled his big face. Then he slumped backwards. Jack moved forward and pulled out the dart. There was a big enough dose to put down a large bull. Wee Kenny was in for a long lie-in.

The exact procedure was repeated the other side of the landing. Liam's dart hit Zippo in almost the exact same place. Tina came awake more slowly. Doyle took hold of her thin arms whilst Liam pushed in a needle. She slumped back. O'Hara and Doyle hefted the sixteen-stone figure out of the back door and into the van. It was four minutes past four.

Zippo's whole command structure had been taken down in less than six hours. By six that morning they were all stripped and laid out in cells ready for the noise and the light to start their work. To all intents and purposes the war was over.

All four of Jack's team slept in that morning. They got up and ate a huge fry-up at eleven o'clock. There was a mood of grim satisfaction around the table. Apart from Moncur, the men in the cell-block up at the top farm weren't kids. They were all hard-men, seasoned criminals who had put the fear of God into a whole town. And they had knocked the whole lot of them over in one night. No fighting. No shooting. Just clean and clinical.

THE CULL

Jack and Liam looked in through the spy holes on the cell doors at noon. Andrew Moncur had been in for 24 hours and he was in a fearful state. The King brothers were little better. Tommy Banks was just about hanging on but it wouldn't be long. But Zippo was different. He was sitting calmly and staring at the door. Waiting. Ready. He saw their eyes at the spy hole and he smiled. He slowly raised his hand and gave them a 'V' sign. He wasn't breaking. Not yet.

They sat in the interrogation room.

"So Liam. What do you think?"

"We'll do Moncur this afternoon. It won't take long. He's had it. We'll get him to make appointments with his secondary distributors and we'll take them in this evening. We'll leave the others till the morning. Should be long enough. They should be ready to make appointments with their men by the late afternoon. That will mean that we can get the rest mopped up tomorrow night."

"Zippo?"

"We'll leave him. He won't be easy."

"Will it get nasty?"

"Probably not. I've got a couple of tricks up my sleeve. You never know. By the day after tomorrow he might just be a pussy-cat."

"That'll be the day. Not that one. He's a hard-case."

"Hey. You of little faith. Remember who you hired? I've nailed harder cases than him in my time. You just wait and see."

By midnight the next night their cells were almost full, Andrew Moncur had made appointments with all of his distributors and they had all been rounded up by the end of the evening. Tommy Banks and the King brothers offered little more resistance. They were soon eager to arrange appointments with all their contacts. By the end of the evening all of them were in the bag. All the men were now wrapped up in their blankets and sat on mattresses wondering what lay in store for them. They were all totally broken. The sheer shame of how they had come apart was eating away at them. They were quiet. All shared the same thoughts. What next? What about Zippo? Had they pulled Zippo? Had they broken Zippo?

The answer, if they had known it, was that they hadn't. It had been over 40 hours now but Zippo was taking it. He had been there before. Never quite like this of course. This was completely off the wall. But he had known solitary. Lots of it. All you had to do was reach inside. Reach inside all the way. Find your strength. And then you could stare them down. They would look in through the peep-hole. And they would wait to see if you were starting to unravel. Well, let the bastards look. They could look for weeks if they liked. Bit of light. Bit of noise. Big deal. So fucking what?

The screaming was a little more alarming. What were they doing? No point in worrying about it. When it happened, he would deal with it. At first his mind had been racing. Who was it? Who the hell would dare? One thing was certain, they were professionals. Not some two-bit amateur outfit. Where the hell was he? How long? Then he had pushed these thoughts aside. No point. At some stage he would have the answers. Why eat himself up about it? Instead he focused all his efforts onto fighting off the cold that was crawling into his limbs. It could have been worse. It could have been January. He could take it. His body would adjust.

What about food? Would they feed him? Yes. They had to. If they had wanted him dead they would have just shot him. No. They wanted to question him. There would be food. After a day and a half the hunger was becoming uncomfortable. He had burned up lots of energy in fighting off the cold. The thirst was worse. His mouth was really dry now. How long would they leave it? No idea. All there was to do was to wait. Give them nothing. Absolutely nothing. No way was he going to ask. No way.

He had no concept of time. At last he had slept. He awoke to another sound over the endless din coming from the speaker. The hatch. The hatch at the bottom of the door snapped open. A hand placed a plate with bread and a plastic glass of water on the floor. The hand was removed. The hatch slammed closed.

Zippo laughed. Bread and water. Did these wankers really think they were going to break him by giving him bread and water? Oh well boys, dream on. He took the plate and cup and sat back down in the corner. He took his time. He sipped the water slowly, savouring every drop. Then he ate the bread. Slowly. Small piece by small piece. Thanks lads. Nice of you. Better for that.

He sat back against the wall and wondered if he could fall asleep again. Maybe he could. Sleep was just a habit. He knew he could learn to block out the sound and the burning light given time. You could adjust to just about anything given time. If you were strong enough. And he was. He knew he was.

Or was he? Very small doubts started to crawl in through his ears. Christ he was cold. Not just a bit cold. Really cold. So cold he felt like he might die of it. Course not. Don't be stupid. But then again. Christ, he could feel it now. There were bits of ice in his arteries. Christ alive, his blood was beginning to freeze. He rubbed his arms and legs as hard as he could, frantically feeling for lumps where the bits of ice were. What would happen when they got into his heart? He would die. He would have no chance.

He looked about frantically at the white walls and the white floor and the white ceiling. And he saw it. Made the terrible realisation. This was no cell. It was a fridge. A freezer. They had him in a freezer. That was why there was ice in his arteries. They wanted to freeze him to death. He leapt to his feet and started rubbing himself as hard as he could. But it was no good. The more he rubbed the colder he became.

What! What was this? The walls. The walls were beginning to come together. They were closing in. Like a car crusher. Like in films. This was no film. They were going to crush him. He threw himself at a wall and pushed and pushed. But it was no good. It kept coming. There was nothing that could stop it. Closing. Closing. Screaming now. Screaming as hard as he could. Make it stop. Make it stop.

Darkness.

Silence.

So dark. Darker than anything he had ever known before. Complete total darkness. Not a chink of light. Not a glimmer of light. The walls. Were they still coming? He felt out desperately. No. They were stopped now. But cold. Dark and cold. Too dark. So dark that he didn't know if he could breathe.

"Light! Light! Light! . . ."

A small light now. A small square of light. Movement. Where was the light? The hatch. The door hatch. Gone now. All dark again. And total silence.

Light.

Light again. Burning agonising light. And what was that. Oh

no. Please no. A rat. A terrible evil rat. In the corner. Staring at him. Eyes straight from hell. Measuring him. Sizing him.

And sound. Terrible ear-splitting sound. The rat goes mad. Completely mad. Demented with sound. Frantically running. No. Keep away. Away! Away! He thrashed to keep the rat away from him. Thrashed and thrashed.

And darkness again. Utter. But still sound. But where was the rat? No. No please. Get it out. Get it away from me! Where was the rat? And screaming, screaming, screaming . . .

No noise now. Silence. Silence and light. The door opening. A black figure. All black. Head to toe black. Evil. From the Devil. From Satan himself. And now Zippo knew. He knew all of it. Every bit.

He was in Hell. He must have died. And this was Hell. He collapsed exhausted and started to cry. The devil in black brushed the rat out of the cell and leant over him. Zippo was gibbering now. "Sorry, so sorry, *so sorry* . . ."

The figure tapped him hard on the shoulder. "No more 'V' signs at the door Eric. No more. You learn to be polite now. Be polite or the rat is coming back. And the rat will be hungry Eric. Hungry."

Zippo's eyes shot open and he grasped at the devil man's legs. He hung on. He wept. He begged. No more rat. Please. Keep the rat away. Keep it out. I'll be polite. I'll never be rude again. You must believe me. You have to. Please believe me . . ."

The devil man pulled his leg clear and left the cell. The door slammed shut. Just light now. No noise. Only light. And silence. And nightmares. And nightmares. And horror for evermore.

Outside, Jack stepped away from the spy hole and shook his head in amazement. "Jesus Liam, what the hell did you do to him?"

"Acid. LSD. Lucy in the sky with diamonds. Loads of it in his water. LSD brings on symptoms of acute terror, insecurity, hallucination and paranoia. Even the best special forces training cannot prepare the mind for it."

"And the rat? How did you know it had to be a rat?"

"I didn't. Statistics prove that the most common of our phobias is a fear of rats. If the rat hadn't worked I would just have had to try other things until we hit pay dirt."

Jack was physically shaken. He had watched Zippo laugh in

their faces for 40 hours and then in the course 60 minutes he had seen him reduced to a complete wreck.

"My God Liam, where did you learn this?"

"I told you. Libya. Hoffman. The research came from the KGB. This was what they did to their dissidents in their mental hospitals. Things have moved on, Jack. There is little need to pull fingernails any more. Not if you know what you are doing. We'll leave him now. The trip will go on for at least another eight hours. Then he'll sleep. Give it twelve hours. We'll see how he is then."

Roger Philips was having an interesting day. A very interesting day. It had started at ten that morning. A very bemused desk-sergeant had shown two visitors in to see him. He was astonished to see Wee Kenny and a thin young girl come into his office.

Wee Kenny had sat down quietly. He wore the confused expression of a big dog that couldn't understand why it was in trouble. The girl did all the talking. She was almost beside her herself. Roger kept trying to get her to slow down, but it was no good. It all came out in a mad, gushing flow. They were like monsters. Great black monsters with metal robot eyes. They shot Zippo and took him away. They shot Kenny too. They did. They did. Show him Kenny. Show him. Kenny duly pulled up his jumper to reveal a massive chest with a livid blue bruise over his left nipple. It went on and on and on. In the end he ushered them away. What the hell was it all about? Somewhere in the girl's hysterics it appeared that Eric Zippo Macintosh had been abducted. Now that really would be something. Philips had more or less made his mind up to go and visit Zippo's house to check when he received another visitor.

This time it was Councillor Walter Moncur. He knew Moncur from the Golf Club and he couldn't abide him. The man was a successful builder who thought that he had become some kind of royalty the day he was elected to the Council. It had only got worse when the club committee had made the wretched man captain two years before. Roger sighed and waited to hear half an hour's worth of sanctimonious shite about how he and his colleagues were rather disappointed with some aspect of police performance.

He was wrong. Instead he got a story almost as far-fetched as the wild ramblings of the hysterical thin girl. Moncur had received a call from a mate at the rugby club. The day before he had thought he had seen Andrew hustled into the back of a van by men in balaclavas. Well the mate hadn't really made much of it. Either he imagined it or it was some kind of prank. But Andrew's posh new car was still there this morning so he had thought that he had better ring. The Councillor had tried ringing his son, and he had been round to his flat. Nothing. The car was still there, but no Andrew.

There had to be some kind of obvious explanation. But could Roger look into it? It was probably nothing. You know these young ones. But could he check? As a favour? To a mate.

When the Councillor had gone Roger was really intrigued. He knew things about Andrew Moncur that his father probably hadn't even dreamed of. He had a file on young Moncur that had been growing steadily for the last two years. It was the usual story. Nothing concrete. Just tip-offs. Nods and winks. Rumours and innuendo. But there had been more than enough to convince Roger that there had to be something to it. Moncur was obviously a dealer and, in all likelihood, an important dealer.

So. Two wild stories of paramilitary-style abductions. Zippo Macintosh and one of his main dealers. It was early days, but still. He made several calls that afternoon. Just unofficial friendly calls. He checked out the homes of Ricky Macintosh and the King brothers and Tommy Banks. And there was nobody home. Stranger and stranger.

He wondered whether or not to make a report to his senior officer. After considering it for a while he decided not to. After all, what real facts did he have? Nothing. Better to wait and let whatever was happening unfold. But still.

Once Zippo's brain had come back to something approaching normality he started to put himself back together again. It wasn't easy. He found it almost impossible to find any reserves of strength to draw on. He had no idea what had happened to him. They had done something. They had taken his brain and liquidised it. It didn't really matter how they had done it. All that mattered is that they had taken him through the gates of Hell. There was no way that he ever wanted to go there again. But he knew that he would have to. And he knew that he would have to find a way to fight it. This was the kind of battle that he had never fought before. These men, whoever they were, were toying with his mind. They were breaking him up piece by little piece. He had to find a way to deal with it. Physically he was more or less completely shattered. He was cold to the marrow and thirsty and hungry. His spirits were becoming dangerously low. But deep inside there was still pride. Somehow he had to keep going. Somehow he would find the strength. Somehow.

He didn't fight them when they came for him. There was no point. There were two of them, and they were both big. He allowed himself to be led to the interrogation room and strapped into the chair.

So this was it. They had finished the mental torture stage. This was when the real stuff would start. In a way physical pain would come as a relief. It was something that he could get his head round. Something tangible. Something that he was used to. It was familiar ground. OK then bastards. Get on with it. His big face broke into a slow smile. He stared hard at the figure in the balaclava at the other side of the table.

The figure looked up from his notes and spoke.

"So, Eric, I hope you're enjoying your little stay with us. Have you been comfortable?"

"Fuck off."

"Oh dear. It's like that, is it? Well is it, Eric?"

"Fuck off you Paddy twat."

"I see. Not in a very civil mood this morning, are we Eric? Not to worry. These things happen. Never mind. I have a couple of things that I want to show you, Eric. I think that you will find them of interest. But first, maybe we should loosen you up a bit. I hope you enjoyed your hallucinogenic experience. Time for another one."

Zippo writhed in the chair as the needle sank into his veins. Damn them. Damn the bastards. It wasn't fair. They were going to fuck with his brain again. He gritted his teeth and fought and fought. But slowly the drug started to pull and tease at his mind and the terrible fear started to set in again. There was nothing that he could do. The more he fought, the worse it got.

Liam sat patiently with his arms folded and waited. He gave it fifteen minutes.

"OK Eric, let's hope you may be a little more civil now. I'll show you what I have. Now, have a look at this."

He reached down to the floor and picked up a strange-looking metal cage with leather straps attached to one end. He got up and walked around the table to the chair.

"Clever thing this, Eric. It fits onto your head like this."

He forced the cage over Zippo's face and tightened the straps at the back of his head. The big man writhed and thrashed, but to no avail.

"There we are, Eric. All done. Now. I thought I might show you a little clip from a film. A bit of entertainment." One of the other men had lifted a TV and video onto the table as Liam had talked. "It's quite an old film Eric, but sometimes the old ones are the best, don't you think? It stars John Hurt and Richard Burton. It's called '1984'. Have you ever seen it Eric? No? Not to worry. It's where I came up with the idea for the cage you see. Let's play it shall we?"

On the screen, a cage not dissimilar to the one on Zippo's face was strapped onto John Hurt's face. All the while the rich, melodic tones of Richard Burton's voice rumbled on. A rat was placed into the other end of the cage. Zippo's eyes widened in terror at the sight of the rat. It was evil-looking and starving-hungry. Burton explained how the only thing that separated the rat from the face was a piece of mesh. If the piece of mesh was removed, the rat would feed on the face. The eyes first, in all probability.

Zippo and John Hurt screamed in unison. Liam picked up a hamster cage from the corner of the room and held it in front of Zippo's eyes.

"Here he is Eric. Your little friend. Your little pal from the other night. He's been in this cage for a couple of days now. I think he must be hungry, don't you Eric? Very hungry indeed. Now I could take him out of this cage and put him into the cage on your face. Would you like that Eric? Would you?"

Zippo didn't hear much of this. He had gone. He had fallen over the edge into a bottomless pit of terror. The small eyes of the rat seemed to stare right into his very soul. And he screamed. He screamed with everything he had. All of his resolve snapped. Anything. He would do anything. Anything to make them take the rat away. Anything. It was over. He didn't care. Just so long as they took the rat away. His brain was spinning out of control. There was only terror. Pure, unrefined terror.

Liam took the cage away and switched off the TV. He walked round the back of Zippo and undid the straps. Then he sat down again.

"I think it might be time for us to talk now. Would you agree, Eric?"

A croak. "No more rat. No more rat."

"Of course, Eric. All you have to do is to talk nicely, and there will be more rat. No more rat ever again. Is that what you want Eric?"

"Anything. Anything you want. Just no more rat."

It took a while for the effects of the drug to wear off, but when they did, Zippo had nothing left. He was broken. Utterly and completely broken. There was nothing left. Nothing at all.

The questioning was easy. Liam knew straight away that he would get nothing but the truth from the big, broken man. Not that there was much to get. They had the whole operation tied up and stowed away.

What came out was a surprise to Liam. What came out was the bank account. A bank account in Switzerland with almost a million pounds. What came out was a man called Taylor. Zippo was beyond caring. He gave them everything. It took hours and hours and by the end Liam's hand was aching from filling in page after page of notes.

It was astounding. Ten Scottish towns. A franchise operation. Franchisees recruited and trained in Barlinnie Prison. Zippo talked with his head bowed. He had been so wrong about himself for so many years. He had thought himself to be nearly indestructible. But he hadn't been. He had been beaten by the rat. He had won so many battles in his life. So many vicious little fights. But this was different. He would never be able to face the rat. Never.

There would be no bar in Spain now. There would be no more nights at the Excelsior. No more Tina. No more suits. It was finished. Completely finished. All because of the rat.

Liam's voice was gentle now. He was Zippo's friend. His confessor. Someone who understood. Who cared.

"You know we can't let you keep this money Eric. You know this?"

"Yes. I know."

"Because if you tried to keep the money I would have to take you back to the rat. You don't want to go back to the rat do you Eric?"

"No. Never."

And so Liam led him through it. Gently. Holding his hand like a little child he took him through the procedures, and when they at last took Zippo back to his cell, the Cayman Island account was swelled by £1,512,647. Zippo curled up on his mattress and wrapped his blanket tight around him. And he slept.

Jack and Liam were quiet together. This was all way beyond the programme. Way beyond. Unbelievable.

At last Liam broke the silence. "So Major. What's your call? Where's the end game?"

Jack was deep in thought. He more-or-less spoke to himself. "I think we have enough. We know where his office is, we know where he parks his car, we know quite a bit about his routine. I say we take him. What do you think Liam?"

"I agree. But you still haven't thought all the way through Major."

"Go on."

"It was Taylor that set up Zippo's account. It was part of the package. Non-negotiable. If Zippo has an account, then the odds suggest that Taylor will have one too. Imagine how much there will be in that."

"Bloody hell."

"Bloody hell indeed Major. Bloody hell indeed."

"Any ideas Liam?"

"Yes. Plenty. But it's your call Major."

Jack heard him out. It was a good plan. A plan that needed doing.

Taking Taylor from the car park underneath his office building in Glasgow proved to be easy. They left the minder Briggs out cold on the back seat of his boss's Mercedes. Breaking Taylor was easy. The man was no hard case. Without his protection he was just a middle-aged lawyer. There had been nothing in his life that remotely prepared him for the ordeal in the cell and in the chair. The very sight of Liam's torture tools almost stupefied him. For a moment they all feared he was about to have seizure.

So they dressed him, and gave him a coffee to calm him down.

Once he stopped hyper-ventilating he talked. He talked for eight hours on the first day, and a further eight hours on the second day. And in the end they had it all. The man's memory was astonishing. Names. Dates. Places. Phone numbers. Account numbers. Everything. An operation that spanned ten Scottish towns and had ruined thousands of lives. And they took away nearly twenty million pounds from him.

He cried when he realised the money was gone. He cried because there was nothing he could do to stop it. Everything he had believed could make him safe had become worthless, his friends in Glasgow, his contacts, his skill at the law, his ex-soldiers, all of it. If he didn't give it all up there would be pain worse than anything he could begin to imagine. He couldn't go there. Not for anything. Never.

They allowed themselves to celebrate that night. Their operation had lasted a little over five days. It had succeeded beyond their wildest. And it had been perfect. Utterly perfect. They ate big fillet steaks and drank can after can of beer. They laughed and joked. They were soldiers and they had won their war. A total victory.

A few hundred yards up the hill sixteen men lay in their cells. They were all clothed now. They all lay on their mattresses under their blankets. They stared at the white walls in what was now a dim light. They had eaten their meals. They had drunk their tea. They wondered what would come next. Not that it mattered much. Their world had been torn apart. They had thought themselves invincible. They thought they were untouchable. They had been wrong. Their fortress had been made from cardboard, not granite. And it had been burnt to the ground.

They had no idea what would happen next. It hardly seemed to matter. Nothing could be worse than the Hell they had come to know in Liam's very own H Block high in the quiet Galloway Hills.

Little did they know. Because after any great victory comes a parade. A ticker-tape parade.

Part Three
Manhunt

"The army tried one last time to bring him back into the fold,
and if he'd pulled over, it all would have been forgotten.
But he kept on going. Kept on winning it his way.
And they called me in. They lost him. He was gone.
All they heard were rumours and random intelligence reports,
mostly from captured VC. The VC knew his name by now,
and they were scared of it. Kurtz and his men
were playing hit and run all the way into Cambodia."

Apocalypse Now

Chapter 9
Parade

The next morning the inmates of the cells received their morning tea laced with crushed-up sleeping tablets and valium. They became drowsy. They became like zombies. Their jailers handled them one by one. When they were told to undress they undressed. When they were told to sit in the chair in the interrogation room they sat. Their jailers were ready with guns, but there was no need for threats. Their prisoners were compliant. They all sat meekly to have their heads shaved.

They were then led out of the cell-block and into the main shed. Again the black-clad figures were there. Quiet. Menacing. Guns levelled. In the shed there were three home-made paddling pools. They weren't much to look at. Their sides were constructed from railway sleepers and the water was held in place by black polythene sheeting which was nailed onto the wood. Each pool was deep enough for a man to immerse himself fully as if he were washing his hair in the bath. The men did as they were told. They stepped in and sat down. They winced at the cold. They allowed their heads to be pushed under the water for a few seconds. None of them liked it a single bit. But they didn't struggle. They didn't fight.

When they were emerged from the water they had become coloured men. Some were red. Some were blue. Some were green. They looked at their limbs with astonishment and rubbed curiously. It wouldn't come off. It was indelible. They looked quite extraordinary. Naked men, all in bright colours.

Once each man was fully dyed he was returned to his cell. All was ready.

Jack pulled his mobile phone from his pocket and dialled Mandy's number.

"Hello."

"Hi Mandy. It's Jack."

"Jack! How are you? I haven't heard from you in ages. Are you OK?"

"I'm OK Mandy. Very busy. What with the clean-up and all. Now Mandy. You need to listen carefully."

The businesslike formality of his tone hit her immediately.

"Yes."

"You need to do two things. Firstly, get hold of one of the photographers that you use at the paper. He needs to do video. Second, both of must you be at the Burns Statue at noon today. There will be a black van. A large black Mercedes van. Have you got that?"

"Yes, but why Jack? What on earth is going on? Why a camera? Why . . ."

"Sorry Mandy, I can't tell you. You just have to trust me on this. You really must. I am talking about your career here Mandy. For the sake of your career you really need to trust me. Will you do that?"

"Yes, but . . ."

"No Mandy. No buts. I can't say any more. You must trust me. Now, it is just after nine now. I will call again at eleven to check that everything is arranged. I know that it's Saturday, but you are a very persuasive girl. We will speak in a couple of hours. Goodbye Mandy."

"Yes, but Jack . . ." She stared at the phone. Nothing. He was gone.

Jack looked at Liam. "OK. She'll be there."

"Certain?"

"Yes. I think I am."

Liam nodded. "OK. Then let's get packed up."

They made their final preparations. Jack stood for a while and looked at the strange structure in the middle of his father's sheep-shed. What on earth was the world going to make of it all? The thought made him smile. He stepped outside and wandered to the edge of the yard and gazed out at the glowing fields.

It was the most perfect spring day. There was a real warmth to the sun and the air filled with butterflies. The fields of Hillside Farm were spread out below him like beautiful green carpets. How many years had he tended these fields? As far back as he could remember. There were those times on the tractor with his father when he was a very young boy. Then when he was older, sweating for hour after hour in the summer sun as they gathered in the hay. And then there had been times with Will. So many times on this very grass with his only son. Summer and winter, rain or shine, year after year. Gathering sheep, or taking the cows down for milking, or cutting their crops of silage.

All the fields were empty now. Asleep. No more animals. Just daisies and dandelions and butterflies. All gone. The cows, the sheep, his son, and now he was about to go as well. Would he ever walk these fields again? Probably not. But life would go on. The bank would auction off the farm so that some new family would come to tend the land.

Hillside Farm and the whole of his life would be long behind him in less than three hours' time. Then there would be pastures new. God alone knew what kind of pastures they may be.

But they would certainly be new.

Jack had been right. The photographer had been adamant. No Mandy. No way in Hell. It's Saturday. I'm going to ride a bike with the kids. And no. Absolutely not. It was a gallant effort but he never really stood a chance. She prevailed in less than five minutes. Jack rang again at eleven.

"Is it arranged Mandy?"

"Yes Jack. By Christ you owe me one for this. The photographer will never forgive me. But yes. It's arranged. We'll be there."

She heard the sound of Jack laughing at the other end of the phone line. It made her smile. It had to be a good sign. She hadn't heard him laugh in ages. "What is it? What's so funny?"

"Oh nothing. Sorry Mandy. It's just the idea of the photographer never forgiving you. He will. I can absolutely assure you that he will. Now there is one more thing. What you will witness will be quite extraordinary. I'm not going to say any more. There will be something of a situation. Don't worry. Nothing dangerous or anything like that, but a situation all the same. As soon as it happens, call Roger Philips. This is his number. 07770 314296. Got that?"

"Yes."

"Don't worry. He'll be close. He is meeting me in the Tam O'Shanter around the corner at twelve. Well, he thinks he is. Let him sort things out." More laughing. "Well. He'll do his best I'm sure. I will call you later Mandy. I will explain everything then. Bye for now."

"Bye."

She never bothered trying to get him explain anything. It was pointless. What the Hell was going on? A black van by the Burns Statue at noon. A situation? Nothing dangerous, just a situation. And Roger Philips, the policeman. What could it be?

She arrived in the square at quarter-to-twelve. It was a typical busy Saturday afternoon. Prams and ice creams and teenagers in tiny tops. Ten to now. She was beginning to get nervous now. What was he up to? She found that she was tapping her foot fast with tension. Five to. Really tense now. Adrenalin. Her instincts told her that something remarkable was about to happen. She tapped the cameraman's shoulder impatiently. "Are you ready? Remember. A black van. Got it?"

He rolled his eyes in exasperation. "Yes Mandy. I've got it. I'm not a bloody imbecile you know. A Merc van at noon. OK?"

"Yes, yes. Just be ready. That's all."

One minute to. A van. A black one. Stopped at the lights. A Mercedes? Yes. A big one? Yes. And there was Jack in the front at the wheel. She rattled the photographer's shoulder again. "There. There it is. That's the one. Start filming now."

The van came through the lights and turned into the area around the tall statue of Robert Burns. It drew up 30 yards past where they were standing, then stopped bang in the middle of the road. Jack jumped out of the door and darted round to the back. He fiddled for a moment with something on the back doors and then jogged over to Mandy.

"Stay clear of the back doors. Enjoy the show. See you around."

"But Jack . . ."

He was gone. He jogged away fast and down a small street. Stay clear of the back door? What on earth was going to happen to the back door.

Bang.

A puff of smoke. And the two doors of the van swung open. A few pedestrians were jumped by the sound. They were looking about. What was it? But Mandy was looking straight into the back of the van with her mouth open in astonishment. Inside were two rows of men sitting facing each other on wooden bench seats.

They were all stark-naked.

They had no hair.

They were dyed from head to toe.

Some were red.

Some were green.

Some were blue.

And they were staring back out at her like rabbits caught in the headlights of an oncoming car. "I really, really hope that you are filming this" she said to the cameraman in a low intense voice.

He was. By God he was. As if his life depended on it. She found that she was speaking to herself very quietly. "Oh Jack. What on earth have you done?"

Seconds ticked by. It was like a stand-off. The men seemed dopey. Drowsy. As if they hadn't a clue what to do. A couple of passers-by had noticed them now and they stared into the van in utter amazement. And still the men gazed out as if in a trance.

Bang!

Everyone jumped. It came from inside the van this time. Louder. What was that? Some kind of banger? A firework? No. Smoke. Lots of smoke. And the men were moving now. Panicked by the noise and the smoke. They poured out of the back of the van and stared about wildly. Everyone in the square noticed them now.

How many were there? About a dozen. No, more than that. Fifteen. Sixteen. All of them naked. All dyed bright colours. There was astonishment in the square now. Every head was turning. Shouts. Laughter. Delighted children. The men clutched their genitals and looked about desperately for somewhere to go. The crowd grew in no time. Like they were gathered to see a fight in a school playground.

The men huddled together, trying to hide behind each other. Their faces were a mixture. Part vacant, part terrified. Then the biggest of them seemed to make a decision. "Quick. This way. Follow me."

The strange bunch shuffled awkwardly across the square with their hands grimly clutched over their crotches. The crowd followed on fascinated, but at a distance. They were across the square now and into the same small street that Jack had run down a few minutes before.

There was small café. The big man darted through the door. The others followed, squashing each other in their haste to escape the stares of the crowd. The door slammed. Mandy pressed her face up to the window. There were not many customers inside. Such as there were gave the painted men one look and fled. The proprietor took a few seconds longer. Then he darted out from behind the counter and followed his customers out of the door. The fugitives packed themselves behind the counter which covered their nether regions from the gaze of all the faces at the window.

There was no back door.

A line of red, green and blue faces stared out at a mass of faces in the window who in turn stared back in. Then Mandy recognised a face. A blue face. It took her a while. The blue and the lack of hair made it difficult. But it came to her. Thin cheeks and wild staring eyes.

It was Ricky Macintosh.

And now she began realise what Jack Sinclair had done. She forced herself backwards through the crowd until she found a bit of space. She dialled Roger Philips's number and stuck a finger into her left ear to keep out the growing noise. She had to shout.

"Mr Philips. It's Mandy Robinson here. I think that you had better take a walk around the corner. There are sixteen naked men holed up in the Statue Café. They are all dyed from head to toe. Some are blue. Some are red. And some are green. Oh, and by the way, one of them is Ricky Macintosh. No, Mr Philips I'm not mad. Quite, quite sane actually. Just walk around the corner. See for yourself."

She hit the "end" button and cut him off. He appeared a couple of minutes later and forced his way to the front of the crowd. The sight that confronted him took his breath away. Almost immediately his eyes were locked onto the terrified stare of Eric 'Zippo' Macintosh. Eric Zippo Macintosh stark, bollock-naked. Eric Zippo Macintosh with no hair. Eric Zippo Macintosh dyed all over green. Eric Zippo Macintosh looking scared out of his wits.

He forced himself through the door and slammed it behind him. He watched the men warily as he dialled up the station on his phone.

"Sarge, it's Roger here. You need to get at least two vans round to the Statue Café as quickly as you bloody well can. I need men. I need vans. And I need blankets. No I can't explain Sarge. Just do it, OK?"

It took ten minutes. In those ten minutes Philips picked out other faces. Andrew Moncur, Tommy Banks, the King brothers, Jesus H Christ. It was a complete haul. What in the name of God was going on?

It took the uniformed officers a few minutes to drive the excited crowd back and make room for the two vans. The strangely coloured figures scuttled out of the café wrapped in blankets. They were met with jubilant cheers. Nobody had the first clue what on earth was happening, but it was a hell of a show.

Mandy's phone rang.

"It's Jack."

"What on earth have you done Jack?"

"That is the question that a great number of people will be asking over the next few days. And you are the one who will have the answers. It's your exclusive Mandy. Take it and run with it. It's my way of saying thanks."

She was getting cross now. "Never mind my bloody career Jack. This all means more than that. What do you take me for?"

She heard him sigh. "Sorry. I put that badly. Of course I know you better than that. I have done things Mandy. Maybe people will think they were crazy things. Maybe they will agree with me. Who knows? But what they think isn't important. I know exactly why I did it and, if you want, you can be the person to tell them."

She calmed a little. "OK Jack. Fair enough. But stop pulling wool over my eyes all the time. Just be honest from now on will you?"

"Yes of course. Now what is happening down there? Has Roger cleared things up?"

"Yes. All the men are in police vans now. I presume they are going to the station."

"Good. Ideal. OK Mandy, this is what to do next. Bob Bennet thinks he is meeting me for a drink at the Golf Club. Get him on the phone and meet him at your office. Show him the video. There is a press release sitting in your email inbox. He will want to sell the story and the pictures as soon as possible so that it will run in one of the Sunday papers tomorrow. As soon as Bob is in the picture leave it all to him. You get yourself up to the Top Farm. You need to go in through the high road. The track from Hillside is blocked off. There is something you need to see and film in the big sheep-shed. Go as soon as you can. You need to get up there before the police. Have you got all that Mandy?"

"Yes Jack. All of it. And I'll do it. But after this we need to talk. Seriously."

"Of course. Later tonight. You're going to be busy for the next few hours."

She met with Bennet in the office 40 minutes later. He looked flustered. "Look Mandy, I can't say that I am happy about any of this. It's Saturday bloody afternoon. First I am supposed to be meeting Jack Sinclair for a pint. Then I hear that it is all some kind of a ruse so that you can get me into the office. This really better be good Mandy."

She gave a small laugh. "Don't worry yourself Bob. This isn't just another of those Mandy wild-goose chases that you like so much. Sit down and watch this."

Bob's face went through all phases of astonishment as he watched the fifteen-minute video. "What the hell is this Mandy? Where was it? And when?"

"Noon today. Burns Statue."

"And who are they?"

"This is a press release that Jack Sinclair emailed to me. I'll read it.

"*In February of this year my only son, Will Sinclair, died at the age of nineteen. His death was caused by a massive overdose of heroin. For what ever reason, his dealer sold him heroin that was 80 percent pure. His system was unable to deal with such an unusually high level of purity. And so he died. As far as the coroner was concerned it was death by misadventure. As far as I was concerned it was murder.*

"*Following Will's death I made numerous enquiries. I discovered that Dumfries has a major drug problem in general, and a growing heroin problem in particular. It became apparent to me that the police find it almost impossible to deal with this problem. It also became apparent to me that there is little or no political will to deal with the problem. It was in the light of this that I decided to take matters into my own hands.*

"*In February of this year the Government ordered the culling of all the animals on my farm. The reason they gave for this murderous action was that it was the only way that the spread of the Foot and Mouth outbreak could be halted. With no living bodies to use as stepping stones, the disease could find no way of spreading further.*

"*With this in mind, I decided that I would adopt a similar approach to halting and eradicating the spread of the heroin disease in the town of Dumfries. I have had extensive military training, and I put much of this training into practice in Northern Ireland in the eighties and the early nineties. Using this training, I have staged an operation to apprehend and interrogate every person involved in supplying hard drugs in the Dumfries area. I authorised all appropriate measures to be taken to extract the required information from each person that we interrogated.*

"*The men who were delivered to the Burns Statue in Dumfries at noon today represent the complete heroin supply chain. The men were stripped naked and dyed three different colours. Green represents a boss or an enforcer. Blue represents a main dealer. Red represents a secondary dealer.*

"*I have collected extensive information, not only about drug operations in and around Dumfries, but also in other towns across Scotland. I will be releasing further details of the operation and the information that I have uncovered over the coming days and weeks. Initially all such information will be made available through Miss Mandy Robinson. At a later date information will be posted on a website. Details of the site will be released in due course. Jack Sinclair, May 2001."*

For a moment Bob Bennet was too stunned to speak. Then his professional instincts kicked in. He looked up to Mandy and the photographer who were waiting expectantly. "Do you understand how things work now?"

"Not really" said Mandy. "Can you explain?"

"Of course. Basically when both of you filmed and witnessed these events you were under the employ of this paper. This means that the paper owns all the rights to the story. Now of course we will run the story just as soon as we can in next week's edition. But you will realise that all of this thing is way, way bigger than that. I have to represent the interests of the owners. They pay my wages and yours. It's as simple as that.

"What that means is that I get on the phone right now and sell the story to the highest bidder. If I did anything else, I would basically be de-frauding my own employers. Do you understand all this?"

"Yes of course." Said Mandy. She was trying to keep her cool, but inside she was churning with excitement. "We better get up to the farm and leave you to it Bob."

"Absolutely. Off you go."

A river of adrenaline surged through Bob Bennet. He had waited thirty long, miserable, under-achieving years for this moment to arrive. And now it was here. His moment. He picked up the phone and enjoyed the best two hours of his life. He managed to get three major tabloid editors into a bidding war for the exclusive rights to tell the story and to use the pictures in their next morning's editions. He closed on a six-figure deal with *The News of the World*. Next, he sold the video footage to *Sky News*, and received a sell on commission for any further sales down the line.

By the time he had finished he was covered in sweat. Mandy returned a little after three. She was pale and seemed rather shocked. She sat down heavily and told him all about the frightening cell-block that she had found in the sheep-shed. She told of how terribly bright the light was when they switched it on. She told him about the white walls and floors and doors. She told him about how they had switched on the cassette player and how the sound that came out in the cells was the sound of insanity. She told him about the interrogation chair. She couldn't understand. She couldn't understand any of it.

The video footage was chilling. The block was so deserted, so empty and yet it carried a chilling threat. "Why, Bob? Why has Jack done this? He is such a good man, such a decent man, and this . . . this is like a nightmare. And why has he left all this for anyone to find? He is condemning himself. I just don't understand. Not any of it."

Bob could see how distressed she was. So young. So very young. Still far too young to know what a stinking cesspool the world could be.

"Jack is a soldier, Mandy. Sure, he left the Army years ago, but he is still a soldier at heart. Look at how he carries himself for heaven's sake. This is Major Jack Sinclair speaking. He doesn't want to hide anything. Soldiers don't. He has acted according to his own personal code. He is unconcerned about what the rest of the world thinks. He has seen a problem and taken action to solve it in his own way. His words are those of a man who is content that what he has done sits well with his own conscience." Bennet was quiet for a moment. "I am beyond their timid lying morality, and so I am beyond caring." He spoke the words softly, mostly to himself.

"Sorry Bob, what was that?"

"That was Colonel Walter E. Kurtz. *Apocalypse Now*."

"Who's he?"

"Oh, just a character in a film. Basically Jack has stepped out over the edge. There is always an edge in our world. A boundary. A tell fence with warning signs. Every now and then someone steps over it. Hops the fence. Sometimes they are deemed to be terrorists, sometimes madmen, sometimes prophets. Sometimes the world loves them, and sometimes we hate them. They are the rebels." Bennet shook his head in wonder at what was happening. "It's early days yet Mandy, but can't you see how huge this could be?"

She couldn't really. He went on. "Jack is the first rebel of the twenty-first century. Look at what he has done so far. He has staged his event and had it videoed. Within an hour I have emailed snips of the video to news editors 300 miles away. The first editions of the paper will hit the streets in the early hours of the morning. Millions of people will wake up to the story less than 24 hours after it happened. He is manipulating the media Mandy.

"Look at the timing. Noon on a Saturday. A guaranteed crowd to watch and plenty of time to make the Sunday editions. And what comes next? More information. More information which will be let out in bite-sized pieces through the mobile phone and the internet. Can't you see the importance of this?"

Again she was struggling. "I don't know. I suppose so."

He smiled. The sheer genius of what Jack had done was beginning to dawn on him. "The dyed naked men represent perfect news. It is the kind of utterly weird event that will make any editor want to sell his grandmother to get hold of. And the readers are going to love it too. Because it's there. Right in their faces. Sixteen multi-coloured men with no hair clutching their bollocks. So who are they? Bad guys. Everybody's bad guys. Heroin pushers. So who did it? A good guy. An ex-soldier. Lost his only son to the same drug that these guys peddle. And he lost all his animals in the Cull. For Christ's sake, it's Gary Cooper in *High Noon*.

"Everyone in the world will want to know more. And this is where it looks like it is going to be different. Whenever anything like this has happened before the person who has done it almost invariably disappears. They either go on the run or they get arrested. Either way they are incommunicado. All any of us can do is speculate about what they did and why they did it. But things have changed. The world is more open. Hell, it's wide open. Jack seems to have sensed that. All you need to communicate with half the planet is a mobile phone and a lap-top computer. Just so long as your batteries don't run out, you can bring the millions into your kitchen. Imagine if Che Guevara had been able to go on-line, or Steve Biko, or Leon Trotsky or Bobby Sands?

"It is so bloody simple. To get anyone to log-on you need to be famous. To get famous you need the media. How do you get the media to make you famous? You dump sixteen naked men in the middle of a town on a Saturday lunchtime. And then you feed the frenzy carefully until you become a source of fascination to just about everyone in the country. And then you give them a web address so that they can all log-on. Christ, Mandy this is genius. Sheer bloody genius."

As Bob Bennet was selling his footage to the editor in London a car pulled up 40 miles away on a small road that ran through thick pine forest. Four men climbed out. Jack opened the boot, pulled out a large rucksack, and hefted it onto his back. The three men from Belfast waited. When he was ready he shook hands with each of them in turn. Doyle and O'Hara climbed back into the car. Liam stood for a moment and looked around at the vast forest that stretched as far as he could see.

"So Jack, I suppose this is it."

"Yes. Thanks Liam. Thanks for everything."

"No need Major. We've all had a ball. Now listen. You have my number. You need anything, you call. OK?"

Jack smiled "Sure Liam."

"I'm serious Jack. You need any help just ring. We'll be here."

Jack could see that he meant it. What a weird, weird way to find a friendship. Here was the man who had been ready to torture him all those years ago. Instead it had been Jack who had sent Liam away for all those years in Long Kesh prison. Somehow they had got away from the 400 years of hate that had put them on opposite sides of the tracks. And now, against all the odds, they had become friends.

They shook hands and Liam gave a small nod. He climbed into the car and drove away. Jack stood for a moment and watched the car disappear around a corner and into the trees. In less than three hours time they would be on the ferry and headed back to Belfast. Now he was alone.

He sniffed the air that was heavy with the scent of pine. All around him was the empty vastness of the Galloway Forest. There were thousands of acres of emptiness all ready to swallow him up. When they came to try and find him he would be like the needle in the haystack. The forest was now his friend, his companion, his family.

He walked for two hours until he reached the first of his camps.

He had set up several camps over the previous weeks. They were all located in places far away from any footpaths or roads. They were all up high, with excellent views of all approaches. They were all well hidden. At each site he had a tent, clothes, a Calor Gas stove, pots and pans and plates, and enough provisions to last him for months. At each site there was a small generator and a healthy supply of diesel. He was completely self-sufficient. He could stay in the forest for a year if he needed to.

He put a kettle on the stove and made himself a cup of coffee. It was a wonderful afternoon. The sun beat down and the ground was warm to lie on. All around was birdsong and the hum of insects. He out pulled his phone and called Mandy.

"Hello."

"Hi Mandy. It's Jack."

"Where the hell are you Jack?"

He smiled. "Right at this very minute I pretty well feel as if I am in paradise. Blue skies and a world of trees and birds. It's beautiful. Really beautiful. This is my new home now. The Galloway Forest."

"I don't understand."

"Well I had to go somewhere didn't I? Someone is bound to come looking soon enough. I decided this was as good a place as any. I've got lots of provisions so I'll be comfortable enough. This is what you need to let people know. I have spent quite a bit of time preparing for this. I have all that I need. It is all very well hidden. They can come looking if they like, but they won't find me. I also have lots and lots of SIM cards for my mobile phone. They are all 'Pay-as-You-Go' and they were all bought with cash over a long period in lots of different cities. There isn't a lot of point in them trying to trace the calls. But they will try of course."

"What are you going to do now Jack?"

"Basically Mandy, I intend to make it as hard as possible for any of these bastards to ever trade their drugs again. You can let everyone know that I have a tonne of information and it is all going to get released tomorrow on a website. The address is 'www.thecull.com'. I'm sure they will try and use it to find me. There is no point. How these things work is quite beyond me, but basically the information is being bounced all around cyberspace.

God alone knows how. The actual server computer is somewhere in Russia I think. I will put all the information out into the public domain. There is no point giving it to the police. Their hands are tied. Just like ours were in Belfast. These people can afford the best lawyers and they almost always get off. The only way is to expose them. Shine a light on them. Put them out in the open."

"But Jack, what about the cell-block? All that light and the loud sound and that horrible chair. How could you?"

"Sometimes you have to fight fire with fire. These men are responsible for ruining people's lives. They destroy families. They hoodwink kids into becoming addicts. They kill people. They killed my son. And as long as they maintain their rule of terror, and have enough money to pay their lawyers, they feel that they are untouchable. Well, not any more. I wanted to show the whole world that these people are not untouchable. They are vulnerable. Completely vulnerable. If we all decide that enough is enough they will have nowhere to hide. I did it because it was time that it was done. All it needed was someone to play them at their own game. I played. They lost."

They talked for a further twenty minutes. There was something about him that chilled Mandy. There were no doubts in him. He was transformed. He had become a zealot. He was living somewhere out on a different plane. The old Jack had been left behind. This was the new Jack. He frightened her.

"There is something that you have to get out Mandy. Something important."

"Yes?"

"Right now there are well over 1,000 heroin addicts in Dumfries who are going to be climbing up the walls. These aren't bad people. They aren't evil people. They are just people. People like me and you. People like Will. They never wanted to become heroin addicts. They made a mistake and they have to pay dearly for that mistake every day of their lives. As of three days ago, there is no heroin in Dumfries. Absolutely none. And I very much doubt if there will be a any for a long time yet.

"These people cannot simply be left to suffer. It isn't their fault. They are the innocent victims of the actions that I have taken and they do not deserve to be. The town has a responsibility. For years it has brushed the problem under the carpet. We must not allow it to happen any more. These people will be going through hell. Just like Will did. They need help, and the help has to be given. They will need their drugs and they will need the chance of rehabilitation. Don't allow them to be ignored Mandy."

"I won't."

Chapter 10
Feeding Frenzy

When it awoke that fine Sunday morning in May the sleepy little town of Dumfries was about to change like it had never changed before. Word had flown around the pubs and clubs the night before. Everybody had phoned everybody else. Pictures of the dyed men had been all over the evening news bulletins on the TV. Who on earth were these men? What was happening? The news people didn't seem to know. All they could do was to guess and speculate. The police confirmed that they had sixteen men in the station. No, the men were not in custody. No, the men had not been charged. No, they would not be releasing any details of their identity.

Each news station speculated and it became apparent that a Sunday paper had bought the exclusive rights to bring the full story to the world. By eight that morning there wasn't a single copy of *The News of the World* to be had in Dumfries.

All through the evening and the Sunday morning, the media started to land in the town. Hotels and guest houses were full in no time. Large TV vans made their home on the car park opposite the police station. The police station seemed to be the only available focal point for the reporters to chase the story. As Saturday night wore on, more and more locals turned out to watch the circus. Various presenters touched up their make-up before stepping into the hard, white lights to broadcast to the world.

It wasn't long before there was something of a carnival atmosphere. The town's burger vans soon caught on, and the smell of deep-fat frying soon permeated the scene. In the pubs and clubs hard-nosed investigative journalists did their rounds, buying drinks and asking questions. So who is this Jack Sinclair? Do you know Jack Sinclair? Have you ever met Jack Sinclair? And yet there was more or less nothing to find out. The fact that they all knew that *The News of the World* had already bought the exclusive made their desperation more tangible. Mobile phones buzzed endlessly. Come on, find something. Anything for Christ's sake.

Then came the dawn and the first editions of the papers. All of a sudden they all knew more. The story fuelled their journalistic appetites. The story was just so perfect. Well, not quite. A few naked women thrown in would have added a nice final touch. Slim ones with great big tits who could be paid to get them out at a later date. But bimbos apart, it was the story that had it all. The morning brought the realisation that the men who were hidden away in the police station were drug-pushers. No names had been released but the whispers started in earnest. One of them was Zippo Macintosh. Who is Zippo Macintosh? And now page after page of notebooks started to be filled.

The journalists now found plenty of people who were more than happy to tell them about Zippo Macintosh. Soon a party had found their way to Sunnybank where Zippo's house had drawn the crowds. Everybody wanted to tell a story. Twenty years of Zippo stories came pouring out. How he would ignite that lighter of his under people's noses, and how many people he had battered, and how he liked to live it up with his skinny little smackhead tart. And there was more. So much more. There was that creep Tommy Banks with his tattoos and his Stanley knife. And there was the big giant Wee Kenny who was madder than fuck and would do anything Zippo would tell him. And there was the little bastard Ricky in his Armani suits and gold watches. There was vengeful glee in the way that the residents of Sunnybank filled in the reporters with stories about the group of coloured men who were hiding away in the police station. Only 24 hours before, Zippo and his cronies had held them all in a grip of terror. The residents of Sunnybank would only dare to talk quietly in ones and twos, outside the Spar, in a quiet corner of the pub, at the school gates. These conversations were accompanied by furtive glances.

Nobody was immune to the wrath of Zippo Macintosh. Nobody wanted the flames up their nostrils.

But now it was different. They had all seen him. Larger than life and dyed bright green on national tele. They had seen him clutching his genitals and looking wildly about. They had seen the fear in his hunched body. They had seen Tommy Banks looking rat-like and runtish. They had seen the King brothers with their big sagging bellies. They had seen Ricky Mactintosh with his skinny little legs and arse. They had seen their tormentors become pathetic. Frightened, coloured men terrified by their nakedness.

The bubble had burst. It was one of those events that brought the community out from behind its closed doors to meet each other. Like a Royal Wedding or peace after a long foreign war. The fact that it was such a gorgeous morning helped. And everybody chose their Sunday best, because they were going to be on the tele. Trays full of tea and coffee and cakes started to come out. Deckchairs. A couple of barbeques.

Someone had spray-painted "OUT SCUM" all over the front of Zippo's house. It gave the crowd a sentiment to unify them. It gave them a target, a goal, an end to aspire to. As they found the freedom to talk to each other, they found that they shared a common purpose. They were all sick of it. They were sick of watching their children and grandchildren and wondering. Have you taken it yet? Have you been offered it yet? Would you say no? Would you dare say no? They found that it was a fear that they all shared. A helplessness that could now unite them.

And now they realised their own power. It was the power of numbers. Once they were together they were strong. Their enemies were no supermen. There would be no more swagger now. Not now that the whole world had seen their pathetic nakedness. Not now that the whole world had seen then huddled together like frightened sheep clutching their bollocks.

A little after nine, a brick sailed gently through the warm morning air and smashed through a bedroom window. The thrower was a little twelve-year-old, skin-headed lad who had been egged on by his mates. For a brief moment the tinkling of the glass was met by stunned silence. Then the cheering started and a hail of bricks rained down. Within minutes every window was put through. The two policemen on duty could do no more than look on anxiously and report back to base. The cameramen caught it all with glee. The crowd was delighted. Delighted that it had become so empowered.

Someone shouted from the back of the house. The back door had opened. Two figures had emerged. One was a giant man. The other a tiny girl. Derision was poured down on them. Wee Kenny looked around at the leering faces in astonishment. He drew the shaking figure of Tina close to him. He had to protect her. Zippo would want him to protect her. She tried to crawl into him. There was so much noise. The faces were so close. There was spit in her hair. She screwed her eyes shut and tried to block it all out. Kenny ploughed on through the crowd grimly. The people came close. But not too close. He was so huge. Nobody dared to get too close. Not to Wee Kenny.

But where should he go? Where could he go? He had no idea. All he could think of was to keep walking. Keep going. Surely there would be a place where the crowd ended. Then there was a voice. A tugging at his sleeve. A hard London accent.

"Come on, mate. This way. In here. In the car. I'll get you away mate. Come on. Quick."

Without thinking he followed the man. The doors were open now. He eased Tina into the back and got in alongside her. The car was rocking slightly. The man got in the front and started the engine. They were moving now. Moving through a sea of leering, shouting faces.

And suddenly they were away. They were driving fast through quiet streets. The man glanced over from the front seat. "You OK back there?"

"Aye" said Wee Kenny simply.

"Good, good. I'm Dicky Tanner. From *The Sun*. Why don't we go and find a nice quiet place to have a chat?"

Inside the police station there were the beginnings of a siege mentality. The Chief Constable had forgone his regular Sunday morning golf game to come in and try and take control of the situation. All he could see was that events were slipping way out of control. Reports kept coming in from Sunnybank of shouting crowds and broken widows. Outside his own front door the media circus seemed to grow by the minute. And in his cells he had sixteen brightly coloured men in borrowed clothes looking scared and bemused. He buzzed for Roger Philips to come to his office.

"Christ Roger, have you seen it out there? What the hell should we do?"

Philips seemed perfectly calm and it annoyed his boss. "Let them go I suppose. There are no charges. We have no reason to hold them."

"Are you mad? Have you seen it out there?"

"Sure I have. They'll be OK. They'll just get a hard time. That's all."

The Chief was open-mouthed. Philips became annoyed. "Look boss, I know every one of them. Well not quite all. I don't know Taylor. But the rest of them I know. I've been chasing all these bastards for three years and I haven't even got close. They're scum. All of them. I say we let them go. Let them get what they deserve. Let them get humiliated in front of all the cameras. Personally I can't think of a better punishment. Just do it now. Get it over with. The longer we keep them the harder it is going to get. It's not our problem boss. There are no charges. No good reasons to hold them. So just let them go. Let them have it."

The Chief Constable agonised for another half an hour and in the end he came round to the Philips point of view. Roger was absolutely right. The men weren't his problem. There was no clear threat against them. They were just in for a hell of a hard time. A complete nightmare in fact. But that wasn't his problem. If they had chosen to push heroin, then they could suffer the consequences. Stuff them.

He left it to Philips to get them out. As soon as they realised what was waiting for them outside they didn't want to go. Not one little bit. They begged him to be allowed to make a phone call, to arrange lifts, to use the back door, anything to avoid the milling circus waiting for them outside.

Philips heard them out with a world-weary look, then he held up his hands for silence.

"Gentlemen, please, quiet will you. Now look, we don't have any obligation whatsoever to do any of these things. We felt that we had to take you in yesterday because you were in danger of committing acts of gross indecency. It is our duty to protect the people of this town, and there were youngsters out there who could have been psychologically scarred for life by the sight of your horrible multi-coloured bollocks. But we got you away, and we've sorted you out with some clothes so that you won't upset anyone else with your hairy arses, and so basically our job is done.

"Now I know from long personal experience that each and every one of you is nothing more than a worthless toe-rag, and so there will be no favours. No phone calls. No lifts. No back door. It's your bed. You made it. You can lie in it. Now piss off the lot of you before I have you thrown out."

And so they made their grand exit. As soon as the crowds of reporters spotted their dyed faces they surged forward. The men reacted differently. Taylor was the lucky one. Almost straight away he spotted the bruised face of his man Briggs. Thank Christ. He pushed quickly through the crowd and into the waiting car. Ten minutes later he was on his way back to Glasgow.

Most of the others simply ran. They pushed and shoved their way through the throng, and legged it back to their flats and houses as quickly as they could. Once home they bolted the doors and had to endure reporters shouting through their letter-boxes for hours to come.

Soon there were only two of them left. Zippo Macintosh managed to pull himself up to his full height and he stared into the lenses and the impassioned faces with an eerie calm. Behind him Ricky Macintosh cowered behind the bulk of his uncle. Zippo stood for several minutes barely moving a muscle. His arms were folded. His face was blank. His immobility soon started to have an effect. The baying of questions died down. When there was near silence he gave a small nod and started to walk.

What happened next was really rather extraordinary. It became a procession. Nobody gave any orders about it. They just naturally followed. Zippo strode out with Ricky scuttling behind, whilst a whole bevy of reporters and photographers and onlookers simply followed. It became like the Pied Piper. Zippo walked with his back held ramrod straight down the middle of the road. Traffic stopped. Pedestrians stopped to watch. Faces appeared in windows. At the front of the following crowd a breathless blonde whispered dramatically into her microphone whilst her cameraman scuttled to keep her head in the frame.

" . . . and so this crowd, which grows bigger by the moment, is simply following the strolling figure of Eric 'Zippo' Macintosh. Nobody knows where he is headed and it seems unlikely that he is intending to make any kind of statement. Everyone here is just following. There must be at least 200 now, and all the time people are joining the throng. Locals tell me that they think that we are making for Sunnybank estate . . ."

Word soon travelled to the mob outside Zippo's house on Sunnybank. He was on his way. Zippo and his nephew Ricky. A shiver of excitement ran through the crowd. He was coming. He was close now. Soon they would see him. Soon he would have to face them. Even though they were so many and he was only one, there was still some fear. Because after all, he was Zippo. 'The' Zippo. Lighter-under-the-nose Zippo.

As Zippo and his entourage were making their way across the bridge at the bottom of Buccleuch Street, the first wisps of smoke crept almost unnoticed out from under the kitchen door of Zippo's house. Ten minutes later the whole place was ablaze. The sight of the flames filled the crowd with all the joy and glee of Bonfire Night.

The excitement hit fever pitch when at last Zippo and his following band were sighted at the end of the road. The Fire Brigade had arrived by now and they were hosing water into the leaping flames. Still Zippo's face betrayed no emotion as he walked steadily down the street.

A chant started. It was slow to start with, but it soon gathered momentum. "OUT! OUT! OUT!" Louder. All the time louder. And louder. Shouted from faces twisted and contorted with rage and hate. **"OUT! OUT! OUT!"**

And then came the eggs and the tomatoes and potatoes. All kinds of food flew through the air and cascaded down on the big man with the green head. Still he kept going forward. His following crowd backed off to avoid getting pelted themselves. Soon his face was dripping with egg yolk and bits of tomato.

And then at last he stopped. He stood very still and stared at the flames jumping out of the windows of his house. Eggs and fruit and veg rained down on him and the chant filled the street. **"OUT! OUT! OUT!"**

At this point Mandy darted out of the crowd and spoke to him. The crowd looked on and wondered what on earth she was saying. "I have a message for you Eric. It's from Freddy. He doesn't want you here any more. He says you should go. Both of you. Go, and don't come back. Because if you stay he will have to bring the rat again. That's what he said. He said he would bring the rat again."

If Zippo's face had not been green it would have drained of all colour. He looked around quickly. His composure was gone now. Mention of the rat made him feel panicky and frightened. For the first time he saw all the faces and the hatred. He became aware of the fruit and the eggs and the vicious chanting. Ricky pushed in close behind him. Mandy spoke again. "There are lots of reporters who would love to give you a lift out of here Eric. Take the ride. Go. Go and don't come back. Not if you don't want Freddy to bring the rat again."

At this point a reporter darted to his side shielding himself under an umbrella. "Hey mate. Maybe you should make yourself scarce. I would if I were you. Want a lift? Get out of town?"

For a moment Zippo seemed not to have heard. Then at last he nodded, and then slowly he and Ricky followed the reporter to his car.

They drove away. They drove all the way to a motel near Ayr where the reporter was able to smuggle the painted men into a chalet-style room. Once Zippo had made his exit the excitement slowly died down. The crowd headed home, excitedly recounting tales of the morning to each other.

He was gone.

Not just for the day or the month. They knew that Zippo was gone for ever. He would never return. Even he wouldn't dare. Not now.

And of course it all made great, great television. Amazing pictures of the eggs crashing into Zippo's set green features as the fire engulfed his house and the crowd danced and shouted. It was just perfect. All of it. The bright sunny morning. The holiday crowd in their bright summer colours. The chanting. The burning house. The firemen. The cascade of fruit and eggs. And in the middle of it all, the two men. One of them big and proud and green. The other small and cowering and blue. Wonderful, fantastic, unbelievable television, and TV channels all over the world wanted a piece of it.

Once the brightly coloured men had scuttled away into hiding, the focus of the media switched. Suddenly there was only one thing that mattered, one goal, one purpose. Editors screamed down mobile phone lines. Every newshound had a new Holy Grail.

Jack Sinclair.

Who was Jack Sinclair? Where was Jack Sinclair? How old? Where from? How tall? Who are his friends? What are his hobbies? Where would he go? Will he give up?

Jack Sinclair had become the man of the hour.

As the reporters started to tear around Dumfries that warm Sunday afternoon, the man of the hour was lying on his back in a small clearing on the edge of a tree-line deep in the Galloway Forest. At his side were several empty cans of lager and the alcohol was buzzing pleasantly around his brain. All the tension of the previous weeks was draining away. He luxuriated in the feel of the warm sun on his face. He smoked slowly and sipped his beer whilst he listened to the radio. He kept skipping from station to station to catch the reports. He had listened to Zippo's return live on the BBC. How right Liam had been. It was a story made in heaven.

Late that afternoon he even found a phone-in show all about himself. Who was he? Hero or villain? Madman or visionary? He kept chuckling to himself. Already he was being built up as some kind of cross between Robin Hood and Joseph Stalin. And Liam had predicted this as well. It wouldn't be long before he wasn't just Jack any more. Not just plain old Jack Sinclair of Hillside Farm. Oh no. Soon he would be all kinds of different Jacks. He would be a different Jack to everybody out there. They would make him who they wanted him to be. Lots of cardboard cut-outs. Pictures would be painted by psychiatrists and sociologists and university professors and talk-show hosts and gossip queens and taxi drivers and women behind the counters in Spar shops. He was about to become a talking point. Talked about over pints in pubs and clubs. Talked about on the lines in car factories. Talked about in the queues in dole offices. Talked about in hairdressers and health clubs and prisons and doctors' surgeries. Everybody would want to talk about Jack Sinclair. Just like Liam had said they would.

He rang Mandy early in the evening.

"Are you OK Jack? You sound odd."

"Hell, I'm fine Mandy. Could barely be better. I've spent a glorious afternoon lying in the sun drinking cans of lager and listening to the radio. If the truth were to be known, I'm a bit pissed."

For a moment she was lost for words. "Jack, have you any idea what's been happening here?"

"Of course I have. I've been listening to the radio. Brilliant isn't it? Couldn't be better. I just wish I could have seen them throwing the eggs. Bloody great."

"This is what you wanted?"

"Of course it is. It's perfect. You don't destroy these people by hurting them. They revel in that. It gives them credibility. Gives them the chance to act hard. No. You have to humiliate them. Make them look small. Make them cringe with embarrassment. Make them seem pathetic and harmless so that they can never intimidate anyone ever again. It will be a long, long time before Zippo Macintosh will be the bully in the playground."

"You really planned for all of this?"

"Every last bit. Well, not all of it I suppose. I never guessed they would burn his house down and pelt him with eggs. But good on them all the same. Serves the bastard right."

"Jesus Jack, what happened to you?"

Suddenly his voice was harder. Crisp. Businesslike. Slightly chilling. "You know the answer to that question Mandy. They killed my son. That makes them my enemies. It's as simple as that. They just picked the wrong enemy. All of them. And I'm not finished yet. Not by a long chalk."

She picked her words carefully. "So what comes next Jack?"

"I'm afraid you're going to have to wait and see Mandy. Everybody is going to have to wait and see. But there will be more. Much, much more. There are a couple of last things that I need to ask of you.

"If you look at your email, you will find that I have sent you a couple of photos. One is from today – a Jack enjoying the sun and the Scottish countryside and a fag and a can of ale photo. The second is an old one. My sergeant took it one day when we were on patrol in Turf Lodge. It's a good one. The papers will love it. I've got all the gear on and I have that 'show me a Provo and he's toast' look on my face."

"Oh Jack . . ."

He laughed. "Sorry Mandy. I'm only messing about. But seriously, the papers will love the photos. This is all about being an enigma. Larking in the sun and patrolling Belfast in the rain. Strange images. An enigma. Me now, me then. The other thing. Make a few calls to the TV and radio stations. Tell them I will be in touch. When I ring I will use the codeword 'Spartacus'. Then they will know it's me, not some prankster. Can you do that for me?"

"Yes Jack. Of course. But *Spartacus*? Honestly."

"What's wrong with Spartacus?"

"Nothing. It's just so typical I suppose. Anything else?"

"Actually there is. How have you got on with getting them to help out the users? Any action?"

"Sorry Jack. Nothing. It's like banging my head against a wall. Nobody seems to care."

"OK Mandy. I thought as much. Leave it with me. I will deal with it tomorrow."

What on earth was he going to do next? She shook her head. God alone knew. There was no point asking. He was wearing his secretive hat again.

"Well I best get on with my chores Major. Just call if you need anything else. Your wish is my command."

His voice was suddenly more concerned. "Look Mandy. You don't have to do any of this. Just say if you don't want to. Really."

She laughed. "This time I was winding you up. Of course I'll help out. We'll speak soon. Bye."

By the next morning the story had made the front page of every paper in the land. Most papers used one or the other of the photos that Jack had emailed to Mandy. There were lots of pictures of the naked men in the square, and of Zippo's dramatic journey home. Headlines followed a similar theme. "Ex-soldier declares war on drugs gang", "Farmer's Drugs Cull", "Red, Green and Blue – The colours of Shame", "Stripped n' Dyed – Ex Major wipes out Drugs gang."

The tone varied. Editorials in two of the broadsheets expressed concern that the dramatic actions could lead to a dangerous rise in vigilantes. Many of the tabloids were almost totally supportive. Bob Bennet had sold the photos of the cell-block to the *Daily Mail*. Their headline was a simple "Inside the Major's torture chamber."

Jack had slept better that Sunday night than he had for a very long time. When he emerged from his tent a little after six the next morning he felt clean and fresh. Once again the sky was an unblemished blue and below him a light mist hung in the heavily wooded valley. He made himself a coffee and then logged his lap-top computer onto the internet to check all the papers. The radio kept on mentioning his name. It was extraordinary. His name was everywhere. His ears pricked up at a little after eight. He was listening to the BBC's *Five Live* channel.

"Nicky Campbell has just come in. Morning Nicky."

"Morning Victoria."

"Tell us a little about this morning's show."

"Well, what else could it be? A story from my own native Scotland is sweeping the world this morning. On Saturday lunchtime, ex-Major Jack Sinclair deposited sixteen naked men in the centre of Dumfries and they were all dyed from head to toe. He claims that these men ran an extensive drugs operation in the town and that they were responsible for his son's death. Already this morning's papers are filled with conflicting emotions. Many tabloids are already hailing Sinclair as a hero. And yet the Daily Mail *carries chilling photos of the home-made torture block on his farm. So what do you think? Jack Sinclair – hero or villain? Black hat or white hat? Call me on 0500 909 693 where the nation speaks its mind. That's the Nicky Campbell show at nine o'clock."*

Jack got connected to a researcher at ten to nine.

"Good morning. I would like to be a guest on this morning's

show. I'm Jack Sinclair and it would appear that the show is about me. Maybe Mr Campbell would find my participation useful. I believe that if you check you will find that the word 'Spartacus' confirms my credentials."

The line was dead for a while and then the researcher returned to inform Jack that Mr Campbell would be delighted to have him on the show. The nine o'clock news cane and went, and then the sport. Then Nicky Campbell started his show.

"Good morning and welcome to the Nicky Campbell show. I have been doing this show for several years now and we have often covered some pretty dramatic ground. But none of it quite as dramatic as the ground we are about to cover this morning. This morning we are discussing what has happened over the weekend up in Dumfries. We were going to try and explore the motives of Jack Sinclair, the man who appears to have rounded up a whole drugs gang, stripped them naked and dyed them red, green and blue. Well, I'm delighted to say that there is no need for us to second-guess his motives because he has joined us to take part in the show. Good morning Jack."

"Morning Nicky."

"And how are you this morning? Somewhat thunderstruck I imagine."

"Actually I'm in tremendous order Nicky. Top of the range. Are you familiar with the Galloway Forest yourself?"

"Reasonably. I've visited it a time or two."

"Well I'm sitting outside my tent with a cup of coffee and a cigarette and the view takes the breath away. Blue sky. Mist in the glen. Buzzards up above. Scotland at its best Nicky. Scotland at its best."

Campbell couldn't help but laugh. "I'm confused Jack. You're supposed to be on the run, but this sounds like a holiday."

"Oh it's both. I absolutely am on the run. No doubt about it. But where better to run? There are thousands of square miles of this forest. I have several camps set up and lots and lots of provisions. If they can find me, then best of luck to them, but I wouldn't bet on it."

A memory stirred in Campbell's brain. "And of course there is a proud Scottish tradition of using the Galloway Forest as a place to run and hide. I do believe Robert the Bruce did much the same there about 700 years ago."

"And they never caught him Nicky."

"No they never did. Not the whole of the English Army. So is that what you are Jack? A new Bruce? A rebel soldier? A defiant Scot fighting the world?"

Jack chuckled. "I wouldn't pretend to be so grand. Maybe it's just a convenient place to hide away. I'm a farmer when all is said and done. I'm used to the outdoors."

"Well we'll be taking calls soon, but first I would like to ask you a couple of questions if I may?"

"Fine. Fire away. That's why I'm here."

"Well the first question is the obvious one. Why?"

"Simple. These men were directly responsible for the death of my son. He was nineteen. He had his whole life ahead of him. And these men caused his death. In my book that makes them my enemies. Simple as that. There was no way that the police were ever going to deal with the situation. Not that I blame them. They do the best they can. But their hands are tied by the politicians. So I decided to take action myself. You have seen the results."

"An eye for an eye then, Jack?"

"Not exactly. My boy is dead. They are not. They will just find it very hard indeed to sell their poison to other boys like Will. This wasn't blind revenge Nicky. This was an operation with clear objectives. I hope that these will be achieved. I would say that part one has been a success."

"But revenge must have been a part of it?"

"Do you have children Nicky?"

"Yes. Yes I do."

"Then you may be able to guess at my feelings. Yes, of course there was an element of revenge. I wanted to punish these men and I did so. But revenge is no good if it is blind. Revenge must be constructive. There must be a purpose."

"And your purpose Jack?"

"I want the people who destroy lives by selling heroin to be stopped. Simple as that."

Campbell was mesmerised. "A worthy goal Jack. But

governments have spent endless millions of pounds on this war, and yet every year the drugs trade seems to grow. How on earth can you change this?"

"I hope to change this in many ways. But I'm afraid that is not a topic for this morning. I must make an admission here Nicky. My main reason for coming on this morning is to promote my website. Now I know the BBC doesn't really allow this kind of thing, but I promise I won't be making a penny out of it. It goes live tomorrow and the address is www.thecull.com. If anyone wants to log on at eight tomorrow night I will be making a broadcast. Sorry about that Nicky."

"Oh I can live with it. You're not going now I hope? There are a lot of people wanting to talk to you out there."

Jack laughed. "No. Not at all. I'm here for as long as you want me. I've got plenty of battery time left on the phone. Before we get to the calls can I just raise one issue please?"

Campbell chuckled. "Of course. Fire away. Feel free."

"Thank you. I believe that there are between 1,000 and 2,000 heroin addicts in Dumfries. These people are not criminals. They are not bad. They have done nothing that means that society should turn its back on them. All they have done is made a simple mistake. They have allowed themselves to become addicted to a drug that is almost impossible to escape from. We all make mistakes Nicky. I have made them. You have made them. Getting hooked on heroin is a pretty serious mistake, but it doesn't mean that society should turn its back on those who make it.

"As of late last week there is absolutely no heroin available for sale on the streets of Dumfries. Soon it will be the same in at least nine other Scottish towns. At this very minute, hundreds of users will be literally going through the torments of hell. This is not right. These people are citizens and they need help. Just because they are addicted to heroin does not mean that the civic authorities have any right to ignore them. Something simply has to be done. There are people out there who need help and it must be given and given quickly. It is quite inexcusable for these people to be left to suffer."

Campbell was confused now. "Shouldn't you have thought

about this before Jack? If you hadn't done what you did all these people would be fine."

"They are not my problem Nicky. They are everybody's problem. We like to call ourselves a caring society. Then we'd best prove it. I want this cancer stopped for the sake of future generations. Nothing I can do will bring my son back. Nothing can help the fact that there are already thousands and thousands of people out there who have seen their lives torn apart. What I can do is to try and stop it going any further."

"But the methods Jack? We are hearing stories of torture and brutality. Let's face it, those pictures of your cell-block are pretty damning."

"Of course they are. I fully expect to be heavily criticised for what I have done in many quarters. It doesn't bother me. I'm not running for Parliament. Popularity is not an issue to me. What I do know is that if I had sat these men down over a cup of tea and had a cosy chat I wouldn't have got very far. These were violent, brutal men. I merely treated them in the way that they were accustomed to dealing with anyone who dared to cross them. It wasn't nice. They didn't like it. Tough. You live by the sword, you die by the sword."

"What about the nakedness Jack? The shaven heads? The coloured dye?"

"As I said before, these were severely brutalised individuals. They used violence and intimidation to keep an iron hold on their operation. And we are not talking about peanuts here. We are talking of a major commercial operation worth hundreds of thousands of pounds every month. Their structure was sound and their procedures pretty tight. They knew full well that the only way that they would ever be caught was if somebody informed on them and was willing to testify against them in court. To make sure this never happened they ran a regime of total brutality and violence. Anyone who crossed them would meet with a fate worse than death either in or out of prison. How would you like someone to light a Zippo up you nostrils? No? Thought not.

"These men made sure that everyone was scared to death of them. They wanted to seem like supermen; indestructible, immune from the law. Well it is pretty hard to act like Superman when your *head is shaved and you are paraded in front of the cameras stark-naked and dyed blue. I wanted to show everyone that these were just men. Show them for the sad, pathetic people they really are. Strip them of their trappings. And we all saw what happened when Zippo Macintosh went home. Nobody was afraid any more. Everyone had lost their fear because they saw him reduced to nothing and taken out of the shadows. I hope the dye lasts for a very long time. These men deserved everything that they got."*

The producer talked to Campbell in his headphones. The phone lines were glowing red. Hundreds and hundreds of callers were trying to get through.

"Well Jack. I think it is time to take some calls. My producer tells me that half the world is wanting to speak to you. You ready?"

"As I'll ever be."

"OK let's go to Jim on the M1. Jim, are you there?"

"I'm here Nicky. Morning Jack."

"Morning Jim. Are you on the road?"

"Yeah, I'm a wagon driver. I've got two words for you Jack. Bloody brilliant. It's about time someone did this. My lad got onto smack when he was sixteen. That was three years ago and we've been through it all, the arguments, the stealing, the violence. It's like a nightmare. People have no idea about how this can break families apart. He's not a bad lad. He was always a good lad. No harm in him. But since he's become an addict he has changed. He wants to get off it, but it is almost impossible. I don't care what you did to those blokes. Whatever it was, it wasn't enough as far as I'm concerned."

"Thanks Jim" said Campbell. "I think we have Lisa on the line from Northampton. Are you there Lisa?"

"I'm here Nicky and I would like to agree with everything that the last caller said. I have two children, one is fifteen and the other is thirteen. I am frightened all the time for them. Drugs are terrible round here. We tell them and we tell them, and they always say that they know all about it, but kids will be stupid won't they? And we all know that these evil people are out there looking to turn our kids in to addicts so that they can make money.

THE CULL

The Government never do anything. The police never do anything. Well thank God you have shown them all, Jack. God bless you. I'm so, so sorry about what happened to your boy, but maybe you have helped stop the same thing happening to my boys."

"Thanks Lisa" said Jack. "What we must all realise is that these people are vulnerable. They think that they will always be protected by the law. But they are wrong. Every day they have to show themselves in order to sell their product. As soon as they show themselves they become vulnerable. The only real protection that they enjoy is the law. Without the law they stand no chance against the likes of me or Jim or you, Lisa. All we need to be strong is to be together. Together we are all strong and they are weak."

Campbell intervened. "Could you explain this Jack? Why is the law the only protection they enjoy?"

"Simple Nicky. Let's say you decide to boost your income by selling heroin. How do you go about it? You take orders on your mobile phone. You arrange a rendezvous with your customer. You never carry more than one or two small bags at a time. Let's say that the police manage to catch you in the act of passing over the heroin. What happens then? You are arrested with a very modest amount of the drug. You can even claim it is only for personal use. But what you do have is a stack of money behind you to hire the very best lawyer you can find. When the case eventually gets to court the lawyer will make a great case that you hardly had any of the drug on you, that it is your first offence, that you are a smashing lad at heart. And if you do get found guilty, what happens then? You'll get a few days community service or at the absolute worst a couple of months inside, where your bosses will ensure that you are left well alone. That is the downside. The upside is that you can earn well in excess of £100,000 a year. Not a hard choice is it?

"On the other side of the fence the law ties the police up in knots. They know full well who are the main players in their town. But they also know that to stand a chance of gaining a prosecution they need a water-tight case because the accused will always hire their fancy lawyers. So the law protects them from both sides. If by any chance they do get caught there are

262

never any severe consequences. And the police, whose job it is to catch them, find it almost impossible to do so, because the law ties their hands behind their backs."

"So what do you do Jack?"

"You find the man at the end of the chain. You find out who is the next link along the line. You shave his hair. You strip him naked. You dye him a bright colour. Expose and humiliate. Once these people are branded, the rest of society can sort them out. A man with a blue face won't get a job, he won't get a girl and he won't dare go into a pub for a drink. The consequences are therefore severe. Getting caught as a dealer means becoming a social outcast, a leper, someone that the kids throw stones at. Now that is punishment."

The calls went on and on. There were a couple who were aghast at Jack's disregard for the law of the land. But it was only a couple. The vast majority of the calls reflected the views of the ordinary British people who so hated the threat of drugs. These were people who were simply frightened for their children and their grandchildren. They were sick of seeing the lives of young people so badly threatened to line the pockets of a few dealers and drug barons in their expensive cars and designer clothes. Sure Jack Sinclair had used harsh measures. So what. About time too. The bastards deserved everything they got. *The Nicky Campbell Show* showed the nation's feelings to an audience of millions.

Before the broadcast Jack Sinclair was well on the way to being a star. By 10.30 that morning he was no longer just on the way. By 10.30 that morning he WAS a star. A huge, huge star.

That night Jack clashed swords with Jeremy Paxman on *Newsnight*. When it was over, and he hit the "end" button on his phone and stared out into the vastness of the Scottish night, he felt as if he had been in a brawl. The following morning he was once again all over the front pages of just about every one of the morning papers. The whole of the country was talking about Jack Sinclair. Who was this man? Where had he come from? Was he a monster? Was he a madman? Was he a saviour? A hero? A Prophet?

Talk, talk, talk and more talk. Experts on studios ranged from baffled policemen to hassled-looking politicians to smug-faced psychiatrists. There was much analysis of the drugs trade. There was much speculation about Jack's mental motivation. There was endless agonising about the rights and wrongs of his actions. Nobody in any position of authority dared to suggest that he could possibly have been right. Going against the law could never be right. All responsible citizens simply had to respect the machinery of the law. There could never be any place for vigilantes in the UK.

But it was becoming increasingly obvious with every interview from every roving reporter that the wider population took an altogether different view. They were fed up with the helplessness of the law. They were sick of how easy it was for the drug trade to flourish all around them. They were frightened. Frightened that all the love and attention and devotion they had given over so many years to their children could be rendered null and void by some sweet-talking pusher. These were the ordinary people who for centuries had guaranteed that Britain would never have a revolution. They were the quiet people, used to abiding by the rules, paying their taxes and working the longest hours in Europe. These were the people who were always taken for granted and made a habit of keeping their heads down.

And suddenly they were coming alive. Because enough was enough. And, when they lifted their heads and took a look around, they found that there were millions and millions of people just like them. People who lay awake at night worrying about their children. The same nagging, eroding worry. What if someone offers heroin to my child? At a party, or in a pub, or a nightclub. Will they be able to say no? Will they dare to say no? Will they want to say no? And what if all their friends take it? And have they really any idea of how it could destroy their lives? And in the new world of the twenty-first century there was no way of keeping children at home wrapped in cotton wool. They all wanted their freedom, they demanded their freedom because the TV and the radio and their pop star role-models and their magazines told them that it was their right. But what would happen once they had this freedom? What demons awaited them? It wasn't just a bottle of Red Martini stolen from the back of the drinks cabinet any more. It wasn't going into one of the old pubs in the back streets which could only ever survive by selling drinks to under-age customers. It was heroin. It was a life destroyer.

On that Tuesday in May these people realised that they were not alone. The airwaves were filled with ordinary people with ordinary jobs in ordinary little towns saying thank God for Jack Sinclair. At last someone had done the thing that they had all dreamed of. Nobody had ever realised that to so many people the heroin seller was the greatest enemy. Governments focused on Irish bombers and evil communists and fanatical mullahs and anti-capitalist anarchists and Balkan War Criminals. But most ordinary people felt little or no threat from these people. They never saw that these bogeymen were going to have an effect on their lives. Why should they? But the shadowy figure loitering near the school gates with his bags of heroin was a very real threat. A threat to their children, their families, their very existence. And nobody seemed to care much. In fact, most so-called experts seemed to want to blame them, the parents. It was the responsibility of every decent parent to make sure that their children would never be so stupid. Had none of them ever had kids of their own? Had none of them ever been kids themselves? Nobody ever seemed to make the realisation that kids would be kids, and no matter how much you tried to tell them something it only meant that they would be that much more likely to do the opposite.

At last someone was saying all the things they wanted to hear. These people, who made their millions from selling heroin to young people, were scum. The only thing to do was to stop them. And if the law was so emasculated that it was incapable of doing this, then other measures needed to be taken. Shave them, strip them, dye them. Perfect. Expose them. Perfect. Humiliate them. Perfect. Brand them for all the world to see. Perfect.

By the middle of the afternoon the media was getting the message. The people were not just fascinated by the story because it involved naked men dyed bright colours. They were fascinated because they approved of everything that Jack Sinclair had done. Hastily arranged polls came back with approval ratings of 80 percent. Jack Sinclair had not just amused the public with a stage-managed stunt. He had tapped into their primordial emotions.

By early evening, all the speculation revolved around the

question of what was going to happen next. Sinclair had hinted that the naked men in Dumfries was only the start. He had claimed that his operation had a long, long way to run. What could he mean? What could he actually do? After all he was just one man, all alone in his tent, protected by a vast empty forest. Gradually people started talking about a new fascination. It came as a slow realisation that he was going to be able to address the world at eight o'clock that night from a mobile phone and a lap-top. And no matter what any of the authorities thought about it, there was not a damned thing they could do to stop it.

And at about this time the penny slowly began to drop with several of the pundits and the analysts. They suddenly saw that what Jack Sinclair had done was truly revolutionary. And like all such actions the genius was in the simplicity. He had recognised the media's voracious appetite for the kind of story he had given them. Then, rather than disappearing from view, he had made himself available to them. He had sent them press releases and pictures and pointed then towards the cell-block. And the media had taken the bait like a hungry fish, and they had given Jack the wall-to-wall blanket coverage he had hoped for.

In the space of three days the TV and radio and newspapers had gifted Jack the most priceless asset in the modern world. Fame. With fame all doors could be opened, and the media cherished the knowledge that it, and it alone, controlled the access to fame. They had made building stars up and knocking them back down into an art-form. And they had been convinced that any star they ever created would always remain their very own exclusive property.

But Jack Sinclair had seen through the myth. He had seen that there was a new, ultimate medium in town. The internet. His eight o'clock broadcast would find an audience of millions and nobody could stop it. Nobody. Not governments, or secret services or regulatory bodies or church leaders or censors. Nobody. Now that he had his fame, the world was all his. The only way that anyone could stop the world hearing from Jack Sinclair was to cut off the world's phone lines. He was gone. Away. Clear of grasping hands.

Jack Sinclair had been granted the gift of fame. Now he could start to make waves.

Chapter 11
Broadcast

"Good evening. I'm Jack Sinclair, and I must tell you that this feels pretty damn strange. At this moment I am sitting under a canvas sheet trying to keep out of the rain. I have a microphone in my hand, and the microphone is attached to a lap-top computer, which is in turn connected to a mobile phone. The experts who have taught me assure me that with these simple bits of kit I can speak to anybody in the world.

"Ridiculous isn't it. I can't but help thinking that I am probably just talking to myself and the odd bird and rabbit. Well, I have to assume that they are right and that there are indeed people out there. If there are, thanks for logging-on.

"If you have taken the trouble to log-on, I assume you will already know why I am here. I can't imagine what you make of me. Maybe you think I'm an absolute lunatic. Maybe you think what I have done is the right thing. I don't know. I hope that I have explained why I did the things that I did. I certainly feel comfortable about it.

"I have been listening all day to what is being said about me on my little portable radio. So was this just a single act of revenge for the death of my son? No. I hope not. So what am I going to do next? Well, clearly I am not in much of a position to do much from a personal point of view. I am hiding away in the forest, and I dare say it won't be long before people come looking for me.

"What I can do is to offer everyone out there an idea. I hope that

I have proved that every drug dealer in the country is completely vulnerable. Every time they show their faces to sell another bag of heroin they put themselves at risk. And they have to show themselves, because if they don't they won't sell anything. This means that lots and lots and lots of people know who these dealers are. In the past these people in the know have contacted the police and passed on their information. And what has happened? Not a lot. The police are under-funded and under-manned. To get a conviction they have to put together an impossibly watertight case. Not their fault. It's just the way it is. Our politicians seem happy to pass laws which allow the drugs barons to do what they please.

"Well all that can change now.

"If anyone out there has any information about any dealer, you can now email it to this website. You will find that there is a simple form to fill in. We want any information you can give us. Who are they? Where do they live? Where do they deal? Movements? Habits? Anything. And give us a postcode. We will then process the information and post it all on this site for the whole world to see.

"When you take a look, you will find that there is already a considerable amount of information on nine Scottish towns. This came from a gentleman called Jeremy Taylor who was interrogated last week. Taylor is both a very greedy man and a very clever man. He made a good living from representing a selection of Gangland clients in Glasgow before he got sloppy with his tax returns. This sloppiness resulted in him being sent to Barlinnie Prison. He used his time in prison to get himself involved in the drug business. He set up a rather impressively co-ordinated franchise system with a network stretching across ten Scottish towns, including Dumfries. Amazingly enough Taylor modelled his franchise operation on McDonald's. He offered a full service, from the supply of quality drugs, to training, to money-laundering, to supplying ex-soldiers to act as enforcers when required. I have to say that Taylor used his legal talents superbly to establish his operation. However, his background was of little use once he became our guest on the 'Block'. He was extremely forthcoming and the information that you can now read was all supplied by him. There are extensive details about all the networks, their personnel and their procedures. This may be used in any way that you feel fit.

"Taylor was procuring his drugs from some very unpleasant men indeed who are long-term members of the Ulster Volunteer Force in Belfast. These men are a very different proposition indeed soon most of the dealers here on the mainland, and I would advise extreme caution to anyone who has any dealings with them. But all their details are available all the same.

"I have a team of people who are going to collate this information and add it onto the site. I am aware that this presents a great opportunity for anyone to have a go at someone they don't like. To try and ensure that the information is as good as possible, we will require at least three independent reports on any individual before we post their details. It isn't foolproof, and there will be mistakes, but that's life.

"The people who we really want to hear from are the policemen. We know just how bloody frustrating it must be for you at the moment. You know exactly who these people are, but there is nothing you can do to stop them. Well, now you have a way. Simply fill in the form and email it in, letting us know that you are from the police. Give us a number where we can contact you to verify that you are who you say you are, and we will post all your information. I can guarantee absolute anonymity. I know you will be really nervous about doing this to start with, but if enough of you do it, there will be far too many for anyone to be able to track down.

"Remember that scene in Spartacus when the Romans say if the real Spartacus will stand up they will let all the others go? Remember? And everyone stands up. Thousands of them. And they all shout 'I'm Spartacus!' Well that can be the same for you guys in the police. Why not let all that work that you have done over the years bear some fruit. These people are scum. They deserve nothing.

"So what happens when the names are posted on the site? Well that is up to you. All of you. Every person in the land. Get yourselves into teams. Plan carefully. Find the one at the bottom of the chain. Make him tell you who the next person is. Strip him. Shave his head. Dye him if you can. And leave him in a public place. Take photos and email them to the site. We will post them for all the world to see.

269

"You see, we're not pussy-footing around here. This isn't a nice cosy type of operation. It's hard and it's nasty. But for me it is worth it. These people have had the free run of our land for long enough. It's time to call a halt. We need to make sure that every person in this country will be scared to death at the idea of selling drugs. If they are scared enough they won't do it any more. Expose and humiliate. We are many. They are few.

"Now I assume that the great and good of the land will not be amused about this. They expect all of us to do as we are told. We must place our trust in our leaders. We must follow and obey the law even when it fails us. We must do as they command. This was the hard lesson that I learned on the streets of a place called Turf Lodge in West Belfast. Me and my men were told to go out and act like hooligans and bullies because our government felt that was the thing to do. And we did it. We did it for year after year and we only made things worse, because every time we smashed up somebody's home or swore at a mother in front of her young children, we helped to create the next generation of men filled with hate.

"I learnt the lesson that governments can be wrong. Really, really wrong. Just like they were wrong for so many years in Ireland where they ordered men like me to do their dirty work for them. But they won't admit it. Never. They will cover up and gloss over. And even though they go on and on about getting rid of the drugs plague, they will never admit that they are losing the battle hands-down.

"I don't suppose they will be very happy when all of us take the issue away from them and sort it out for ourselves. I expect that they will want to make my life rather difficult. This means that this will have to be my last live broadcast. A mobile phone signal in the middle of this wilderness is too easy a target. A rather easy beacon to home in on with a helicopter full of likely lads from Hereford.

"So when I finish tonight, I move. I will be able to record further broadcasts and have other people put them on the site. I will be able to respond to messages that I receive through the message boards, and I can watch as our database of information builds up. From now on I will have to stay on the move. The stakes will keep going up. Any help that anyone can give me about suspicious-looking groups of men heading into the forest would obviously be useful. Just email them in.

"This website is now open. It a resource for all of you. It will stay open and nobody can stop it. It belongs to everybody. If enough people out there feel the same way as me, it will soon become a powerful weapon. Information is power. Power for every last one of us. Let's use it. Let's break these people into pieces. Let's never again allow them to spread their cancer amongst us. Expose. Brand. Humiliate.

I wish you all well. Thanks for listening."

Jack had already packed all his gear. He quickly got the computer into his rucksack and started to move. The rain was falling steadily and visibility was poor. A thick mist wrapped itself around the pine trees. He moved quickly for two hours. All the time his senses were on high alert. His ears strained for the old familiar thump, thump sound of helicopter rotors. But there was nothing. Only the muffled silence of the rain. He would have been surprised if they had been ready to track him. Before tonight he hadn't been much of a threat. He was just a bizarre side-show freak that appealed to the tabloids. But now it was different. Because now he had challenged them. He had tossed down the gauntlet. He had incited mass disobedience. And that would never be tolerated.

He had no idea whether or not his appeal would be effective. In his heart of hearts, he rather doubted it. It seemed too absurd. This was the United Kingdom after all. But Liam had been adamant. He had been certain that out there they would find millions of willing recruits. He remembered the soft compelling Irish voice. "It's never the working classes that change the world Jack. Never. That's just a myth. Whenever the working classes try to rise up they get squashed. Always. No, it's the middle classes. When the middle classes feel threatened enough to organise themselves they are almost unstoppable. Who is there to stop them? The police? The Army? The courts? Of course not. These are the middle classes themselves. Look at Hitler's Nazi party in about 1929, Jack. Who were they? They were students and businessmen and small farmers and shopkeepers and accountants and policemen. And they were unstoppable. These people can be your army. Jack's army. They are all scared to death that heroin will ruin their lives. They are scared for their children. They are angry and frightened and they feel powerless. All they need is someone to show them a way. You can be one Jack. You can be the Pied Piper."

Well he had certainly played his pipe. He had played it as hard as he could. There was nothing else for him to do. The ball was now in another court. If the people took up the baton, all there was for him to do was to stay free. He had lit the kindling sticks. Others would have to feed the fire. All there was left now was to become a talisman. A phantom.

He reached his second camp a little after ten. Darkness was closing in all around. The rain sprinkled down onto the tarpaulin that he used as a shelter. He pulled a can of beer out of his case of provisions and turned on the radio.

Now he would see if it was starting to work.

Voices on the radio were outraged. This was diabolical. Of course it would never happen. Not here. Not in Britain. A very flustered Home Secretary gave a hurried statement. No, they were not concerned. The British people were far too mature to be influenced by this kind of extremism. Yes, they would be taking immediate steps to locate and apprehend Jack Sinclair. No, he had no concerns that any member of the constabulary would ever consider divulging information to this crazy website. He concluded with a statement saying that the British people would never forget the value of the democracy they enjoyed, and that they would never dream of taking the law into their own hands.

And he got it wrong. Absolutely, utterly, completely wrong. All over the land people saw a smug face telling them that he knew better than them. Just like Jack Sinclair had predicted he would. And all he could think of was to treat Jack Sinclair as if he was some kind of terrorist. Millions of people had listened to Jack's broadcast. It had hit a chord. It had appealed to deep instincts. When the Home Secretary rubbished it so smugly and glibly, people became angry. Who did he think he was? Typical arrogant politician. Thinks he knows everything. Well, we'll show the cocky bastard.

And so at the very moment that numerous pundits in numerous TV and radio studios were in the process of explaining how it could never happen, it actually started to happen. Hundreds and hundreds of emails started to land on Jack's site. Liam's contact in New York had put together a team of four people to handle the traffic. It was quite impossible. Soon the information coming in became a flood.

It came in all that night, and by the next morning the website was starting to fill up. Names. Addresses. Details. Hundreds of them. After a few days it was thousands. And the "Spartacus" plea had worked. Policemen talked to each other discreetly. If you will, I will. And they did. They opened up files that had taken years to put together and passed them over to the public that they served.

Liam and Jack had decided that it would be unwise to use the mobile phone much from now on. The signal would be far too much of a giveaway. To check the website he would have to make long walks to the edge of population areas where there would be more phone signals. It was bound to be tiring and risky, but there was no other way. He would have to record his broadcasts and mail them.

When he listened to his radio the next evening he found that these measures would not be necessary after all. An email had been sent to the website during the morning. It came from a volunteer who had promised to drive into the forest every evening at eight o'clock and use his mobile phone. The volunteer asked for more volunteers. And more had came forward. The radio reporter was talking from inside a pub in New Galloway. The place was heaving with people grabbing a couple of quick pints before heading into the vastness of the forest to use their phones at eight o'clock.

And so Jack was able to broadcast after all that night. He thanked the volunteer who had come up with the idea. He thanked all the others. He said that he was amazed by the support. He told everyone that he was staggered by the amount of information that was pouring into the website. From now on he would be able to broadcast every night.

The first incident came on Thursday morning. Three naked men were tied to some railings in Stranraer, a small port 70 miles to the west of Dumfries. Their heads were shaved, but instead of dye they had been sprayed with green paint. Their photos appeared on the website by Thursday lunchtime.

On Friday there were more incidents. Arbroath, Kilmarnock, Burnley, and Stevenage.

THE CULL

By Saturday morning naked men had appeared in over 50 British towns. And in high places, panic was beginning to set in. It wasn't just a British story now. It was a world story. Reporters from all over the planet were flying in. It was astonishing. Amazing. There were bound naked men and women seemingly everywhere. Exposed. Branded. Humiliated.

The Prime Minister called his Cabinet into Downing Street that morning. There was an air of unreality in the room. At last the Foot and Mouth crisis was finally beginning to die down. And now there was this. In some ways it seemed similar to the Foot and Mouth epidemic. That had started with an isolated incident up by Hadrian's Wall, and seemingly in no time at all it was sweeping across the country at breakneck speed. This new problem promised to be the same. But much, much worse.

When the Dumfries men had first appeared on TV, the Prime Minister had watched in amazement along with the rest of the country. It hadn't worried him. It was an isolated incident. A dramatic incident to be sure. But nothing to concern him. It was a Scottish matter when all was said and done. It would have to be the decision of his counterpart in Edinburgh as to how this Jack Sinclair was to be pursued.

Monday had made him more nervous. He listened to Sinclair on *Radio Five Live* and on *Newsnight*. He was good. Amazingly good. But was he going to be a one-day wonder? Surely he was. This was just another crazy wallowing in his fifteen minutes of fame. The webcast worried him quite seriously. He had made enquiries the afternoon before the broadcast was due to go out. Could it be stopped? It couldn't. Could they track it? Could they find the people who were running it? Maybe, but probably not. If it was being run by professionals, there would be almost no chance. The Prime Minister began to feel a prickling unease. He had never ever considered it possible for anyone to be able to broadcast to the nation other than him. It seemed outrageous. All he could do was to lean on the TV and radio stations to ensure they would not relay the broadcast live on the conventional media network. It had been difficult, and the media bosses had been hopping-mad about it, but in the end he had prevailed.

It had been a wasted effort. At tea time CNN started announcing that it would be carrying the broadcast live. By eight o'clock the word was out. In just about every pub in the country the TV was tuned into the American News channel. Besides that, there were millions and millions of people on-line at home and able to tune in. The rest of the media broke ranks at ten o'clock. They were fuming that the Yanks had been presented the broadcast as an exclusive. No point in holding back now. It was already in the public domain. So they replayed the broadcast word for word. And they dissected it and analysed it and played-through again and again and again.

The Prime Minister felt like a fool. He had used all his power to try and keep Jack Sinclair off the air, and it had only lasted for an hour. In the end Sinclair's words had got out anyway. The next day he talked to the leader of the Scottish Parliament who assured him that everything possible would be done to apprehend Sinclair quickly. He had spent the best part of the morning ensuring that all the necessary tracking devices were put in place to triangulate Sinclair's position as soon as he used his phone. He had also autho-rised the movement of a helicopter and four-man SAS team to West Freugh Airfield on the Mull of Galloway. By the evening his officers gave him assurances that the team could reach Sinclair within ten minutes of him using his phone.

This news enabled the Prime Minister to start to relax a little. Not for long. The next misery was Prime Minister's Question Time. It came as no surprise when the leader of the Opposition taunted him mercilessly about the Sinclair affair. Had he found time to see just how much information was being loaded onto the Cull website every hour? Had he considered the consequences if the public did indeed follow the lead Sinclair had given them? Did he not agree that this was yet more evidence of the British public growing sick and tired of a government that was so arrogant and aloof? All the Prime Minister had been able to do was to grit his teeth and give assurances that he was doing everything in his power to apprehend Jack Sinclair. He stated that he was confident that the British people would abide by the rule of law, and that they would never stoop to this kind of dangerous vigilante-type behaviour.

And of course the opposition MPs had loved every minute of it. Laughter had cascaded down on him from the green benches across from where he spoke. Jack Sinclair was making him look like a fool, and they all knew it. Damn the bloody man. Damn him to hell.

As soon as Question Time was over he had reviewed the situation. God only knew what mayhem the website was going to cause, but at least they could stop the bloody man broadcasting to the nation like some kind of modern-day Roosevelt. This sense of relief lasted two hours before reports came in of many cars being driven into the Galloway Forest by members of the public who were determined to use their mobile phones at eight o'clock. Rapid consultations soon confirmed that it would be impossible to recognise Sinclair's signal in the midst of so many others. Damn. Once again the country tuned in to Jack Sinclair.

By Saturday morning the situation was beginning to drive the Prime Minister demented. He had to handle several calls from other European leaders wanting to know just what was happening. He could not miss the amusement in some of their voices, particularly that cocky bastard from Paris. It was all getting way beyond a joke but what on earth was he to do? Well, that's why he had a Cabinet. Maybe someone could come up with something. He was certainly all out of ideas.

This hope was quickly shown to be forlorn. His plea for suggestions caused many heads to turn downwards to study pens and note paper. Silence. Nothing. Jesus. Here they were, supposedly the people that ran the country, and not a single one of them had the first idea how to stop some crazy Scottish farmer from running rings round them. He tossed his pen down on the table angrily.

"Is that it? Nothing? Not one of you has anything to say?"

They hadn't. Not one of them. The Prime Minister blew out his cheeks in exasperation.

"Bloody marvellous. Well you better come up with something soon. I want some ideas by next Tuesday morning." He stared at the Secretary of State for Defence. "Talk to the Army. What can they do? Can they find him? Make sure that they know that it has to be discreet. If we send hundreds of soldiers into the forest we will look terrible."

The Minister spoke up. "What about all the people going in there in the evenings to use their mobile phones? Can we stop them? Seal off the forest? Technically it is still a high risk Foot and Mouth infection area. All the footpaths are closed. Why don't we close off the roads as well?"

"Are you crazy? How do you think it is going to look if we start sealing areas off with the Army? The Press will have a field day. No. No way. Whatever we do has to be discreet. Very discreet." He looked over to the Home Secretary. "I need you to look at any options at the Home Office. Talk to the Special Branch. Talk to MI5. We pay enough money for these people to build their little empires. Surely they can find out something."

The Home Secretary made a point of fiercely scribbling on his jotter and nodded vigorously. The Prime Minister sighed. So much for his hopes of finding inspiration from around the table. "OK. So what should I do? I need to say something. Outside Number 10? Or on some programme or another? Suit on or casual?"

This was easier ground. A debate started up. In the end they agreed on a quick Press Conference that afternoon in casual weekend clothes outside Number 10. The tone would be relaxed. The Cabinet was duly dismissed until Tuesday morning.

The Prime Minister strolled out of Number 10 two hours later in jeans and a golfing jacket. His smile was easy as he faced up to the ranks of the world media. He gently gestured for their questions to wait until he had made his statement.

"Good afternoon Gentlemen. Thank you for coming at short notice. I feel that it is appropriate that I should say a few words about what has been happening in towns all around the country over the last few days. We are of course greatly concerned that this kind of vigilante behaviour has broken out in our country. However I must emphasise that this is not a crisis. I have spent this morning discussing the situation with my Cabinet colleagues as well as the Chief Constables of various Police Forces. We will not tolerate this kind of behaviour. Those responsible for these acts will be vigorously pursued and prosecuted. I refute all allegations that members of the police are supplying any information to this lunatic website, and I can assure you all that if any member of the police is caught doing so they will face severe consequences. We are investigating all avenues by which we can seek out Jack Sinclair, and I am confident that he will be

*in custody very soon. To conclude, I ask the British people to show
their responsibility and maturity. We don't go in for lynching in
our great Country. We respect the rule of law. We always have and
we always will. This is what makes our democracy one of the
greatest in the world. Now, are there any questions?"*

A barrage of shouts broke out immediately. The Prime Minister
pointed to a journalist from the *Telegraph*. "Prime Minister. Can
you confirm that you have authorised for an SAS team to be sent
to West Freugh Airbase near Stranraer?"

His stomach nearly dropped through the pavement. How the
hell did the bloody man know that? His smile tightened on his
face. "You know very well that I never comment on any security
issues, especially those involving the Special Air Service."

Every journalist in the crowd gasped. He had basically said yes.
Bloody hell. They had deployed the SAS. Next question.

"Prime Minister, you keep referring to Jack Sinclair as a
madman and a terrorist. Are you aware that he was once
presented with the Military Cross? Are you aware that every poll
that has been conducted this week gives him approval ratings of
over 80 percent? Have you stopped to consider that he might be
more in step with the nation's feelings than you and your
Government?"

Thank you very much. A nice question for a sunny Saturday
afternoon. He took a deep breath. "Popularity does not mean that
the law can be ignored. Our laws have been drafted by our
democratically elected Parliaments over hundreds of years. We
are the very cradle of democracy. My government is the custodian
of these laws, and our Country's proud tradition of freedom and
democracy. There is no way that I, or my Government, will fail in
this duty. The law of the land must be upheld at all costs. There is
no room for vigilantes or lynch mobs here in Britain."

He was rather pleased with that. Not bad for off-the-cuff. The
journalist came straight back. "So I can take it that Jack Sinclair
is correct. The law does protect the drugs trade and you will
ensure that it continues to do so?"

Outrageous. How dare he? "No. That is not what I am saying
at all. It has always been the determined policy of this government

to stamp out the evil of drugs from our society. But this is a job for the proper authorities, not teams of vigilantes."

He nodded for the next question. "Prime Minister, there are many people who would say that Jack Sinclair has done more to eradicate drugs in a week than any government has managed in twenty years. How would you respond to that?"

How indeed? "Obviously it is far easier to achieve supposed justice when one decides to by-pass the courts and all the other vital elements of our Judicial system." Damn. Damn. Damn. As soon as he closed his mouth he knew he had walked straight into a nightmare. Damn. He had just agreed with everything the bloody man Sinclair had been saying. Idiot. The journalist was like a dog with a bone. "Surely, Prime Minister, that is the exact point that Mr Sinclair has been trying to make. Is it the case that you in fact agree that the law makes it easy for the drug trade to thrive?"

Sod it. "No I do not agree. All of our police forces are fully committed to stamping out the evil of drugs, and they will achieve this."

Next. "Prime Minister. Do you agree that if things continue as they have over the last couple of days there won't be any problem for the police to stamp out. Do you agree that Jack Sinclair may well have do their job for them?"

"No I do not agree. There is absolutely no evidence that the people who have been abducted and subjected to such appalling treatment have anything to do with drugs whatsoever. There is no evidence because the proper process of the law has not been followed. For all any of us know, these people may be entirely innocent. Next."

"Prime Minister. Jack Sinclair has been in touch with me this morning and has asked me to put a proposal to you about this very issue." There was a buzz of excitement in the crowd. Sinclair had done it again. He had primed a fellow journalist to put a question direct to the PM. Christ, this was some operator. The chosen journalist carried on. "Mr Sinclair shares your concerns that there may be some miscarriages of justice. He says that the last thing that he wants to see is for any innocent people to be exposed. With this in mind he suggests that the police can have the opportunity to monitor all names before they are uploaded onto his website. If they believe that any of the information will lead to an innocent person being wrongly exposed, then they can request that it is held back. Obviously if the police abuse this facility by knocking back all names, the offer of co-operation will be removed."

What on earth was happening here? How dare he? This was getting more outrageous by the minute. "There is absolutely no question of any such co-operation. We do not do deals with terrorists or vigilantes. That has always been our position."

"So will you take responsibility for any innocent person that is wrongly exposed?"

"No I do not take any such responsibility. The responsibility lies squarely with Jack Sinclair. He is the one who has started this madness."

"But Prime Minister, this is surely the whole point. Jack Sinclair fully accepts the responsibility. He is very clear on this. He is simply asking that the government does what it can to ensure that there are no miscarriages of justice."

The Prime Minister was fuming. By God when they got hold of this bastard Sinclair he would make sure he was sent away to rot. "I repeat, I do not talk with terrorists. That is final. If Mr Sinclair is so concerned about innocent people then I suggest he shuts his site down and stops inciting the population. Thank you gentlemen. I must go and attend to other business."

As he re-entered the famous door to his residence he felt like a rabbit scuttling back into its warren. Damn. Damn. Damn. He had been made to look a complete and absolute fool. He could barely believe it. After all these years, his reputation was being shredded by a farmer in a tent in the woods. It defied all belief.

That night Jack really hit the big time as he appeared live on the *Larry King* show in the United States. There had been the first appearances of spray-painted, naked men in four American towns that morning. The show was prime time, and millions tuned-in. And the Americans just loved the amusing laid-back Scotsman. He was very much their kind of guy. The man alone. This time he used his web cam, and many felt that his hard, craggy face reminded them of Gary Cooper in *High Noon*. In the course of half an hour Jack earned the priceless tag of being "big in America". The Prime Minister watched in something approaching utter misery, particularly when King asked, "Jack, you managed to relay a message to the Prime Minister this afternoon. Rather ingenious I must say. How do you feel about his response?"

"To be honest Larry, I have a great deal of sympathy for him. None of this is his fault, but it all lands up at his door. I wasn't trying to make things awkward for him. I was just hoping to be constructive. There is no way that I am giving this up so long as I stay at liberty. No way at all. I just wish that he could accept this and do what he can to ensure that it is only the bad guys who get exposed. The police know exactly who these people are. I realise that it must be hard for him to be put on the spot by an upstart like me, but maybe he will come around to my point of view. I like to think that a bit of co-operation might well be the lesser of two evils. By the way. The same deal goes for your President and the DEA. I never anticipated that Americans would start to use the site, but it seems like it is going to happen. I'm quite happy to work with your people as well."

King chuckled. "You certainly have the knack of putting politicians into the hot seat Jack. Tell me, aren't you getting scared. Let's face it, you're getting up some pretty powerful noses."

"Scared? Not really. You see, I am a man with nothing much to lose. My boy is gone. My animals have gone. My wife went years ago. When Will died something died in me too. I suppose that is why I was ready to do all this. Remember, Larry, I have been under fire before. I can assure you that the streets of Belfast seemed a damn site more hairy than the Galloway Forest. And in those days I had a wife and young boy to worry about. Not any more. There's only me now. No. I'm not scared. Anyway. Who's saying I'm going to get caught? That's not a part of my programme Larry."

It was one in the morning when the Prime Minister had to take a call from the President of the United States. The occupant of the White House wasn't amused. Not at all. He didn't appreciate being put on the spot by some unknown Scotsman on prime-time TV. He very much hoped that this Jack Sinclair would be caught and caught quickly. He didn't need these kinds of problems in America.

And so ended the Prime Minister's worst-ever day in politics. It had started badly, it had got worse in the middle, and it had ended with a ticking-off from the White House. Suddenly it was all his fault. And all because of a man in a tent. Sleep took a very long time in coming that night for the British Premier.

The next day was a Sunday. And it was dramatic. The news was again dominated by the Jack Sinclair story. Early-morning bulletins were filled with reports from all over the country of stripped and branded dealers being dumped in town centres. All the government's efforts had come to nothing. They had pleaded for restraint but they had woken up to an epidemic. That morning the Sinclair phenomenon went national. Virtually every town and city in the UK was affected. Jubilant crowds turned out to taunt the terrified victims. The country had discovered its bloodlust. By noon on that dramatic Sunday the drug trade in the UK was to all intents and purposes completely broken. Those whose names were on the list fled their homes in terror. Those who were further up the chain, but still retained their anonymity, did the same. It only took one name in any organisation to send panic all the way up the ladder. Victims were treated mercilessly. Fruit was thrown, crowds mocked and jeered and laughed, children danced and cheered in delight at the spectacle. Restaurants and fast-food joints which had been named as money-laundering outlets were boycotted at best, and stoned and spray-painted at worst.

All over the country, stretched police forces collected naked men and women in their vans and took them away to the sanctuary of the stations. Nobody could quite believe what they were seeing. It was reminiscent of old grainy black and white films showing the French people rooting out collaborators in the wake of their liberation at the end of the Second World War.

The second piece of dramatic news came from *The News of the World*. The front page ran a banner headline 'My Torture Hell'. The paper had bought the exclusive rights to tell the story of Andrew Moncur. All the other Dumfries victims were still hiding away, but Moncur had decided to cash-in. The story told in graphic detail how he had been subjected to appalling torture during his stay in the Block. He told of how his genitals had been clamped in a vice. He told how he had been given electric shocks. He told of how he had been mercilessly beaten with rubber hoses.

The paper concluded that maybe Jack Sinclair wasn't such a hero after all. How could he be? These were the kind of stories of terrible cruelty that usually came out of the Balkans or the Middle East.

As the sunny afternoon wore on, doubts began to spread about Jack Sinclair. Many rubbished the story from the Sunday tabloid. Of course Moncur would say these things. But why should he be trusted? He was just a no-good dealer. He would say anything for the money. So what if he was tortured? He deserved it.

But there were others who found it harder to take. The chilling descriptions of brutality and torture shocked them. Of course drugs were an evil, and so were the people who sold them. But still, it hardly justified torture. That was going too far. Sinclair had stepped over the line. The debate raged across the air waves and everyone waited impatiently for eight o'clock when the man would speak for himself. Would he defend himself? Would he be brazen? Would this be the moment when the people would turn their backs on him?

That evening the Galloway Forest was like a great sprawling carnival. People had flocked in from all over the country with tents and camper vans. Foot and Mouth restrictions and No Camping policies were impossible to impose. Police estimated that over 5,000 people were camping out in the forest. Barbeques burned, music blared out and beers were guzzled. It was one big party counting down to eight o'clock, like New Year's Eve revellers waiting for midnight.

It was to be Jack's most listened-to broadcast. It was heard all over the planet from Scotland to Singapore, from Dumfries to Darjeeling, from the Galloway to Ghana. Nobody ever really knew just how many it was. But it was a lot. A hell of a lot.

"Good Evening. So here we all are again. But now it is a bit different isn't it? It's different because a lot has happened over the last 24 hours. There is a lot that I want to say about what happened all over the country this morning. But first I think that I should talk about Andrew Moncur. I gather that is the subject that a lot of you are keen to hear about.

"Torture and brutality. The kind of stories that we associate with the Gestapo or the KGB. Not nice is it? Not very British at all. So did it happen? Is that what I did? Is Jack Sinclair a monster? Well, I'm afraid that the answer to your question is yes

and no. Did Andrew Moncur undergo the kind of terrible physical torture that he has claimed in today's News of the World? No. Of course he didn't. And don't worry. I can back this up. The full video of Mr Moncur's interrogation will be posted on the website at nine o'clock. Watch it if you wish. It isn't particularly pleasant, and it will be very embarrassing to Mr Moncur, but it proves conclusively that he wasn't physically harmed in any way whatsoever. The voices are muted to protect the identity of one of my associates.

"We found out quite a lot about Mr Moncur during his stay with us, and to be honest he is a thoroughly unpleasant young man. He has absolutely no excuse for what he did. He comes from a wealthy family and he has had every chance in life. Basically, he has never been interested in any career that involves hard work. It was during his time at university that he discovered the financial rewards of peddling drugs. He was caught and thrown out. However he was not deterred. On his return to Dumfries he picked up where he had left off in Edinburgh. Andrew liked fast cars and nice suits and an easy life. Heroin offered him all of these with a minimum amount of work. He has probably been lying and cheating ever since he was no doubt a thoroughly nasty, spoilt little boy. He has lied and cheated the News of the World, and I sincerely hope that they have not been so foolish as to pay him anything yet. If they have, they will have to sue him. Not my problem.

"I said that the answer to your question was yes and no. Actual physical torture? No. Acute mental torture? Yes. I will not deny it. We stripped these men naked and put them in cold concrete cells where we subjected them to extremes of light and noise. Once it was clear that fear was eating them alive, we took them for questioning. We told them quite graphically what we would do if they didn't co-operate. We had already simulated the sounds of human terror and there were pools of pig's blood on the floor. We put these men through a mental hell. I do not deny it.

"So was this right? Well, that depends on whatever your own personal views are. As far as I am concerned these men were responsible for endless mental torture among the addicts that they created. They were also responsible for many acts of physical brutality. I was willing to make them suffer extremes of fear and anxiety to make them talk. I was not willing to resort to actual physical abuse.

"So there you have your answer. You must make of it what you will. I will move on. This morning we have all witnessed remarkable events. People not only in this country, but all over the world, have basically said that enough is enough. I think that we have sent a clear message to governments of every colour and hue. We are not children. So please do not treat us like children. If you do, then you must beware. We are more than capable of telling what is right from what is wrong. If you are unwilling to stick your heads over the parapet to do what is right, then you have to accept that the people may decide to do it themselves. The last ten days have proved that the Internet gives every single one of us the power to talk to millions of others. All you need is for people to know the address. The era of censorship and D-notices is over. If we want it, power belongs to us. All of us.

"Things have moved fast today. Information is pouring into the website and we have seen those who sell drugs exposed and branded all over the world. I believe that today will prove to be a decisive day. A day like El Alamein. On that day the Eighth Army proved to all the world that the Germans were not supermen. I like to think that we have all done much the same with the drug trade today. These criminals are just people. Nasty people, greedy people, often brutal people, but people all the same. They are subject to fear and anxiety just as you and I are. From today there is a harsh light shining into the dark corners where they like to hide.

"The light is the website, and it will never be switched off. Even if I should drop dead today the site will continue. Money is no problem. We have received huge numbers of donations. This was not something that we asked for. People have given simply because they want to give. My job was to establish the site. It doesn't need me any more. It has its own life and it belongs to everyone.

"I would like to finish by talking about money. We took a great deal of money from Eric Macintosh and Jeremy Taylor. Taylor in particular had stowed away a vast fortune in his Swiss bank account. It is time to put these funds to use. Tomorrow there will be a Press Conference to announce the establishment of a new foundation. My boy was called Will. His life was wasted. Nothing *can ever bring him back. Out there are many, many thousands of boys and girls like Will. They need help. Often they are desperate to find help. And by and large they are ignored.*

"I have decided that a right and proper way to use Jeremy Taylor's nest-egg is to create a Foundation to help these people. It will be called 'Where there is a Will, there is a way.' I hope that it will mean that my boy's death was not in vain. The Foundation will start its life with one Director. This is Mandy Robinson. Mandy is a fine young lady who I once hoped would become my daughter-in-law. Heroin took that possibility away from both Mandy and myself. I will leave everything to her, and I have absolute faith that she will do a magnificent job. The Foundation will start its life tomorrow with £18,000,000 in the bank. Yes, you heard right, £18,000,000. That was the kind of money that Macintosh and Taylor were making from peddling misery and pain.

"It is a huge sum, but it is only a start. I urge you all to give if you can. We all bear a responsibility for what we have done. The good news about today is that our country has become a very bad place for the drug trade. The bad news is that there are many, many thousands of people out there who will now suffer because they cannot buy the drugs that they need. Please let's not forget them.

"I have one more donation. Maybe this is me looking for atonement. I don't know. Maybe. For many years now I have felt bad inside about many of the things that I did during my time in Ireland with the Army. It is all history now. Long Kesh Prison is no more. But there is still a shameful legacy. Well, to do my bit I am making available a million pounds worth of Taylor's dirty money for youth projects on the Turf Lodge estate in Belfast. There will be many who find this confusing. Well so be it.

"So where do we go from here? To be honest, I don't really know. Life will go on. It always does. The site will stay open, and I will continue to hide in the forest. How long for? Again, I really don't know. I will keep broadcasting every now and then just so everybody knows I'm still here. If all goes quiet, then I suppose it means that I am gone.

"Bye for now."

That was very much the crescendo of the Sinclair phenomenon. Everybody seemed to realise that the battle was already won. The fact that Jack's website was never going to close meant that the dealers would always have to look over their shoulders. The next day a terrified-looking Mandy duly announced the new Foundation to the world and money came in at an impressive rate. The morning brought another spate of naked dealers up and down the country, but not as many as Sunday morning. Not nearly as many. All over the country Social Services and doctors' surgeries struggled to deal with thousands of desperate addicts. Virtually nobody dared to offer drugs for sale on the streets.

Over the days and weeks that followed it became more and more apparent that Jack Sinclair had won his war.

Chapter 12
Endgame

The Cabinet met on Tuesday morning in sombre mood. They felt damaged. They felt belittled. Most of them had gone on TV to appeal to their people to show restraint and to ignore the words of Jack Sinclair. And they had been ignored. The people had turned their backs on them. Every poll highlighted massive public support for Jack Sinclair. Every poll showed contempt for the feeble efforts of the Government to stop him. Jack Sinclair's face had appeared on the front cover of Time magazine that week. He was the man of the hour and they all felt foolish.

The Secretary of State for Defence explained that the army could see no way that they could do anything discreetly to locate and apprehend Sinclair. The forest was crawling with sightseers and day trippers. It would be impossible to move troops into the area undetected. Besides, the forest was vast. Enormous. Even with a free hand they could not guarantee to be able to flush him out. Of course if the eight o'clock crowds could be taken away, and if Sinclair continued to broadcast, them maybe things could be different. All the Minister could do was to report that there was basically no military option. He could see that the Prime Minister was in a towering bad mood. He had been going to go a little further, to explain that the generals had been concerned that their men would have little stomach for the task. The soldiers saw Sinclair as one of theirs. He was a decorated officer. Even if a team were to find him in the forest, the odds were that they would turn a blind eye. The Minister decided to keep this to himself.

The Prime Minister turned to the Home Secretary. "So. How about the Home Office? Anything?"

The Home Secretary looked anxious, almost embarrassed. "Yes Prime Minister. Well, maybe. I have talked the matter through with several organisations as you requested. I have been recommended a man called Wilson."

He couldn't maintain eye contact with his leader. He looked down guiltily to his notes. The Prime Minister was impatient. "Yes. A man called Wilson. Please go on. Who on earth is Wilson?"

"He is a 'Defence of the Realm' man. So they tell me."

"And what on earth does being a 'Defence of the Realm' man entail?"

Now the Home Secretary almost squirmed in his seat. "He deals with people who are deemed to be a threat to the Defence of the Realm. He finds them and, well, he makes them go away. I believe he did a lot in Ireland. In the past that is. During the bad times."

The Prime Minister rolled his eyes. "Good God, do these people never go away? Who on earth does he work for? Who authorises him?"

"He doesn't exactly work for anyone Prime Minister. At least not specifically. Technically he represents the Monarch. As to authorisation, well that is down to you Prime Minister."

"Me !"

"Yes. Only Downing Street can authorise these kinds of special measures."

"So what is this man? A soldier?"

"I don't believe so. More a detective. Wilson identifies and locates. If further action is required, he arranges for third-party contractors to come in and do the job. These people are never connected to the Government in any way. They are generally from overseas. Wilson ensures that there is never a trail. Well, so I've been told."

The Prime Minister leaned back in his chair and pondered. He thought of all the speeches he had made through twenty years of being a politician. Fine ideas about open government and transparency. And now here he was in the hot-seat. In a corner.

Being advised that the only way out of the whole mess was a man called Wilson who didn't actually work for anyone. A man who disappeared people on behalf of the Crown. A man who never left a trail. A 'Defence of the Realm' man.

"OK. I want to see him. Tonight. Arrange it please. Now, we have other things to deal with. We have thousands and thousands desperate addicts on the streets and we are going to have to do something to help them. Bloody Sinclair is going to force us. So we better come up with some ideas about what measures we can take and it better be fast . . . "

Wilson came at nine that night. He came through the tunnel that was used by visitors that were not to be seen. He was a nondescript looking man in his early 50's. He was largely bald and he stood just under six feet tall in a sober grey suit and highly polished shoes. He was a man who would never attract a second glance. There were countless Wilsons to be found on the tube every weekday morning making their way into offices and government departments.

The Prime Minister nodded for him to sit. He did so and crossed his legs.

Up close he frightened the Prime Minister. There was an air of coldness about him. He pretended an attitude of subservience, whilst at the same time maintaining a kind of arrogance. This wasn't the first resident of Number 10 who had called him in. No doubt it wouldn't be the last. Politicians came and went. They owed their borrowed time to a fickle electorate. Wilson didn't have to worry about votes. He was a fixture. They never liked him, but they always needed him. It was only ever a matter of time before he got a call. Eventually they all wound up in a hole. Then they turned to him.

The Prime Minister looked up from his desk. "Have you been briefed?"

Wilson nodded. A small gesture. No wasted energy

"And?"

"Too early to say I'm afraid sir. On the surface it looks difficult. Your target is hiding in an area of very desolate countryside. He is meeting nobody. As far as we can tell he has no direct support team. He isn't staying in a hotel or using a credit card or eating in restaurants. These are all areas where I usually look. This is a more difficult case, but I dare say not impossible."

A flat voice. Almost no expression. Essex somewhere, the Prime Minister thought. Cold. Empty and cold. He tried to address the man with as much authority as he could muster. "When you find him you do nothing. You report to me. Understood?"

"Of course sir. That would be quite normal. If you don't mind me saying sir, I wouldn't like to be too optimistic about my finding Sinclair. I am not a Bushman. Maybe the best you can expect is that I can find a way to reach him. That might be all sir."

"Well if that is all then so be it. Just do your best. I await your report. Thank you Wilson. That will be all for now."

When the man left he left a slight smell of cologne. The Prime Minister felt dirty. At times he hated his job.

How pathetic thought Wilson. Pathetic. All of them. Each one of them was desperate to believe that they would be different, that they would never stoop so low. But in the end they all did. And then they were ashamed. They so wanted to believe their own publicity. But when it came to the straight choice between getting a lousy press and making a problem go away, they always chose the latter.

As he made his way back to his flat he decided that there was no hurry. They would want a rush job of course. They always did. They would want Sinclair tomorrow. But they would have to wait. These things took time. The most important thing was always to try and get under the skin of the quarry. Learn all about him. Good times. Bad times. Hopes. Lost dreams. Thwarted ambitions. Unrequited passions. Moments of triumph. Strengths. Weaknesses.

The only way to do this was to talk to people. He would talk to them indirectly. Find out the small things. Half-forgotten events. And out of these things he would start to paint his picture. And as the image of his quarry would emerge, he would start to know him. To understand him. Only when he could understand the man could he begin to think of finding him.

This one was interesting. A terrorist with a difference. Wilson was in no doubt that Jack Sinclair was a terrorist. There was only one definition of a terrorist that he considered to have any relevance. It was someone who threatened the status quo. Whether they were right or wrong was immaterial. Right and wrong was not his job. He left that to others. He was happy to represent the status quo. If somebody was bothering them, he would do his best to make it stop. He had given up worrying about what was right and what was wrong years before. There was nothing to be gained by asking moral questions. All those roads lead nowhere. He had seen the men like him who asked the questions. They were the broken ones hiding away at the bottom of their gin glasses.

What made Sinclair different was that he was the perfect terrorist. Every terrorist aspired to do something so dramatic that it would force the people to wake up and consider their cause. That was step one. Step two was that the people would agree with the cause and adopt it. Step three was that the people would become an army and overthrow which ever government or institution that the terrorist hated in the first place.

It was a wonderfully simple theory but one that was hardly ever successful in practice. The media would almost always side with the forces of the status quo. With the media on board, the government would be able to paint their pictures of the terrorists as being mad, crazy fanatics. These pictures would frighten the people and make them pull away in horror and disgust. This always made the terrorists feel alienated and misunderstood. Like spoilt children denied the toy of their choice, the terrorists would then become angry and petulant and violent. They would always do something beastly out of sheer frustration. And at that moment their battle would be lost. The people would step back in horror. The Government would be given a free hand. The terrorists would become marginalized and hunted and their cause would be forgotten. The media and the authorities would patiently turn them into bogeymen. Then they would hunt them down like dogs.

This was how it had always been before. But not this time. Jack Sinclair had stayed ahead every step of the way. Initially he had played the media with the skill of a snake charmer. He had conned them. By giving them the story of their dreams they had all gone too far, too fast. And once they had put Jack Sinclair into every living-room in the country, he had walked away from them. He had simply created his own media by broadcasting direct. All that the rest of the media could do was to try and play catch up.

Every step of the way he had set the agenda. He never gave anyone time to draw breath, let alone time to work out how to dismantle his image. It had all been so fast. Just a few days. And in those days Sinclair had made himself a hero. A loveable rogue. An eccentric. A brave loner. Pure Hollywood. And nobody had the faintest idea how to deal with it. Well, not quite. They had decided to call in Wilson. Just like they always did.

As he sat in his flat that night he thought about everything that Sinclair had done. He was sure that the answers would be found from Jack's time in the Army. That was where he would look first. This was where the man had been made. Somehow, almost certainly purely by accident, the British Army had spawned the perfect terrorist. Wilson decided that he would start his patient search at the Regiment. Somewhere there he would start to find the loose threads. Then he would tug them.

As May drifted into June, it was remarkable how the stories of the Foot and Mouth epidemic and the Sinclair phenomenon mirrored each other. In the early weeks of Foot and Mouth, the crisis dominated the news. Pictures of burning cattle, sheep and pigs were everywhere. The pictures were the very images of Hell and they horrified and fascinated people in equal measure. And then all of a sudden it didn't seem so dramatic any more. Burning animals? So what? Big deal. Seen it all before. Foot and Mouth statistics dropped steadily down the news schedules until they merited no more than a quick five-second snatch just before the sport, or a couple of column inches on page thirteen.

The disease was still roaring up and down the country and animals were still being slaughtered and burned by the thousand. It just wasn't newsworthy any more. It quickly became something that happened every day. Something that was a shock to start with and then became taken for granted, like pound coins or footballers earning £50,000 a week.

After a fortnight much the same had happened when naked bodies would appear most mornings tied to lamp posts or railings in town centres up and down the land. There were not so many

any more. But there were always some. They had become something normal. Something to be expected. Oh look, there are some more dyed drug pushers. Blue this time. Very nice. How did Villa get on last night?

Jack became a fixture too. He only broadcasted every other night and only to answer occasional specific questions. Many said that the tension had gone out of him. He was more relaxed. More humorous. Less driven. More or less every night he would appear as a guest on some show or another and the Americans couldn't get enough of him. But the edge had gone. He had scored the winning goal in the World Cup Final and now he was enjoying the plaudits. He still had plenty of followers. Every night the forest was full of campers in their "Jack" T-shirts merrily chatting away on their phones.

The papers were now filled with carefully crafted articles that assessed and analysed the Sinclair effect and what it meant. And so Jack slowly became a fixture. Everybody's favourite guest. Always polite. Always witty. Always out there, the perfect thorn in the side of authority.

Wilson arrived in Dumfries more or less unnoticed. Over the next couple of weeks he quietly picked his way around. He talked to all kinds of people, but nobody thought much of it. He always announced himself as being from the Home Office. He just had one or two questions. Nothing very detailed. He was hardly at the forefront of things. Oh no. Not at all. He was just putting together some information. Routine stuff. Boring stuff. Typical civil service stuff.

He seemed such a grey, boring man. Nobody had any desire to spend any more time with him than they had to. He asked boring questions in his flat voice and he jotted away in his note book in his neat handwriting. They had forgotten him almost as soon as he had gone. You see, by this time almost everyone in Dumfries had got used to talking to strangers. The town was buzzing. There were hundreds of reporters from all over the world. Then there were policemen of course. And there were thousands and thousands of visitors who were sucked in by sheer curiosity. Every one of these strangers asked their questions. Did you know Jack Sinclair? Did you ever meet him? Did you know any of the men he abducted? What was it like that day? What is it like in the forest? Is it really as wild as they say it is?

It took about a week for Jack to become an industry. From being desperate and deserted, the town was now booming. There was never a hotel bed to be had, the pubs were heaving, and tables in restaurants almost impossible to find. And all the visitors wanted to talk and talk and talk. They would take their day-trips out to the forest and gaze up in wonder at the thickly-wooded hills. Normally the landscape would not have meant anything to them. But now it did. Now it was filled with mystery and magic because Jack Sinclair was somewhere out there. Maybe he was only a few hundred yards away. Maybe he was up on that hill. Maybe he was watching through binoculars.

When they drove back into town for a night in the pub they were buzzing and glowing. They had actually been there. They had seen the forest where he was hiding.

They had posed by signposts for pictures and taken videos of each other. They had grabbed a little piece of history. I went to the Galloway Forest in 2001 when Jack Sinclair was still hiding out. Jack Sinclair: the legend. Jack Sinclair: the outlaw. Jack Sinclair: the Robert the Bruce of the new millennium.

In the forest every night was party time. There were lots of unofficial camp sites. These were places where people let their hair down. Everybody talked to everybody else. There was a terrific feeling of shared excitement. Every night was a party. And more and more people came simply because they fancied a party.

And amidst all the excitement Wilson quietly got on with his job. He talked to farmers who knew Jack. He talked to teachers who had taught Will. He chatted in the bars of the golf club and the rugby club. He talked to the policemen. And all the while his picture of Jack Sinclair was becoming clearer.

Not all of them were co-operative. The farmers in particular gave him nothing. They took an instant dislike to him with his flat Essex vowels and his neat grey suit. The kidnapped victims were much the same. Some had vanished. Others were hidden away with parents who hated them for the shame that they had brought. But then there was Andrew Moncur. He was different. He sensed that the bland man from the Home Office was more than he seemed.

ENDGAME

Moncur was hiding away at his parents' house. He never went outside. In fact he barely left his room. His humiliation was complete. Not only had the *News of the World* stopped his cheque before he could bank it, but a worldwide audience had logged on to see his lies cruelly exposed. Worse still, they had seen him spread-eagled and bound in the chair, naked and begging and crying. Every day he scrubbed and scrubbed at his skin to try and remove the dye. Slowly it was beginning to fade. His hair was coming through his blue scalp in a stubble. But he simply couldn't imagine ever going out again. Never. He could never face anyone. Not when they had seen him. Seen him like that.

He had all the time in the world for the quiet man from the Home Office. He hoped that this man would be able to find Sinclair. Find him and destroy him. He only wished he could get the chance to put Sinclair in that chair himself. God how he would have his revenge.

Wilson took him through his story quietly. He showed no emotion. He showed no surprise. He never passed comment. All he wanted were the details. How did they take you? How fast? What was the cell like? Did they ever speak to you? What kind of food? How were they? What was their demeanour? Did they swear? Did they hit you? Did he shout the questions? What kind of questions? How long . . . ?

He went along steadily compiling his notes. He picked out the details. He examined the small things. And suddenly after three hours the clouds were swept from the sky and he could see it all.

Clear. Pure. Perfect.

So utterly, utterly obvious. It had been staring into all their faces all the time. But of course it was always the hardest thing to see. The thing that is so obvious. He betrayed no emotion to Moncur. He thanked him politely and left.

He drove to the farm. It was dark now and raining. The policeman at the entrance seemed surprised to see anyone out on such a rotten evening. He examined Wilson's credentials, then let him by. Wilson parked up and pulled a torch from the boot of his car. He went into the cell-block and walked around slowly, thinking hard. After twenty minutes he entered the interrogation room and sat down at the desk.

THE CULL

All the time he had been looking through Sinclair's past to find where he had learned to become the perfect terrorist. He had tried to understand where his man could have learned to design and build the block. He had tried to understand how he could have learned so much about the art of interrogation. And now he knew.

Jack Sinclair hadn't learned any of these things at all. He had subcontracted the job out. He had found himself an expert. And he had gone right to the top. He had called on Liam Kelly. Everything Wilson had learned about Jack made the scenario fit. Brave. Headstrong. Stubborn. A maverick. Always a maverick. And only a maverick would walk into Turf Lodge to seek out the man he had sent to Long Kesh Prison for ten years.

So obvious. So very, very obvious. He couldn't help but smile. The sheer, undiluted audacity of it. And now he had found his way. He was sure of it.

He drove back to London the next day and arranged to see the Prime Minister the following evening. He ran through his findings slowly and carefully. When he had finished the Prime Minister was silent for a while.

"How can you be sure of this? Surely it is merely a theory."

"I'm quite sure" said Wilson.

"Why?"

"Because this is what I do. I am not wrong."

"So what do you suggest?"

"You told me that you wanted the Sinclair problem to go away. I believe that I know how. If you approve of my ideas then I will proceed."

"Then please explain. I'm all ears."

Two days later Wilson arrived in Belfast. He was collected from the airport and taken to an office that had once been very familiar to him. The MI5 head of station looked at him coldly as he entered the room.

"Ah. Wilson. Can't say I'm glad to see you. Thought we'd seen the back of you this side of the water. But I see you're like a rash. A rather nasty thing that won't go away. What do you want?"

"I want a meeting with the Chief of the Belfast Brigade."

"Well you can piss off. Try the Yellow Pages. Nothing I can do."

"Oh really?"

"Yes. Really. So if that's all, you can get back of the plane and bugger off back to the hole you crawled out of."

"I don't think so actually. I've been rather well briefed you see. And I have all the authority that I need."

The MI5 man snorted. "I doubt it. I doubt it very much indeed."

"That may be so. I was briefed inside Number 10 by the Prime Minister himself. He told me all about how things are these days. How you chaps and the Provisionals are all the best of buddies now. How you are working ever so hard with each other to dispose of those dreadful maniacs in the 'Real IRA'. So please, let's stop the silly charades shall we? I have a letter if you need to see it. Or you can make a call to your superiors in London if you wish. But I can assure you that neither course of action is necessary. It is hardly something that I would lie about."

"I'll see what I can do."

"No you won't" said Wilson. "You'll do better than that. You'll do it and you'll do it quickly. After all, it involves the Defence of the Realm, and you know how important that is. So why not be a good chap and set it up."

It took two days. The meeting took place in a small pub in the countryside 50 miles from Belfast. The Chief was a big, hairy man in his middle-50's. His hands swallowed his pint glass and smoke drifted up from the ashtray on the table. He was all sullen hostility.

"So go on then. Get on with it."

Wilson took his time. "I need you to relay a message to one of your people. Liam Kelly."

"Never heard of him."

Wilson shook his head slightly. "How very odd. Your memory must be playing tricks on you. He was one of your senior people right through the nineteen eighties. In your Brigade. Up in Ballymurphy and Turf Lodge. One of your better people. That is until he fell for a sucker-punch. Though personally I always doubted that. I always felt that the order for him to apprehend and interrogate Major Jack Sinclair must have come from higher up. I could never quite believe that Kelly would have been so foolish. Don't you think?"

The Chief took an ill-tempered swig of his beer. He couldn't get used to having to talk with these people. "Don't push it. What makes you think I can get a message to him? Kelly's out. Retired. He's a fucking accountant now, last I heard."

"Oh is that what you heard? Well, I'm afraid you are rather out of touch. Kelly walked out of his job many weeks ago. He left his flat. He locked the door. Switched off the lights and nobody has seen him since. Once upon a time that kind of thing would have had us worrying. But not any more. Not now we are all friends."

"So you said it. Kelly's gone. He's away. How the fuck should I know where?"

"You know. It's your job to know. However there may be things that you don't know. Mr Kelly has been up to quite a lot of late. Amazingly enough he has teamed up with the very same Major Sinclair who was his downfall all those years ago. Whoever would have thought it? The very man who sent him away for all those years in Long Kesh prison. It really is a very strange world at times. I dare say you have been watching the news. The pair of them have caused quite a stir."

The expression on the Irishman's face was one of utter incomprehension. "Don't be so fucking stupid. Liam would never do that. You're off your fucking head."

"Actually I'm not. And Liam Kelly did do that. All of it."

"Jesus fucking Christ."

"Indeed. Now I need you to pass on a message. As you can well imagine, my people are not at all amused about what has been happening. It has been an embarrassing and difficult time. Basically they want it to stop. No more broadcasts. No more talk shows. No more interviews for glossy magazines. In short, they would like Mr Sinclair to disappear in a puff of smoke. They would really like to see his irksome website closed down as well. They really would. But I told them that I didn't believe that would be an option. A very stubborn man Mr Sinclair. Very stubborn indeed.

"They have agreed a deal. Sinclair vanishes. Not for a while. For ever. The site can stay. If he does so, after a month my superiors will see that his Fund will receive an anonymous donation of twenty million pounds. And then we will be willing to forget him. We will wipe the slate clean. For ever."

The Chief was silent for a while. "What makes you so sure that Liam will be able to contact him?"

"To be honest I'm not sure. But I have a strong gut feeling that he will. In fact he is going to have to isn't he?"

"Oh is he now? And why is that? What if they both just turn round and tell you all to fuck off?"

"Then we will not forget them. Either of them. If they reject this proposal I have the authority to find them both and dispose of them. It may take some time. It may even take years. But in the end I will find them. That I can promise. And when I do find them, I will have them killed. That is what will happen."

The Chief stared into the dead eyes of the man across the table. He thought of all the comrades who had been quietly executed in the past. This man would do it. That much he knew. He was the type. Oh yes, he was the type.

"OK. I'll do what I can. Give me a number. I'll let you know one way or another." The Chief got up and left the bar. Wilson sipped at his orange juice. All there was to do now was to wait. And that was something he was good at.

It was ten o' clock in the evening on the first of July when Mandy was surprised by the door bell? Who the hell could it be? She wasn't expecting anyone. She made her way down the stairs and opened the door.

There was something familiar about the man. Slight build. Thin wet hair. When he spoke she knew. A soft Irish voice. "Evening Mandy."

"You're Liam?"

"Yes. I'm Liam. Can I come in? Bloody wet out here."

They went upstairs. He was soaked to the skin. He had been watching to make sure that she was alone. She made coffee. He took an appreciative drink from his mug. "Jesus, that's welcome." He looked at her and smiled. "So we meet at last. You're a special kind of lady Mandy. "

She felt uneasy, unsure of what to say. Unsure why he was there "Kind of you to say so. But I don't suppose you came all this way to say how terrific I am. What do you want?"

"To kick off with I could murder another coffee."

She made him one and he filled her in. He told her about how he had been contacted by the Organisation. He had met up with the Chief and he had been briefed all about Wilson and the deal that was on the table. "So as you can see, I need to meet Jack. He calls me from time to time, but I don't have his number. I don't think that I could persuade him over the phone. You know how he is. Crazy, stubborn bastard. He mentioned that you were meeting him fairly often. I need you to take me there. Take me to him. You see, he has to take this deal. I hope you realise that."

She thought for a while. Liam was obviously right. Jack had done more or less everything that he had set out to do. He was only in the forest now because there really wasn't any other place to go. But he liked it there. He was at home. And he was having the time of his life getting up the noses of the authorities. But Liam was right. He had to take this deal.

"I'm meeting him tonight. At midnight. I'll take you with me."

It was a wild, wild Scottish night. The rain cascaded down as they passed several of the campsites. Everyone was huddled in their tents and nobody took any notice of Mandy's old car. The rendezvous was in a lay-by on a wooded stretch of the road. They pulled up a little before twelve and waited. Jack would come when he was ready. He would come from the forest like a ghost and tap on the window. Mandy was worried that he may not come at all when he saw that there was someone in the passenger seat.

At ten past twelve there was a tap on the window. Liam opened his door.

"Well what a pleasant surprise. To what do I owe this pleasure Mr Kelly?"

"It seems that I just couldn't live without you Major. Are you well?"

"Aye. Fine. Come on, let's get away from the road."

They walked for a couple of hundred yards through the wet trees to the place where Jack had made one of his makeshift camps. He made coffee and laced the tin mugs with whisky.

Liam told him all about Wilson and the deal in his soft Irish voice.

"So Major, that's how things stand."

"What do you think Liam?"

"Take it. The mission is all finished. You hit all your targets. There isn't much more for you to do. I suppose you could carry on with the talk-show circuit but they'll find you in the end. Then it will be a bullet in the back of the head and a grave in a quiet corner somewhere. Maybe that's what you want. I don't know."

Jack was silent for a while. "Not really Liam. In a way I like it here. But I can't stay for ever. But I can't think what to do next. Where to go? Who to be?"

"Come over the water with me. You can hide up somewhere. We're used to hiding people over there. We've had years of practice. I think I can guarantee your safety after your little donation to the kids on Turf Lodge. Take some time. We still have tonnes of money. I can fix you a new identity. Passport. Credit cards. Birth certificate. The lot. We'll give you a bit of a make over. Cut your hair. Dye it black. Coloured contact lenses. And you can be somebody else."

"You must think that they are being serious?" Said Jack.

"Oh yes. Like cancer. The Brits are always serious about these deals. It upsets their sense of honour if anyone turns them down. They will find you in the end Jack. And then they will execute you. Believe it."

"So what's next? What if I agree?"

"I'll go back and make a few arrangements. I'll get the Chief to pass on the word that you're agreeable to their proposal. I'll arrange a boat to take us across, probably from the Mull of Kintyre. And then I'll come and pick you up. Hey, it all fits in Major. I seem to remember that your man Robert the Bruce hopped over the water in a small boat once upon a time. I'll pick you up a week from now."

Jack stared long and hard into his mug of coffee. At last he spoke "OK fine. I'll be ready."

And so it was that the air waves went quiet. Nobody thought much of it for a couple of days. But by the third day there were whispers. By the fourth day they were louder. Where was Jack? No broadcasts. No interviews. No nothing.

Rumours and theories started up. They must have found him. Maybe it was the SAS? Something must of happened. Mandy saw him twice more that week and they finalised the arrangements. It seemed strange on the last night. So much had happened so quickly. And now it was over. Liam was due the next day. And Jack Sinclair would leave the Galloway Forest.

When it was time to go they were both awkward. There was a silence. A difficult silence. A million things to say and so very hard to start sying them. Mandy broke it.

"I don't want the goodbye yet Jack. Not here. Not now. Contact me when you are over the water and safe. Contact me before you disappear for good."

"I will. That's a promise."

They hugged briefly at the edge of the tree line. As she drove away she could see the figure of a tall man in the moonlight in her mirror.

And then he was gone.

Weeks passed and then months. Other news came to keep the media occupied. The Sinclair story slowly faded away. Articles still came and went. In-depth documentaries were made to look back on the remarkable events of May and June. And on most mornings bound and naked figures would turn up in a town square somewhere. The camp sites in the forest emptied and after a while there were only a few diehards who would make the eight o' clock pilgrimage to use their mobile phones.

After a while everybody accepted that he was gone. On September 11 terrorists drove planes into the twin towers of the World Trade Centre and the Pentagon and the world forgot all about Jack Sinclair. Autumn came and Dumfries slipped quietly back into obscurity. Once again the streets were empty. The town quietly settled down to wait another seven hundred years for something to happen.

There were concrete legacies of course. The "Will Foundation" purchased a vast country house with 100 acres of land and renovations were soon well under way, When it opened it would offer superb facilities for over 100 addicts. There were several similar projects under way, up and down the country. The Government had introduced several new measures and had allocated considerable funds to help those of its citizens who were addicted to hard drugs.

ENDGAME

Most importantly, the drug trade itself had gone into a terminal decline. The police soon got into the habit of using the website. Why go to all the bother of dragging the thing to court when a simple email would solve the problem. The price was far too high for anyone thinking about dealing. Anyone who dared to try it risked being watched by fifty million eyes. Exposure was more or less inevitable. Jack's website acted as an eternal policeman.

Mandy gave up her job with the paper. It was soon apparant that her work with the "Will Foundation" was going to take every minute of her time and every ounce of her energy. Then one day she received an email.

"Giant's Causeway. 8 a.m. Friday."

She caught a ferry from Stranraer on Thursday afternoon and drove up to Ulster's North Coast. She awoke to a perfect Autumn morning. There wasn't a cloud in the endless blue sky as she parked her car and walked along the path at the bottom of the cliffs to Britain's most outrageous geological attraction. It was still too early for tourists. She felt as if she was alone in the world with the gulls stooping overhead and the waves slapping gently into the grey pavement of basalt.

There were towering cliffs and a sky and sea that seemed to stretch into the outer reaches of nowhere.

And then they were there.

Jack's hair was now black and cut short. He had grown a beard and he wore glasses. Jack and Liam. Two men in their 40's who had shaken the world. The soldier and the terrorist. A big man and a slight man. Such a strange pair.

"So where to now Jack?"

He smiled. Just like he had always smiled. And the glint was still in his eyes. "Oh I don't know. Here and there. This and that. You know."

"Both of you?"

He chuckled. "I think so."

She left them. At the top of the track she looked back. They were matchstick figures sitting on the rocks staring out at the water. And she knew that she would never see them again.

Mandy went back and started her new life. It was a life that she was born to. Over the weeks and months and years that followed she would often find her mind wandering away from whatever task it was addressing. And she would stop for a moment or two and wonder where they both were. The soldier and the terrorist. And whenever she wondered she would always find the same picture in her mind. A picture of two men sitting on the rocks staring out at the deep blue sea.

The soldier and the terrorist.

THE END

Other titles available
from Glenmill Publishing

One Man's Meat
by Mark Frankland

"Frankland turns crisis into drama"
Sunday Telegraph

November 1997 and British Farming
is being ripped apart by the BSE Crisis.
Vast areas of the countryside are facing devastation.
Finally one man decides that enough is enough.

Sir Alistair McIntyre, owner of the vast McIntyre
Holdings Corporation, makes the fateful decision to
save the Beef Industry. He hires a team of Mavericks
who claim to be able to solve any problem.
Their prize is massive. So is their task.

As their campaign gathers momentum
thousands of angry farmers at last start to fight back.
The story sweeps across the globe at breathtaking speed
from Argentina to Matabeleland,
from the windswept Scottish hills
to the shanty towns of Brazil,
from the Cabinet Room in Downing Street
to the Boardroom of a Supermarket giant.

Every step of the way the team are sucked into ever
greater danger until their path inexorably leads them
to the lair of one of the most dangerous men on earth . . .

**To order a copy complete
the order form at the back of the book
or tel. 0776 149 3542**

£5.99 plus £1.00 P&P

Red Sky in the Morning
by David Cherrington

"Red sky in the morning, shepherds warning . . ."
Harry Sinton mumbled to himself noticing the sunrise.
Minutes later he was standing over two lifeless
bodies, clutching his shotgun, and shaking in disbelief.

Harry Sinton was a quiet man leading a quiet life
on his farm in his quiet piece of England,
until one fateful morning when he stumbled across
a gang of thieves stealing his machinery.
Within seconds two thieves lay dead,
a third was running scared,
and Harry Sinton could not believe what he had done.

Red Sky in the Morning is a gripping tale
of how a single incident can transform a life.
As the story sweeps to its climax, the reader,
like the jury, has to make some hard judgements . . .
Who is the victim?
How far can any of us go to defend ourselves?

*"The story is enjoyable, thought-provoking and so strongly
written that it seizes the reader's attention in the first chapter
and holds it in a vice-like grip until the final moments."*
Charlotte Smith, Hampshire Chronicle

*"A gripping read, the more so because it is so chillingly
close to the fact. Mr. Cherrington's book raises
controversial questions about how far anyone has the right
to go to in order to defend themselves and their property."*
Angela Turnbull, Salisbury Journal.

**To order a copy complete
the order form at the back of the book
or tel. 0776 149 3542**

£5.99 plus £1.00 P&P

The Drums of Anfield
by Mark Frankland

"A fantastic adventure book for all young
football lovers – even one as young as me!"
Sir Tom Finney

Once in every generation a great new star emerges
into the world of football. Out of the slums of Sao Paulo
came Pele. Out of the bullet-scarred streets of Belfast
came Georgie Best. Out of the shanty towns of Buenos Aires
came Maradona. When Liverpool's veteran captain,
Tony Hobbes, suffers a crippling injury and receives a long
ban for violent conduct, he decides to take his son to Africa.

He expects to find lions and elephants amidst the Dark
Continent's endless wild plains. Instead, far away in the East
of Uganda under the shadow of the Mountains of the Moon,
he finds a boy called Simon Matembo. He knows that the
boy's talent is so huge that he could become the greatest
of them all. He knows that this boy can take Liverpool back
to the great days. But first he has to find a way to take him
back, and to do this he must overcome many huge challenges
from the tribe, the club, and even the forces of nature.

"Anyone who loves football will love this book.
Football is about passion, unrelenting excitement
and, more than anything else, it is about dreams.
Exactly the same can be said about 'The Drums of Anfield".
Gerry Marsden, from 'Gerry and the Pacemakers'

"Genuinely hard to put down", **FourFourTwo Magazine**

To order a copy complete
the order form at the back of the book
or tel. 0776 149 3542

£4.99 plus £1.00 P&P

Order Form

Name ------------------------------------

Address ------------------------------------

Telephone ------------------------------------

Email ------------------------------------

Please send me ------------------ **Copies of**

Please send me ------------------ **Copies of**

I enclose a cheque for ------------------------

**Please make cheques payable to:
'Glenmill Publishing'**

Return this form to:

**Glenmill Publishing
Glenmill
Dumfries
DG2 8PX**

Or Telephone   0776 149 3542